MONEY FOR LOVE

MONEY FOR LOVE

A NOVEL BY
PETER S. BERMAN

ISBN-13: 978-0-9907456-4-8

ISBN-10: 0990745643

Published by Merseyside Press.

Contact us at **merseysidepress@gmail.com**

Visit the authors page on Facebook at **Peter S. Berman**, or check in with us on Facebook at **Merseyside Press.**

AUTHOR'S NOTE

This novel is a work of fiction in its entirety. All characters, settings, dialogue, incidents and other story elements are wholly imaginary. Following an old literary tradition, I have honored some of my friends by using their names to identify fictional characters, but there is no connection between my imaginary characters and my real-life friends. Any resemblance between the fictional contents of this book and real people, companies, institutions and places is strictly coincidental.

This story is dedicated to the men and women of the Los Angeles Police Department who I have had the distinct pleasure of having worked both for and with throughout the last forty years.

Your daily and selfless acts of heroism are greatly appreciated.

***

It is also dedicated to my friend Don Flynn, former Assistant Director of the Secret Service, who passed away.

Real friends like Don are hard to find, and he is sorely missed.

"We are so accustomed to disguise ourselves to others, that in the end, we become disguised to ourselves."

— Francois De La Rochefoucault

"Dishonesty, cowardice and duplicity are never impulsive."

— George A. Knight

MONEY FOR LOVE

PROLOGUE

During the summer months in Saint Petersburg, Russia, the darkness was always slow to arrive, so when the sun finally set that evening at just about ten p.m., it left behind a city that would still have to deal with an hour or so of gradually diminishing twilight before becoming engulfed by total darkness.

The month was August; a time of year that was synonymous with frequent and heavy rain showers that floated in from the adjacent Gulf of Finland; and this particular night was no exception. The sky was heavy with dark, bloated clouds that would soon open up on this historically significant piece of land known as the *Venice of the North.*

Alexei Kuznetsov was seated on a mattress that lay on what passed for his side of the bed; one that he reluctantly shared with Nikolay, his ten-year-old brother, who for the moment was sound asleep. Their room was part of a two-bedroom, dingy flat that they'd come to accept as their home. A window in the South facing corner of their bedroom was intended to afford a view of the city, but the exterior of the glass was crusted with so much grime that what made it through the window was a filtered form of pale half-light.

"Alexei?" came the growl. *"Get in here…now!"*

His earphones were wedged tightly into his ears, enabling him to listen to a track of heavy metal music from the American band called the *'No Name Gang.'* The music came from an illegal download provided by a friend of his from school. He was so into the beat of the song that he didn't hear his stepfather's order, but apparently, his little brother did.

A now wide-awake Nikolay—whose eyes expressed the panic he was feeling—reached over and grabbed Alexei by the arm. Something was up, and seconds later, when the bedroom door came crashing open, Alexei quickly pulled out his earphones and sat up straight, his eyes landing on his stepfather's angry face.

Zakhar Lebedev was a bully and a typical drunk; a swiller of vodka from morning to night. And even though this functioning alcoholic managed to hold down his job as a mechanic on the city's electric trolly system, he had a cruel

1

streak that always managed to bubble to the surface whenever he was around the two boys.

Zakhar reached the side of the bed in three strides and grabbed the fourteen-year-old Alexei by the arm. He dragged him from the bedroom and into the front room where he violently pushed him down on the floor.

"Cigarettes," he muttered in a deep, gravely voice. He dug into his pocket and came up with a handful of rubles that he pitched in Alexi's direction.

"Go get them for me now."

This was nothing new for Alexei. He was often ordered to do things like this, and he was so grateful that the man had not battered him that he was willing to do what was being demanded, including going out on a wickedly cold night to get the stupid bastard his cigarettes. Even if it was only to be able to escape for a short time from their eighth-floor walk-up apartment.

Alexei collected the scattered rubles from the floor, and as he got to his feet, Zakhar grabbed his shoulder and slurred a final demand.

"Come right back. Understand?"

Alexei nodded tersely. He grabbed his heavy coat, then made his way out through the metal front door and into a darkened hallway full of stale air and cooking smells. This was followed by a long trip down an equally oppressive, urine-smelling stairwell.

At first glance, Saint Petersburg was full of massive, majestic, and formidable old-world buildings that were crowded together and sectioned off by almost a hundred canals and tributaries. But this superficial beauty was grossly misleading, for many of the buildings were in a state of appalling disrepair. And just like the city's architecture, Saint Petersburg's reputation as a bastion of Russian culture was a mask that concealed an uncomfortable secret. For all of its posturing and claims of first world sophistication, the vast majority of its people were forced by economics to live in noticeably substandard and overcrowded conditions. Many blue collar workers—the backbone of any community—often went hungry, particularly in the winter. It was truly a place of unfulfilled promises; where many of its young men were often burdened by a sense of overwhelming hopelessness.

Holding his breath while he tried to ignore a puddle of urine that had pooled on the steps of the lower floors, Alexei reached the bottom of the stair-well and made his way outside. He was immediately struck by a blast of cold wind that forced him to tighten his coat collar around his neck before plunging his gloveless hands deep into his pockets.

The streets were unusually quiet for this time of night, as most people were already safely inside in anticipation of the pending storm. He glanced up at the sky and instinctively knew that the start of the rain was imminent, so he length-ened his stride as he made his way down the main road, crossing mid-block to shorten the journey. His goal was to reach the tiny convenience store that was two blocks away, and at this time of night, it was the only one still open for miles around.

The *nebol'shoy rynok goroda,* or small neighborhood market, was visible from more than a block away, and the light that poured through the store's front window bathed the sidewalk in a warm, yellow glow.

Alexei briefly stopped for a moment when he spotted a lone male figure lounging up against the market wall, just outside the front doorway. The man was wearing a black leather jacket and dark jeans, and he was casually smoking a cigarette. The streets in this neighborhood were never completely safe—espe-cially at night when they became the hunting grounds for addicts and common street muggers—so Alexei was instantly on guard.

His choices were few. He could turn away now and go back home without the cigarettes, but that would certainly result in a beating from his drunken step-father, or he could keep on going and hope that the stranger would pay him no mind. But that, too, was risky, for in Alexei's limited experience, a lone stranger on the street at this time of night—particularly when a dangerous storm was about to unload—was likely to be someone who was up to no good.

He watched the man for another quiet minute while his mind churned over his predicament. His heightened sense of awareness was now warning him to be cautious; that the stranger presented a real and very credible threat. But what could he do? Any other stores that might be open were too far away to get to safely, and while the option to keep going was not attractive, it was better than facing the bastard's wrath back home.

He really didn't have any choice. He had to continue on to the store and take a chance that the man would turn out to be completely harmless.

It was moments like these when he wished his mother was still around. Aside from his younger brother, she was the only person who had ever truly loved him, and she would have known exactly what to do. But after Alexei's real father had passed away, she took up with Zakhar, and later, when it was too late to admit that she'd made a big mistake, she had turned to drugs as a way to lessen the pain of the man's abusive tantrums.

Alexei had watched his mother's slow decline into the oblivion of addiction, and on a freezing night six months in the past, when a light dusting of snow had concealed the outward grime of the city's streets, a syringe containing a batch of contaminated heroin finally took its toll.

Alexei increased his pace. The man lounging in front of the store was still a good fifty meters away, so Alexei couldn't tell for sure if he was friend or foe. There was always a chance that he was one of the guys from the neighborhood, but he'd need to get closer to make that determination.

With his hands still stuffed into his pockets, he made his way forward, keeping close to the curb by the street. If he had to run, he would do so. He didn't fancy a beating for a pack of cigarettes.

He got close enough to the man to realize that he wasn't someone he knew, so he picked up his pace, confident that if he could make it into the store without a confrontation, he would likely be okay.

The man watched him approach, took a final puff on his cigarette, then discarded the butt into the street with a flick of his middle finger and thumb. He then turned away from Alexei and walked around the corner going out of sight.

Alexei breathed a sigh of relief. He made it to the front of the store and climbed up the two steps that put him safely inside.

The cigarettes were in a rack off to the side of the front doorway where an elderly night counterman from Kazakhstan sat on a stool behind an old, western-style, American cash register.

Alexei grabbed a pack of *Belomorkanal's*, the cheapest and strongest of the Russian brands still made at a factory in the city. He held it up for the man to see before placing the rubles on the counter. The shopkeeper gave him a silent nod, then watched as Alexei tucked the cigarettes into his pocket before making his way towards the door.

When he stepped outside, Alexei was surprised to discover that the man he'd been so worried about was once again lounging against the front wall. He appeared to be in his late twenties, and he was clearly much taller and stronger than Alexei.

The man's eyes had now fallen on Alexei, and his stare was as cold as the wind from the coming storm. There was a cruelty inherent in his smile that made the hair stand up on the back of Alexei's neck.

The man watched him closely as Alexei came down the stairs.

"You have cigarettes?" he asked, moving closer.

"For my father," Alexei answered, voice quivering.

The man's smile grew larger as he held out his hand and motioned with his fingers for Alexei to hand them over.

Alexei shook his head, his mind busily processing all available routes for escape.

The man seemed to look past Alexei who noticed the direction of his glance. He turned quickly to see two other young toughs who had come up quietly behind him.

Alexei looked back at the first man who said, "Give us the cigarettes and all of your money."

One of the other two came up from behind and grabbed him around the neck.

Alexei bit his arm and kicked backward at the man's shin, but the first man quickly charged him and struck him in the face.

Alexei went down and the three men began to kick him. He tried to cover his head, but one of the kicks to his face finally knocked him unconscious.

He awoke a few minutes later: dizzy; spitting out blood and pieces of his two front teeth; not sure where he was or what had happened. He tried to sit up, but everything hurt, especially his ribs.

He was on the sidewalk, about twenty feet away from the store. There was no one around, and he was soaking wet from the rain that had already started to fall while he'd been unconscious. It took a few moments, but as dizzy as he was, but began to remember exactly what had happened and what they'd done to him.

His attackers were long gone, and when he checked his pockets, so was his CD player and his earphones. He then thought about the cigarettes, and what the bastard was going to do if he tried to come back without them.

He got to his feet and used the wall to help him maintain his balance, and in that single moment, he made a decision that was about to cost him dearly.

He staggered back down the sidewalk and made his way into the store.

The old man behind the counter saw him and stared at him in open disbelief. Alexei knew that he was probably a frightening sight. He was covered with blood, and one of his eyes was now completely swollen shut. He went directly over to the rack of cigarettes, grabbed two packs, and started for the door.

The man behind the counter stepped out from behind it and tried to stop him. He grabbed his arm, but Alexei would not be detoured. He turned into the man and gave him shove which sent him sprawling down to the floor.

He glanced down at the still speechless man, then made his way out into the worsening storm.

****

Thirty-five minutes later, he was sound asleep in his bed when his bedroom door came flying open. His little brother came over to the side of the bed and tapped him several times on the arm. Nikolay softly whispered to Alexei to get up, but Alexei was too sore to even try to move. He pushed his brother's hand away and angrily told him to let him sleep.

Loud voices from the front room then slipped into Alexei's conscious mind. He tried to make out what they were saying. His stepfather was clearly drunk and yelling at someone, and that someone was threatening to take him away if he didn't produce his son.

Alexei suddenly knew what was going on and tried to sit up, but it was just no use. He was too beat up to even try to move.

Moments later, three uniformed *politsiya* came into the room, hauled him up into a sitting position—cuffed his hands in front of him—then dragged him forcefully out of bed.

One of the men made an unkind reference to Alexei's battered face which caused the other two men to laugh roundly.

When they led him from the bedroom and into the front room, his stepfather just stood there, saying nothing, smoking one of the cigarettes that Alexei had stolen just about an hour before.

With all the dignity he could muster, Alexei stood up straighter and never gave the bastard a second look.

Nikolay cried softly as Alexei was taken away.

****

Ninety Days Later

Alexei was chained to a ring in the floorboard of the prison bus that was on its way from the courthouse in St. Petersburg to the *Kolpino* youth prison, fifteen miles away. The bus was designed like an armored car, with narrow slits resembling gun portals which replaced the traditional windows. Tri-color in design, white over blue over silver, there was no missing what it was when it lumbered down the highway.

Kolpino was a detention facility for sentenced young offenders between the ages of fourteen and twenty-one. More than half of the boys there were convicted of crimes of theft, including those who'd stolen items as trivial as flour and eggs. The practice in Russia was to impose jail sentences on all first-time youthful offenders, and they were often unusually heavy; three to five years was considered to be the average.

The inmates at *Kolpino* were rented out to private businesses as a cheap source of labor, with most of the inmates earning just fifteen cents for a full day of work. This practice was publicly touted as one that helped the young men to gain the kind of work experience and discipline that they would need after leaving the prison, but those who understood the system knew that it was nothing more than a form of modern day slavery.

A coffin making company ran one of the workshops in *Kolpino* and that was especially worrisome to some in the government since organized crime was known to have infiltrated the various business aspects relating to the industry of death in Russia. Competition between the different Mafia gangs was often fierce, so having a workshop on land controlled by the Justice Ministry offered the *Kolpino* syndicate a measure of guaranteed protection.

It was also a fertile ground for Mafia recruitment.

None of this was yet known to Alexei, but he would learn soon enough that his world was changed forever.

Alexei was seated next to a physically bulky young man who appeared to be a few years older than he was. Very few of the other juvenile convicts on the bus were talking, as most were terrified by what would await them, but the boy that was seated next to Alexei seemed completely unfazed by where they were going or what they should expect when they finally arrived.

He leaned in closer and whispered to Alexei.

"What's your name?"

"Alexei Kuznetsov."

"Never tell anyone your full name," he confided. He studied Alexei cautiously. "You from *Petersburg*?"

Alexei nodded, still wondering why he shouldn't be free to give his full family name?

"First time for *Kolpino?*" The older boy virtually spat out the prison's name.

Alexei nodded again.

"First time for you?" he asked the older boy.

"No, I was here before for two years, and this time I'm down for eight more." He studied Alexei's face. "Once I get to twenty-one, they'll transfer me to a fucking *Gulag* where they can watch me build roads or some shit like that."

Alexei was impressed. The boy seemed to know a lot about *Kolpino*, and he certainly appeared to be unconcerned about his very long sentence.

Perhaps this wouldn't be so bad.

"Is it hard?" Alexei finally asked.

"It won't be easy. The staff's okay, but some of the older cons can be real bastards. It's survival of the strongest, so you'll need to bulk up if you can?"

He then glanced out through the slit that served as a window on the side of the bus, as if watching the last vestiges of freedom as it slowly slipped away.

Then he turned back to face Alexei.

"How long did they give you?"

"Five years," Alexei replied.

"Five years for a first offense?" He studied Alexei more carefully. "Who'd you kill?"

In spite of his palpable anxiety, Alexei found himself smiling.

"I didn't kill anyone. I was stealing cigarettes for my stepfather, and I gave the old man behind the counter a shove."

The boy continued to eye him with a new found respect, clearly not buying the explanation.

"Smart. Play it down. Never tell anyone what you really did or how long a sentence you got. Understand?"

He didn't, but this older boy seemed to be pretty sure of himself, so it was probably good advice.

A long silence settled in as each boy considered where they were headed, but five minutes later, the older boy turned to face him again.

"It can be difficult at first at *Kolpino*, especially if you don't know your way around. The gangs inside are tough, and a boy like you could end up getting hurt real fast." He shot Alexei a crooked-toothed smile. "I'll tell you what. You stick with me when we get there, and I'll watch your back. I've got a few good friends inside that shit hole, so when we arrive, you stick with me. Okay?"

Alexei nodded. To his way of thinking, having a friend—especially an older one who knew the ropes—was the first positive thing to happen to him since that horrible night three months ago when the police first took him to jail.

He smiled to himself. Maybe this wouldn't be as bad as he thought, and while he would sorely miss seeing his little brother, he would not miss that asshole his mother had married.

"What's your name?" Alexei whispered.

"No real names, remember?" The boy said with a crooked smile. "You can call me *Dima,* and I will call you *Ubiytsa*."

Ubiytsa translates to *Killer*.

The bus turned off the highway and drove up the road that led directly to the prison where a few scraggly birch trees fought for their lives near a beat up basketball court. There were some sturdy looking buildings, but other than that, the facility was desolate and appeared at first glance to be landscaped in slabs of dirty concrete.

They came to a stop in a caged unloading area, and a guard began to unchain the prisoners from the bolts on the bus floor. They were ordered to step off the bus in single file, and they did so hurriedly, most of them driven to do so by fear.

Once outside, they were frog-marched indoors to a reception area where they were forced to disrobe, cavity searched, then told to get dressed in all black uniforms that would now become their everyday clothes.

Inmate leaders from the four sub groups of a company composed of a hundred prisoners were brought into the holding area to escort their respective charges to their dormitory rooms. In exchange for additional privileges, it was the responsibility of the inmate leaders to see that the boys in their groups remained quiet and orderly.

Those who resisted their iron-fisted brutality received the label of "the humbled." Those designated as such would be forced to do the dirty work in the prison, like cleaning the toilets and floors.

Kolpino was a typical Russian juvenile prison where survival first was the rule of law; where the physically strong would continually dominate over the weak. And in those first few moments in the reception area, Alexei was made to understand that if he wanted to survive this ordeal, he was going to have to find a way to become a force to be reckoned with.

CHAPTER 1

Twenty Years Later, October 10, Morning

Shari Thompson pulled the dark blue Crown Vic over to the curb in front of a Spanish-style triplex on a tree lined street on the South side of Beverly Hills. The building was old, built in the nineteen-thirties, but was meticulously maintained by the current owner. Access to the building's garages was through an alley behind the building, but she wasn't parking. She was there to pick up Jennifer Donahue, her partner in the Robbery-Homicide Division.

The older of the two by three years, Thompson had assumed the role of Donahue's big sister in their very close relationship. At five-foot-five, she was shorter than Donahue by about three inches but had a fuller figure then Donahue who by any measurable standard was athletically thin.

She and Donahue were best friends and had been now for several years, and theirs was a relationship that long since brooked no personal secrets; a fact that often led to poignant but merciless kidding between them.

She reached for her cell phone, typed in a text message—*I'm out front*—then settled back into her seat where she listened to an all-news radio station until a knock on the passenger side door snapped her back into the moment.

She hit the button which unlocked the door and smiled when Donahue opened it up.

Donahue settled into the front seat, hooked up her seatbelt, then folded her arms across her chest. She was dressed in a well-tailored black pants suit worn over a crisp white blouse. She had opted for flats instead of heels, due in part to how she was feeling. Her badge was pinned to her gun belt which she wore around her waist, concealed beneath her jacket. A pair of dark sunglasses covered her eyes.

"Not even a *'good-morning'* or *'thanks for coming by to pick me up,'*" Thompson asked.

Donahue continued to silently stare out the window.

Thompson studied her for a moment longer.

"Okay. What's up, Jen?"

"Can't we just go?"

"Not until you tell me what's wrong."

Donahue sighed. "I've got a splitting headache and my stomach's upset. Is that what you wanted to hear?"

Thompson studied her best friend carefully.

"Lift up your glasses," she said with authority.

Donahue turned slowly towards her direction, then lifted the glasses to reveal her bloodshot and watery eyes.

Thompson frowned.

"Have you been drinking?"

"Maybe."

"You wanna tell me what's wrong?"

She shook her head.

Thompson considered that response for a moment then started up the car. As she pulled away from the curb, she said, "You know you're gonna tell me eventually, so why not do it now and get it over with?"

Donahue exhaled slowly.

"He walked out," she said in a tiny voice.

"Who? *Doctor Head Case?*"

Head Case was the nickname that members of the squad had given to Donahue's latest boyfriend; a neurosurgeon that she met in the Cedar's-Sinai Emergency Room when he'd been working on the victim of a robbery who eventually passed away.

Donahue removed a tissue from her purse and blotted the tears that appeared at the corners of her eyes.

"When I got home last night I discovered that he'd packed his things and moved out." She sniffed back her runny nose. "He didn't even leave me a note."

Thompson knew the history of their relationship and that they'd been together for almost six months. Both of them had continued to maintain separate residences, a stroke of luck considering the current outcome, but most of the time when they were staying together it was over at Jen's place rather than his.

"Did you see it coming?" Thompson asked.

Donahue shook her head.

"So...call him up and ask him why?"

"I tried, but he's not answering my calls."

Thompson looked over at her friend, then reached out with one hand to give her arm a squeeze.

"Did you guys have a fight about something?"

Donahue shrugged her shoulders.

"Just the usual... *'How come you always have to work so late?'"*

"Didn't you say that he was gonna cut back on his hours?"

"He did," Donahue replied, looking over to meet Thompson's gaze. "But we were arguing about was *my schedule*, not his."

Thompson's face reflected her concern. For the past two months she knew that Jen's relationship had been on shaky ground. Both she and the doctor had been working long hours and that had been causing them to drift apart. Donahue obviously thought it was something that they could weather through: a miscalculation that hadn't worked out.

"When was the last time that you guys spent the night together?"

"Two weeks ago," Donahue replied.

Thompson could only shake her head.

"Well, that kind of explains things, doesn't it, Jen?"

"Yeah, I guess it does."

Thompson studied her friend's face.

"You look really pale, Jen. If you're not feeling well, I can take you back home?"

"Just keep driving. Okay?"

Thompson drove in silence for a while, then said, "You know we have to qualify this morning. Right?"

Donahue nodded. "I know."

"You wanna stop for some breakfast first? Maybe something to eat will help settle your stomach."

Donahue didn't respond.

"I don't know why you're beating yourself up about this, Jen. You're smart, single, and still hot in sort of a conservative way." She smiled. "You'll find another guy in a couple of weeks."

"Not this time, Shari. I'm done with dating. I need time to figure out why I missed all the signs."

Thompson knew that her partner was putting too much pressure on herself. Jen had never been married and what she wanted most of all was to find a husband and have a couple of kids. Pressure like that was destructive, and it contributed mightily to her partner's recent bouts of heavy tequila imbibing.

"Let me save you the trouble of going through months or years of self-analysis. Do you really wanna know why you missed all the signs?"

"You gonna be the one to tell me why?"

"Sure, and it won't cost you an arm and a leg."

"And I should listen to you…*why?*"

"Why? Because I've spent the last two years in marriage counseling and I think I've learned a thing or two."

Donahue almost smiled.

"Fine. Enlighten me. Let's hear what doctor Shari has to say."

"Okay. You missed all the signs because you really cared for this man and it blinded you to all of his flaws."

Donahue frowned. "So you're saying it's all my fault?"

"No! Of course not. It's just that during the first stages of a relationship, we all tend to fall for the image that the person we're dating is projecting, and it's not until much later—when the bloom is finally off the rose—that our eyes are open, and we see him or her for who they really are."

"So you're saying he saw me as…*what?*"

"Good question, Jen, and I'll give you the answer. He saw you as a woman who cared more about your job than you did about him."

"That's not true—"

"Let me finish." She paused for a long moment. "If you really cared about Doctor Head Case, you would have found a way to make time to see him. And conversely, he would have found the time to be with you. But the two of you are already wedded to your careers, and neither one of you cared enough about the other to make the kind of changes that would make things work." She looked over at her partner and shrugged. "You didn't miss the signs, Jen, you just ignored them. And you did so because deep down you knew that he wasn't the right guy for you."

Donahue didn't respond. Thompson's words had struck a nerve, and the sad thing was ...*she was probably right.*

Thompson cocked her head, then smiled.

"Cheer up, sweetie. You fell off the horse, and if you want to keep riding— and I know you do—then what you have to do now is get right back up in the saddle. And since I've been in your shoes more times than I care to admit, I can tell you from first-hand experience that the best remedy for a breakup is a roll in the hay with a handsome stranger." She looked over at Donahue and smiled. "All I'm sayin' is that sometimes all a girl really needs is a good fuck."

Donahue suddenly reached over and tapped Thompson's arm.

"Pull over, Shari."

Thompson immediately assumed that she'd gone too far with her unsolicited advice.

"I didn't mean anything by that, Jen. I'm just saying—"

"Now!"

Donahue raised her hand to cover her mouth.

Thompson suddenly realized what was going on and her eyes went wide.

"No, Jenny! Please! Not in the car! I just got it washed."

As Donahue turned to roll down her window, Thompson made a quick lane change, cutting off a driver who laid on the horn. Seconds later she pulled up to the nearest curb and watched as Donahue bolted from the car and promptly threw-up.

*****

Forty-five minutes later, after battling their way through the early morning rush hour traffic, they arrived at the Police Academy shooting range in Elysian Park. The facility was nestled in a hillside setting that included fountains, waterfalls, an outdoor pool, large pine trees, picnic tables and benches, and a couple of Spanish-style buildings set on twenty-one acres.

After finding a parking spot in one of the two lower parking lots, they made their way up a paved road on foot, passing under the famous Academy arch, before arriving at the range where they occupied two of the thirty individual shooting stations where they planned to qualify with their handguns.

They each picked up a clean target sheet which was then attached to a cable before they sent their respective targets by a pulley setup to a predetermined spot downrange. A small tray-sized platform in each of the stations provided them a place to put down their extra ammunition while they waited for the others to get ready to shoot.

They were required to qualify quarterly with their handguns, and there were twenty-eight other officers and detectives present at the range who were also trying to get this mandatory task out of the way before the close of the deployment period.

As Thompson picked up a set of headphones intended to be used to dampen the sounds made when the shots were being fired, she said to Donahue, "Why don't you come over tonight, Jen. I'll put the boys down early, and you can have a good cry on my shoulder."

"Thank's anyway, Shari, but I think I'll just stay home tonight. I need to think about what you said."

Donahue finished loading two clips, then slammed one home into her 9 mm Sig Sauer.

"Besides," she added, "if I did go to your place, you'd pull out the tequila, and God knows I don't need to be doin' that again for a while."

Thompson chuckled. She was glad to see that Donahue appeared to be coming out of her funk. Maybe her drinking to excess during the past few months had been her way of glossing over the fact that her relationship with Head Case was headed for the rocks.

"You're probably right, Jen, but just remember, the offer stands."

They finished putting on their headphones, and both of them put on the clear plastic shooting glasses which were designed to keep gunpowder particulate from blowing back into their eyes.

"Ready on the left?" came the voice over the loudspeaker.

The two women then settled into the familiar routine of qualification by facing their downrange targets.

"Ready on the right?" said the same voice.

There was a momentary pause as the rest of the entire shooting line readied themselves to begin firing.

"Commence firing," came the command.

All thirty officers began firing at once, and the sound of the guns going off echoed throughout the entire Academy campus. But within a ten-seconds, when twenty-nine of the officers had completed firing their requisite five shots, only one lone gun could still be heard as the shooter continued to blast away at her target.

Shari peeked around the partition to watch as Donahue kept on firing until her clip was completely empty.

No one said anything, but all eyes were on her. She was oblivious to the stares as she popped out the clip, inserted a fresh one, then waited in silence for the next verbal command.

But the Range Master had seen it all, and he came out from his overwatch perch and slowly walked up behind her. He was a uniformed Sargent with thirty-four years on the job. He studied Donahue's face for a moment, then hit the button on the side of the protective divider which called back Donahue's target.

Taped to the center of the bullseye was an eight-by-ten photograph of a man in a pair of doctor's green scrubs. The area around the man's groin had been completely obliterated by Donahue's precision shooting.

The Range Master shifted his eyes from the target and the photo over to Donahue.

"Is there something I should know about?" he asked with a touch of amusement in his voice.

Donahue shrugged.

Thompson tapped him on the shoulder.

"Her boyfriend, a doctor, by the way, moved out last night and didn't even bother to leave her a note."

The Range Master nodded slowly, then shifted his attention back to Donahue. He took another peek at what was left of the photo.

"He's a doctor?"

Donahue nodded.

"Then he should know better." He met Donahue's eyes unflinchingly returned her stare.

"Well, I'll say this, detective. That's an impressively tight grouping, but don't you think it's just a little low for a shooting assignment that calls for center mass?"

"My sights must be out of alignment, Sarge," she told him with a straight face.

"That must be it. Get it corrected."

Then, as he turned to go, he mumbled softly to himself, "Remind me never to piss you off."

CHAPTER 2

October 19, Late Afternoon

Donahue was ready to call it a day.

She'd been at her desk in the squad room for the better part of the afternoon, trying to track down a drug using witness who'd bailed out of jail the week before, but who had failed on his promise to call her with his new contact information. She'd tried calling all of the usual haunts—the flophouse hotels along skid row—but none of the front desk clerks had seen him, nor, she suspected, would any of them say so if they had.

She leaned back in her chair and checked her watch. It was approaching four-thirty p.m., and if she left the squad now, she might just make it to an important appointment set for five-fifteen.

It had been nine days since her meltdown over her boyfriend's moving out, and to be perfectly honest, once she was over the shock about the way it occurred, she was actually glad that it had happened that way. She had taken to heart her partner's words, about how neither one of them had made time for the relationship, and she had to admit it made sense. Theirs had been a match driven by mutual physical attraction, but beyond the bedroom, they really had very little in common. If he hadn't made the move so decisively, they might still be wasting time in an impossible struggle to try and make something out of nothing.

For the last three days, she'd been feeling pretty good about herself and the way things were going. The weight of their complicated relationship had been lifted from her shoulders, and while she hadn't changed her mind about backing away from dating for the foreseeable future, she had come to believe that she was on the right path.

She took a moment to stretch, then glanced at her watch.

Donahue was lanky in stature but physically fit. A jogger by choice, she would often take long runs to gather her thoughts and to deal with the stress that came with the job. Recently, she'd taken to wearing her dishwater blond hair in a ponytail. Her eyes could best be described as translucent blue, while her well-defined high cheekbones and generous smile seemed to be a magnet for the attentions of men.

At forty-one years of age, she seemed to be at a point in her life where she was genuinely happy with her career. She had once considered studying law—the career that her father had chosen—but she changed her mind during college to pursue a degree in sociology, and to pick up a teaching credential. But right after college, she suddenly changed her mind and signed up with the Los Angeles Police Department, and once she got a taste of the streets, she knew that she'd made the right decision. Her one and only goal was to become a detective, and now that she was one, and working homicides, she hoped that it would never end.

She'd done five years in patrol, two years in Community Relations, and three years working in Vice. During the latter assignment, she'd been placed on loan to Sex Crimes for almost a year; an experience that strengthened her empathy for women who found themselves working in the world's oldest profession. After that, she was given a slot in divisional homicide, and one year later, she was brought in to work a case at RHD.

She'd proven herself during that first investigation, and now in her fifth year of working on major cases, she was considered by her supervisors to be an independent thinker; one who more often than not used her considerable mental prowess to unravel the most complex of cases.

She got to her feet and looked over the divider and into Thompson's cubicle.

"I'm out of here, Shari," she said casually.

Thompson looked up from her computer screen.

"You're leaving pretty early, aren't you?"

"Got stuff to do."

Thompson caught her glance and smiled.

"Let me guess. You're finally getting back on the horse, aren't you? That's it, isn't it? You've got a date!"

Donahue pulled her holstered firearm from out of her desk and strapped it around her waist.

"How in God's name did you ever arrive at that conclusion?" she asked.

Thompson smiled again. "Your demeanor the last few days; visibly anxious this afternoon; talking out loud to yourself; constantly checking your watch; that dreamy, far away expression on your face. I know all the signs, Jen. You're considering getting naked for a man."

Donahue cocked an eyebrow, her pale blue eyes fixed firmly on her partner.

"All your years as a detective and that's the conclusion you arrive at?"

Thompson ignored the jibe, clearly pleased with herself. She leaned back in her chair, a smug expression on her face.

"I'm right, aren't I? Details, girl. I want all the details."

Donahue picked up her purse, checked her watch, then lowered her voice to a whisper.

"You want details, huh? Okay. It just so happens that in about forty-five minutes, I'll be on my back, buck-ass naked, legs up in the air, moaning softly, while *Carolyn* pokes and probes me in God-only-knows how many different ways…"

"What the—?" Thompson's mouth flew open in complete surprise. "*Holy shit! I never figured you for a…*"

She wasn't quite sure how to phrase it.

"*…for that!*"

Thompson got to her feet and stepped around the waist-high partition and into Donahue's cubicle to keep their conversation as private as possible. It was common knowledge that because of the design of the squad room and the use of low-walled cubicles, there could be no expectation of privacy. Everyone in the squad knew everyone else's business because even speaking in a normal voice, everything said above a whisper could be easily overheard.

Thompson glanced around to make sure that none of the other nearby detectives were tuning into their conversation.

"When did this happen?" she whispered.

"When did *what* happen?"

"You know…you and this *woman*?"

Donahue appeared to be giving the question some thought while she slid an errant strand of hair behind her ear.

"Oh, I don't know for sure. Maybe about five years ago..or something like that."

"*What?*"

Thompson was having a great deal of trouble processing this startling revelation. Her mouth was open in stunned amazement.

"But what about all the different guys you've been with?"

Donahue smiled.

"What about 'em?"

Thompson's hand went up to her mouth.

"You never said you were *bi*, Jen. Don't get me wrong. I'm not making a judgment call here. You know I don't care about a person's sexual orientation, but I just can't believe that you didn't let me know?"

Donahue burst out laughing, no longer able to maintain the charade.

"Some detective you are. *Carolyn* Carter is my gynecologist. I've had this appointment scheduled for the past three months, and I'm not about to miss it."

Thompson, who was smarting from Donahue's prank, was in the process of flipping Donahue off when the phone on her desk began to ring. It was the office's common line—one that ran to everyone's phone—but when no one else bothered to pick it up, she stepped back into her cubicle and grabbed it just as Donahue waived and headed for the door.

Thompson listened for a moment, then covered the receiver with her hand.

"Hold on, Jen," she called out. "It's for you."

"Take a message," Donahue said, still heading for the door. "I can't stop now. I'm late."

"She says her name is Nika Kaminski and I'm supposed to tell you that it's very important."

Donahue stopped, thought about it for a moment, then headed back to her desk, clearly unhappy.

She picked up the receiver. "Hey, Nika, what's up?" she said in a cautious voice.

"I need to talk to you, detective. It's really important."

Donahue tried to remember the last time she'd even run into Nika Kaminski. It had to be…*what?*…four…*no*, maybe five years ago?

"Are you in trouble?" Donahue asked, sitting down in her chair.

"Not on the phone." Kaminski had lowered her voice to just barely above a whisper and Donahue was having trouble hearing what she was saying.

"Speak up, Nika. I can't quite hear you."

"I need to talk to you," she said as emotion flooded her voice. "You're the only one I can trust. Can we meet somewhere?"

Donahue winced as she checked her watch again and thought, *I just can't break this appointment.*

"Listen, Nika. I've got something I have to do, but I should be finished about six p.m. Why don't we get together then for a bite to eat? It'll be my treat."

"I'm at work now," Kaminski whispered, "but I'm going straight home. Can you come by my place? It's important."

When Donahue said yes, Kaminski gave her an address for an apartment in Hollywood, then hung up the phone, leaving Donahue momentarily staring at the receiver.

"Everything okay?" Thompson asked.

Donahue was lost in thought, wondering what could possibly be putting Nika into such a panicked state.

"Jen?"

"Huh? What?"

"Is everything okay?"

"Yeah, I guess so," she said. A deep frown appeared on her face. "That was Nika Kaminski. You ever deal with her?"

Thompson racked her brain, but no connection came to mind.

"I don't think so."

"Five-six, brunette, really pretty. Turned tricks out of a condo over in mid-Wilshire."

"Is she an informant of yours?" Thompson asked.

"Not really an informant, but I helped her out once when I was working Vice. She was a high-end escort at the time; Russian-born, a sweet Jewish girl. Forced into the game by the Russian mob. They set her up in LA, and if I remember correctly, her street name was *Sasha.*"

"Still doesn't ring a bell."

"Anyway, I helped her get out of the life back then, and now she want's a meet."

"Want me to go with you?" Thompson asked, already wondering if her nanny would stay on for a few hours longer to watch her three boys.

"No, but thanks for the offer. She probably just wants a few bucks and to have a good cry on my shoulder about some guy."

Donahue checked her watch. "*Damn!* I've got to get out of here, Shari."
She quickly got to her feet.

"Enjoy your probing," Thompson said, flashing her a sly little smile.
Donahue stuck out her tongue then hurried off.

CHAPTER 3

October 19, 5:00 p.m.

Nika Kaminski was scared. No, scared was too soft a word to describe how she actually felt. She was absolutely terrified.

She'd been through a great deal in her twenty-seven years of life, but nothing she'd experienced in her checkered past had spooked her quite as much as this.

After speaking to Donahue, she left her office in North Hollywood and drove her five-year-old Chevrolet Sonic over the hill from the Valley to the Westside of Los Angeles where she lived in an apartment in Hollywood proper.

The sun was just setting over the Pacific Ocean, and the high clouds took on a gray cast against the red-orange glow of the western sky. Halloween would soon be arriving, and in LA that usually mean colder weather and strong winds. But Nika was oblivious to the beauty that surrounded her because she had too much on her mind.

Instead of using her spot in the underground garage, she parked at the curb several buildings away, walked quickly and deliberately to her building, all the while looking around to see if anyone was watching her. Satisfied that she had not been followed, she entered the building, climbed three flights of stairs to her unit, and quickly unlocked the door.

Inside, she turned on the lights and took off her coat.

Nika's life had been very hard. Born in the city of Moscow, she'd been raised by parents who held low-level government jobs in the Kremlin. Her father had been a trade attache and her mother a secretary in the Ministry of Defense. Nika was an only child—only slightly spoiled—and because she was a bit of a rebel during her years of secondary education, she'd turned to running with a fast crowd, and eventually that led her to drugs. Her parents kicked her out when she wouldn't stop using, and she ended up meeting a man who 'knew a man' who was looking for a girl who would clean his house in exchange for her drug of choice. With very little money accessible to her since her falling out with her parents, Nika took the job and moved into the man's *dacha* in a private residential community along the Black Sea coastline.

But the house cleaning duties included sleeping with the owner, a task she endured for the steady supply of drugs, and when he tired of her and moved on to someone new, she was passed off to another man who promised to get her work as a nanny in America.

Unknowingly, she'd fallen for the mob's cruelest gambit.

She was flown to Tijuana, Mexico, where she was forced into a life of prostitution. The beatings to compel her compliance were frequent, but without money of her own, and without access to her passport, she was forced to do what her keepers demanded. They fed her a steady supply of heroin, kept her high while they forced her to service as many as twenty different men each day in a shit hole of a flop house behind a cheap bar that featured live sex shows with humans and animals. After six months of this, when her self-esteem had fallen through the floor, and her compliance was no longer an issue of concern, the men responsible for keeping an eye on her forced her to go through a medically supervised program of drug withdrawal which slowly cleaned her up. Two months later, when she started to feel normal again, they told her she was too good looking to work in the high volume brothels and that they had bigger plans for her in mind. They were going to send her off to Los Angeles where she'd be given a condo to work from in exchange for her role as an escort. She would be servicing high-end clients, and as a part of the deal, she would be allowed to keep ten percent of her earnings.

They smuggled her across the border by using a well-funded coyote operation and she was delivered to a condominium project in the heart of the mid-Wilshire neighborhood of Los Angeles. The condo was clean and professionally decorated for use with the upscale clients. She was given a much less luxurious abode to actually live in—a two bedroom apartment on the eastern edge of Hollywood—that she was forced to share with a Ukrainian girl who'd been brought into the business in the same brutal way.

She'd done what they asked her to do, all the while saving her share of the money she'd earned so that one day she could make her escape. But that became unnecessary when one of her Johns took things too far, causing her to end up in the Emergency Room at Cedar's Sinai Hospital with several broken ribs. That was when she'd met up with Detective Jennifer Donahue, and after that, her life completely changed.

Nika took a quick walk-through her apartment, then went into her bedroom where she stripped a few pillowcases from the pillows on her bed and began stuffing them with her belongings; mostly clothes, some cheap jewelry, and a small stuffed animal that she'd bought one night on a whim. She wanted to be ready to leave the apartment just as soon as her meeting with Donahue was over.

Her cell phone rang, and she checked the caller ID.

"Where are you?" Nika said when she answered. There was a note of desperation in her voice.

"I'm just leaving work," replied Eliska Rodinova. She was in the parking lot of her employer, walking towards her car.

Eliska was her closest friend and confidant, and she was acutely aware that Nika had been anxious and preoccupied the last few days, thus explaining her continued agitation.

"Are you still at work?" Eliska asked her.

"I'm already home," she said stiffly.

"What's wrong? You sound upset."

"I need a place to stay, Ellie. Can I move in with you for a while?"

"Yeah, sure, I guess," but Eliska was confused and starting to worry. "What's happened? Why do you need a place to stay?"

"I'll tell you later. Can you pick me up?"

"What's wrong with your car?"

"Please, Ellie. I think I'm being followed…"

"*What?*" Eliska's worry now rose to a heightened level. "By whom?"

"*Not now, Ellie. Please?*" She tried to tone down her exasperation. "I'll tell you when you pick me up."

Eliska stopped walking towards her car. "You're scaring me, Nika. What's going on?"

"*Jesus! Ellie, I said I'll tell you later.*"

Eliska ignored Nika's rudeness. Instead, she chose to chalk it up to her penchant for being overly dramatic.

"Fine. Be that way," she sighed. "I'll pick you up in half an hour—"

"No! Wait! Don't come by until six-thirty. I have to meet someone here at six."

Eliska frowned. "Oh? And who are you meeting?"

Nika sighed. Ellie was so insecure about things. If she didn't say something, she would never let it go.

"I'm meeting with Jennifer Donahue. You don't know her."

"Who is she?" she said suspiciously.

"She's a detective with LAPD. I'm going to tell her about that stuff I already told you about. She's the only one I can trust."

"I thought you trusted me?" Ellie said.

"You know what I mean." Nika was getting angrier by the second. She didn't have time to deal with Ellie's jealousy. "I've got to hang up now, but when you get here, don't come to the door. Send me a text and I'll come right down. *Oh*…and park down the street. Don't park in front of the building. Okay?"

Eliska sighed. Even for Nika, this drama was starting to be a little too heavy. They were gonna to have to talk about it sometime soon.

"Fine," she finally said. "I'll see you at six-thirty."

Eliska rang off, and Nika moved over to her closet. Too many clothes and not enough time to take them all. She reached for a bathrobe, decided it was probably essential, as was the blue dress she bought last summer.

She never heard the man when he entered her apartment. In fact, she never even heard him when he crept into her bedroom.

When she turned around to put the blue dress into one of the pillow cases, the man's sudden appearance a few feet away brought about a strangled scream from deep within her throat.

She stiffened as he fired, a quick shot to her forehead, then he watched as she quickly fell to the floor.

He then stood over her body, and when he became aware that she was still drawing a ragged breath, he shot her one more time.

CHAPTER 4

October 19, 7:40 p.m.

Thompson turned right onto Westmount Drive in the city of Hollywood and pulled up next to the yellow crime scene tape that had been tied to two trees and stretched across the roadway. The neighborhood was in the flatlands, south of Santa Monica Boulevard; full of three and four story apartment buildings as well as an equal number of small, mid-century, single family homes.

The evening temperature had dropped quickly, going below the anticipated mid-sixties to the high fifties, catching most Angelenos by complete surprise.

She climbed out of her personal car, a black GMC SUV, adjusted a muffler around her neck to ward off the evening chill, then showed her ID to a uniformed officer who was holding back a group of neighbors who were desperately craning their necks to see what was going on. She walked up the front pathway to the security gate leading into the white, four-story apartment building.

Thompson was five-five in her flat shoes, with auburn hair that she preferred to wear in a ponytail. Now in her early forties, she was recently divorced with three young sons, but she still had the figure and the youthful good looks of a woman ten years her junior.

Her emerald green eyes had a bluish tint, and they flashed brightly as she took in the scene that played out before her.

There were a dozen or so officers going in and out of the building, and standing up by the exterior door, she spotted Detective Ulysses Gibson holding court with several uniformed officers: handing out assignments, making suggestions, and otherwise directing the canvassing investigation.

Gibson was her acting Lieutenant. He was formerly Donahue's partner and a mentor to her as well. To those he worked with, he was known as "Gibby."

"Where is she?" Thompson asked him, not bothering to wait for a break in the group's conversation.

Gibson pointed to a blue Plymouth parked a dozen cars away, down the street.

Thompson nodded, then made her way back to the sidewalk and over to the car. She tapped softly on the closed driver's side window, then opened the door. Jennifer Donahue was seated in the front passenger seat, and in the reflected glow of a nearby streetlight, Thompson could see that she was crying.

"You okay?" she asked, shutting the door and leaning in to give Donahue a hug.

But Donahue didn't answer, and Thompson could tell that she was lost in thoughts that were miles away.

"I came as soon as Gibby called," Thompson told her. "He said you found her?"

Donahue slowly turned to face her, her dark mood clearly evident on her face.

"I should have canceled the damn doctor's appointment and gone to see her when she called."

"Don't beat yourself up about it, Jen. If you'd shown up earlier, it could've been you lying up there, too. It's not your fault."

She opened her purse, took out a tissue, and handed it to Donahue. "Your mascara's smeared," she said.

Donahue used the tissue to blot around her eyes, but the tears continued to flow.

"Let's get out of here," Thompson said without hesitation. "You need a drink, and we can talk it out."

"I can't leave." Donahue wiped at her runny nose with what remained of the tissue. "I'm supposed to stick around to be interviewed."

"Who's running the case? Hollywood?"

Donahue shrugged.

"You stay right here." Thompson cracked open the driver's side door. "I'll talk to Gibby, and we'll see what can be done."

She climbed out of the car and made her way back to the apartment building. Gibson was nowhere in sight, so she spoke to a uniformed officer who guided her up several flights of stairs to a third floor unit near the back of the building.

She spotted Gibson in the front room along with two other detectives that she didn't know. When he spotted her, he signaled for her to sign in and join him.

She located the log-in officer who was having a smoke on the exterior balcony walkway, showed him her ID card, had him log her in, then she entered the living room of the apartment.

"How's she doing?" Gibson asked. As an acting Lieutenant in the Robbery-Homicide Division, he was always given a call concerning cases that affected or involved detectives who were under his supervision.

"She's pretty upset, Gibby. Blames herself for not coming right over when the victim called."

"What's the story about that call?" asked the taller of the two detectives who was standing next to Gibson.

Gibson recognized the look on her face, the one that silently asked... *who are these guys and should I actually be speaking about this in front of them?*

"This is Ron Grayson and Jack Tucker from Hollywood Division," Gibson said, introducing the two detectives. "They're gonna handle the case."

He turned to Grayson. "Thompson is RHD. She and Donahue are partners."

Grayson nodded, then said to Thompson, "Did Donahue tell you what the victim's call was all about?"

"I was there when she got it," Thompson replied. "The victim wanted to speak with her, but Jen had a doctor's appointment, so she told her she'd come by here after that. But from what Jen told me, the victim never mentioned what she wanted to talk about."

She noticed that Tucker was taking notes. She looked over at Gibson.

"I'd like to get her out of here if it's okay with you?"

Grayson interjected, "It's okay with me. I'm sure that what she knows can wait until tomorrow."

Gibson told them that he could make her available in the morning, and after a brief negotiation, they settled for nine a.m. at the Police Administration Building (PAB).

Thompson glanced over towards the bedroom door where a Coroner's Investigator was just finishing up his examination. The others noted her shift in attention, and soon they had all edged over towards the doorway to hear what the investigator had to say.

Blake Fletcher, the Coroner's Investigator, was a heavyset forty-two-year old man with thinning brown hair, a small thin mustache, and a prominent double chin. He was sweating profusely in the stifling heat of the apartment.

He pulled off his purple nitrile medical gloves, removed a linen handkerchief from his jacket pocket, then slowly wiped his face and brow.

"From what I can tell, she took two to the head. Her clothing appears to be intact, so this is probably not a sexual assault, but we'll run the standard tests just to confirm."

"Any sign of defensive wounds?" Tucker asked. He noticed that Fletcher had fastened clear plastic bags around both of her hands.

"Not that I can see, but we'll do fingernail scrapings. Hopefully, she clawed whoever did it."

"There was no sign of forced entry," Gibson said as he turned toward Thompson.

"You think she let her killer in?" she asked.

"Maybe, or she might have left a window unlatched."

"No sign of that," Tucker told them. "I checked that out. Everything is locked up tight."

"Maybe a boyfriend with a key?" Thompson suggested. She had a habit of thinking out loud.

Tucker met her glance. "We'll look into that," he said, not hiding his scowl.

Thompson ignored the rebuke. Tucker was simply reminding her that the case was their's and that they knew what they were doing.

She gave him a tight smile, then pointed off to her left.

"What's that on the bed?"

"Pillowcases full of personal stuff," Grayson said. "Some items dropped down on the floor. I think that someone got in; was stealing what they could; she walked in, surprised whoever it was, and got clipped for her trouble."

Thompson shook her head. "I don't agree."

All four of the men gave her questioning looks.

"The bags are full of clothes; some of them look like they're from *K-Mart* or *H&S,* not exactly high couture items. And on that dresser over there is an iPad, untouched. That's the first thing a prowler would want to take." She shot them a tight, little smile, then pointed in the direction of the headboard. "And in that second bag over there? That fuzzy little thing on top is a stuffed animal."

Tucker's brow went up. "Meaning?"

"*Meaning* she was packing up her own stuff to get out of here, and it looks to me like she was in one hell of a hurry."

"And how do you conclude she was in a hurry?" Tucker asked.

"Because she didn't take the time to fold up her things. She just stuffed them in the pillow cases."

Tucker looked over at Grayson who shrugged. "Makes sense to me, which means that she might have been afraid of someone, and maybe that's what she wanted to talk to your partner about?"

Gibson turned to Thompson.

"Did Jen tell you anything about the victim's background?"

"Her name is Nika Kaminski; street name was *Sasha*. At one time she was a Russian escort. Jen ran across her when she was working in Vice. Said she helped her out of the life."

"Maybe we should talk to Donahue now?" Grayson said to his partner.

Tucker shook his head. "It'll keep until tomorrow. We'll be working here for the rest of the night."

Thompson nodded, then turned for the door and Gibson followed her out.

"Hold on, Shari." He caught up to her and lowered his voice. "No tequila, you understand? She needs to keep her wits about her for tomorrow's interview."

Thompson nodded then gestured with her head towards the apartment. "She was running away from someone, Gibby. The call to Jen was a call for help."

"Yeah, I agree. Too bad she didn't tell Jen what it was about."

"If I know Jen, she's gonna wanna be involved. Two to the head seems pretty personal to me."

Gibson shook his head.

"We'll monitor things from time to time, but this is not our case. Understand?"

"We'll stay clear," she promised, but Thompson had her fingers crossed behind her back.

*****

Donahue licked the skin on her left hand between her thumb and forefinger, sprinkled a small pinch of salt onto the saliva, picked up a slice of lime with the same hand, then licked the salt, downed the shot of *Patron*, and followed it up with a quick bite of the lime. She then tossed her head back, swallowed all of the tequila in one big gulp, then shivered while she wiped her mouth by using the back of her hand.

It was the fourth shot in just under thirty minutes, and Thompson was beginning to wonder if Donahue was close to reaching her limit.

Thompson worked on her second glass of wine while Donahue took a few moments to look around the room. When she spotted the waitress—an overweight but attractive young woman who was working nights at the bar while doing stand-up comedy on the weekends—she waived her arms frantically, caught her attention, then signaled that she wanted another shot.

They were in the lobby bar of the Mandarin Hotel in Beverly Hills. At this hour of the night, there were very few patrons, so they were seated on a couch in the middle of the room where they had a good view of the piano player who had just finished a muted rendition of the Sinatra classic...*It Was a Very Good Year.*

"How are you doing, Jen?" Thompson asked with a touch of concern in her voice.

Donahue's eyes were starting to take on a forty-yard stare and Thompson couldn't tell if their glassiness was the result of all the crying that she'd been doing or if a new round of recriminations was on the way.

"Why does everything in my life turn to shit?" Donahue mumbled.

Oh, boy!

"I mean, that poor girl, Shari. She was good people. She didn't deserve to get killed that way." Donahue sniffed loudly and used her hand to wipe her nose. "She went through so much... too damn much." Her voice grew louder as the soliloquy continued. "It isn't fair. She finally gets her life back, and some asshole has to come along and shoot her in the head."

The few patrons who were seated on a nearby couch began casting concerned looks in Donahue's direction.

Thompson leaned forward and whispered, "You're talking too loud, Jen."

"Too loud? I'm not too loud." Tears formed at the corners of her eyes. "It's just not fair!"

"You're right, Jen. It's not fair."

Donahue folded her arms across her chest. "I'm tired of seeing dead people."

"You sound like that kid in the Bruce Willis movie, what was it called? *The Sixth Sense*? Yeah, that's it....'*I see dead people.'*"

But Donahue wasn't listening. She was adrift somewhere in muddled thought.

A different waitress walked up and said to Donahue, "Can I get you another *Patron*?"

Donahue nodded.

"Hell, yes, and get her one too," she added, gesturing towards Thompson.

"Not for me," Thompson said, catching the waitress's eyes. "And I'm pretty sure the other waitress was already going to bring her one."

Her eyes then shifted to Donahue. "You sure you want another, Jen? You've got that interview with the Hollywood guys pretty early in the morning."

"I can deal with it," she said, defensively. "And besides, I'm not driving, so there."

She stuck out her tongue.

The waitress walked off, and Thompson's next thought was how pissed off she was going to be if Donahue got sick in her car while she was driving her home.

Donahue leaned forward, nearly toppling off the couch.

"What's happened to my life, Shari? Chris was such a great guy—"

Uh, oh! Here we go.

Thompson rolled her eyes. Donahue's most recent breakup with the neurosurgeon was now making its way to center stage of her current pity party.

Donahue cocked her head to the side, closed her eyes, and rocked unsteadily.

For a moment, Thompson thought she might fall right off the couch, but her eyes popped open and she suddenly smiled.

"He brought me flowers on our first date. He's such a sweetie."

Thompson shook her head and spoke bluntly.

"He walked out on you without even saying good-bye." She reached out and patted Donahue on the hand. "I'd say that takes him out of the category of 'sweetie,' don't you think?"

Donahue studied her, then smiled.

"You're right. He's shit. I'm better off without him."

Thompson nodded. "Just a speed-bump, Jen. You'll bounce back soon enough. You always do."

"You're right. And that's why you're my best friend. You know that, don't you? You're my best friend, and I mean that, Shari. I really mean that."

Thompson smiled. Donahue was hammered. It was time to get her home.

She signaled to the waitress who came right over.

"Check please," Thompson said.

"Did you want that other drink first?" the girl asked, looking over at a now stoic Donahue.

Thompson summoned a smile. "Not unless you're prepared to clean up the mess when she throws it all up."

"Right," said the waitress as she quickly scurried off. "I'll get your check right now."

"I'm gonna take you home now, Jen," said an impatient Thompson. "Can you stand up?"

Donahue nodded, but her eyes were closed.

"I don't feel so good."

Thompson quickly stood up and grabbed Donahue's arm to get her up and off to the nearest bathroom, but an empty stomach and too much tequila were a deadly combination that wouldn't wait.

Donahue started a series of projectile heaves that were so loud and violent that the few remaining patrons quickly made a hasty retreat, leaving Thompson to deal with a very distraught bar manager.

*****

CHAPTER 5

October 20, 10:15 a.m.

"I thought I might find you in here."

They were in the women's restroom on the fifth floor of the PAB. Donahue was hunched over the sink, splashing cold water on her face and using a palm full of water to rinse out her mouth. She had just finished another bout of hangover heaves, and her skin was as pale as a ghost.

"You don't look so good," Thompson said without sympathy. She pulled three or four paper towels from the dispenser and handed them to Donahue who wordlessly wiped her face and hands.

"You're gonna want to touch up your lipstick," Thompson said. She was leaning against a nearby sink, arms folded across her chest.

Donahue looked over at her above the top of the paper towels that she was still holding up to her face.

"You know you could've stopped me at two," she said.

Thompson smiled. "There was no stopping you last night, sweetie. You needed to get whatever it was that was bugging you completely out of your system."

"I'm afraid I got more than that out of my system."

Donahue threw the crushed up wet towels into the nearby receptacle while Thompson failed miserably to suppress a grin.

"I never knew a human of your size and weight could make such deeply disturbing noises while throwing up. You sent patrons and staff running with your antics last night."

"I did?" A look of concern passed over Donahue's face. "I don't remember much of anything."

Thompson let out a short, exasperated laugh.

"Maybe that's for the best."

"From now on I'm through with tequila," Donahue pronounced, then she involuntarily gagged, and her hand flew quickly up to cover her mouth.

"Oh, my God," she said after regaining control. "Just saying that word makes me retch."

"What word?" Thompson said with a wicked smile.

Donahue looked over and held her glance. "Really, Shari? Some friend you are. You're enjoying my misery, aren't you?"

"Immensely," Thompson replied.

They made their way back into the squad and settled in at their desks. The room was extremely large, with many dozens of individual cubicles set up in parallel rows. Each cubicle was three sided with waist high partitions which offered little in the way of privacy for the individual detectives.

Donahue got out of her chair and leaned over the top of their shared partition to speak to Thompson in a very hushed tone.

"Nika was doing so well, too. What the hell could have been so important that she couldn't tell me on the phone?"

"I have no idea, but if it makes you feel any better, we can ask Hollywood to give us updates on their investigation?"

Donahue nodded. "I may have to poke around a bit on my own."

"Not smart, Jen. That could get us in a whole lot of trouble."

"You don't have to get involved," Donahue told her.

"Yeah, right, as if I could let you do it on your own."

But Donahue wasn't listening. She was thinking about Nika and what they knew.

"The double tap to her head has the feel of a professional hit," Donahue said. "Maybe that's what we should be exploring?"

Thompson reached for her now empty coffee cup.

"I'm gonna get a refill. You want a cup?"

"Yeah, thanks. Black with sugar." She handed Thompson a ceramic cup that needed a good washing out.

Thompson took it, then frowned at the prospect of having to scrub it clean.

"When was the last time this cup was cleaned?"

"I don't know," Donahue said, not really caring. "Never mind, I'll do it myself."

She got to her feet and put out her hand.

"Don't get your thong in a bunch," Thompson proclaimed, holding on to the cup. "I'll get your coffee."

She started for the door, then turned back, a sympathetic look on her face. "You need a couple of aspirins?"

Donahue shook her head. "I loaded up before this morning's debriefing." She studied Thompson's face. "Thanks for helping me out last night. I guess I overdid it a bit."

Thompson smiled. "That's what friends are for. Just don't tell Gibson you were drinking tequila."

"He gave you the lecture?"

"More like an order."

Donahue almost laughed. Gibson couldn't resist playing the role of everyone's father. It seemed to be part and parcel of his DNA.

Thompson walked off to the coffee room while Donahue checked her emails and her telephone for messages. When Thompson returned, she handed Donahue her coffee, then pulled her own chair around the divider and sat down next to Donahue's chair.

"Does Hollywood Division have any leads?" Thompson asked.

"If they do, they didn't bother to say so when they interviewed me." Donahue put down her cup. "That reminds me. When Nika called me yesterday afternoon, she told me she was at work, and when I asked her what was going on, she said, 'not on the phone.'"

Thompson sat up a little straighter. "Did you mention that to the boys from Hollywood?"

"Yeah, and they asked me what it meant, and I said that she was probably afraid that someone at her work might overhear what she wanted to say."

Donahue studied her fingernails for a moment and came to the conclusion that she was in desperate need of a perfect manicure.

"You got anything going on this morning?" she asked Thompson.

"Not really. What did you have in mind?"

"I thought maybe we could take a drive over to Nika's place of employment. Maybe someone over there might know something that could explain what was going on?"

Thompson shook her head.

"Gibson warned me last night that we had to stay clear of Hollywood's investigation, and he wasn't kidding, Jen. He made that perfectly clear."

"We won't be investigating, Shari. Her boss is an acquaintance of mine, so I thought we might just pop over there and say hello."

Thompson shook her head.

"You're gonna to get us into so much trouble..."

*****

CHAPTER 6

October 20, 11:00 a.m.

The West Coast headquarters of the *American Standard Life Insurance Company* was located in North Hollywood on Ventura Boulevard, a miles long, east-west thoroughfare in the San Fernando Valley that sported all kinds of retail establishments as well as high-rise office buildings. *ASL,* as it was referred to in TV and radio commercials, was a twelve story facility housing more than four hundred full-time employees.

When Donahue pulled up in front of the building, she parked in a red zone on Ventura Boulevard and draped the police microphone cord over the rear view mirror to alert any parking meter officers prowling the neighborhood that the car was, in fact, a police vehicle, and that they were there on official business.

She and Thompson marched into the granite floor lobby of the building, flashed their credentials, and asked to meet with Nicholi Grushik, the Vice President of claims for the Western Region. Five minutes later, a secretary showed up, introduced herself, then led them to the top floor where they were escorted into his office.

Grushik was a forty-five-year old American of Russian descent with short dark hair, a swarthy tan, a strong chin, and high cheekbones that framed a dark, bushy mustache. His dark suit was *Dolce & Gabbana,* his cuff links from *Tiffany,* and his shoes were highly polished black wingtips from *Louis Vuitton.*

"Detective Donahue?" He walked out from behind his polished wood desk, approached her and shook her hand. "It's a pleasure to see you again."

Donahue introduced Thompson and Grushik invited them both to sit.

His office was luxurious by anyone's standards. They were guided to a pair of matching couches that were separated by a glass top coffee table. The office had a commanding view of the northern side of the San Fernando Valley. Both women took seats on one of the couches while Grushik sat on the other.

"How have you been, Nicholi?" Donahue asked.

"I'm doing well, detective. Are you still working with the Sex Crimes

41

Division?"

"Actually, I'm not. Detective Thompson and I work in Robbery-Homicide. We're here about the murder of Nika Kaminski."

Grushik's eyes moved from one to the other. It was evident to them that he was processing what she had said.

"Nika Kaminski? The young woman who works for us? You're saying she's dead?"

Donahue nodded. "She was shot to death last night. We wanted to talk to some of the employees she works with to see if they can help us out."

Grushik appeared to be stunned.

Donahue waited, but when he didn't answer, she said, "Can we talk to the people she worked with?"

"What?" Grushik shook his head. There was a long pause. "I'm sorry, detective. I'm afraid my mind was wandering. I was thinking about when she started working for us. Such a nice young woman, but such a tragic life history. How could something like this have happened?"

Donahue turned to Thompson.

"Nicholi was kind enough to hire Nika to work here. She was brought in as part of a training program for women who were victims of domestic violence or otherwise physically exploited; women who needed a second chance."

She looked back over at Grushik.

"Was she a good employee?"

"Very intelligent. She was in line to be an adjuster."

"What's an adjuster?" Thompson asked.

"A person who reviews claims that are submitted and makes a determination about the payout." Grushik smiled. "Miss Kaminski was an intake specialist, the position just below full adjuster. Her job was to do a preliminary analysis of any new claims and to set up the file for easy review by the adjuster."

"Do you know if she had any problems in the workplace, any disputes with anyone?" Donahue asked.

"As far as I know, there were no problems, but I didn't have daily interaction with her. I've been told that she got along well with the other employees." He looked off for a few moments. "I just can't believe it. Do you know if she has any family nearby?"

Donahue shrugged. "Hollywood detectives will handle that. They may be contacting you soon to see if you have contact information in her personnel file."

"I'll have it pulled and set aside for them," he said. "Is there anything else you might need?"

Donahue nodded. "The people she worked with? We'd like to talk with them."

Grushik smiled tightly. "That's right. You asked about that. I can arrange for you to speak to her direct supervisor, Leigh Cherlina. Perhaps she can help you identify Nika's closest friends."

With that, he got to his feet, walked over to his desk, punched in a number, then spoke for a few moments to someone before hanging up the phone.

"Leigh will meet you in the fifth-floor conference room."

Donahue and Thompson got to their feet.

"Thanks, Nicholi," said Donahue. "We appreciate your assistance."

"Just find the person responsible," he said with a scowl. "She was a nice young woman. This shouldn't have happened."

*****

They caught an empty elevator, and on their way down to the fifth floor where a large conference room was located. On the way, Thompson said, "So how do you know this guy Grushik?"

"I was speaking at a fundraiser for the *Rape Foundation* in Santa Monica, and he was in the audience. Afterward, he came up and introduced himself. He suggested we set up a program to help victims who needed to get back out on their own. Initially, I think he was contemplating a program for victims of do-mestic violence, but once his company got behind it, it quickly expanded to in-clude women who were victims of human trafficking."

Thompson appeared skeptical.

"Did anyone ever take a look at his background?"

Donahue nodded. "He's married with two kids. College educated, no criminal record. From what I understand, he has very little actual interaction with the women in the program. Everything is handled by their HR department."

Donahue suddenly frowned.

"Why? You think there was something nefarious going on?"

Thompson smiled.

"*Nefarious*? I like that one, but no, not really. I guess I'm just skeptical by nature."

"He's a good guy, Shari. You know, some guys really don't have ulterior motives."

"Ha! Next time you meet one, point him out."

The elevator stopped on the fifth floor, and when the door slid open, they were met by a very prim and proper looking secretary who motioned to them to follow her, then led them to a nearby conference room.

They entered the conference room and spotted the woman they were there to see. She was seated in one of a dozen chairs that were grouped around a dark, walnut conference table. As Donahue walked over to introduce herself, she took a few moment to size the woman up.

Leigh Cherlina was conservatively dressed in a pale green sweater and a pair of dark brown slacks. She wore a single strand of pearls around her neck and a small silver watch on her wrist. Her shoulder length brown hair was worn down and framed a pleasant face, the most striking feature of which was a pair of warm brown eyes.

"Ms. Cherlina?" Donahue said as she extended her hand. "I'm Detective Donahue. This is my partner Detective Thompson."

Cherlina got to her feet.

"Please, call me Leigh." She smiled then shook their hands, and as she and the two detectives took their seats, she said, "Can you tell me what this is all about?"

Thompson looked at Donahue, saw the okay nod, then took the lead.

"I understand that you are friends with Nika Kaminski?"

Cherlina looked from one to the other.

"That's right. I'm her direct supervisor." There was a brief pause as she put two and two together.

"Nika didn't come in today. Has something happened?"

Thompson studied her briefly, then said, "I'm sorry to have to be the one to give you this news, Leigh, but we're here because we're investigating her death."

"Death? Nika's dead? *Oh my God!* How did it happen?"

"We believe it's a homicide," said Thompson. "We're hoping you can tell us a little bit about Nika and whether or not she had any enemies or problems here at work?"

Cherlina closed her eyes, then began to cry. Donahue and Thompson waited her out, and when the tears finally subsided, Thompson opened her purse and passed her a packet of tissues.

Cherlina blotted her eyes, sniffed a few times, then said, "I knew there was something wrong. Nika was upset about something for at least the last month. She tried to pretend that nothing was wrong, but I knew that something was up."

"Did she ever tell you what was bothering her?" Donahue asked.

"She never said."

"Did she have any problems with anyone here at work?"

"Not that I'm aware of. Nika was a hard worker and a quick learner. She was due to be promoted to a full Adjuster." She held Thompson's glance. "Can you tell me what happened?"

Thompson answered with another question.

"How about her family? Did she ever say anything about them?"

"I'm pretty sure her family is still in Russia." She studied the two detectives. "Do you know much about her background?"

"A little," Donahue said. "Did she confide in you about her past?"

Cherlina nodded. "She told me what happened to her before she started working here."

Donahue was relieved. She had no intention of telling anyone about Nika's past, but if Cherlina already knew about it, they would be able to explore that topic without setting off a wave of gossip among the workplace employees.

"What did she tell you?" Donahue asked.

Cherlina looked concerned, then said, "About her being a victim of human

45

trafficking. I don't think she confided what happened to her to anyone else. In fact, the only reason I knew anything at first was that she came to us from the program you guys set up with the company."

"Did she ever say anything about running into the people who did that to her, or anything else like that?" Donahue asked.

Cherlina shook her head. "She was done with that life, and she seemed pretty happy...until, like I said, a few months ago."

Thompson leaned forward and lowered her voice.

"Tell me something, Leigh. How did Nika get along with Mr. Grushik?"

"Fine, I guess. There was nothing going on between them if that's what you're asking?"

"How about friends here at work? Anyone else she was close to?"

Cherlina shifted her gaze, then folded her arms across her chest.

"Nika didn't really socialize with anyone from work. She was friendly enough; it's just that she really didn't want to get too close to people she worked with because she didn't want to worry about having to answer questions about what she'd been through."

"Makes sense," said Thompson who leaned back in her chair. "How about boyfriends? Did she have someone she broke up with recently or maybe a guy who might have been stalking her?"

Cherlina's eyes went wide before she shook her head and chuckled.

"Is that funny?" Thompson asked.

Cherlina locked eyes with her.

"Nika was gay, detective. She was seeing a girl named Eliska Rodinova. I think she's a hair stylist somewhere in Sherman Oaks."

Cherlina glanced back over at Donahue, then slowly shook her head.

"After what she went through in her old life, she once told me that she had no desire to ever be with any man again."

CHAPTER 7

October 20, Afternoon

Donahue and Thompson left the insurance company and found their way to a local eatery known as *Gino's* where both of them had salads and sweet iced teas. During the drive downtown to the PAB, they spoke only about Thompson's three sons and what a load of grief her ex was giving her when it came to his lack of willingness to take the kids when she was forced to work overtime.

They trudged into the squad about two in the afternoon, and when Donahue arrived at her desk, she found a *"See me"* note from Gibson that was scotch-taped to her office telephone.

Thompson found one taped to her phone, too, so after asking around, they were told that he was in one of the interview rooms with a couple of detectives from Hollywood Division.

The former Lieutenant in their particular unit had recently retired, and with a promotional freeze currently in effect because of budgetary shortfalls, the Captain in their division, Tommy Elwood, had seen fit to select Gibson to be the acting Lieutenant for the foreseeable future.

To say that Gibson was displeased by the decision was an understatement. There was no additional pay, he hated the paperwork that came with administrative duties, and it took him out of the field when all he wanted to do was nothing more than to be left alone to work on unsolved cases.

They made their way out of the squad to the interview rooms that were clumped together off one of the major hallways. The door to one was open, and Thompson, who was first to reach the door, immediately spotted Grayson and Tucker, the two detectives from Hollywood Division that she'd met the night before. Gibson was seated across the table from them, and when she knocked on the doorframe, the conversation inside the room immediately ceased.

Gibson invited them in, and when Thompson and Donahue took seats at the table, Gibson asked the two Hollywood detectives if they would mind waiting outside for a few minutes while he had a little chat with his detectives.

Grayson and Tucker stood up, and as they went out, Grayson closed the door behind them.

"What's up?" Donahue asked once they were alone.

"I got a call during the lunch hour from the Officer-in-Charge at Hollywood Homicide. Seems as though you two went behind my back and conducted an interview with a guy named Grushik at over at Nika Kaminski's place of employment."

Donahue cleared her throat.

"I asked Shari to go with me, Gibby. I wanted to find out about her next of kin so I could send them a note. Nicholi Grushik is a friend of mine as well as her employer, so I paid him a courtesy call, and we talked for a while about Nika."

Gibson slowly shook his head, an involuntary gesture that spoke volumes about what he thought of her story. Donahue was an excellent investigator, and she had a real gift when it came to rationalizing her behavior, but he could smell a pile of bullshit from a mile away, and at the moment, he was knee deep into it.

"What you two did was to conduct an interview with Grushik. The Hollywood detectives got there just after you left, and when they started asking him questions, he said several times that you had already asked him the same ones."

Donahue shrugged while Thompson stayed mute. This was a conversation they weren't going to win.

"She was my friend," Donahue told him by way of admission. "I figured Grushik might be more inclined to give us something important if I was the one asking the questions."

Gibson pressed his lips together and carefully contained himself.

"It's not our investigation, Jen, and because you were acquainted with her, you may have a conflict of interest if you work the case." He shifted his gaze over to Thompson, who lowered her eyes to her lap to study her hands. If she could have crawled under the table, she would have.

"And you," he said sternly to Thompson. "I thought I made myself perfectly clear last night that you were not to let her get involved in the investigation."

Thompson cleared her throat.

"We just wanted to get her next of kin info, Gibby. The rest just sort of happened."

"Like the interview of her co-worker?" he said slowly and with mock surprise.

Thompson knew they were sunk. Her mind raced to find a way out of their situation.

"We just figured that since we were already there, we could do a quick interview, then come back here and write it up. We didn't think the guys from Hollywood would get around to doing those interviews for a couple of days, and if there was something good, we thought they might need it right away to move things forward."

Gibson rolled his eyes, then looked from one to the other.

"Did the two of you put your stories together on the way over here, or are you just making up this BS as you go along?"

Neither one answered, and he knew he'd made his point. He leaned back in his chair and slowly shook his head.

"I want you to write up the details of the two interviews and have them on my desk before you leave here today. And I want it completely understood that neither one of you is to involve yourselves in any way in Hollywood's investigation of Kaminski's death. Is that clear?"

"Yes, sir," they replied in unison.

Gibson shifted his gaze between them, then told them they could leave.

On their way towards the door, he said to their backs, "Ask Grayson and Tucker to come back in. I'll try to smooth their feathers before this goes up the chain of command."

Donahue found the two detectives waiting in the hallway about ten feet away.

"Gentlemen, would you mind going back in?" she said. They came right over to the door, and Donahue whispered, "Sorry about the misunderstanding. We'll write everything up and get it over to you guys this afternoon."

"Did you get anything useful?" Tucker asked.

"You can probably rule out a jilted boyfriend," Thompson said. "Her supervisor says she was gay."

"Really?" Grayson seemed surprised. "But I thought you told me she was a hooker?"

Donahue frowned.

"Technically, she was enslaved by members of the Russian mob who forced her into prostitution with drugs and threats to kill her family back in Moscow." She said it with such intensity that both men unconsciously took a step back.

Thompson added, "And the fact that she was forced to have sex with men has nothing to do with her sexual preference."

The two women then walked off leaving the two Hollywood detectives stunned and speechless.

"Idiots," Thompson muttered underneath her breath.

"Would you mind writing up the interview reports?" Donahue asked. "I want to see what I can find out about Eliska Rodinova, Nika's girlfriend.

Thompson stopped in her tracks.

"You heard what Gibby said, Jen. We don't need to be doin' this."

"We're not gonna go out and talk to her," Donahue said with a wink. "I just want to find out what we've got on her in the system."

"You're playin' with fire," Thompson shook her head.

"Will you do it for me, Shari?"

Thompson studied her for a moment, then said, "I'll take care of it. You want me to mention to *Frick and Frack* back there that the girlfriend's name is Eliska Rodinova?"

"No, don't give them her name. They're hot shot detectives, let them go back to Cherlina and get that for themselves."

Thompson shrugged her shoulders, "You're positively evil."

CHAPTER 8

October 21, 1:30 a.m.

Milan Petrovich knew that he'd had too much to drink, but it was getting late, and he was not about to leave his new Mercedes overnight in the parking lot where vandals could get to it, or worse, where someone could drive it off.

The lot was just to the west of an old warehouse that had been converted at great expense into a popular nightclub called *Siberia.* It was primarily a dance club, featuring techno music, several long bars, and lots and lots of beautiful Russian women and attractive, well-dressed men. It was also a favorite haunt of underworld types from various assorted eastern European countries.

Petrovich had just spent a long evening inside *Siberia* making small talk with a number of attractive young women, all in an effort to recruit the better-looking ones for his lucrative dating service. He had freely purchased them drinks, laughed at their silly stories, handed out dozens of his business cards, all the while knowing that if this night's efforts were to ultimately prove successful, he would need at least one or two out of the dozens he'd talked with to actually follow-up with a call to his office.

He walked unsteadily past two hulking, bald men dressed in dark suits who stood sentry duty at the front door of the club, then awkwardly, but carefully, he made his way down the front steps to the sidewalk on Hollywood Boulevard. A group of about thirty young men and women still stood in line, hoping against hope to get inside the club before it closed down at two a.m.

As far as Petrovich was concerned, this particular club had turned out to be a fairly good one for recruiting purposes, so he made it a point to drop by at least several times a week, even though he had almost a dozen other clubs to visit on a monthly basis.

He walked through the parking lot, stopping briefly at the valet stand to slip the attendant a ten. While he made use of the valet lot, he didn't want any of the minimum wage car jockeys behind the wheel of his brand new baby, so months ago, he cut a deal with the lot boss to pay extra for the use of their space in exchange for parking his own car.

The lot was still half full, but with the club closing in less than thirty minutes, it would soon be filled with revelers who would stand around in boisterous groups, hoping to keep the party going into the early morning hours. But he would be long gone by then, and his car would still be in perfect shape… that is, assuming he could get it out of the lot in his present state of inebriation.

He fished through his pockets for his keys, found them, then pressed the remote. The headlights came on and the doors unlocked. He admired it for a moment, a sleek gray beauty with an all black leather interior. It was the first truly expensive car that he'd ever owned and for him, it was a symbol of his new found success.

Petrovich was forty-five years old; tall and well built, but starting to get a little soft around the edges. His hair was shoulder length, but he kept it pulled back and tight on his head with the use of a rubber band. He was a Russian immigrant, an engineer by trade, who had stumbled inadvertently into a cash cow business investment. He was supremely happy with what he had, and with what he'd accomplished thus far, but in the back of his mind he knew that he still had a ways to go to reach the level of wealth that he felt that he was entitled to. His hope was to expand his burgeoning business to other major US cities, and as long as he could find the right kind of women to sign up as dates, he could triple or even quadruple his yearly profits within a couple of years.

It was all going well, perhaps too well, for during the last two years he'd attracted the unwanted attention of men he knew were connected to the local Russian mob. But he had no intention of sharing his good fortune, and he'd made that point clear enough to that leech who was trying to shake him down. The man had friends, of that he had no doubt, but Milan was no fool, and he had friends of his own. If they wanted to force him to give up his business, they were in for a surprise, for he had taken the first step towards ridding himself of their troublesome interference, and soon he would be free to conduct his business without having to look over his shoulder.

He opened the door to the Mercedes, slid into the comfortable leather seat, struggled briefly with the seat belt, then closed the door and engaged the ignition.

The resulting explosion was massive.

Car alarms were set off for several blocks, and windows in the immediate area imploded with the force of the blast.

The Mercedes itself was briefly lifted off the ground before a secondary explosion caused by the violent rupture of the gas tank turned the car into a fiery inferno.

CHAPTER 9

October 21, 6:30 a.m.

Donahue was driving the blue Crown Vic while Thompson was still putting the finishing touches on her makeup using the mirror attached to the passenger seat visor. The sun was up, but the morning air was chilly, so both women were wearing jackets over their dark pants suits and blouses.

As Donahue parked the car about a block away from the scene of the explosion, Thompson continued to express her concerns about having to prevail upon her babysitter to come over at six a.m. to watch her kids and get them ready for school.

"I just don't know how much longer she's gonna agree to cover for me during these call outs." She glanced over at Donahue, seeking affirmation, but Donahue was looking straight ahead.

"I might have to put in for a transfer," Thompson said with a sigh. "Maybe Community Relations might have an opening. I'm pretty sure that they're still an eight to four operation."

Donahue didn't bother to volunteer a comment; it would have been futile. The truth was that her partner was addicted to the drama of being a homicide investigator, which meant with just about absolute certainty that she'd never give up her current assignment, not if there was any possible way of hanging on to it.

They walked the rest of the way to the nightclub, crossing under the yellow crime scene tape that was stretched across the street a hundred yards on either side of the explosion. There were a large number of curious spectators standing behind the crime screen tape, waiting for something to happen, which of course, it never did. A photographer from the police department was busy taking photos of the spectators since there was always a chance that the parties responsible would return to the scene to study what was going on.

They signed in with the patrol officer whose duty it was to log in all personnel with access to the scene, then made their way over to the parking lot where the explosion was reported to have taken place.

As usual, Gibson was already on the scene. They found him standing by the hood of a black and white patrol unit that was serving as a temporary field command post. Along with Gibson were several uniformed officers from Hollywood Division who were coordinating the canvassing of the neighborhood for possible witnesses. Inside the nightclub, a few more officers were finishing up with the interviews of the last of the patrons who'd been inside the club at the time of the explosion. As the witnesses were individually released, they staggered out into the daylight like creatures from an alternate reality.

Donahue thought, *How sad. They look like characters from Alice in Wonderland who've just climbed out of the rabbit hole.*

Gibson spotted Donahue and Thompson approaching and waved them over. The uniformed officers took off to deal with their assignments, so the three of them were free to huddle about what was going on.

"So what have we got?" Donahue asked. Her eyes were drawn to the wreckage in the back of the lot.

"Bomb in a car went off about 1:35 a.m. The Fire Department put out the blaze then turned things over to Hollywood Division when they discovered human remains in the car."

Gibson pointed at a man with a tiny black and white Boston Terrier who was slowly walking through the wreckage.

"ATF is going over the scene now, looking for explosive residue."

"With that?" Thompson said as she pointed to the terrier. "It looks like a toy of some kind."

Gibson smiled. "I'll grant you it's not a Lab, but the handler says his dog will find it if it's there."

"I don't know," Thompson replied, shaking her head. "He looks awfully small."

Donahue rolled her eyes while Gibson tried not to smile.

"I'm told that size doesn't matter, Shari," he said.

Thompson winked at Donahue and cracked, "That's what you men always say."

Donahue laughed. "It has to do with the dog's training and ability to smell,

Shari. Boston Terriers are really intelligent, and their sense of smell is uncanny. Another small breed, Beagles, are often used to sniff out explosives as well."

Thompson turned to Gibson.

"And this is coming from a girl who doesn't even own a dog." She then shifted her attention over to Donahue, "I'm not even going to ask you where you picked up those little tidbits."

"You'll get an answer anyway," Donahue replied. "I went to an ATF seminar a few years ago. They talked a lot about the different breeds and their varied abilities."

When the ATF handler completed his search, he made his way over to Gibson and the detectives.

"All finished," he said. His Boston Terrier was on a leash, and he took a seat right next to his handler.

"Can I pat him?" Donahue asked.

The handler nodded.

"His name is Jake."

She bent down and patted the dog on the head, and Jake immediately rolled over onto his back and exposed his belly for further patting.

"Just like a man," Thompson snorted.

Everyone laughed while Donahue scratched the dog's belly. She then straightened up.

"Find anything useful?" Gibson asked the ATF agent.

"There's residue. I've marked the pieces I want for collection. I'll be able to give you some specifics in a day or so."

Gibson nodded. "Are we okay to go up to the remains?"

"I'm finished," the handler replied. "Just watch for my marker cards. I'll be collecting my samples just as soon as I get Jake back to the car."

He turned and walked off with his dog.

Thompson quipped, "I think you made a friend there, Jen."

"Story of my life," she said. "I've always been a dog magnet."

Before Thompson could respond, Gibson asked, "Are you two ready to take the scene over?"

Donahue nodded, now all business, and both women pulled notepads out of their purses.

"Okay. What have we got?" Donahue asked him.

"One victim in the car. The remains will have to be identified by the Coroner as the body was almost entirely consumed by the resulting fire. But the license plate comes back to a new Mercedes registered to one Milan Petrovich, age 45. The staff in the club say they know him as a regular. He comes in here once or twice a week. He was in last night, and one of the doormen says that he walked out of the club about two minutes before the explosion."

Donahue looked over her shoulder. "Any security cameras set up?"

"Only inside," Gibson responded. "I've got the night manager pulling the tape for us, but no such luck in the parking lot."

"I see a valet stand," Thompson declared. "Any chance the victim is the valet?"

Gibson shook his head.

"The valet says that the Mercedes owner paid him to let him park and lock his own vehicle. He saw him head to the car, then turned away and started counting his tips when the explosion went off."

"Was he hurt?" Thompson asked.

"Possible concussion. He was knocked to the ground, but miracle of miracles, he wasn't struck by any shrapnel. The guy was lucky as hell."

Donahue looked over at Thompson. "We'll need to talk to him to find out if he saw anyone near the car?"

Thompson nodded in agreement.

'So why are we taking this one, Gibby?" Donahue asked. "Can't Hollywood take it on?"

"The Captain at our Organized Crime Intelligence Unit called the Chief this morning. He said the likely victim, Milan Petrovich, along with his partner, a woman, operated a dating service for wealthy men interested in dating Russian women. An OCI investigation of the business was recently started, so considering the complexity and possible organized crime implications, the Chief feels it's complex enough for RHD to take it on."

He looked at the two of them then winked.

"And with your prior experience with the sex workers in the Russian community and their connection to the Russian mob, I figure you and Shari just might have an interest in taking on this case."

Donahue smiled. For all practical purposes, the door would now be open for them to look into any possible mob involvement in the death of Nika Kaminski without stepping on the toes of *Frick and Frack* as she and Thompson had taken to calling Grayson and Tucker behind their backs.

"You think there may be a connection between Nika's death and this guy Petrovich?" she asked.

"Both victims are Russian, and while there may be some differences in their respective business models, both have, at their core, the relationships between women and men." He shrugged, then smiled. "So, in answer to your question, it can't hurt to explore that possibility."

"Artfully put, Gibby." Donahue smiled at the way he'd given her the green light to look into the Kaminski case. "But Nika was out of the life."

"She may have been out of it, Jen, but that doesn't mean she didn't have the kind of info about it that might have brought about her death."

Donahue nodded. You could drive a train through this now open door.

"Okay, boss. We'll take it from here." She caught Thompson's glance. "You ready to take a look at the victim's remains?"

"Not really," Thompson said with a grimace. She hated charred body cases. The smell of burnt flesh always made her gag. She took a handkerchief out of her purse and held it in her hand, ready to put it over her mouth and nose at the very first whiff of that horrible, unmistakable smell.

"Let's just get this over with," she said halfheartedly.

"You're not gonna blow breakfast, are you?" Donahue asked.

Thompson stared at her through rheumy eyes.

"I won't lie, Jen. Right now it's just about fifty-fifty." She looked over at the wreckage. "Make that sixty-forty."

Donahue sighed. "Just hold your breath Shari, and we'll make it fast."

They slowly walked over to the remains of the car, and carefully picked their way through the debris.

CHAPTER 10

October 21, 2:00 p.m.

Back at her desk in the squad room, Donahue took a sip of her coffee and checked her watch. They'd skipped lunch, and she was starving, but once you caught a fresh homicide, it was important to stay with it as long as physically possible because the passage of time usually resulted in the loss of possible evidence.

The best approach was to go all out until you couldn't go any longer.

This "drop everything and stay the course" attitude created enormous stress for most of the people who worked homicides. It destroyed many marriages, caused personal psychological breakdowns, and impacted the health of many investigators. And yet, in spite of the fact that these tolls were well known to the detectives who did this type of work, if asked about the pitfalls of working homicides, almost to a man or woman they would respond quite proudly that they had no worries about the probable consequences of their career choice, because "they" would certainly end up being one of the exceptions to the rule.

Another ten minutes passed while Donahue put the finishing touches on her follow-up report on the Petrovich homicide. The ATF conclusion was that the bomb had been remotely detonated when Petrovich had climbed into his car. It would take another day or two to analyze the explosive residue recovered at the scene, but the ATF agent who'd combed over the crime scene wreckage was fairly certain that the explosive used was a form of *plastique*. But confirmation of that would have to come later.

A search of the neighborhood by detectives called in to assist with the investigation turned up no eyewitnesses to the explosion. There were no CCTV cameras on any of the nearby buildings, so they didn't catch a break when it came to video of the perpetrator coming or going from the scene.

The valet had been tracked down at the hospital where he was being observed because he'd shown signs of a concussion, but he readily admitted quite candidly that lots of people wandered in and out of the lot during the course of the evening and he couldn't keep track of all of them. Of one thing he was adamant: he hadn't seen anything suspicious as it related to Petrovich's car.

She leaned back in her chair, listened to her stomach growl, then resolved to get up and find something to eat. But just as she got out of her chair, Gibson walked in with two large bags of take-out food from an Italian restaurant around the corner from the PAB.

"Lunch is served," he said.

He walked straight to his desk and began opening the takeout boxes of pasta, laying them out next to a stack of paper plates and plastic forks.

Donahue was the first to take advantage of his generosity, piling a plate high with pasta primavera. Thompson was right behind her, and soon both women were seated back at their desks, enjoying their first meal of the day.

Mitzi Roberts, a detective who enjoyed a reputation for being the electronics wizard in the unit, commandeered a chair from a nearby cubical and took a seat in the aisle between them.

Roberts was an attractive brunette with a warm smile and a wicked sense of humor. Quiet and professional when she was working, she was a closet hell-raiser when on her days off.

"I tracked down that hairdresser for you," Roberts said. "I ran her through DMV. There was only one Eliska Rodinova. The address given is an apartment building in Sherman Oaks." She handed the DMV printout to Donahue who stopped eating long enough to glance at the results before passing the slip on to Thompson.

"Are we going to mention this to the boys at Hollywood?" Thompson asked between mouthfuls.

"Not a chance," Donahue said. "We're going to talk to her because she *may* have info that *might* be helpful to us in our bombing case."

"You're gonna get us in trouble, Jen. We can't keep this from the Hollywood guys forever."

Donahue thought it over as she took another bite of her pasta.

"Tell you what. If we learn something of value about Nika that would help their case, we'll pass it on. Okay?"

"Much better," Thompson declared.

Roberts shook her head. "I hate to interrupt this fascinating discussion about inter-office cooperation, but if you ladies are through, I've got the rest of the information you asked for."

"Did you want some pasta?" Donahue said, looking up from her plate.

"Thanks, but I already had lunch."

"Cranky," Thompson said, gesturing with her head in Robert's direction. Donahue nodded. "Might be low blood sugar."

"Are you done yet?" Roberts asked with an exasperated smile.

Donahue grinned. "Lay it on us."

"Okay. Your possible victim, Milan Petrovich—and I say possible because a positive ID is still pending—emigrated to the USA ten years ago from Russia. He worked for a while as an engineer at Raytheon, then left his nine-to-five almost four years ago to partner up with a female Russian named Irina Konstantinov. They set up an upscale matchmaking service based here in Los Angeles which caters to wealthy men looking for Russian women. Actually, that's not quite correct. The women on their site are from Russia as well as the now independent countries that used to be a part of the greater Soviet Union."

"You mean like the Ukraine and Georgia…countries like that?" asked Thompson.

"Very good, Shari," Roberts added in a patronizing tone, "and that's surprising since it's coming from you."

Donahue laughed, then licked the tip of her finger and made an imaginary hash line in the air as if keeping score on a blackboard.

"That's one for Mitz," she said.

"There's more," said Roberts who tried to get the conversation back on track. "The name of their dating service is *Trophy-Wife Matchmaking*."

"Catchy," said Thompson who turned to her computer and typed the company name into her search engine.

"*You get what you pay for…* is probably the corporate motto," Donahue suggested with a half-suppressed laugh.

"I looked at the site, and I'm guessing that they recruit the women from the waiting rooms of plastic surgeons," Roberts said.

Donahue laughed again. "Nice, Mitz! You're on a roll."

"*Wow!*" Thompson leaned back in her chair. "You need to check this out, Jen."

Both Donahue and Roberts got to their feet and studied the website from over Thompson's shoulder.

Thompson had clicked on the heading *Member Photo Gallery* and the photographs that came up were head shots or full body shots of women whose physical beauty was of jaw-dropping quality. They appeared to be mostly in their twenties and thirties.

"Meet the competition, ladies," said Donahue.

"The average woman doesn't have a chance," Roberts added.

"I'll bet they airbrush these photos," Thompson mumbled.

"They must," agreed Donahue. "These girls are just too perfect."

"I think we need to talk to Petrovich's business partner right away," Thompson suggested, her eyes still glued to the screen. "What did you say her name was?"

"Irina Konstantinov," Roberts said.

Donahue stood up straight, no longer focused on what was on the screen.

"Before we do that, I want to follow up with the Captain of the OCI Unit. I want to know what his investigation was all about, and what they know about Petrovich and Konstantinov."

"Does that mean we can put off interviewing Konstantinov and Nika's girlfriend Eliska Rodinova until tomorrow?" Thompson asked, shutting down her computer.

Donahue nodded. "Yeah, I guess so. I wouldn't want your sitter to throw a fit."

"You're all heart, Jen."

"I know."

CHAPTER 11

October 21, 3:00 p.m.

Captain John Odom was a twenty-six year veteran of the LAPD. Currently head of the Organized Crime Intelligence Unit, he had an affable personality that seemed to go well with his tall, lanky frame and his neatly parted snow white hair. His face was weathered by his outdoor lifestyle that included frequent boating on the Colorado River and horseback riding three times a week on an energetic colt named 'Sniper' that he boarded at a ranch in the city of Calabasas.

Odom's office was located in a nondescript industrial building on Sixth Street, about two miles from the downtown civic center. Also housed at that same location, but on a different floor, was the Intelligence Surveillance Unit, a group of specialists who followed organized crime figures for the purpose of gathering information on their contacts, haunts, and activities.

Donahue had called ahead, so Odom was waiting for them in his office when she and Thompson arrived. He welcomed them in and had them sit in chairs in front of his desk.

The office was without windows and furnished with old metal desks that had been salvaged from Parker Center, the former headquarters building for LAPD that served as the focal point of the Department before the construction of the PAB. Rank came with privileges, Donahue noted with irony, but apparently not when your unit was stuck in a building that was old and not staffed by the senior administration.

"Did you confirm that the victim was Petrovich?" he asked as soon as they were settled.

"Not yet," said Thompson, "but there's almost no doubt."

Donahue said, "We were told that your people had opened a case on Milan Petrovich. Any chance you can tell us what was going on?"

Odom smiled. "That's not exactly what happened. Petrovich came to us with information on a subject named Vladimir Komarov, so we opened the case on him."

"What was it about?" Thompson asked.

"Petrovich said about five years ago he entered into a partnership with a female named Irina Konstantinov. Together, they set up a dating service using her connections in the dating industry and his financial assets to recruit young Russian and Eastern European women, all professionals, to sign up with their agency."

"Professionals as in *sex workers*?" Thompson asked.

Odom chuckled.

"No, we're talking about accountants, interior designers, engineers, doctors, and according to Petrovich, they even recruited a rocket scientist. The women were asked to go out with fee-paying clients. Petrovich was adamant that the girls were legitimately looking for husbands or a serious relationship. Supposedly, they were told that if they engaged in sex with the clients before the fourth date, they would be dropped from the agency for good."

"But sex was okay after the fourth date?" Thompson asked.

"I guess they figured that four dates were considered the start of a real relationship," Odom replied. He leaned back in his chair and smiled. "Seems to me that it would be a little hard to enforce, but what do I know?"

"How did the agency make their money?" Donahue asked.

"A yearly fee for the male clients. He told us the minimum was ten thousand dollars, and for that kind of money, the customers were guaranteed a new introduction every month."

"That's a lot of money," Thompson said with a roll of her eyes.

"Petrovich bragged that more than a few of their male clients pay up to twenty-five thousand a year in exchange for *unlimited introductions* during the twelve month period."

"Who are these clients," Donahue asked, "and why can't I meet men like that?"

Odom laughed. "He said that his clients are lawyers, doctors, and successful businessmen; the kind that don't have the time or the social skills to go out and find a match on their own."

"With that kind of money to spend, it's no wonder the agency is able to recruit such beautiful and talented girls."

"Petrovich said that women who are raised in Russia and Eastern Europe have no qualms about dating much older men. They are primarily concerned with security, so looks and age are not as important as they seem to be for western women."

Donahue shook her head and smiled.

"So you're saying that this agency catered to older men who get their jollies off by dating beautiful and much younger women?"

"That would be my take," Odom said with a smile. "Petrovich was also quick to say that the agency boasted more than a dozen marriages since they started up the business."

"Hence the name...*Trophy-Wife Matchmaking,*" said Thompson.

"Anyway, Petrovich stated that when they first started up, he handled the male clients while his partner recruited the women. Apparently, she had experience at another agency, and she siphoned off some of the women she had previously worked with. But after a while, they needed more women, so he started going out to clubs on a regular basis and discovered that he had a talent for recruiting the girls. He also realized that the male clients preferred to have female counselors, so they recruited young women to help them work with the men, and once they did, the business took off. Apparently, there was no shortage of clients."

"So what was the nature of his complaint?" Donahue asked.

"Their business was so profitable that members of the Russian mob got wind of what they were doing. Petrovich walked into the Hollywood Division about a week ago and complained to the Watch Commander that a guy named Vladimir Komarov had cornered him at a nightclub in Hollywood and told him that since he was dipping into their talent pool, *his people* wanted a share of the business. Petrovich said that someone told him that Komarov was Russian OC, but he turned him down flat without hesitation. He said Komarov seemed to take it well, but the day after that meeting, Petrovich had second thoughts about what he'd done, so he came to us and filed a complaint, hoping that by doing so, these mob guys would leave him alone."

Odom looked from one to the other.

"I told my guys to get a line on Komarov. That was about three days ago. Then the bombing happened, so that's where we're at."

"Apparently, these mob guys don't fool around," Thompson said.

Donahue asked, "So this guy Komarov is actually mobbed up?"

Odom shrugged.

"We did a preliminary check. Seems he emigrated from Russia about six years ago. Since then, he appears to have flown under the radar. Not much is known about this guy, but if he is involved in organized crime, my guys believe he *may have* hooked up with a group called *Solntsevskaya Bratva*."

"That's a real mouthful. Who are they?" Thompson asked.

"For simplicity, we call 'em the *SB*. They got their start in the *Sointsevo* District of Moscow back in the 1980s. And while they got their start in Russia, over the years they've spread out like a cancer into the Ukraine, Hungary, the Czech Republic, Israel, the UK, France, Spain, Western Europe, and of course, the USA. Hollywood likes to portray these guys as well organized—you know 'em if you see 'em hoods—and to some extent, they are, but around here they tend to operate more like a loose-knit coalition. They've got about a hundred members in LA whose heritage goes back to Russia and other Eastern Bloc countries, and they maintain ties to other groups all over the world."

Odom leaned forward in his chair.

"When we think of organized crime in this country, we think of well-defined groups like the Italian families or the Japanese Yakuza. But the Russians aren't set up that way. The best way to describe them is to say that they are a loosely knit group whose individuals come together to pull off scams or other illegal activities. When the scam or crime has run its course, they move on to the next scam with other, new and different partners."

"Do they kick up the chain to a hierarchy?"

"In selective situations, the answer is yes. But for the most part, they don't. That's what makes working these guys so difficult."

"What's their structure like?" Thompson asked.

"There's an Elite Group, led by a *Pakhan* who's involved in management, organization, and ideology. He oversees everything, sort of like the mafia Don. Below the Elites are the Security Group, and the leader of that is called the

Krysha, which literally translates to 'roofs.' He would be an extremely violent enforcer who's job it is to protect a business from other criminal organizations. The third level is the support group, and the leader of that group is charged with watching over the working unit, collecting the money while supervising their criminal activities. This group has equal power with the Security team, but they will plan a specific crime for a specialized group or choose who carries out an operation. Below them, at the bottom of the barrel, are the Working Units. These are the burglars, thieves, and street gangs."

"What kind of crimes do they tend to be involved in?" asked Donahue.

"Human trafficking, bank fraud, theft from the elderly, narcotics, money laundering, insurance fraud, gasoline truck hijacking, murder-for-hire, and extortion. You name it, they're into it." Odom shifted in his chair. "In fact, I saw a recent Federal report that says that they've apparently been in collusion with the Columbian cartels to ship meth and cocaine into the US of A."

"I don't envy you guys," said Donahue. "It sounds like it's almost impossible to make a case."

Odom gave her a terse nod. "Thank God for the feds and the racketeering statutes," he said. "That's about the only way to go after these guys as a group."

"Do your people work the human trafficking cases," Thompson asked, "or is that left to the Human Trafficking Unit?"

"Our HTU usually works the street prostitution cases. They deal with the young runaways who are being pimped out by locals. We handle the intelligence gathering when the trafficking involves organized crime, and if we come up with something workable, we pass it off to the appropriate unit. For example, if it's an Asian gang involved, then it would go to the Asian gang unit. But if its Eastern European or Russian mobsters, then we tend to hold on to it because of the complexities of working a case with significant international ramifications. We have the connections to get foreign assistance, while HTU doesn't focus on that."

"So what about this guy Komarov? Could he be a key player?"

Odom shook his head. He shifted in his chair, made a show of massaging his lower back, then leaned forward, putting both elbows on the desk.

"My guys tell me he set up a trucking business of some kind. That's about all we had developed before the bombing went down. But because we didn't know about him before Petrovich walked in, I would doubt that he's more than a low-level thug, part of a Working unit."

"Can you get us an address and a photo of Komarov?" said Donahue.

"I'll take care of it," he replied.

The two detectives got to their feet and shook his hand.

"Let me know if I can be of any further help," Odom said. "I've got a really top-notch undercover guy here who knows a lot of the players, so give me a call if you've got any questions or if any other names come up, and I'll have him get back to you."

"Thanks, Captain."

Donahue hung her purse strap over her shoulder.

"We certainly will."

Once they were clear of the station, with Donahue behind the wheel, Thompson said, "I just don't understand this whole organized crime thing. If law enforcement knows who these guys are, why not just go arrest them and throw away the key?"

"The law," said Donahue. "We have to get evidence of a crime."

"No, I mean like over in Russia, where they aren't hamstrung with the niceties of decisions like the Miranda rights, or bail?"

"Spoken like a true right winger," Donahue said with a smile.

"You know what I'm getting at," said a frustrated Thompson. "They don't have the same stringent rules, and yet when they don't do something about their problem, it spills over to the rest of the world."

"There are some experts who would say that their failure to act is the direct result of the involvement of their political leaders." Donahue caught Thompson's glance. "In other words, it's a mafia-run country, Shari, and we would be wise to keep that in mind."

CHAPTER 12

October 21, 11:30 p.m.

The *Siberia* was allowed to reopen the night after the bombing. Considering the size of the explosion in the parking lot, it was surprising that the building itself was none the worse for wear. A cement block wall on the western side of the building had taken the brunt of most of the shrapnel, and while small pieces of metal were imbedded in the wall, the interior of the club had not been damaged. The city had come out and inspected the building, and once the mess in the lot was cleaned up, the managers of *Siberia* were given the official okay to resume their daily operations.

But for the fact that it catered primarily to the Russian expat community, the *Siberia* was a typical Hollywood dance club.

After the fall of the Soviet Union, a large number of Russians and eastern Europeans had emigrated to the United States, with many of them settling in southern California. There were two major enclaves. The largest, by far, was in the city of Glendale, a suburb in the eastern San Fernando Valley. The other contingent was based at the eastern end of Hollywood, and since Hollywood was known as a base for the clubbing crowd, the owners of the building had deemed it to be the logical place to establish the club.

Exactly who the owners were was not readily determined. On the surface, the club was owned by a shell corporation, which in turn, was owned by another shell. Had anyone tried to follow the trail to its end, they would have uncovered an attorney who was paid to use his name by owners who were living in Moscow. Who they were was not really known, and the source of their financial where-with-all was considered to be of dubious origin.

Yuri Pavienko slammed down a shot of vodka and followed it with a champaign chaser. The men and women whose booth he had joined did the same. They were drinking to *'the Motherland.'*

Pavienko was thirty-five years old, six-foot-two in height, two hundred and fifteen pounds; a formidable presence wherever he went. His hair was black, his face clean shaven, but his eyes were something of a mystery. While they could be warm and generous most of the time, on other occasions, they were cold and unreadable.

Personality wise, he was considered a charmer; a ladies man who exuded supreme confidence in social situations.

Pavienko was wearing a long sleeve black shirt, black jeans, and a pair of black *Frye* boots. The top two buttons of his shirt were open, and around his neck was a thick gold chain supporting a solid gold Russian Orthodox crucifix.

He was seated at the table with Vlad Komarov who had invited him over to meet a friend of his named Martun Hagopian. Two long legged blond females, both in their early twenties, wearing crop tops, short skirts, and platform heels, completed the group.

There was techno music playing softly in the background, but the dance floor was empty while the DJ took a break. Most of the hundred or so young men and women were gathered around the bar, and the chief topic of conversation was the bombing the night before.

Komarov filled everyone's shot glasses with vodka again, and the group immediately pounded them down.

Komarov, thirty-nine, was a bit shorter than Pavienko, but his weight, while similar, was concentrated around his middle. He wore a long sleeve white shirt, a pair of dark blue jeans, and black boots.

Hagopian, was much shorter than both men, but his darker skin and long, unkempt dark hair, reflected the toughness and suspicions of a man whose hardscrabble life had seen its share of violence.

Komarov leaned forward towards Pavienko and spoke softly so as not to be overheard by the women at the table.

"Martun is from *Dagestan*. Mutual friends of ours asked me to help set him up in business."

Pavienko glanced over at Hagopian who appeared to be busy feeling up one of the blonds.

"What did you have in mind for him?" Pavienko asked.

"He'll make the rounds of the clubs, maybe sell some *E* or *Meth*. I haven't decided."

"Better clean him up a bit," Pavienko told him, his eyes still glued to Hagopian. "His looks don't fit in for working the club scene. He'll stand out like a sore thumb."

Komarov, who prided himself on looking as though he just stepped out of the pages of GQ Magazine, shifted his glance to Hagopian.

"Mmm, you might be right, Yuri. I'll have to give that some thought. Maybe I'll just have him run a few girls."

Pavienko was getting bored. He'd reached his limit of vodka for the evening and the small talk with Vlad Komarov didn't really interest him. He checked his watch, then made a show of yawning.

"I'm going to take off, Vlad. I didn't get enough sleep last night."

Pavienko smiled. "You with that girl I introduced you to? What was her name? The one with the beautiful tits?"

"Marusya?"

"That's the one," said Komarov with a leer. "How was she?"

Pavienko smiled, then shook his head.

"I was alone last night, Vlad. A neighbor's dog was barking all night."

"Easy to fix," he said with a laugh. "A little poison meat over the fence should solve your problem, Yuri."

Pavienko smiled and got to his feet.

He nodded to Hagopian who was still so busy with the blond in the booth that he paid him scant attention.

"Later, Vlad," said Pavienko, his eyes now locked on Komarov. "Thanks for the *Stoli.*"

He reached into his pocket and pulled out a wad of bills to pay for the drinks, but Vlad waived him off.

"Not tonight, *Apyr.*"

Pavienko smiled at being called 'friend'. He reached out, bumped fists with Komarov, then made his way out of the club.

He walked out to the lot, gave the valet his ticket, paid the eight dollar fee, then stood on the sidewalk, studying the passers-by, until his black BMW pulled up.

He got in, pulled out into traffic, then turned right at the first corner, pulling up at the curb.

A man in black jeans and a long sleeve gray shirt and black leather jacket walked up to the car and got into the passenger seat. He stubbed out his cigarette in the ashtray, fastened his seatbelt, then looked over at Pavienko as he pulled away from the curb.

Clay Young was thirty-five, an all-American, mid-western male with a sprinkling of freckles across the bridge of his nose. His shoulder length sandy blond hair was intentionally worn slicked back to show off a half caret diamond stud which adorned his right earlobe.

"Who's the new guy?" Young asked, "the one who looks like *Rasputin the Mad Monk*."

Pavienko laughed.

"His name is Martun Hagopian, a recent arrival from *Dagestan*. Vlad says he's going to help him out for a friend. The guy's a low level soldier, no real skills. Nothing for us to worry about."

"Unless you ran across him in dark alley," Young muttered.

Twenty minutes later, Yuri pulled into the driveway of the industrial building on Sixth Street, about two miles from the downtown civic center, where the Organized Crime Intelligence Unit made their home. He pressed a code into the keypad of the security gate box, nodded once in the direction of a concealed security camera, then waited while the iron metal gate slid open to allow them into the lot.

He parked the car next to several others, and the two of them walked to a nondescript door where he punched another code into a security box, then pulled open the door to let both of them inside.

The building held units that worked in the field of organized crime. Their Captain, John Odom, was housed on the upper floor, but Yuri's unit was housed in the basement, away from everyone else.

They entered a small squad room where they got a nod from an officer who was sitting at a desk with a monitor screen that showed four separate camera views of the parking lot.

"Hey, Yuri," the officer said as he waived a piece of paper. "I got a message for you from Captain Odom."

Pavienko took the note out of his hand and walked over to his desk. He removed his coat, hung it on the back of his chair; pulled a handgun from the waistband at the small of his back, slid it into his desk; then opened the note and read it.

He turned to Clay Young.

"Start a background check on Hagopian. Check with Interpol, and contact our friend at the FSB (Russian Federal Security Service). See if they've got a file on him?"

"What does the Captain want?" Young asked.

"He wants me to give a detective named Thompson a call tomorrow morning." He looked at the note again, memorized the number, then crushed it up and threw it in a wastebasket.

"Want me to come along?" Young asked.

"I can handle it." He looked over at his partner and smiled. "Why don't you go ahead on home? Burn some of your overtime. The boss says you're already over your monthly accrual."

"Yeah, okay, sounds good. I can use the sleep. You got something going on?"

"Just paperwork, and as soon as it's done, I'm going to crash."

CHAPTER 13

October 22, 9:00 a.m.

The *Vanilla Bake Shop* in Santa Monica, California, was nationally known for among its' buttercream frosted cupcakes and gigantic chocolate brownies. So it went without saying that Shari Thompson suggested to Yuri Pavienko that they hold their face-to-face at a location that was miles away from Hollywood which was where he operated in his undercover capacity. When he agreed to the location, she dragged Mitzi Roberts along to introduce her to the guilty pleasures of *Vanilla* while Donahue took a separate car to try and track down the whereabouts of Nika's girlfriend, Eliska Rodinova.

Thompson and Roberts were seated at a small table for two inside the public area of the bakery.

"This was a big mistake," Roberts said while she greedily forked a bite of a '*Meyer-Lemon'Raspberry'* cupcake into her mouth.

Thompson smiled. She took a sip of her coffee, then put down her cup.

"I told you these were the best. Try a bite of this one, it's called *'Blackberry Passion Fruit.'* It's to die for."

Roberts reached across the table and cut off a piece of Thompson's cupcake just as Thompson's phone began to ring.

"Your ring tone?" Roberts said. She listened for a moment longer. "Tell me that's not…'*It's Raining Men*?'"

Thompson grinned as she pulled her phone out of her purse.

"It is, isn't it?" Roberts rolled her eyes, then in a reference to Thompson's bosom, "For you and your twin girls, I suppose it always is."

She popped her fork into her mouth and closed her eyes as she savored the taste of the bite from Thompson's *Blackberry Passion Fruit* cupcake.

"Hey, Jen," said Thompson into her cell phone. "What's up?"

"I went to the address for Eliska developed by Mitzi, but there's no one there. She hasn't been seen for a couple of days. A neighbor says she works at a beauty shop somewhere in Encino. I'm on my way back to PAB. I'll work the phones once I get there and maybe I can track her down." She paused to take a breath. "How's it going with the OC undercover?"

"Sergeant Pavienko is late," Thompson said, stealing a glance at her watch. "So we're just killing time by sampling a few cupcakes."

"Where are you? At Vanilla?"

"Yep."

"Bring me a couple, will you?" Donahue asked.

"What flavors do you want?"

A man walked into the shop, and both Thompson and Roberts turned to watch him approach. His good looks were not lost on the women. In jeans, a black T-shirt, a dark gray linen sports coat and motorcycle boots, he seemed to glide effortlessly across the floor.

"Gotta go," Thompson said.

"Do they have the Cinnamon Vanilla or the Red Velvet cupcakes?" Donahue asked.

Click!

The line went dead, and Donahue was left staring at her phone.

"You must be Yuri?" Thompson said as she put down the phone and got to her feet. "I'm Shari Thompson, and this is Mitzi Roberts."

Yuri smiled and shook their hands. He pulled up a chair from a nearby empty table then joined them. When he did, Roberts said, "Care for a cupcake?"

He looked at her, smiled briefly, then shook his head.

"Maybe I'll get one to go."

He looked back over at Thompson, sizing her up.

"So, thanks for coming all the way out here," Thompson said. "I figured this is about as safe a place for a meet as we could find."

"It's fine," he said, looking around. There was a line of customers waiting to purchase cakes and cupcakes, but the table they were at kept them out of public earshot.

"What was it you wanted to know?" He directed his question to Thompson.

She immediately recognized the signs. He was attracted to her, and for her part, he wasn't bad looking at all. She smiled brightly and turned on the charm.

"I was hoping you could tell us a bit about the Russian mafia here in Los

Angeles. I tried to get some facts off the internet, but they didn't have much of substance."

Yuri nodded. "Anything in particular?"

"Everything," said Roberts, and Thompson shot her a withering stare.

Yuri chuckled.

"Okay. Russian gangs tend to be very loosely organized. The LA scene is predominately run by Armenians, but for the last fifteen years or so the SB or *Solntsevskaya Brotherhood* has been moving in and infiltrating the rackets. They're allied with groups all over the world which give them powerful backing. The players come and go, cutting deals with their cohorts in Europe and South America. Occasionally, someone here tries to get things better organized, but for the most part, the crimes committed here are loosely organized, and the perpetrators don't answer to a formal chain of command."

"Are they all Russians?" Thompson asked.

"No, they have members from most of the Eastern European countries, but quite a few of them are specifically from Russia."

Thompson was hanging on to his every word, so Roberts interjected with a more direct follow-up question.

"We heard that a guy named Vladimir Komarov was trying to muscle in on Petrovich's dating site. Did you ever come across that guy?"

"I know who he is. I've run into him a few times when I'm working the club scene. The guy's a low level pimp. He also sells drugs." He looked back over at Thompson and smiled. "Personally, I'm not buying into Petrovich's story. It doesn't make a whole lot of sense to me."

"How so?" Thompson asked.

Yuri leaned back and inhaled deeply.

"Well, for starters, Komarov is small time. He's all flash and bling. The guy's got a coke habit, and he loves the young women. The pimping and the drug sales keep him in the money, but he just doesn't strike me as the type who'd want to take on the headaches of a legitimate business." He leaned in closer to Thompson and lowered his voice. "And secondly, it wouldn't surprise me if Petrovich and Komarov got into a beef over something else, like maybe Petrovich's recruitment of a young woman that Komarov had designs on."

"You think that's what happened?" Thompson asked.

"I don't know, but if he wanted to get Komarov to back off, then what better way to do it than to file a complaint with us and have us start nosing around in Komarov's business."

"You've got a good point, Yuri, but we've got to look at him anyway," said Thompson. "If it turns out he wasn't involved, can you talk to some of your informants and see what the word is out on the street?"

"I can try, but it won't be easy. These guys aren't like the local street gangs. To warrant a death by bombing, Petrovich must have done something that really pissed someone off. If his killing is somehow mob related, we might never find out who actually did it. The kind of guys who order a hit like the one you're working on don't need to dirty their hands. For very little money, they can fly in outside talent from the Caucasus or Western Europe, get the job done, then get the hitter back on a plane to their homeland before we can even manage to clear the crime scene."

"I had no idea they were that sophisticated," Thompson said.

"They are. These guys are a bunch of ruthless bastards and they have no respect at all for our laws or institutions." He gave Thompson a smile. "Maybe you should come by our squad sometime? I can show you a flow chart we're putting together to identify the more significant LA players."

Roberts folded her arms across her chest and thought, *he's actually trying to hit on her.*

"Maybe I will," Thompson said with a smile.

Roberts rolled her eyes, then said, "Don't forget the other case, Shari. You know, the one that Jen is working on?"

"Oh, yeah," Thompson looked back at Yuri. "Is there any street buzz about the death of Nika Kaminski?"

"Kaminski?" He pondered the question. "Was that the hooker found dead in her apartment in Hollywood?"

"*Former escort,*" Thompson said by way of correction. "She was an escort at one time, but got her act together and left the life behind."

He studied her for a moment, then said, "Isn't Hollywood working that case?"

Thompson nodded.

"Then what's the interest for you guys?"

"A couple of dead Russian expats in the same week? That's unusual enough for us to wonder if there's any possible connection?"

"I really don't think the two are related, but again, I'll keep my ear to the ground."

"By any chance, did you know her personally?" Roberts asked.

He shook his head.

"Hollywood asked our Captain if we knew anything about her associates, but we had nothing on file. In fact, they're the ones who told us she was a hooker...er, former escort."

He smiled at his faux pas, then gave Thompson a wink.

"Sounds to me like you may have known her," he said. "What's the connection?"

"She called my partner the night she was killed and wanted to meet, but by the time we got over to her place, someone had already gotten to her."

"So she was a CI?" he asked, a note of surprise in his voice. A CI was short for a confidential informant.

Thompson shrugged. She had no idea whether or not Kaminski had ever given Donahue intelligence information, so she decided not to answer.

"Okay, then," he said as he glanced at his watch. "If there are no more questions, I really need to crash. I've been up all night and I'm due back on duty tonight at seven."

"I think we're done here," Thompson said with a generous smile. "Thanks for your help."

"One more question, Yuri," said Roberts. "Nika supposedly had a girlfriend named Eliska Rodinova. We're told she works at a beauty shop in the Valley. Does that name ring any bells?"

"Did she ever work the streets?" he asked.

"No idea."

"Nothing comes to me now, but I'll see if we've got anything on her back at the office."

He pulled a loose slip of paper and a pen from his jacket pocket and wrote down a telephone number.

"Here's my office number," he said handing it to Thompson. "Call me if you've got more questions."

"You don't give out your cell?" Thompson asked, taking the paper.

Yuri smiled.

"I only give the cell to my Russian contacts." He got to his feet, nodded to Roberts, then gave Thompson a wink before heading for the door.

"A total narcissist," Roberts whispered when he was out of earshot, "but he certainly seemed interested in your chest."

"I didn't notice," Thompson replied.

"I was watching his eyes," Roberts added. "He was totally fascinated."

Thompson laughed.

"Well, he's a major bad boy, Mitz, that's for sure, but my goodness, he sure is cute."

"That he is." Roberts stood up. "You ready to go?"

"I need to get some cupcakes for Jen. You want to take some back to the squad with you?"

"Try and stop me."

CHAPTER 14

October 22, 11:00 a.m.

"Whose car is this anyway?" Thompson asked. She was squirming around uncomfortably in the passenger side front seat. "It smells like my kid's dirty clothes hamper."

They were riding in a brown Crown Victoria that looked clean enough, but the inside was showing the trappings of extended wear.

"Bengtson and Jackson loaned it to us while ours is being serviced," said Donahue. "They were going to walk to court today so they said we could use it."

"Well, I don't know who's been riding shotgun in this heap, but this seat has no support. I feel like I'm sitting on a piece of wood...and there's a spring or something that's poking me in the ass."

Donahue snickered. "I'm not gonna even touch that line, Shari."

"You better not." She loosened her seatbelt so that she could slide closer to the door and off the busted spring.

"No wonder they decided to walk to court." She looked over at Donahue. "And I thought our car was a piece of crap."

"We're almost there," Donahue said, fighting to keep the smile off her face.

The sky was clear outside, but the weather was cool. Both women were wearing coats, and Thompson sported a wool scarf.

"When did they say our car would be ready?" Thompson asked.

"Later this afternoon or first thing tomorrow."

"Well, it can't come back soon enough to suit me."

They rode in silence for a couple of minutes before Thompson spoke up again.

"How many salons did you have to call before you tracked Eliska down?"

"Six," Donahue replied, not taking her eyes off the road. "I got lucky. She wasn't there yet, but her shift was starting at ten, so she should be there now."

Thompson nodded, thought for a moment, then said, "I'm driving back when we're done."

They arrived at the *Miguel Ortec* salon in Encino and found a spot at a meter on Ventura Boulevard. As was her custom, Donahue hooked the radio microphone cord over the rear view mirror to avoid getting a parking ticket.

They made their way into the shop and walked up to the check-in counter. The salon was small but modern enough. There were eight chairs, a shampoo bay, and a row of seats with dryers. The staff was young, more male than female, but the youthful energy they exuded was contagious. It looked as though it was a fun place to work.

"Hi," said Donahue to an attractive Hispanic girl who looked to be no older than twenty-one. "I'm looking for Eliska Rodinova."

"She's not in yet," said the girl, "but Christina just had a cancellation so I can work you in for a shampoo and trim."

"No thanks," said Donahue.

Thompson, who was studying Donahue's hair, said, "How much to take care of her roots?"

"*Shari!*" Donahue was in no mood to be playing the game. She shook her head no and addressed the girl.

"Is the manager in?"

The young woman frowned. "I'm the manager. What can I do for you?"

Donahue flashed her ID card.

"What time do you think Eliska will get here?"

The girl shook her head, now wary of saying too much. "She was due in at ten a.m., but she must be running late."

"Does that happen often?"

"No. She's usually early."

"Do you have a phone number for her?"

The girl nodded, then looked up the number in a small book she removed from a drawer in the reception stand. She gave them the number, which Donahue wrote down.

The girl said, "I've tried her number a couple of times but it just goes directly to her voicemail." She looked from one to the other. "Has something happened to Ellie?"

Donahue shook her head. "We just want to talk to her about someone she might know."

"Oh," said the girl. That seemed to satisfy the young woman's curiosity.

"What can you tell us about Eliska?" Thompson asked.

"She's missed the last few days of work," the girl told them, "but overall, she's a hard worker, always on time, and the customers really like her."

The two detectives exchanged a look.

"A couple of days?" Thompson asked with a note of concern in her voice.

The girl nodded. "Like I told you, I tried calling her, but I got no answer."

"Has that happened before?"

The girl shook her head. "I just figured she needed a break. Doing hair is a very stressful job, and sometimes some of the stylists need to walk away from it for a while." She shrugged. "What can I say?"

"When she's not working, what kind of stuff does she like to do?" Donahue asked.

"She's studying engineering at UCLA. Part time, of course. She pays her way through school by cutting hair."

"Engineering? Nice. Smart girl." Then, with all the subtlety of a freight train, Thompson asked, "Does she have a boyfriend?"

The girl smiled and shook her head.

"Ellie's gay."

"Do you have a current address for her?" Donahue asked.

The girl read it off and Donahue confirmed it was the same address that they already had from the Department of Motor Vehicles.

"Here's my card," Donahue said, handing it to the girl. "She's not in any trouble or anything like that, but if she comes in after we leave, would you please ask her to call us at her earliest convenience?"

The girl agreed and the two detectives made their way back out to the car.

"My turn to drive," Thompson said when they were almost there.

Donahue waived the keys in the air as she made her way around to the driver's door.

"Not yet. You said you were gonna drive *back,* and right now we're going to go over to Eliska's apartment before we head back to the barn."

"Not fair," said Thompson, but she was arguing a losing position as Donahue got into the driver's seat and shut her door, effectively closing off any further discussion.

Thompson got in and said, "You know, you really could use a root job."

"Bite me," said Donahue as she pulled away from the curb.

*****

The drive over to the apartment in Sherman Oaks took less than fifteen minutes. The building was a three-story, thirty unit structure with outdoor walkways, stucco siding, and a flat roof. It was shaped like the letter U, and there was a small swimming pool in the center between the units that was surrounded by a waist-high, wrought iron fence.

Thompson checked the building register.

"Figures," she mumbled. "Every place we go to is always on the third floor."

They made their way up the staircase and down the outer walkway directly to a dirty beige front door. Donahue knocked and rang the bell, but there was no answer.

"Let's try the neighbor," said Donahue.

"I thought you already spoke to the neighbors," Thompson said.

"There was no one home at this one," said Donahue, gesturing to the one directly next door. She knocked on the door, and a few moments later a young woman responded.

She was short and frumpy, with thinning black hair.

"Hi," said Donahue, flashing her badge. "I'm Detective Donahue, a friend of Eliska's, the girl who lives next door. Over there is my partner, Detective Thompson. We were supposed to meet Eliska for lunch today and she's not answering her door. I'm wondering if you've seen or talked to her in the last few days?"

The girl pulled her pale blue housecoat a little tighter.

"Ellie's gone out of town. She left two days ago. She said she had to visit a sick relative. She left her cat with me, but she should be back in another

83

day or so, at least I hope she is. The damn cat scratched the hell out of my boyfriend and he's threatening to turn her loose if Ellie doesn't come get back soon."

"What's your name?" Donahue asked.

"Karen. Karen Rodgers."

"Well, it has been nice talking to you, Karen." Donahue handed the woman her business card. "If you see Eliska, would you give her this and ask her to call me right away. It's very important."

Rodgers accepted the card, looked it over, and nodded.

Donahue then added, "Oh, and you can tell your boyfriend that if anything happens to Eliska's cat, I'll be back to arrest him for cat endangerment."

She walked back to where Thompson was still peeking into Eliska's front window, and when Donahue joined her, Thompson whispered, "Cat endangerment?"

"Sounded good. At least we know that Eliska's alive."

"So she goes out of town on the same day that Nika gets killed. You think she might have been involved?"

"It's possible, but it could be just a coincidence."

"Yeah, maybe. Just the same, we better add her to our possible suspect list. This might be nothing more than a case of domestic violence."

As they started for the stairwell, Thompson said, "You think we should let the guys over at Hollywood know about Eliska?"

"Absolutely! We'll let them work that part of it while we concentrate on the death of Milan Petrovich."

"And you propose that we do that... *how?*"

"Well, we'll start with Irina Konstantinov."

CHAPTER 15

October 22, 3:30 p.m.

Irina Konstantinov was a fashionable woman, always dressed in designer clothing with her hair coiffed and her makeup flawless. But today she was still in her bare feet, dressed in a pair of jeans and an old baggy shirt. It was early afternoon, and she'd been drinking vodka for most of the day. She was too distraught to go to work, the foremost thought in her mind being the death of her business partner, Milan Petrovich. She'd read accounts of the bombing, had known that he was being squeezed, and to say that she was terrified was a gross understatement. And while she didn't know exactly who had blown him up, she had a pretty good idea, and the meaning of that killing to her personally was more than crystal clear.

Someone wanted a piece of their business, and they were willing to murder to get it.

She had come to America from Moscow six years before. A friend of a friend had offered her a job in a retail store, and while working there, she spoke to a girl from the Ukraine who was working as a recruiter for a dating agency. The girl had talked about her own personal situation, how she was dating American men who had jobs and disposable income, and for Irina, that seemed a real novelty.

From her time as a young woman in Moscow, she'd come to realize that the economic system in Russia worked against the young men because it stifled their chances to move up into the middle class. What Russian women wanted was economic security, and when they couldn't find it in Russia, they went elsewhere. There was a serious exodus of educated Russian women who sought a better life in countries where the men offered protection and comfort. America—in particular, Los Angeles—was a destination full of wealthy men who were looking for younger women who had the ability to see beyond a man's chronological age or past his physical shortcomings.

The idea came to her in a flash, and Irina was quick to nurture it. She watched, listened, and spoke to the young female emigres about what they wanted and how hard it was for them to meet the highest quality men. She even took a job at an agency that featured American-born women to see how the business was run.

Irina concluded that the demand was there, so she developed a blueprint for a dating service that would specialize in accomplished women from Eastern Europe who were seeking out men of financial means.

Because she needed money to get things started, she turned to a man she'd met when he was a customer at the agency she'd previously worked for.

Milan Petrovich was an engineer who had been bored with what he was doing. He told her he had saved up some money and was looking for an investment. He turned out to be a personable man, and they hit it off right away, so she shared with him her vision and later took him on as a partner.

The business started off slowly, but by the end of the first year, they were turning a profit. But Milan wasn't satisfied with the way things were going. He wanted to attract an even wealthier cliental. He borrowed the money needed to take the next step, and by the end of the second year, their business was thriving.

Thanks to Milan's expanded vision, the focus on the internet had proven to be a boon to the matchmaking field, and they set up a website that glamorized the women that Irina signed up for introductions to the men. Milan focused his recruiting on what he called the big fish; the men with large amounts of disposable income, while Irina continued to focus her efforts on recruiting the most attractive girls. But after about six months, their responsibilities shifted when Milan turned out to have the type of personality that lent itself to bringing in the best looking women.

As the business continued to grow, they hired significant staff, and within three years, they were firmly established as an agency that delivered results.

When Irina finished off the last swallow of vodka in her glass, she got off the couch and made her way over to her living room bar.

She lived in a three-bedroom home in the Hollywood Hills. The view from the back of the house was stunning at night; a sea of twinkling lights that stretched as far as the eye could see. It had cost her a great deal of money, but as far as she was concerned, the view itself was worth every single cent.

Her doorbell rang, and without giving it a second thought, she made her way over and opened it up. She'd been expecting her personal assistant, a beautiful young woman who sometimes went out on dates with their better-looking clients, but it wasn't her assistant. When she opened the door she discovered two imposing male figures whose very presence at her home made her heart skip a beat.

"We need to talk," said the first man.

He walked into her house without being invited. The second man took a last look out towards the street, then he came in behind the first man and shut the door. They made their way into the living room, and the first man paused briefly to study the view of the city below.

"Very nice," he said in a thick Russian accent. He turned back to face her. "Do you know who I am?"

Irina shook her head.

"My name is Vladimir Komarov, and this gentleman is Martun Hagopian. Milan was a good friend of mine, and we heard about what happened, so we came by to express our condolences."

A chill ran down Irina's back. She had a sudden premonition that these two scary men were the ones that Milan had been worried about, the ones who might have blown him up.

"That's very nice of you," she managed to say. "I appreciate your concern, but I'm afraid I'm not dressed for company. So, if you don't mind, perhaps you can come back some other time when I'm in a position to be a proper hostess."

Komarov gave her a cold smile.

"We won't be more than a few minutes," he said. "I did some asking around, and from what I've been hearing, it appears that Milan was screwing around with one of the girls he recruited. I'm told that her boyfriend may have taken exception."

But Irina wasn't buying it.

"You tried to force him to give up part of our business," she said, although where this lack of caution came from she wasn't really sure. She could only guess that the vodka had loosened her tongue.

"Is that what Milan told you?" Komarov smiled and shook his head. "Can you believe that, Martun?"

"It must have been translation problem," Hagopian said with a deep, thick, Eastern European accent.

Komarov nodded in agreement. He turned back to Irina.

"Several years ago, I loaned your partner the money he needed to expand your business. He had fallen far behind on paying me back, so I recently offered to buy him out in exchange for what he owed me. He said he'd consider it, and that's where we left it, but now that he's gone, and I'm afraid that everything has changed."

"But Milan was very clear. He said that you were pressuring him and—"

Komarov stopped her mid-sentence by raising his hand in protest.

"I had nothing to do with what happened to him, and you would be wise to remember that."

Hagopian spotted the bar and Irina watched as he walked over and helped himself to a healthy pour of vodka.

Komarov smiled as he reached out and touched her arm.

"I know you're in a difficult situation now that Milan is gone. He was your financial partner and finding a new source of funding to keep your agency going is going to be difficult."

Hagopian laughed, and Komarov silenced him with a stern look, then tightened his grip on Irina's arm.

"Fortunately for you, I have the money you'll need to keep you going."

"I'm not interested in taking on a new partner," Irina told him. Her voice was shaky and didn't even sound very convincing to her.

"Let me finish," Komarov said.

Hagopian walked over and stood by his side, and Irina sensed that he was the most dangerous of the two.

"I'm willing to take over Milan's share of the partnership in exchange for the money he owed me. You can keep recruiting the male clients, and I'll help supply you with some of the girls. You can keep your same front office staff, and I will see to it that no competitors get a foothold in our market."

Emboldened by her previous statement, Irina declared, "But I don't need a partner. I can handle the business on my own."

"But you can't." His words were said with such a degree of ferocity that she knew his offer was non-negotiable.

"You're a smart woman," he said, softening his tone while holding her stare. "Milan spoke a great deal about how critical you were to the operation, so I see no reason for you to go. But my offer is a one time proposition, and should you decide not to accept it, well... that would certainly be a major mistake."

Irina shuddered.

Her options were crystal clear. She could tell him *no*, send him on his way, and wait for the pale horseman to pay her a visit; or she could tell him *yes* and hopefully hang on to her half of the business.

She'd grown up in a culture where bullies like this were connected to all aspects of everyday life. Some were common street thugs, but most were connected with the very agencies that were supposed to protect the people's rights. These men before her were no different from the men back home, and to fight them or resist them was both futile and dangerous.

Give in to their demands and I will probably live. Tell them no and I'll likely die.

"I accept," she said dejectedly. "We will be equal partners."

"Sixty, forty," Komarov responded, and when her brows went up in shocked surprise, he added, "My associate here, Mr. Hagopian, will be working with you in the front office. He will help to close the deals with your male clients, and since that will reduce your workload, it's only fair that the extra ten percent should come out of your half."

Irina didn't respond. There was nothing she could say that would change what was happening, and if she managed to come out of this with a forty percent share, then that was still much better than losing her life.

She slowly nodded her assent.

"An excellent decision," Komarov said. He looked over at Hagopian and smiled. "I think we should drink to our new business arrangement. Would you mind doing the honors?"

Hagopian made his way back to the bar, and Irina locked eyes with Komarov.

"If he's going to be working in the front office, he's going to have to clean up. He's too rough looking. He'll need a hair cut, designer suits—"

Komarov silenced her again with his hand.

"That won't be a problem. I'll see to it that he looks the part."

"And the girls in the front office? They must be off limits." Her eyes were now glued on Hagopian. "Their work and skills are too important to risk any problems that might arise."

Komarov's eyes revealed a brief flash of hostility, but just as quickly, the moment passed.

"Always thinking about what's good for the business. I like that." His eyes bore into hers. "He will not be a problem."

Hagopian returned with three glasses, each one filled with two fingers of vodka. He passed one to Komarov and gave a second one to Irina.

Komarov raised his glass and smiled tightly.

"To your continued good health."

CHAPTER 16

October 23, 10:00 a.m.

The following morning, Mitzi Roberts showed up at Donahue's cubicle in the squad room.

"You guys got a moment?" she asked.

Donahue, who was writing up a search warrant for Milan Petrovich's townhouse and office, typed a few more strokes, then leaned back in her chair.

"Sure, Mitz. What's up?"

Thompson, who was working in her own cubicle on the other side of the partition, stood up at the divider to listen in.

"I'm having no luck building a dossier on Komarov. The DMV has a photo and a residence, but I checked the address out on *Google Maps* and it comes back to a trucking company warehouse in Compton. The business name on the building says *SB Trucking*. I ran the company name through the California Corporate Index, but I didn't get a hit. It's not a registered business."

"You think he's living in that warehouse?"

"Not likely. You can say a lot about Compton, but a Russian community it's not, and as I understand it, most immigrant populations tend to group together geographically, so based on simple demographics, it's highly likely that he's living in the city of Glendale or in good old Hollywood, both of which have sizable Russian enclaves."

"I got an email this morning from Captain Odom at Organized Crime Intelligence," said Donahue. "He sent a photo of Komarov and an LA address. I didn't think to give it to you Mitz. I guess I just assumed it was going to be the same as the one on his driver's license."

Donahue retrieved the email, copied down the address, then handed the copy to Roberts.

"Let me see the photo?" Roberts said.

Donahue held it up.

"That's much better than the one I got from the DMV. Can you forward that to my email?"

"Yeah, sure."

"I'll get some copies printed up," said Roberts, "so we can hand them out to the search teams."

While Donahue forwarded the email, Roberts stepped into Thompson's cubicle and typed the new address into *Google Maps.* The result that came up was an apartment building in Hollywood.

"Much better," said Roberts to Thompson who was watching from over her shoulder. "I'll get someone out there to check the building directory, and we'll see if we can pin down the actual unit."

Roberts moved away from the computer and returned to reviewing her notes. "He's got no CII record, and the DOB on his license may or may not be accurate."

"Is he here on a visitor's visa?" Donahue asked.

"I put a call into Homeland, but they haven't called me back yet."

Donahue nodded. Her mind was working overtime. They needed to get a search done right away on Petrovich's home and workplace, but at the same time, with Komarov emerging as a possible suspect in the bombing, it was equally important that they try and get a search warrant for his home and workplace—if he even had one—just in case there was evidence that he could destroy that might connect him to the bombing.

"Try Homeland again, Mitz. If you don't get a response, let me know. I may know someone who can cut through the red tape."

Gibson walked up and addressed the three women. "I got a call from Tucker over at Hollywood. They finished the autopsy on Nika Kominski yesterday afternoon. They removed two slugs from the brain pan, both of them too damaged to make a comparison."

"Did they find any casings?" Donahue asked.

"None," he replied. That meant that the killer had collected them before leaving, or that he had used a revolver to keep them from being ejected.

As Gibson walked off, Donahue turned to Thompson. "While I finish up the search warrant for Petrovich's townhouse and office, why don't you give Yuri Pavienko a call and see if he can tell us more about where Vlad Komarov lives or what he drives?"

Thompson smiled. "You want *me* to give him a call?"

"He gave you his number, right? In fact, try calling him on *FaceTime* or *Skype.*"

Thompson's eyes widened. "Why would I want to do that?"

Donahue smiled. "Well, according to Mitzi, he spent most of the previous conversation talking directly to your chest, so you might want to let your boobs do the talking for you."

Thompson flipped her off, then stuck her tongue out at Roberts. She pulled the slip of paper with his number out of her purse and punched his number into her desk telephone, but when it went directly to voicemail, she was forced to leave a brief message.

Ulysses Gibson walked back over and joined them again.

"Gather 'round," he said. "I just got an email from ATF. They've concluded that the bomb was set off by a remote-controlled device. The charge itself was attached under the car by a magnet. They believe it was directly under the driver's seat. They found traces of PVV-5A, a plastic explosive that's Russian in origin." He looked up from his notes. "That doesn't mean that it was set off by a Russian, but it does suggest a place to start."

"We're way ahead of you," Donahue said with a smile. "We're working on a search warrant for the residence of one Vlad Komarov." She went on to explain to him Komarov's tenuous connection to the case.

"That's pretty thin on probable cause, Jen?" he said. "You think a judge will sign off on something like that?"

"It's all we've got at the moment, but if I word it right, I think I can sell it."

"Good luck." He ran a hand through his hair, a gesture he was known to make when his mind was racing.

"Any indication that the Hollywood murder is in any way connected to the dating agency?" he asked.

"Not yet," Donahue replied. "In fact, it's always possible that Nika Kaminski's killing was the result of a domestic dispute."

She told him about Eliska Rodinova, Nika's supposed lover, and how she hadn't been seen since the day of the murder.

"That reminds me…" Donahue turned to Mitzi Roberts. "Can you call over to Hollywood Homicide and see if they booked Nika's cell phone into evidence? If so, we should run a check of all her calls, both in and out, and see if any of the numbers come back to any of our players?"

"I'll take care of it," Roberts said.

Gibson turned to Thompson.

"They've scheduled the autopsy on the bombing victim for eleven this morning. Since Jen is writing up the search warrant, and with Mitzi looking into the phone stuff, I guess that leaves you to handle post." He looked at his watch. "I'd suggest you take off now. They're gonna start in fifteen minutes."

"But I have to talk to the OC undercover guy to get more info for Jen's warrant?"

"Don't worry about that, Shari." Donahue smiled wryly. "When he calls back, I'll take down the information."

Thompson rolled her eyes. The smell of burned human flesh always made her sick to her stomach. This would not be good…not good at all.

"Call me when you're done," Donahue teased. "I'll take you to lunch. My treat."

Thompson pursed her lips and slowly nodded.

"Just keep it up, Jen. Payback's a bitch."

When Gibson laughed, Thompson had a light bulb moment. She looked over at Donahue.

"I wondered why you were so insistent on writing the warrant." Her gaze then shifted to Gibson. "You planned this with her, didn't you?"

Gibson shrugged.

Thompson shook her head in disgust. "You guys are something else."

She got to her feet and packed up her stuff.

"Ten bucks says she loses it," Donahue whispered to Gibson in a voice intended to be overheard.

Thompson looked over at Donahue and smiled broadly.

"I'll catch you later."

She was already planning her revenge.

CHAPTER 17

October 23, 11:00 a.m.

Thompson entered the Coroner's Office building with the firm intention of making it through the autopsy without getting sick.

The Los Angeles County Coroner's Office was situated on a parcel of land adjacent to the hospital campus of the University of Southern California and the County General Hospital. A state-of-the-art high-tech medical facility, the Coroner's Office conducted close to 9,000 autopsies a year. To meet the demand, autopsies were handled on a prioritized basis, and the death of Milan Petrovich was not considered a priority since it was generally assumed that the cause of death was the explosion. But after prodding by the Los Angeles Police Department, the autopsy was bumped up to accommodate the serious attention the case was getting from the general public and the press.

Thompson signed in with a receptionist who sat behind a counter topped by a bullet-proof pane of glass. The woman checked her ID, had her sign in, then electronically admitted her to the restricted area. Thompson followed the hallway to the main autopsy room where she spotted the assistant coroner, Dr. Annabel Corrander, who was just about to enter the special room for decomposed and bloated-body autopsies.

Corrander was an exceptional doctor whose pursuit of the cause of death in troublesome cases had made her the coroner of preference in difficult, high profile deaths. A diminutive figure physically, she more than made up for her five feet of height with a larger than life personality, one that often endeared her with the detectives who she came in contact with on a regular basis. She was also known for a positively evil sense of humor which somehow cropped up in the most unlikely and politically incorrect situations.

Behind her back in the legal community, she was referred to as *Annabel the Cannibal,* a nickname she received when a homicide detective spotted her eating a cheeseburger in the walk-in freezer where the bodies were stored before being autopsied. Her actions were explained by the fact that she'd been eating her lunch on the run while looking for the subject of her next autopsy, but that mattered not to the detective who'd witnessed it, so the nickname stuck, much to her chagrin.

She spotted Thompson entering the room and waived her over. "Are you Thompson?"

Thompson nodded.

Corrander studied her carefully over the tops of her eyeglasses.

"You look a little peaked, detective. You sure you can handle this?"

Thompson slowly nodded. The truth was her courage was flagging, and she wasn't at all sure she was going to make it through the entire procedure. The view at the crime scene had been bad enough, but the smell had been the real killer. The smell of burnt flesh and fat content, mixed with the odor of burning hair, had cost her the contents of her stomach out at the crime scene, and her fear was that it would happen again.

Corrander could see the concerns on Thompson's face.

"I've decided to do Mr. Petrovich in the wind tunnel, so you don't need to worry about the smell."

Thompson immediately brightened up. The special room, jokingly referred to as the wind tunnel, was constructed to ensure that the air inside was vented completely at a high rate of speed. It was specifically designed to prevent the smell of decomposition from becoming overwhelming. Once the air left the room, it was filtered to prevent the odors from being released into the adjacent community. By conducting the autopsy in such a facility, Thompson would be able to use minimal measures to disguise the residual smells.

She opened her purse, pulled out a small bottle, and put a little dab of *Vicks VapoRub* on her upper lip.

"You guys still use that stuff?" Corrander asked.

Thompson nodded. "I'm told it helps."

Corrander smiled.

"I prefer the foolproof method, to put myself into a Zen state and pretend I'm out in a field of roses."

"And that works?" Thompson asked, surprised.

"Of course not," Corrander said with a smile, "but you'd be surprised how many of your colleagues I can string along for a time when I'm in the mood."

Thompson shook her head. Everyone was a comedian, and this was not a joking matter. Her stomach was starting to do flips, and it was beginning to look as if things were gonna get worse.

"Your first time standing in on a burn case?"

Thompson nodded.

"I thought so. It seems to be a right of passage with you guys…always sending over the newbies. So, okay. Relax and take a deep breath. When we enter, you can take a seat on a chair over by the wall. I don't want you to pass out on me as it would slow me down. I'll be dictating as we go along, the same procedure as the usual autopsies, and I'll try to talk loud enough so that you can hear me over the sound of the ventilation system. Any questions?"

Thompson shook her head, afraid to speak. The anticipation was only making things worse. Her heart was racing, and her breathing had become shallow.

Keep it together. Keep it together.

"You'll be fine," Corrander told her. "And since this is gonna be your first time, I'd like to direct your attention to the waste basket over by the wall. If you're gonna puke, feel free to use it. I don't want to have to clean up your breakfast."

Corrander slid on a nose plug and pulled a clear plastic shield down over her eyes. "You all set detective?"

Thompson inhaled deeply, then nodded.

"Good."

Corrander opened the door, pulled a mask up over the lower portion of her face, and spoke to Thompson from over her shoulder.

"By the way, Detective, I hear the special today in the cafeteria is ground beef smothered in brown gravy. After we're through here, you wanna join me for lunch?"

Thompson lost it, and Corrander smiled to herself. How she dearly loved to torment those who were first-timers to the infamous wind tunnel.

*****

The autopsy proceeded slowly due to the horrifying condition of the body. The first order of business was to take x-rays of the remains. This was done to give Corrander a visual roadmap of the pieces of shrapnel that she was going to remove from what was left of the victim.

The standard procedure was to cut a "Y" incision in the chest, followed by the removal of the organs which were then weighed, carefully examined, and dissected with samples taken for microscopic analysis. Blood and bodily fluids were collected, as were foreign objects discovered inside the body. In Petrovich's case, that meant pieces of metal, plastic, glass, and fabric which had entered his body during the initial explosion.

The secondary explosion, caused by the rupturing of the gas tank, had incinerated the corpse as well as the car. Portions of the body were charred beyond recognition, but all the parts that remained burnt but identifiable were carefully studied to determine the cause of death.

At two p.m., Thompson arrived back at the squad room, bound and determined not to mention to anyone what had happened to her at the Coroner's Office. After throwing up a few times, she had made it through the rest of the autopsy without incident, and if the truth be told, it wasn't half as bad as her imagination had made it out to be.

She walked over to her desk, put her gun in the top drawer, then settled in her chair to check her messages.

Donahue peeked at her over the top of the partition.

"You okay?"

Thompson turned and smiled.

"Of course. Why? Shouldn't I be?"

"Who did the *Post*?" Donahue asked.

So that was it. They knew it was going to be Corrander and her evil sense of humor!

"Annabel Corrander. Interesting lady. Very informative."

Donahue smiled.

"So it all went well, then?"

Thompson smiled back, and in her smoothest voice, said, "Of course it did,

Jen."

Donahue nodded. She knew her partner well enough to know that she was not about to admit getting sick.

"So what was the cause of death?"

Thompson leaned back in her chair. "As you can imagine, the explosion pretty well shredded him below the waist, but the Coroner says that severe burns and bleeding were secondary to smoke inhalation."

"Smoke inhalation?" Donahue was taken by complete surprise. "That's what killed him?"

Thompson nodded. "Critical were the lungs—or what was left of them— and the trachea; all three showed signs of soot that was caused by exposure to the burning that resulted from the fire. Apparently, he was alive for a bit after the initial blast."

"Unconscious, I hope." Donahue cringed. "*Jesus!* What a horrible way to die."

Thompson nodded in agreement, and after a moment of mutual silence, she said, "So, did we hear back from Yuri Pavienko?"

"Not yet." Donahue was still thinking about Petrovich's horrible death. "But the warrant for Milan Petrovich's condo and his office is complete, and the warrant for Komarov's apartment and the Compton warehouse is almost done." She shrugged. "I just wish we knew what kind of car he drove?"

Thompson's desk phone rang loudly. "Robbery-Homicide," she said when she answered it.

Yuri Pavienko smiled through the phone.

"Detective Thompson? This is Yuri. I'm returning your call."

"Yuri, great, thanks for getting back to me."

She waived to Donahue that it was him, then spun around in her chair to face her own desk.

"We wanted to know if you guys have determined where Vlad is working or what kind of car he drives?"

"The guy doesn't work," Pavienko said. "He runs a few girls in Hollywood, but that's about it."

"How about a car? How does he get around?"

"Same answer. I don't really know. I've only seen him inside the *Siberia*. But I'll look through our files and we'll see if anyone else around here has made contact with him while he was mobile."

"Your Captain already gave us an apartment address from your files." She then read off what they had from a piece of paper on her desk. "Does that location ring any bells?"

Pavienko was impressed. Thompson was a go-getter; the kind who would go to whatever lengths it took to pursue her investigations.

"If the Captain sent it to you then it must be the most recent info we have on file. Did you run him through DMV?"

"Yeah, but came back to a warehouse in Compton. We're gonna search that place, too."

There was silence for a moment.

"You're doing a warrant?" he finally asked.

"Yeah. We want to look for explosives residue." She paused for a moment. "You want to come along?"

Pavienko laughed. "I'd love to, but I think it would blow my cover."

Of course, it would!

Thompson winced.

He said, "Tell you what. After you wrap it up, if you'd like to get a drink or talk about what you find, I can probably shake loose for a while?"

"Thanks anyway, Yuri, but I've got three kids at home who'll be waiting for me."

"Three? Wow!"

They spoke for a few more moments, then Thompson hung up and turned to face Donahue's partition.

"Well, that was a waste," she said.

"Anything we can add to the warrant?"

"No. Either he's being very closed mouth or their intelligence gathering really sucks."

Donahue looked over the partition. "Probably both."

"Are we ready to see the judge for a signature?" Thompson asked.

"In a couple of minutes. I just need to print it out. Is our car ready?"

"Yeah, thank God. They got it done early, so I used it for the ride over to the Coroner's Office. It works just fine."

"That's great! You mind driving? I want to proof the affidavit on the way over to the judge's chambers."

"Yeah, sure. Why not?" Then under her breath, "Now that we get the good car back, you're gonna let me drive? Figures..."

"Pardon?" said Donahue looking up.

"Nothing. Of course I'll drive."

Donahue got up and walked over to the printer and waited for the last pages of the warrant to pop out. She picked them up and stapled them together.

"Okay, partner. Let's do this."

CHAPTER 18

October 23, 4:30 p.m.

The roll call for the search was held in the auditorium next to the PAB. Technically, it was part of the same structure, but on the outside, it appeared to be a stand alone building.

Because of the possibility of explosives being found, the Captain of the Robbery-Homicide Division, Tommy Elwood, had pulled out all the stops. He'd had his people working on a tactical plan all day, and everyone involved was now present for last minute instructions.

A contingent from SWAT and one from the Bomb Squad were present, as were two Platoons from the Metropolitan Division. Handlers from ATF were providing the explosives-sniffing dogs, and a dozen detectives from RHD were being pressed into service to help with the search. Units from the LA City Fire Department, including Paramedic personnel, would be present at several of the search locations, as would Officers and Fire officials from the City of Compton, the place of the *SB* warehouse. All in all, more than seventy people would be involved in the operation.

The plan had boiled down to doing a simultaneous search of Vlad's apartment in Hollywood, the warehouse in the City of Compton, and Milan Petrovich's townhouse in the Hollywood Hills. The warrant could be served at any time during the next ten days, so it was decided early on that a search of Milan's office, the location of the matchmaking agency would keep until another day when the focus would not be fundamentally directed towards Vlad and the possibility of explosives.

Donahue and Thompson were assigned to handle the search at Vlad's apartment location, while Detectives Bengtson and Jackson would assume responsibility for the search at the Compton warehouse. Mitzi Roberts and Gina Divak, another detective from RHD, were chosen to handle the search of Milan's apartment, where they would be looking for any evidence that might help them determine the motive for his killing.

At Vlad's apartment and at the warehouse, Metro Units would be used to seal off the surrounding neighborhoods. Once that happened, nearby neighbors would be evacuated for their safety. This would be critical at Vlad Komarov's apartment building, as it was likely that some residents would be home and at significant risk if explosives were discovered. Once the property was cleared, SWAT teams would then be used to make entry at the apartment and the warehouse, and after that, if the all clear were given, the detectives would be allowed to enter the locations to conduct their respective searches.

Once the briefing was concluded, and the individual teams had a chance to discuss their operational plans, the personnel involved left the auditorium and made their way to designated staging locations close to where they would be conducting their searches.

Donahue and Thompson sat quietly in their Crown Victoria in the parking lot behind a *Pavilions* Market in Hollywood. A preliminary check of the apartment location had been completed, and what they were waiting for now was word from downtown that the operation could get underway.

The lot was filled with squad cars, both black and whites and undercover vehicles, two fire engines, one paramedic unit, and a Mexican food service truck that was doing a bang up business with the hoard of officers who had no idea when they'd have the time to get their next meal. There were several command personnel vehicles, including their Captain and a Deputy Chief.

Donahue frowned as she looked out the windshield at the collection of personnel and assets that were gathered around.

"This whole thing has gotten awfully complicated. I sure hope to hell we come up with something good."

"Relax," said Thompson. "Most of these boys love the chance to play army. They don't give a damn if we come up dry." She looked over and smiled. "Besides, it's good practice for the day when it really counts."

"So you don't think we're gonna find explosives?"

"I'm not saying that," Thompson cautioned. "It's just that you and I both know that nothing ever gets handed to us on a silver platter, so I'm just not gonna get my hopes up."

Donahue started to nod, then noticed that the Metro Units assigned to their location were starting to leave the lot.

"Looks like were on," she said.

Gibson walked towards them from the passenger side of their car, so Donahue rolled down her window.

"We got the go sign," he said as he leaned in to talk to them. "Metro is going to block the streets and clear the building. As soon as they're done, we can follow SWAT in, but they're going to hold us outside the building until the Bomb Squad makes sure that the place isn't booby-trapped."

"That's nice of them," Thompson quipped.

"So hang tight here for a while longer," Gibson told them. "I'll let you know when we go."

He walked away and the two detectives settled back in their seats, their anxiety starting to soar.

*****

Thirty minutes later, Thompson and Donahue arrived at the location. Behind them, in another car, were Gibson and Capt. Tommy Elwood.

SWAT had assisted the Metro teams in evacuating the building. It had taken a little longer than anticipated, but that was because movement was detected in Komarov's apartment by an alert Metro officer who had seen a curtain move. SWAT arrived in two armored vehicles, then took over the evacuation of the residents who lived in the apartments immediately adjacent to Komarov's. They were better armed and had more sophisticated body armor, so they carefully approached the apartment, and using riot shields for cover, they evacuated three women, an elderly man, and two small children, all of whom were taken to a safe location two blocks away.

Gibson walked over to their car to tell them that SWAT was presently ordering any occupants of Komarov's apartment to come out. Donahue had rolled down her window, and they could just hear the tail end of the order being given over a bullhorn. It took a few more minutes, but word soon came out over the Rovers that the subject was successfully taken into custody.

Donahue and Thompson got out of their car and made their way with

Gibson and Elwood over to Komarov's building. They arrived just in time to see two SWAT officers escorting Komarov down the last of the steps.

"He came out without a struggle," one of the SWAT officers told the group.

Thompson stopped in her tracks and shot Donahue a look.

"Wow!" she said. "Check out his tats."

Komarov was shirtless. He was wearing jeans, his feet were bare, and his entire upper body was completely inked. Not like the Japanese Yakuza, whose gang tattoos tended to fill every square inch of exposed skin, but more like a mural of symbols and individual scenes that were clearly Russian in style.

His hands were cuffed behind his back, and as he got closer, Donahue could see that the tattoo's appeared to be very different from what she was used to seeing on American prisoners and gang bangers. Komarov's tattoos were far more stylized, and they included on his front what looked like Onion Dome spires mixed in with numerous religious figures.

The SWAT team officers stopped a few feet in front of the detectives. One of them said, "You want us to take him to our car? We can hold him there for you until you're ready to take him downtown."

"I'll get some of our people to take him off your hands," said Donahue. She looked around and spotted Detective Bryan Berman and his partner Liz Camacho who were standing nearby, waiting for an assignment or an order to search.

She called them over.

"Would you guys run Mr. Komarov down to the PAB for me?"

"No problem, Jen," said Berman, walking over. "You want us to put him in a holding room?"

Donahue nodded. The PAB hallway just outside of the squad room had half a dozen interview rooms and a comparable number of holding cells where people in custody could be kept until the detectives were ready to conduct their interviews.

She turned her back to Komarov and said to Berman under her breath, "Get someone from the photo lab to take a full set of stills of all of his tattoos. There's nothing on file for this guy."

Berman nodded. He walked over to the two SWAT detectives and thanked them for their help.

Camacho took one of Komarov's arms and they began to walk him down the street to their car.

"Can we go inside and search now?" Donahue asked the SWAT team officers.

One of them spoke into his shoulder mike, and the answer that came back was negative.

He explained, "The apartment still has to be checked for booby traps, and after that, the explosive sniffing dog will go to work. But since the unit has only one bedroom, I'm pretty sure it won't take too long."

*****

Donahue stepped out of the apartment to get a breath of fresh air. The place smelled of body odor from dirty clothes and unwashed sheets. She hated pouring through peoples living spaces. It was like going on a treasure hunt, while at the same time it felt like a full on invasion of someone's private life. Embarrassing things were often encountered, from unkempt living quarters to personal medical or sexual information. It disgusted and interested her at the same time, and she could only imagine how she would feel if a bunch of strangers was allowed to pour through her personal space.

Thompson came out to the walkway and joined her.

"*Nada,*" she said, disgustedly. "No computer, no cell phone, no address books, no weapons, and according to ATF, no explosive residue. We're back to square one."

She pulled a cigarette from her purse and lit it up.

"I didn't know you smoked?" Donahue said.

"I don't," Thompson replied, taking a drag.

Donahue reached up and held out her hand.

"Neither do I."

Thompson passed the cigarette to Donahue who took a drag that made her cough, then she passed it back to Thompson who paused for a moment then crushed it out.

"I don't know why I lit that up," she said. "I really don't smoke."

"Neither do I," said Donahue as she pulled her cell phone out and dialed a number.

Detective Rich Bengtson answered on the third ring.

"Rich? It's Jen. Did you guys come up with anything?"

Bengtson held the phone to one ear and used the palm of his hand to cover the other.

"The warehouse is empty," he said. "Lots of dust, but no explosives. How'd you guys do?"

"Goose egg," she said. "Are you breaking down the scene?"

"Everyone's already gone. We're just hanging out here while a carpenter boards up the front door. SWAT took it down, so we have to secure the building." He paused. "Did you at least get Komarov?"

"We got him. He's down at PAB, so we're gonna head over there now and see what he has to say."

She hung up her phone and turned to Thompson.

"Let's head back to the barn."

Thompson nodded and they started off towards their car.

"What a waste of time," said Donahue. "Not a damn thing to help our case."

"Not surprising, though," Thompson replied.

"Meaning... *what*?"

"Meaning he had plenty of time to dispose of any evidence."

"Yeah. I guess you're right."

"I'll say one thing, though." Thompson wrinkled her nose. "That boy needs to spend a little time at the laundromat. I'll bet his bedsheets haven't been washed in more than a month."

"That may be." Donahue flashed her partner a smile, "But I'm sure it was a whole lot better than what you smelled when you were down at the Coroner's Office."

But Thompson was not about to fall into that trap.

"Smelled like roses," she said, not giving an inch.

"So that's your story and you're sticking to it?"

"Precisely."

*****

On the ride back downtown, Donahue placed a quick call to Mitzi Roberts who advised her that they'd found nothing earth shaking during their search of Milan Petrovich's townhouse. He had a personal computer which they had taken into custody, but it was password protected, and Mitzi decided she'd work on getting past the password once everything settled down.

CHAPTER 19

October 23, 4:30 p.m.

Thompson was not above begging, and this time she pulled out all the stops.

"C'mon, Marcelina," she said into her cell phone. "I'm really in a jam here. Did you watch the news tonight about the arrest we made in the bombing case?"

She listened for a few moments, while her babysitter, Marcelina LoCiero, told her that she'd been too busy refereeing Thompson's three squabbling sons to turn on the TV news.

Thompson sighed. "Well, a man was killed in Hollywood when his car blew up in a nightclub parking lot. You like to go to nightclubs, don't you?"

"Of course," replied the twenty-two-year-old girl.

"Well, just between you and me, stay away from the *Siberia* for a while. It might not be safe."

"Is that where it happened?" Marcelina asked, now interested.

"Yep, that's the place. Anyway, I've got the possible bomber here at the station, and I have to talk to him, so I'm gonna be another few hours." She paused. "So please, if there's any way you can hang in there for me, I'd be ever so grateful."

"Just how grateful?" the girl asked.

"Double your usual rate?"

"I'll stay," she replied.

"Thanks, Marcelina. I'll give you a call when I'm on my way home."

"Take your time, Mrs. Thompson. I've got your back."

Thompson hung up the phone and looked over at Donahue.

"What a vulture. *'Take your time Mrs. Thompson, I've got your back.'* Yeah, right. She's got my back as long as I'm paying her double. Bit by bit that girl is picking the flesh off my bones."

"You're lucky she didn't charge you triple. I've seen your little men when they're wired up." Donahue gave her a smile. "When we get a little time, I'll help you get a backup sitter for when this happens again."

"You know someone?" she asked.

"I've got a few ideas, but that's for later. Let's get this over with."

They got to their feet and headed off to the interview room where they ran into Bryan Berman who was standing out in the hallway.

"He's in room two," said Berman. "The SWAT guys emptied his pockets, so I brought up what they found." He handed Donahue a plastic bag containing an iPhone, a short-blade pocket knife, a wallet, and three hundred dollars in cash. "I haven't booked it in yet. I thought you might want to look it over first."

"Thanks, Bry," said Donahue. "Did you get time to photograph his tattoos?"

"I did and they're really unusual."

"Unusual? In what way?"

"They don't look anything like the one's we're used to seeing. They're more...I don't know... fairytale in design."

Donahue nodded. She walked over to her desk and pulled out a box of blue latex gloves. She put on a pair, as did Thompson. She then opened up the envelope and removed the cell phone.

"Where's Mitzi?" Donahue asked.

Thompson waived her over and after Mitzi had put on a pair of the gloves, Donahue handed her the phone.

"Is it password protected, Mitz?"

Roberts played with it for a few moments and discovered that it wasn't.

"Lucky break," said Donahue. "Okay. Look it over and get me a list of all his recent calls."

"Are you planning on booking him tonight?"

"Not likely. Unless he confesses, we've got nothing to tie him to the crime."

"Well, the search warrant allows us to book the phone, so I'll see if anything jumps out, but I'd like to explore it properly and go through everything on here tomorrow when I've got more time."

"That sounds fine to me, Mitz."

Thompson reached into the bag and removed Komarov's wallet. She started to go through it and came up with a scrap of paper that had what appeared to be Russian writing on it.

"Does that look like an address or phone number to you?" Thompson asked as she handed the piece of paper to Donahue.

"I have absolutely no idea what language this is," Donahue replied.

"It's *Cyrillic*," Roberts said authoritatively. "Looks like the Russian version."

Both Donahue and Thompson were open mouthed.

"You know what this is?" said a surprised Donahue.

"I don't know what it says," Roberts told her, "but I do know it's Cyrillic."

Still stunned, Donahue said, "Well, okay then." She handed the piece of paper over to Thompson. "Give Pavienko a call. Get him to translate it for us."

"Assuming the guy can read," said Thompson.

Roberts frowned.

"He hasn't been all that helpful so far," Thompson said by way of explanation. To Donahue she added, "I'll call him right now."

She walked over to her phone and dialed Pavienko's cell. He answered on the second ring.

"Yuri? It's Shari Thompson."

"You ready to meet for a drink?"

"I can't. We've got Vlad Komarov here and we're about to see if he'll talk with us."

"Want a little tip?" he asked.

"Sure."

"There's no problem with you sitting in on his interrogation, but you might want to have a male take the lead for the interview. From what I've seen about the way this guy acts towards women in the clubs, you'll get more out of him if a male appears to be in charge."

When she didn't respond, he added, "It's cultural Shari; a Russian thing."

Chauvinistic, she thought.

"Okay, Yuri. Thanks for the help."

For once he'd told her something useful.

Yuri asked, "Did you get anything good during the search?"

"Nothing," she replied. "The guy was completely clean. But he had a piece of paper in his wallet and we think there's Cyrillic writing on it. Can I fax over a copy of it and have you translate it for us?"

"Sure," he said. He gave her his fax number. "I'm not in the office now, so as soon as I can pick it up, I'll get a look at it and call you back."

"How about if I just take a picture of it with my iPhone and text it to you now?"

"I'm using an old phone on the job," he said. "No frills, so just fax it over."

She said goodbye and walked over to the nearest fax machine and forwarded a copy to Pavienko. She then reported what he said to Donahue.

"Should we find Gibby to handle the interview?" said Donahue.

"Can't hurt. Let's track him down, then let's see what we can squeeze out of Komarov."

*****

While Thompson and Donahue were going into the interview room, Grayson and Tucker, the Hollywood Homicide Detectives, showed up in the squad room where they were directed to the desk of Mitzi Roberts.

"Are you Roberts?" Grayson asked.

"I am."

"I'm Ron Grayson and my partner here is Jack Tucker. You called us about Nika Kaminski's phone?"

"Oh, yeah. Did she have a cell?"

"Actually, she did. We found it in her jeans pocket." He produced a manilla evidence envelope and handed it to her.

"Did you get a look at the contents?" Roberts asked.

"It's password protected, but we hear you're the guru of all things electronic so we brought it over here hoping you can open it up for us?"

"Well, I might be able to get it open, but it depends on what kind it is. If it's an iPhone, I don't think I can do it. We'd have to get the company involved, and that would take a warrant. On the other hand…"

"It's a Samsung," Tucker said.

"Oh!" She smiled. "Okay. I can crack that one."

She opened the envelope and pulled it out.

"How long will it take?" Grayson asked.

"About twenty seconds, once it's warmed up."

"Bullshit," said Tucker. "No one can do it that fast."

She looked up from the phone and said, "Wanna bet lunch on it?"

Grayson looked at Tucker who said, "I'll take half that action."

"Okay," said Tucker. "Twenty-seconds." He held up his arm and looked at his watch. "Tell me when?"

Roberts punched in a ten digit code and handed the phone to Grayson.

"She did it," he said, showing it to Tucker.

"But how—?" Tucker was completely mystified.

"Samsung set up the phone with a code. You punch it in and all passwords on the mobile are deleted and the phone memory is reformatted to accept a new password." She smiled. "The new password is '*UOWEMELUNCH.*'"

Grayson laughed. "Is that legal? I mean, having a master code like that?"

"It is."

"Can you give us that number or code or whatever it is?" Grayson asked.

"Nope, but now that you can see what the number is for her phone, you'll need a search warrant for Sprint to get a complete set of her records. And if you want a little tip, go back for at least six months. Sometimes a pattern—if that's what you're looking for—goes back a long way before the killing."

Grayson nodded. His own cell phone rang, and he turned away to answer it.

Tucker said, "Was there some reason you initially called us about the phone?"

"Yeah. If she had one, we wanted to get a look at the call register for the day she was killed."

"Be my guest." Tucker handed her the phone. "You've earned it."

Roberts smiled and took the phone over to her desk. As she scrolled through the call register, she started copying down call numbers and names, beginning with the last one made that night and moving backward.

Grayson put away his cell phone and rejoined them.

"We've got to go," he told Donahue. He turned to Tucker. "We just picked up a fresh one, a body in a car."

Tucker turned to Donahue, "How long will you need the phone?"

"At least a couple of hours to do it right. Can I get it back to you tomorrow?"

"You willing to call us square on the lunch?" He was smiling.

"Sure."

"I was just kidding about the lunch. If you come by tomorrow before noon, then maybe we can schedule it then."

"Thanks," she said.

When the two detectives walked off, she turned her attention back to Komarov's phone. She made a copy of his cell phone log, then forwarded it on to her computer.

After that, she left a note on Donahue's desk saying what she had done, then quickly packed up her things. She'd been working for almost fifteen straight hours and she needed to go home and get some sleep.

*****

Vlad Komarov had arrived at the PAB both shirtless and shoeless, so Det. Camacho located a t-shirt in the basement locker room's lost-and-found which he put on before he was left alone in a locked interview room with one hand cuffed to a metal ring that was solidly embedded into the wall.

The air conditioner was on full blast, but Komarov still managed to fall asleep.

He wasn't intimidated by this cooling-off period. He knew the uncertainty brought on by the wait time was designed to make him nervous. He almost laughed out loud at this thought. He'd done serious time in a Gulag in Russia, where the brutality of the system and the sadists who ran it knew a thing or two about real intimidation; something the Americans and their system of justice would never consider approaching.

No, he wasn't worried about how they would treat him, and he was even less concerned about the search. His apartment was clean. There was nothing to connect him to any kind of crime, and whatever it was they were looking for, it wasn't there.

He heard the door open and slowly raised his head off the table.

"Mr. Komarov, I'm Detective Gibson, and this is my partner Detective Thompson. Can we get you a cup of coffee or a glass of water?"

Komarov smiled. "No water, but have you got a *Stoli Elit*."

Gibson confused, turned towards Thompson for clarification.

"*Stolichnaya Elit*," she said, "a very expensive Russian vodka. One of the best."

"Ah," said Komarov, now looking at Thompson through a new set of eyes. "You know your vodkas."

Thompson smiled. The opening was there for her to address him, so in spite of Yuri's admonition, she took the opportunity to make a connection.

"So do you," she said. "Here in America, it's all about wines, so it's nice to meet a man who knows a thing or two about Vodka."

Komarov smiled. She was a good looking woman, especially for a cop, but *she was a cop* and he would have to keep that in mind.

"I'm afraid vodka is not on the menu," Gibson told him. "Do you have any idea why you're here?"

"Not at all," he replied.

Gibson nodded. He knew that wasn't true.

"You're in here because of your connection to Milan Petrovich. You know who that is?"

Komarov nodded. "I met him a few times. He hangs out at the *Siberia.*"

"Did you know that he's dead?" Gibson asked.

Komarov smiled. "Of course. Word spread quickly after it happened." He shifted his gaze to Thompson. "I read the newspapers, too."

"You speak English very well," Thompson said with a smile. "How long have you been in the country?"

"A few years, and I'm here legally if that's your next question."

"When was the last time you saw Mr. Petrovich?" Gibson asked.

Komarov closed his eyes in thought. "I guess about a week or so before he died. We met to discuss an offer I wanted to make him for a share of his business."

"The matchmaking business?" Gibson asked.

"That's right. I wanted to invest, and he said he'd think it over."

"Did you know that he filed a complaint with the police? He said you tried to force him to turn over a percentage of his business."

Komarov shook his head, but the hint of a smile never left his face.

"That's not true."

"Where were you on the night Mr. Petrovich died?" Gibson asked.

"Around," he said, shrugging his shoulders. "I was out that night, but I was drinking, too, so I can't really tell you where I was at any particular time."

"Can anybody vouch for your whereabouts that night?"

"I'll have to think that over." He looked over at Thompson and smiled. "Is he always so formal?"

Thompson knew that he was playing them. This was going nowhere and he was giving them nothing that was particularly useful, so she decided to try another tact.

"Were you ever in the military, Mr. Komarov?" she asked.

"They didn't pay enough."

"Do you have any idea who might have wanted to kill Mr. Petrovich?"

"I hear he dated some of the women at the clubs. Maybe someone's husband or boyfriend got upset."

"Did he date or try to date a woman you were interested in?" Gibson asked.

Komarov laughed out loud. "If he had, I would have handled it with a talk."

This was going nowhere, and Gibson was tired. He turned to Thompson. "I'm going to step out for a few moments. I'll be right back."

He planned to consult with Donahue who was watching the interview in the squad room on a closed circuit TV, while his departure would give Thompson a chance to see if she could get anywhere while he was out of the room.

When he left the room, Thompson smiled at Komarov and began with a bit of flattery.

"When they walked you out of your apartment, I noticed that you had a lot of tattoos. Any chance I can get a closer look?"

Komarov smiled. "My hands are cuffed."

"Only one is, and it'll have to stay that way," she said in her sweetest voice, "but you can raise your shirt up with your free hand."

Komarov lifted up the front of his shirt and held it up just under his chin.

Thompson studied his chest. "Is your back tatted up as well?"

"Of course," he said.

She got to her feet and came around the table to get a quick glance at the artwork on his back.

She then had him turn so she could look at his stomach and chest.

"Do you like buildings?" she asked, pointing to the eight onion domes on his upper chest. Underneath the eight domes was a Knight in armor, possibly a Crusader.

He grinned at her, and for the first time she noticed how crooked and dirty his teeth were. She'd heard or read somewhere that Russian dental hygiene was horrible, and it appeared to her that Komarov was living proof.

"The buildings are the domes of churches. Eight spires, to signify the number of months I spent in prison."

Thompson's eyes grew wider.

"Was that back in Russia?"

Komarov nodded. "The Crusader is for protection from misfortune." He was looking down at his chest.

"And the tiger?" she asked.

He looked up and smiled. "The one on my back? It's "for strength."

"What were you in prison for?"

"Here in America, you call it domestic violence."

"Can I get a better look at the ones on your back?"

He leaned forward in the chair while she walked around behind him and lifted up his shirt. On his back, in addition to the tiger, was a full-sized mural of what looked like a church. A man dressed as a monk was pulling the chords of two large bells.

"This one is quite beautiful," she said, admiring the detail.

"The bells mean that I have found the calling from God, that I have given up the criminal life."

Yeah, right, she thought. He's feeding me a load of shit.

She made up her mind that she would get ahold of the photos of the tattoo's and have Yuri Pavienko look them over. She would be interested to know his take.

"Did you get these while you were in prison?" she asked.

He nodded. "I was young and foolish, but you did what you had to do to survive."

Thompson noted that he had two stars, one on each side of his upper chest just below his shoulders.

"What about the stars?" she asked, returning to her seat on the other side of the table. "What do they represent?"

"They mean that I'm made of stardust, just like everyone else."

"When you applied for a driver's license, you gave an address for a warehouse in Compton. What's that all about?"

"I was staying there when I first arrived. I was hired as a night watchman."

"What kind of business was operated out of there?"

"Freight storage."

"You know, it was empty today when we searched it."

"I haven't worked there for many months."

"How do you make your money," she asked?

"Odd jobs."

"Okay." She too had grown tired of the game. "You stay seated. I'll be back in a few minutes."

Komarov nodded. He knew they were almost through.

She stepped outside and locked the door behind her before making her way into the squad room where Donahue and Gibson were waiting for her and still watching Vlad on the TV monitor.

"I think we should book him," Thompson said to Donahue.

"For what? We've got nothing to hold him on."

"Murder," Thompson replied. "It'll never stick, but we can keep him in for forty-eight hours. I want to get a set of his prints and I think we should get a saliva sample and push for a DNA profile."

"But we haven't got anything to link him with the crime, Shari."

Thompson shrugged it off. "What about his phone? Anything on there that would help?"

"We don't know yet. Mitz is going to work on that tomorrow. She's taken off for the rest of the day."

"There you go," Thompson said. "We're still investigating a homicide and he's a flight risk. We've got enough PC to hold him. No one's gonna complain. Besides, we need to check out his immigration status, so what do you say? Shall we book him?"

Donahue looked over at Gibson for guidance.

"She makes a good argument," he said.

"Get someone to walk him down to the booking cage," Donahue said to Thompson. "I'll start writing up the arrest report."

CHAPTER 20

October 23, 11:40 p.m.

Eliska Rodinova quietly unlocked the front door of her apartment in Sherman Oaks. She took a quick look around, entered, then closed the door and switched on the front room overhead light. She made her way straight to her bedroom, and after turning on the light, she opened the closet door, retrieved a good sized suitcase, and carried it over to the bed. She systematically worked her way through the four drawer dresser, quickly selecting items such as panties, bras, scarves, tops, and jeans. She stuffed them into the suitcase until it was full, then made her way into her bathroom where she emptied the medicine cabinet of prescriptions and over the counter products. She planned to take everything she could carry, then come back for the rest when it was safer.

The knock on her front door completely froze her with fear. Her eyes squeezed shut as she considered her options. The window was out, too high above ground. She quickly looked around for a weapon, her eyes falling on a small metal lamp on the dressing table. She reached out to get it just as a voice called out.

"Ellie? It's Karen. Open the door, hun. I've got a message for you."

The knocking continued, and worried that she'd wake up everyone in the building, Eliska went back into the front room and peeked out through the front window curtains. When she was satisfied that it was, in fact, her neighbor Karen and that there was no one else standing beside her, she unlocked the door and opened it up.

"Hi, Karen, what's up?"

"Is everything okay?"

"Yeah, it's fine. You said there was a message?"

"Yes, a couple of police detectives came by yesterday. They wanted to speak to you." She handed Eliska the card that Donahue had given her. "This one asked me to give this to you as soon as you came back. She said it was important. I think she said her partner was a woman named Thompson."

Eliska studied the card. The name Thompson meant nothing, but Donahue was the woman that Nika had intended to meet with. She slipped the card into her pocket.

"Is everything okay?" Karen asked again.

"Yeah, fine, I was a witness to a traffic accident. I'm sure that's what it's all about."

Karen nodded. It was a perfectly reasonable explanation.

"I'll go get Coco for you," she said, turning to go.

"Can you take care of her for a few more days?" Eliska asked. "My granny's not doing so well and I have to go back."

"Oh, gee… I don't know, hun. Coco scratched the hell out of Mickey's face and I don't think he'll take too kindly to her staying on much longer."

"Just a few more days, Karen, I promise. I have to spend most of my time at the hospital, so I can't take care of her. It would be for just a few more days until I can get things straightened out."

Karen thought it over. Ellie was a good friend and a good neighbor. She could do this for her in her time of need, as she was sure that Ellie would be there for her if the situation were reversed.

"Okay. I'll hang on to her, and I'll say a few prayers for your Granny."

"Thanks, Karen."

Eliska backed into the apartment and without another word she shut the door.

She returned to her bathroom, gathered up what remained of her belongings, stuffed them into the suitcase, turned off the lights, then let herself back out of the apartment.

Down in front of the building she took a quick look around. Satisfied that there was no one nearby, she kept to the shadows and made her way past two of the adjacent buildings to a beige Toyota that was parked at the curb.

She opened the rear door, put the suitcase on the back seat, then got into the front passenger seat.

"Got everything?" the driver asked as she started up the engine.

The driver was Svetlana Lazarev, a thirty-six-year-old brunette whose too thin, model-like body was the direct result of a year's-long battle with an eating disorder.

"For now," Eliska told her. She fastened her seatbelt. Her hands were trembling.

"You okay?"

"I'm fine. Let's just get out of here."

Svetlana slowly pulled away from the curb.

Unbeknownst to either of the two women, a car parked half a block away took special care to follow them away from the building at a safe distance.

*****

They arrived at a multi-story apartment building in the city of Tarzana. The drive there had taken a short ten minutes because the streets were not crowded at this time of night.

Tarzana, Encino and Sherman Oaks were all nestled in the foothills and the flats of the San Fernando Valley. All three were major residential communities transected by Ventura Boulevard which served as the primary business hub for the Valley's understated, nightlife scene.

Svetlana guided the car into the underground parking lot and into the stall reserved for her use. The garage was well-lighted at night, so Eliska was the first to get out of the car. She took a careful look around, but noticed nothing out of the ordinary, so she retrieved her suitcase and followed Svetlana to the elevator which required a passcode number. Once they were inside the elevator and the doors were closed, Eliska sighed with
relief.

"Are you hungry?" Svetlana asked.

Eliska nodded. "But I need something more than the rabbit food that you've been eating for the last few days."

"It's healthy," Svetlana said.

The elevator arrived at the third floor and the two women made their way down the interior hallway to Svetlana's unit.

Once inside, Eliska found her way to the bedroom, while Svetlana went into the tiny kitchen.

"I've cleaned out one drawer for you to use," Svetlana said, over her shoulder. "I'm sorry there's not more space."

"It's fine. I really appreciate your helping me out like this. I won't forget it."

Eliska placed her suitcase on the floor and took a seat on the side of Svetlana's bed. She pulled Donahue's business card out of her pocket and placed a call from her cell.

"Robbery-Homicide Division," said a strong, male voice.

"Can I speak to Detective Donahue, please?"

"I'm sorry," said the voice. "Detective Donahue works days. She won't be in until tomorrow morning. Can I take a message?"

"It's an emergency," Eliska told him.

"I'll connect you with 911," he said.

"No." She stopped him from disconnecting. "Not that kind of emergency. I need to talk to her about Nika."

The night detective, Tony White, wasn't sure whether or not this was a crank call, a drunk, or something possibly important, but he'd been trained not to make a judgement too quickly, so he began by trying to calm her down.

"Maybe I can help, you?" he said. "I'm Detective White. If you can tell me what this is all about, maybe I can try and reach her at her home?"

Eliska racked her brain for the name of the other detective that Karen said had been at her apartment with Donahue.

"Does someone named Thomas or Thompson work there?" she asked.

"Thompson?" White scratched his head, then checked RHD personnel roster, a printed list that was taped to one wall of his cubicle.

"Yeah, you must mean Detective Shari Thompson. She's Donahue's partner, but she works days, too." He took a deep breath. "Would you like me to leave them a message?"

Eliska thought it over. It would be dangerous for her to say too much. She had no idea who Thompson was, and Nika had told her that the only person she trusted was Donahue. Still, if Thompson was Donahue's partner, and they'd come out together, then Thompson, by association, was probably okay.

"Okay, can you tell Donahue or Thompson, either one, that I need to talk to them about what happened to Nika."

"*…what…happened…to…Nika.*" White was repeating it out loud as he wrote it down.

"I will only speak to Thompson or to Donahue. What time do they get in?"

"They should be in by nine a.m."

"I'll call back then," she said.

"*Wait!*" said White. "You didn't tell me your name or give me a number they can reach you at if either one of them calls in tonight?"

She didn't want to leave her number but decided that if she left her name, then the detectives would know who she was, and perhaps, they might actually wait around for her call tomorrow morning.

"Just say Eliska called."

She hung up her phone.

CHAPTER 21

October 24, 10:00 a.m.

Donahue drove to the PAB directly from her doctor's office in West Los Angeles. She was running behind, so at every traffic stop along the route to the freeway, she spent time putting on her face and combing out her hair. She managed to get her lipstick on straight as she entered the freeway onramp.

The traffic was a little lighter than usual, and considering that it was already after the rush hour, she made good time. She parked under the building instead of the usual lot a block away because she intended to pick up Thompson and go right out to the *Trophy-Wife Match* offices in Beverly Hills to interview Irina Konstantinov.

She made her way up the elevator to the fifth floor, then used her magnetized identification card to gain entrance to the RHD offices. She headed for her desk, stopping twice along the way to exchange pleasantries with colleagues that she hadn't seen in a while.

When she finally reached her desk, it was just about ten a.m.

"I thought you might have taken a sick day," Thompson said when Donahue reached her desk.

"No, I had to make a stop at my doctor's office this morning for a mammogram."

"Is there a problem?" Thompson asked, immediately concerned. She recalled that Donahue had gone through a gynecology visit just the other day.

"No, I'm fine. The doctor wanted me to get a baseline set of images to use for comparison in the future."

"You sure?"

"I'm sure, Shari. I'm fine."

"Well, that's a relief." Thompson got to her feet. "I thought—"

"What's this?" Donahue said, cutting her off. She picked up a note that was taped to her telephone.

She looked over at Thompson. "Did Eliska Rodinova call here this

125

morning?"

"Not that I'm aware of. Why? What's up?"

"This note. It's from Tony White on the night desk. It says Eliska called last night to speak to me about Nika's death. Said it was an emergency, but not a 911 type. Won't talk to anyone but us. Will call back when we get in at 9:00 a.m. She refused to leave a number, but her number popped up on Tony's caller ID." She looked over at Thompson. "Tony wrote down the number she called in from."

Thompson turned to face the room and yelled out, "Did anyone take a call this morning for Jen or me from a girl named Eliska Rodinova?"

All she got were blank stares and head shakes, no verbal responses.

"I guess she didn't call," Thompson said. "You wanna try calling her now?"

Donahue nodded. "I was gonna suggest that we go serve the warrant on the matchmaking agency this morning and see if we can talk to Irina Konstantinov, but we can do that after we talk to Eliska."

Donahue reached for her desk phone, but before she could make the call to Eliska, Gibson showed up.

"What was the name of that girl you were just asking about?"

"Eliska Rodinova," Donahue said. "Why? Did you hear from her?"

Gibson sighed deeply.

"No, but I'm afraid I've got some bad news."

Donahue got a sinking feeling while Gibson held her stare.

"I just got off the phone with a West Valley detective. There's been a shooting death of a young female this morning, a girl with the same name. Apparently, the ID was made from a drivers license she had in her purse, and your business card was found in her pocket."

He reached out and grabbed ahold of Donahue's arm. She had gotten to her feet but suddenly looked wobbly.

"You okay?" he asked.

She nodded slowly. "Where is she?"

"In an underground parking garage in Tarzana. I told them to hold the scene until you arrive. But if you're—"

"I'm fine," she said, gently shaking off his arm, but he wasn't sure that she was.

"Are we to take it over?" Thompson asked. She had overheard the conversation and had walked over to join them.

"No." He focused on Donahue's emotional reaction. "Let West Valley Homicide take it."

"She called here last night," Donahue said, aloud.

"Who called here? Rodinova?"

Donahue nodded and handed him the note.

Gibson read it over, then said, "I'll talk to the Commander. We may need to put a task force together. Fill in West Valley with what you know and put them in touch with the Hollywood guys. We need to figure out what the hell is going on."

*****

Donahue and Thompson parked in front of the apartment building in Tarzana and made their way over to the log-in officer.

The street had returned to normal. The curious neighbors had disappeared when the patrol cars left the scene to return to their regular duties. Only one black and white and two detective units remained at the scene, and all three were parked at the curb in front of the building. With the exception of the log officer who dutifully noted their names and ID numbers before letting them down the driveway and into the garage, few people would know that a homicide had taken place in this quiet, middle-class neighborhood.

They trudged down the driveway into the underground garage and noted the three detectives who were standing next to a row of parked cars. Donahue counted the cars in the garage. There were fourteen and two empty slots.

One of the vehicles in the garage was a transport wagon from the Coroner's office. That likely meant that two of the three men in suits were detectives and one was the Coroner's representative.

They started to make their way over to the detectives, but one of them met them halfway.

"You must be from RHD," he said.

"I'm Jennifer Donahue, and this is my partner, Shari Thompson. Are you Joel Price?"

"I am," he replied. Price was the head of the Homicide Unit at the West Valley precinct station.

Price was a DIII in grade, a good looking man with a full head of graying black hair. He had a cheerful personality, warm brown eyes, and a soft spot in his heart for victims of violent crime.

"Can you tell us what you know?" Thompson asked.

"When Gibson called he said you'd be filling me in on your interest in the case."

Thompson explained to him what they knew about Nika Kaminski and that Eliska Rodinova and Kaminski were lovers.

"Are you working the Kaminski homicide?" he asked.

"Hollywood has got that one. We're working on a car bombing that killed a Russian expat named Milan Petrovich. We're not sure if our case is connected to these two, but it's possible that they're all related."

Donahue explained to Price how Nika Kaminski had been a victim of human trafficking by Russian mobsters, and how she had given up the street life several years ago.

"She asked for a meeting with me the night she died," Donahue said with a touch of sadness. "I couldn't meet with her until later that evening, and by the time I got to her place, she was dead."

She reached into her purse and pulled out a photocopy of the note that had been taped to her phone.

"This was a call that your victim made to me last night."

Price read the note, then looked up at Donahue who said, "We went out to her place a couple of days ago. We wanted to ask her about Nika Kaminski. She wasn't there, so I left my card."

"You mind if I book this copy of the note?" Price asked. "It might be evidence of motive."

"No, go ahead."

He looked from one to the other. "So what makes you think this might be related to your bombing case?"

"Because of Kaminski's connection to the sex trade, and because the victim of our bombing case was part owner of a dating service featuring Russian women. We're thinking there might be a connection of some sort. We just haven't put it all together."

Price nodded. "Okay. Let me tell you what we've got. A neighbor found the body this morning about eight a.m. The first unit on the scene checked her out, but there was no pulse."

"How'd she die?" Thompson asked.

"It looks like two to the head. We haven't moved her yet. The Coroner's rep is all done, but your Captain asked us to wait for you before we let him move the body."

"Two to the head. Just like Nika Kaminski," Thompson remarked.

"Any casings?" Donahue asked.

"Not that we've found, and we really looked carefully."

Donahue knew that there were no casings left behind at Nika Kaminski's homicide scene. She told Price as much.

"If the bullet is still in the body, you might want to have it compared to the two that were taken from Nika's head. She was killed by two .22 caliber rounds, but I've been told they were too damaged to be used for a formal comparison, but maybe the lead came from the same batch."

"I'll do that," he replied.

The three of them walked over to the body and stopped about five feet away. She was lying between two parked cars, fully dressed, her purse still draped over her shoulder.

"Her roommate says she was on her way to work. Left the apartment about 7:30 a.m." He looked down at the body. "There was no sign of robbery. We found money in her wallet which was still inside her purse."

"You said *roommate*?"

Price nodded. "Svetlana Lazarev. She lives in this building; an upstairs unit."

"Hold on?" Donahue said. "Eliska has a place over in Sherman Oaks. So what's she doing here?"

"Svetlana Lazarev was a friend of Eliska's from work. She told me that

Eliska called her four days ago and begged her to let her stay here for a couple of days. Eliska said that a girlfriend of hers had been murdered and that she was afraid to stay alone at her place in Sherman Oaks."

"Where is this Svetlana Lazarev?" Donahue asked. "We need to talk with her."

"I had her taken down to West Valley Station," Price replied. "I still have to do a full interview with her, but you're welcome to sit in."

"Should we head over there now?" Thompson asked.

"You can if you're finished with the scene. I've got another twenty minutes worth of stuff to do here, so why don't you get yourself a cup of coffee somewhere and meet me at the station in another forty-five."

CHAPTER 22

October 24, 11:45 a.m.

Behind the West Valley Police Station was a secure parking lot where offi-cers left their personal cars while they worked on duty. Having left the scene of the murder of Eliska Rodinova, Donahue and Thompson stopped off at a Star-bucks for a pair of lattes that they were slowly consuming in their car which was parked under a shade tree in the West Valley Station lot.

"You think the two women were killed by the same person?" Thompson asked.

"Sure looks like it. Both of them wanted to tell us something, so I can only conclude that they were killed for that reason."

"So if we look at this objectively, Nika Kaminski calls you and wants to meet, but before that can happen, someone kills her. Eliska Rodinova then dis-appears, ostensibly because she knows something about what Nika wanted to tell you. She decides to tell us whatever it was, and she ends up dead." Thomp-son shook her head in disgust. "How did the killer know where to find her?"

"Find who? *Nika*?"

"No. Eliska. If she went into hiding right after Nika was killed, how did the killer find out she was staying with this woman, Svetlana?"

"Didn't Price say that Eliska and Svetlana worked at the same beauty shop?"

"So maybe Svetlana told someone?"

"Remember to ask her that," Donahue said.

Thompson took a sip of her latte. "Oh, that reminds me. I forgot to tell you. I got a call from the Captain out at Wilshire Division. They've got an opening coming up in their community relations program."

"You're still thinking of transferring out?"

"I've got to do something, Jen. I've worn out my welcome with my sitter. She's getting tired of putting in four or more hours of overtime every time we get called out on a case."

"Even when you pay her double?"

"No, when I pay her double, she's willing to watch them twenty-four hours a day, but I can't afford to keep doing that."

"And your ex?"

Thompson gave her a look that said… *Are you serious?*

Donahue studied her latte. There was very little she could say to that. The job was at odds with personal lives, and that was multiplied in spades when you worked in Homicide.

Donahue knew that she'd sabotaged more than one of her own relationships because of the hours that she put in on her cases. Had it been worth it? The jury was still out on that one, but the job was still the one constant in her life. It was what made her feel fulfilled, and catching killers was not only satisfying, it was her forté, a skill that it seemed she came by naturally. It made her feel useful and productive, so much so that she could never envision working as a nine-to-fiver again.

She had sympathy for Shari's dilemma, but she also knew that transferring out was not the right answer. *Tracking down killers* was Shari's personal motto; it was engraved upon the fabric of her soul. If she ever gave it up—if she worked at some lesser position just to get by—she'd regret it for the rest of her life.

"What if we could find you a couple of other sitters? You know, get you a list that you could work from? There's safety in numbers, Shari. You could work your way down the list every time you need one, always confident that someone would be willing to watch your boys."

"Sounds great, Jen, but I don't even know how to start finding other babysitters. I've asked around at my kid's school, but the other mom's don't share that kind of information. They don't want the highest bidder to steal their sitter away."

"Really? I had no idea it got that cutthroat."

She reached into her purse and pulled out a couple of pieces of paper which she handed over to Thompson.

"What's this?" Thompson asked, scanning the pages.

"Mount St. Mary's University in Brentwood maintains a list of women students who are willing to take babysitting jobs in the community. As you can see, there are a few hundred names on that list, and they include the days and times they're available, and the price each girl wants to charge."

"*Oh my God!*" Thompson's expression quickly mirrored her joy. "This is gold, Jen! How'd you find out about this?"

"I'm a detective, and I'm good at my job."

"No shit your are! This is great! But how did you hear about this?"

"Two minutes on the internet. Just typed in the keywords...and *bingo!*"

"I owe you a girls' night out for this," but Thompson quickly amended her offer when she took a closer look at the list.

"Considering how much these women want per hour for watching three kids, we'll have to settle for an ice tea at McDonald's."

"*Bullshit!* You make more than enough working overtime to cover their fees. It's your solution, Shari. Embrace it."

"You're right. This is great."

She leaned over and gave Donahue a hug, and in her exuberance, she nearly spilled what was left of Donahue's latte.

A knock on the window made them both jump, and this time Donahue's latte sloshed on her jacket.

"*Shit!*" Donahue grabbed a napkin from the console and furiously began to blot.

Price knocked again and Donahue rolled down her window.

"You scared the hell out of us," she said. "Where'd you come from?"

Price smiled. "I drove in through the other gate. When I didn't find you inside, I figured you were probably out here somewhere." He gave them a tiny smile. "Sorry about that, and I'm not even going to ask what you two were up to."

Donahue opened her door, bumping him as she did so, then climbed out, still blotting her jacket.

"Shari's got three boys and I gave her a list of babysitters. She got carried away with gratitude."

"No kidding?"

Price looked over at Thompson who had climbed out on the other side of the car.

"Any chance I can get a copy of that list? My wife is always complaining that none of the other moms will part with their sitters. Half the time we want to go out, we can't."

"Over my dead body." Thompson waived the list like a matador waves a red cape in front of a bull. "This list is gold, and its mine, *all mine!* Go out and get your own."

Price looked shocked and Donahue rolled her eyes.

"Absolute power corrupts," she said to Price, and then to Thompson, "You're kidding, right?"

"Of course I am." Thompson smiled. "I'll be happy to *sell* him a name or two."

Price laughed and led them inside.

*****

Svetlana Lazarev sat by herself in an interview room equipped with a two-way mirror. She was dressed in jeans and a sleeveless top, her jacket slung over the back of her chair. One of the Detectives from the Burglary Detail had thoughtfully brought her a cup of coffee and a sandwich from a vending machine in the coffee room. She'd gratefully accepted the coffee but had no appetite for food.

Price entered with Donahue and Thompson, and all three took seats at the table. Price introduced the two detectives, then began the questioning.

Donahue studied her carefully as Price went through the basics concerning her background. Svetlana was attractive, in an edgy sort of way, with a short, spiky haircut, an eyebrow piercing, and large hoop earrings that hung down to her shoulders. She was rail thin, with several tattoos visible on the backs of her shoulders.

This girl has an eating disorder, Donahue thought. *Someone needs to get her some help.*

Price's questioning disclosed that she was originally from Czechoslovakia, an immigrant whose parents had fled the Communist Regime when she was only six years old. She'd become a citizen in her early twenties, and had worked as a hairdresser at various shops in the greater Los Angeles area for all of her adult life. Married and divorced, she had no children, and she said that she'd been living alone for just about the past three years.

"Ellie called me four days ago," she said. "She told me someone killed Nika, her girlfriend. She was very upset and afraid to be alone. I told her she could come over and stay with me, so she drove straight over and she's been here since then."

"Ellie? Is that her nickname?" Price asked.

"That's what her friends call her."

"Did you know Nika personally?"

"Not well. I met her a couple of times, once at a party at the salon last Christmas, but that's about it."

Svetlana had a tissue balled up in her hand and as her eyes teared up, she gently blotted them dry.

"Did Eliska ever tell you anything about what happened to Nika or what might have been the reason for her death?"

"No, sir, I know she was shot. I read that in the newspaper, but she never said who did it or anything like that."

"Where was she headed this morning when she left your apartment?" Price asked.

"She said she was going to go to a coffee shop on Ventura Boulevard to call someone at the Police Department. They've got a pay phone there, and she didn't want to use her cell."

"Why was that?"

"She didn't want anyone to be able to track her back to my apartment."

Price's eyes narrowed. "What was she afraid of?"

Svetlana shrugged. "I don't know, but whatever or whoever it was, she was really terrified. She was talking about quitting the salon and going to Texas where she has a few friends."

After twenty more minutes of questions that produced no further leads, Price turned to Donahue.

"I've got what I need. Do you want to ask a few questions?"

Donahue nodded.

"Svetlana, do you have any idea how the killer knew that she was staying with you?"

Svetlana shook her head. "We were so careful. I just can't imagine."

Donahue moved on.

"Do you know if Eliska ever belonged to a matchmaking service called *Trophy-Wife Match?*"

Svetlana looked surprised, and just for a moment, Donahue had a feeling that she was about to say yes, but she slowly shook her head.

Svetlana crossed her arms over her chest, and said, "No. Ellie was gay. She and Nika have been together for the last eighteen months." She looked from Donahue over to Price, then back to Donahue.

"I used that agency for a while. Are they involved in this?"

Donahue was entirely surprised. She leaned forward in her chair, trying to keep the excitement out of her voice.

"Tell me about the agency, Svetlana. How did you get connected with them?"

"Another girlfriend of mine told me they were looking for single women who were interested in meeting upscale men. She said she'd been on a few dates, and while they never resulted in a connection, she got to have dinner at a couple of really nice restaurants, so I thought it might be fun."

"Was there any pressure on you to sleep with these dates?"

Her expression hardened. "I'm not a prostitute if that's what you're inferring. It wasn't like that."

"Oh? So what was it like?" Thompson asked.

"It was a chance to meet men who were financially secure. The idea is to try to find a real, love relationship. I want to get married, detective, but for me the money isn't the sole reason."

Thompson looked skeptical.

"In this country, men only want women with a beautiful face and a great body. No one seems to criticize that. Where I come from, security is the most important factor for a woman. The men in Russia...how do you say it... they are flakes. But just because a guy has money doesn't mean I want to spend the rest of my life with him. It's just a nice starting point, and after that, if there's mutual chemistry, then maybe it works out."

Makes sense, Donahue thought. Women were no different then men in that respect. There were certain baseline criteria for each gender, criteria based on life experience, self-worth, and past experiences. Who's to say if it's right or wrong.

Perhaps I need to take a closer look at my own personal criteria. If I didn't put so much stake in how physically attractive a man might be, I might actually find a guy who could really make me happy.

"So you never worked as an escort?" Thompson asked, but her skepticism was still reflected in the tone of her voice.

"Never."

Svetlana's eyes narrowed. She was clearly unhappy at the direction the questioning had taken, and Donahue could see that the interview was quickly deteriorating, so rather than lose her, she shifted gears to bring her back into the fold.

"We know you weren't," she said. She reached out and touched her hand. "And we're not passing judgment on anyone who was. We have to ask these questions because we need to be sure that you weren't connected to that agency. We're looking at them as a possible link between Nika's and Eliska's deaths."

Svetlana appeared to soften. She put her hand over her mouth for a brief moment while she tried to marshal her thoughts.

"I'm being honest with you, Detective. The way it was explained to me, everything was legitimate. I'd like to find a husband. I want to have kids, but I'd never sell out for the money. Money doesn't make me happy. It makes some things easier, but it's not as important as being with someone you really love."

Amen to that, thought Donahue.

"Are you still using the service to get dates?" Donahue asked.

Svetlana shook her head. She clasped her hands in her lap and looked down.

"They told me they couldn't set me up anymore." She looked up and frowned. "I lost a lot of weight. They said I was too thin; that their clients would be put off by my body type."

Donahue nodded knowingly. "Do you have an eating disorder?"

Svetlana squeezed her eyes shut as if the answer was too painful to give. "I'm anorexic. I'm seeing a therapist, but it's really hard."

"Who's the therapist?" Donahue asked.

"Doctor Shari Bauer."

Donahue smiled. "I know her personally. She's really good. You stay with it. You're a beautiful woman, Svetlana, and if anyone can get you through this, it's Shari Bauer."

"Thanks." She noticeably brightened up. "I needed to hear that."

Thompson, too, had suddenly softened her feelings for Svetlana. She was turning out to be a warm and sensitive woman, not one of the flakes they so often encountered.

"Do you have a support person assigned to help get you through the high-stress moments?" Thompson asked.

Svetlana shook her head. "Right now it's just one on one with Doctor Bauer, but I'll be going into a more formal program in another few months."

Thompson slid her business card across the table.

"Well, in the meantime, if you get in a bind, you can always give me a call. I'm a pretty good listener, and as Jen will attest, I'm a damn good cheerleader, too."

Svetlana was dumbfounded. This was coming from the woman who had just inferred that she was a prostitute. She was really touched.

"Thank you, Detective Thompson." Her gaze dropped down to the card. "I appreciate that more than you'll ever know."

Thompson smiled. "Call me Shari, okay?"

"Okay." Svetlana smiled. "Same name as my therapist. Easy to remember."

"Well, I think we're about done here," Donahue said.

"Hold on," said Svetlana. "I don't know if this means anything or not, but I just remembered something. About two months ago, I was visiting Ellie over at her place, and Nika was there. We got to talking, and Ellie was asking me about my non-existent social life. I told her that after the agency dropped me, I decided to get my life straight first before complicating things by starting to date again." She looked over at Thompson and smiled. "Anyway, Nika asked me what agency I was with, and when I told her it was *Trophy-Wife Match*, she warned me not to go back to the agency. She said there was something going on there; that I should stay away."

Thompson wrote furiously to keep up with what Svetlana was saying.

"I asked Ellie later if she knew what Nika was talking about, and she said that Nika ran into someone from there and that the person she spoke to said it was dangerous."

Her eyes shifted back and forth between them; she had their complete attention.

"I didn't ask her what she meant by that because I knew the agency would never take me back, so her warning didn't really resonate with me."

Donahue and Thompson exchanged an excited glance.

"The person Nika supposedly ran into…" said Thompson with a moment's hesitation, "…did she say whether or not it was a man or a woman? Or did she happen to mention a name?"

"Not that I recall." She looked over at Price who was also taking notes. She held his glance. "I'm sorry I didn't remember this sooner. I just hope it helps."

Donahue nodded. "You've been a big help, Svetlana. If anything else comes back to you, please give us a call. Okay?"

"I will."

The three detectives got to their feet.

Price said to Svetlana, "I'm gonna step outside to talk to the detectives for a few moments, but I'll be right back and then I'll drive you to your home."

He followed Donahue and Thompson out of the room.

"Sounds like you've got at least a tenuous connection to your bombing case, so how do you want to handle it?"

"For the time being, keep what we learned to yourself," Donahue said. "I want to talk to my Captain, and I want to run a few things past OC Intelligence. I'm pretty sure we're going to have to set up a task force with the Hollywood guys, too, so I'll get back to you today or tomorrow morning to let you know what the boss has in mind."

"Great," said Price. "I think that's the best way for us to go."

Thompson and Donahue had already started for the back door of the station when Price called out.

"Detective Thompson? Hold on a minute." He walked up to them and said, "The list? Can I trouble you for a couple of those babysitters' names?"

Thompson smiled.

"Sure, how much have you got in your wallet?"

CHAPTER 23

October 24, 11:45 a.m.

After a quick bite to eat for lunch at *The Lettuce Patch,* a restaurant known for having a high-end salad bar, Donahue decided that they would shoot over the hill from the Valley and make a stop in Brentwood where the headquarters of *Trophy-Wife Match* was located in an office building on San Vicente Boulevard.

On the ride over the hill, Thompson used the passenger seat mirror to touch up her makeup.

Donahue glanced over at her several times. This was no quick touch up. Thompson was being very careful and deliberate.

"What are you doing?" Donahue asked.

"Need to look better than the competition," she replied as she slipped her lipstick tube back into her purse.

Donahue scoffed. "We can't compete with those twenty-somethings, Shari. For Christ's sake, they still don't have a single wrinkle at the corners of their eyes."

"They're not wrinkles," Thompson said, checking hers out in the visor mirror. "They're called character lines."

"*Whatever...*" said Donahue with a laugh.

They found the building—a modern glass and steel structure that was ten stories tall, and after consulting the lobby directory, they made their way up to the penthouse suite.

They stepped off the elevator and walked over to a pair of oversized doors that bore the logo of the *Trophy-Wife Matchmaking Agency, LLP.* The doors were locked, but there was an intercom phone and a security camera on the wall adjacent to the right-hand door.

Thompson pushed the call button and a gentle female voice answered with a soft, "Hello?"

"Hi, there," Donahue said. "We're here to see Irina?"

"Do you have an appointment?" the woman asked.

Donahue held up her badge for the camera.

"This is our appointment."

There was no verbal response, and as the seconds ticked by, Thompson said, "Goin' all *Dirty Harry* on her like that might have been a mistake."

"Perhaps, but it '*made my day*.'"

Thompson rolled her eyes.

They could hear footsteps approaching from behind the office door which was suddenly opened by a very attractive blonde who immediately invited them in.

"Ms. Konstantinov is just finishing up with a client. She asked me to have you wait for her in our VIP Lounge."

She escorted them to a room that was furnished like a five-star hotel living room with a spectacular view of the Santa Monica Mountains. The floors were dark hardwood, and the two leather couches were placed on an expensive Turkish rug made of hundred-year-old wool; the pattern of the rug being a copy of a royal design from the fourteenth century Ottoman Empire. Between the couches sat a costly coffee table made from highly polished black piano wood.

"That receptionist is stunning," Donahue said when the girl was out of earshot. "If that's the hired help, the female's doing the dating must really be hot."

On the table were two leather-bound photo albums, and each of the detectives picked one up and thumbed through the pictures of the women the agency claimed were available for matches.

"*Holy crap*," said Thompson. "These girls are gorgeous." She looked over at Donahue. "No wonder all the guys we get to date are second tier. Who'd want to go out with a cop—particularly one with three hyper children—when they could go out with a woman who looks like this?"

She turned her photo album for Donahue to see, and the picture she pointed to was a professionally taken headshot of a girl who had the kind of looks one might see gracing the cover of a magazine.

Donahue sighed. "I still think they photoshop these pictures." It sounded like sour grapes, but she didn't care. "I know LA has got more than its fair share of beautiful women, Shari, but the number of beautiful women in these books defies statistical probability." She looked over at her partner and smiled. "To look this good, a woman would have to spend hours each day on makeup and hair, and judging from their bodies, at least two workouts a day."

"Ya think?" Thompson muttered.

" And, of course, most of these girls have had surgical alterations."

"Hey! Don't be throwing stones."

Donahue smiled. "None of them have ever nursed three boys, so you've earned the right for enhancement."

"Damn straight," Thompson replied, leaning back on the couch. "Girls like these are so into themselves that they're probably lousy in bed."

Donahue gave her an incredulous look.

"Don't touch my hair," Thompson said in a falsetto voice. *"Hurry up and get this over with, I still have to do my nails."* She smiled broadly, now completely into the role. *"You want me to do what? Sorry baby. Not this girl. That's just plain nasty."*

Donahue laughed so hard that her tears had started to mess up her mascara.

A door opened upon an inner wall of the room and a heavyset, balding man with an uneven smile—wearing a very expensive designer, double breasted suit —came into the VIP room. He spotted the two detectives, then his gaze settled on Thompson, which stopped him in his tracks.

He made a beeline over to where they were seated and gave Thompson a broad, lascivious smile.

"Are you in the book?" he asked, gesturing with his hand to the leather bound album that she was looking at. His accent sounded middle-eastern.

"Neyt," she said, mimicking a bad Russian accent, "but maybe soon."

She gave him a smile and stuck out her chest.

"You like?"

"Oh, my God!" said Donahue under her breath and she started to laugh again.

"Very much," he replied, ignoring Donahue; his eyes now glued to the obvious.

"Good," Thompson said, continuing the accent, "because I'm a package deal. I've got three boys, all under the age of ten; and of course, my parents and two sisters who live in Saint Petersburg would want to come over here to live with us—"

The man beat a hasty retreat out of the VIP room and into the main reception area accompanied by the unrestrained laughter of both Donahue and Thompson. Neither of them realized that Irina Konstantinov was now standing in the doorway that led to her private office, hands on her hips, a stunned and angry look on her face.

"*Vhat are you doing?*" she said. Her Russian-accented English sounded so much like Thompson's mimicry that both detectives burst into laughter again.

Donahue was the first to regain her composure. She got to her feet, straightened her jacket, then walked over to Irina and introduced herself   .
Thompson immediately joined them and apologized profusely for what she claimed was just poor judgement on her part.

Irina was mollified somewhat, and knowing from her receptionist that they were the police, she reluctantly invited them into her office where the three of them took seats in a grouping of red velvet easy chairs that were positioned to take advantage of the view.

Donahue noticed right away that Irina appeared to be extremely nervous. She supposed it was a natural reaction. Her partner had been murdered, and the penchant for Russians to distrust the police was common knowledge throughout law enforcement circles.

"Is this about Milan?" Irina asked.

Donahue nodded. "I'm sorry for your loss. We've been assigned to find out who's responsible, so we'd like to interview you about Milan."

"He was a very good man," she told them. "He invested in my business and handled the recruitment of our female matches."

"Did the women have to pay a fee to be listed with your agency?" Thompson asked.

Irina shook her head. "The women don't pay. We carefully screen them to make sure that they are sincerely interested in finding a long-term relationship that would someday lead to marriage."

"Do you get many marriages?" Thompson asked.

"Since we started four years ago we've had nineteen introductions that have led to marriage. And of course, we've had many more long term relationships that will likely result in marriages sometime in the future."

Irina pointed to a cork wallboard on an inner wall of the office. A number of photographs were pinned there, and all three of the women got to their feet and moved over to the board.

"These are pictures of the women who've gotten married to our clients," she said. "I'm very proud of our success rate. We are a legitimate matchmaking service."

She gave the two detectives time to study the photographs. All of them appeared to have been taken at weddings. The women were dressed in wedding gowns and the men appeared to be happy.

Donahue was looking at the men with the women. They seemed to be what western culture would deem to be some serious mismatches. Some of the men appeared to be significantly shorter than their brides, while others were obviously much older. And while all of the women looked like Barbie dolls, she counted only one male in the photos who came even close to looking like a Ken.

Thompson, on the other hand, was studying the women, and as her gaze moved through the photographs, she spotted one that garnered her immediate attention.

She thought, *Hey! I know that girl.*

But before she could ask a question, Donahue said, "Tell me about your male clients, Ms. Konstantinov? How do you first make contact with them?"

"Most of them discover our internet site. We follow up with everyone who searches through the online photographs." She looked from one to the other. "Of course, word of mouth brings in quite a few, and once we conduct interviews with the men, we decide on a fee, and if they can pay up front, we take them on as clients."

She smoothed her skirt, then turned and walked back towards the couch. Donahue followed, but Thompson chose the moment to surreptitiously remove the photo of the girl she thought she recognized before putting it into the pocket of her jacket.

"We charge a great deal of money, ten-thousand dollars for twelve introductions, one a month. Some of our clients, the ones who are exceptionally wealthy, prefer a more individualized approach. For twenty-five thousand dollars, they get unlimited access to all of the girls in our registry, and we will send out staff from my office to personally hunt down women who match their ideal profile."

"How do they do that?" Donahue asked.

"They scour internet dating sites, local universities, hospitals, casting calls, other agencies; you name it, we search everywhere."

"Any of your *very* wealthy clients ever end up on the marriage board?" Thompson asked.

"A few," Irina said, "but we have two more that are now in long term relationships, so I'm hoping we'll have good news very soon."

"Well, if any of the still unattached ones are looking for a hot female cop with three kids, you can send 'em my way."

Thompson had said it with such sincerity that Irina didn't know whether to take her seriously or just to laugh.

Donahue rolled her eyes. "Don't mind her. She's just trying to be funny."

Konstantinov nodded, a false smile on her face, and the three of them settled back into their chairs.

Donahue cleared her throat. "Irina? Can I call you that?"

Irina nodded.

"What can you tell me about Vladimir Komarov?"

"I don't know that person," she said, looking down at her lap.

"That's not what we've been told." Thompson leaned forward. "Milan reported to the police that Komarov was attempting to muscle his way into your business. Surely, he discussed that with you?"

"I don't know what you're talking about? Milan never discussed anything like that with me."

"You sure about that?" Donahue decided it was always possible that he didn't tell Irina, but she thought that was quite unlikely.

"I'm sure," Irina insisted.

"We were also told that Milan might have been having a relationship with one of the girls and that the one he was involved with might have had a jealous boyfriend?"

Irina adamantly shook her head. "Milan was not dating any of the women, at least none of the women here in the office. We agreed, up front, that they would always be off limits."

"What about the girls he recruited? Could he have been seeing one of them?"

"It's possible," Irina told them, "but if he was, he never said anything to me."

"Did he have any male friends? Anyone we could talk to who might know a bit more about his personal sex life?"

"I don't think Milan had many friends outside the job. He was always working the clubs, looking for women he could recruit. I'm afraid I don't know any of his male friends."

Donahue realized they were making very little progress. They could serve the warrant now and conduct a search of the office, but she suddenly had a better idea.

"C'mon Shari," she said, giving her a cautionary look and getting to her feet. "I think we've taken up enough of Irina's time...*for now*."

"What about—?" Thompson started.

"Later," Donahue said.

Thompson got to her feet, and as Irina showed them to the door, Donahue said, "I think you're afraid, Irina, but you need to know that Vlad Komarov won't stop until he's muscled his way into your business, and after that, he'll muscle you out."

She paused for effect.

"I'd hate to see you end up like Milan, so if you change your mind and decide you want to tell us about him, give me a call."

She pressed one of her cards into Irina's hands, then she and Thompson made their way out of the office and down to their car.

Once they were underway, Thompson removed the photograph from her purse, the one she'd liberated from Irina's marriage board.

"What's that?" Donahue asked, looking over.

"I think I know this girl, and if I'm right, she was seventeen when I last saw her. She was working the streets when I worked Hollywood Vice, so she'd be in her early twenties now."

"A Russian emigre?" Donahue asked.

Thompson nodded. "I don't remember her name, but I'll stop off at Hollywood Station tomorrow and I'll see if I can pull her card and get her file."

Donahue returned her eyes to the road as she moved through the pre-rush hour traffic.

"Did you notice how nervous Irina was?" Thompson asked. "She nearly peed-her-panties when you mentioned Vlad's name."

"She's holding back," said Donahue. "I just hope she comes to her senses before she loses everything."

"Can you drop me off at my car?" Thompson asked. "I've got to take the boys to a birthday party at *Chuck E. Cheese* tonight."

"No problem."

Thompson slid her sunglasses up, then checked herself in the visor mirror.

"What the hell do you suppose Nika knew about the agency that made her warn Svetlana off?"

"I don't know," Donahue said, "but I plan to find out."

CHAPTER 24

October 24, 11:50 p.m.

Yuri Pavienko arrived at the Organized Crime squad room and walked directly over to his desk. He took off his shoulder holster and placed his 9 mm semi-automatic handgun in his side desk drawer, then he reached down to his right ankle, raised his jeans pants leg, and removed his five-shot Smith and Wesson .38 *Airweight,* a backup gun that he carried around... *just in case.*

After he had locked the drawer containing both firearms, he checked his desk for messages. There were several of no real importance, so he set them slide, grabbed a cup of coffee from the lunch room, then went in search of his partner, Clay Young.

He found him alone in a room they used for interviews. He was seated at a table where he was reading the fourth page of a stack of photocopied pages.

"What's all that?" Yuri said, referring to the stack of documents.

Clay looked up. "I finally heard back from our contact at the FSB. He said they checked their files on Martun Hagopian..."

Yuri sat down at the table across from him. He took a sip of his coffee, then put the cup down. "You've got my attention. Go on."

Clay leaned back in his chair, still reading the page he was holding in his hand.

"Weren't you under the impression that this guy was a foot soldier with connections to the SB?"

"That's what Vlad inferred."

"Well, they've got nothing on file, and I mean *nada.* This guy apparently stayed completely below the radar."

Yuri sat up straighter. He added a little packet of sugar to his coffee while he mulled over what Clay had just told him.

"So maybe he's not SB," Yuri said. "Maybe he's just a common crook who never got busted in Russia?"

"Who knows? But it looks like he's our problem now."

Yuri nodded in agreement.

"So what did that detective want?" Clay asked.

"What detective?"

"You know, the one the Captain said wanted to ask you some questions?"

"You mean Detective Shari Thompson." Yuri's expression suggested a look of smug satisfaction.

"I know that look." Clay smiled. " Pretty, huh?"

Yuri nodded.

"You seeing her?" When Yuri didn't answer, he smirked, "You kill me."

When it came to women, Clay knew that Yuri was incorrigible, a real hound with a preference for a different woman every week. But this was the first time he'd known him to hook up with another cop.

"What'd she want to know?" he asked.

"Not much. A little background on Russian OC, but she'll be checking out Vlad, so I think it's best if we keep our distance from him for a while."

He caught Clay's concerned look.

"I'm just thinking there's no sense our getting caught up in their investigation. We don't want to be stepping on anyone's toes."

"That's fine with me," Clay replied. "We've been spending too much time on that prick as it is. I'd rather we went after a higher up instead of messing around with that guy."

"That's precisely why we're doing what we're doing, Clay. You've got to turn the Indians to get to the chiefs."

"I know you really believe that Yuri, but these guys would rather die then turn snitch. For my money, the only way to take down the heavyweight players is to sit on 'em night and day until we catch 'em red handed."

"That'll never happen. Trust me on that. I keep trying to get you to understand that the people we want to target never do anything themselves. They rely on the hired help to run their dope and to work as muscle."

Clay pursed his lips. They'd had this discussion several times already and Yuri never changed his position, and because he spoke Russian while few others on the force could, his impressions and opinions had the ear of the Captain and the upper echelon of the department. He had become the *resident expert* on all things Russian, and because of his so-called *expertise,* he was the go-to guy whose opinions always carried a great deal of weight.

To Clay, it seemed like LAPD was no different than any other enterprise. If you held yourself out as an expert, people tended to believe that you actually were one without ever seriously questioning your credentials.

Clay squirmed in his chair. "So we keep our distance from Vlad. Okay. I'll buy into that. But what about Hagopian? Do we need to forget about him, too?"

Yuri nodded in the affirmative. "For the time being, we'll stay out of the way of RHD. Let them do their thing, and once they're through, if they don't or can't make a case, then we'll put Vlad and Hagopian back on our radar. But until that time, we'll find other things that we can look into that are worthy of our time and effort."

Clay knew that trying to get Yuri to consider working with RHD was a losing battle, so he made a quick decision to keep his mouth shut and his thoughts to himself.

What else could he do?

*****

CHAPTER 25

October 25, 9:00 a.m.

Jennifer Donahue strolled into the squad room at ten after nine a.m. She was dressed in a knee-length black skirt, a pink silk blouse, and a black leather jacket designed by *Alexander McQueen*. Her black heels were suede pumps by *Manolo Blahnik*.

Thompson watched her walk in and her jaw hit the floor.

"Good morning cover girl. And here I thought maybe you'd just overslept."

"Nope, I went for a run this morning." She looked over at Thompson as she placed her gun in her desk. "After getting a look at the competition yesterday, I decided I'd better spend a little more time on self-maintenance."

Thompson laughed. "So I see, but I gave it a lot of thought last night, Jen, and those girls are just fishing in a different pond. The guys might all be rich, but I guess that most of them don't have the social skills or the degree of personal confidence to find someone on their own."

"You heard the pitch," Donahue said. "Her clients are too busy to get out and meet women on their own."

"That's a load of crap. Men who like women make time for the hustle. It's in their DNA." Thompson stood up and leaned over the partition to carefully look at Donahue's shoes.

"Are those *Manolo's*?"

"Uh, huh." Donahue smiled. "You like 'em?"

"*Hell yes!*" She studied her friend with an appraising eye. "You really do look good, sister."

"Thanks."

Donahue flipped a wayward strand of hair back behind her ear. "I'm gonna make a sincere effort to spend more time on myself, starting with a spa day next Saturday. You wanna join me?"

"Love to, but I've got three soccer games and another birthday party." She shrugged, then smiled. "But you've just reminded me of something. I think I know someone you might like to meet?"

"Oh, brother, here we go..."

"No, wait, hear me out. I know the last guy I set you up with didn't work out so well, but—"

"*Ha!* That's an understatement."

"Oh, come on. It wasn't that bad."

"You weren't there. The guy had nothing to say after 'hello.'"

Thompson laughed. "Okay, maybe he was a little shy. But he was awfully good looking."

"He was gay, Shari."

"Don't be that way." Thompson struggled to suppress a smile. "I suppose that's possible, but this other guy is different. He's a fireman. He saves little kitty cats that climb up too high in trees."

"Good start, but now you're going to tell me that he's never been married and currently lives with his mother?"

Thompson frowned. "He's a widower, Jen. His wife died of cancer a few years ago."

"Oh?" Donahue's contrition was immediate. "I don't know, Shari. That widower stuff comes with a whole different set of problems."

"I know, but he's really stable. He's a bit older than the guys you usually latch on to—"

Donahue smiled again and shook her head.

"I knew there was a catch somewhere. Thanks, babe, but I don't go in for geriatric cases."

"Not true. You always seem to date older guys. But he's not that old. He's got two kids in school with my brood. I see him at the soccer games." She searched Donahue's eyes for any glimmer of interest. "I think you'd like him."

Donahue folded her arms across her chest. "If this guy's so great, then why aren't you doing him?"

"I've got a hard and fast rule against playing in my kid's school sandbox, but if it wasn't for that..."

"So basically, what you're really trying to say is that he's not your type."

Thompson gave that a moment's consideration. "Yeah, I suppose he's a little too sedate for me."

"*Sedate?*" Donahue returned her smile. "You mean responsible, don't you?"

"Got me there! But give it some thought. I think it might work."

"Thanks for the offer, Shari. I know you have my best interests at heart, but I'm still intent on a cool-down period. I really need to take a break."

Mitzi Roberts walked over from her cubicle and joined them.

"You guys got a few moments?"

"Sure, Mitz." Donahue turned to face her. "What's up?"

"I had a chance to take a quick look at Vlad Komarov's cell phone call log. Turns out the guy's a real talker. Dozens and dozens of calls in and out every day. The call record on his cell only lists about a hundred numbers, but I'm gonna write a search warrant and get his calls for the past few months from his carrier. It's gonna take a lot of work, but it might be a gold mine of information."

Donahue nodded. Her face reflected a heightened excitement. If Vlad was involved in criminality, then that many calls would likely reveal some tangible results.

"Let me know if you need some help—" Thompson started.

"Hold on. There's more." She lowered her voice to just above a whisper. "I began with the call record of his outgoing calls made around the time of the bombing incident. I was working my way backward, just correlating the numbers, looking for multiple calls to the same number, and it turns out that one of the numbers got called three times in the hour before the bomb went off."

"And…?" said Thompson.

"*And...* I called a friend of mine at *Sprint.* He owed me a favor. He said the number comes back registered to a company called *Baseline Productions—*"

As Roberts was speaking, Donahue was already typing the name into *Google* on her desktop computer.

"—a company that doesn't show up on the California Department of Corporations register," Roberts said.

Donahue confirmed with a nod that it didn't. She turned back to Roberts.

"So what does that mean?"

Roberts smiled. "My friend at *Sprint* checked the confidential file and told me that it's a registered front number for the LAPD."

"*What?*"

Both Thompson and Donahue had said it simultaneously.

"*Shh!*" said Roberts. She looked around, but no one was paying them any attention. She lowered her voice.

"It's used for phones supplied to our undercover operatives." She looked over at Donahue. "You worked Vice, right? Didn't they give you a cell phone?"

Donahue nodded. "But we kept the phones clean. No traceable callback numbers."

"Old phones," Roberts said with a smile. "Nowadays, if you get one and lose it, if someone checks on the registration, it comes back to a dummy company. The UC's are instructed to say that the phone was a stolen and that they bought it on the street." She looked from one to the other. "Each UC operation gets a different front company name so there's no overlap that might give them away."

Donahue felt her stomach begin to knot up. She briefly closed her eyes and gently shook her head.

"So how do we find out which UC operation he was calling?"

Roberts looked around again, and once she was satisfied that no one else was within earshot, she whispered, "*Baseline Productions* is the front company currently being used by our Organized Crime Intelligence Unit."

*****

11:00 a.m.

The Internal Affairs Group of the Los Angeles Police Department was established in 1949 with a mandate to maintain the public confidence by investigating all complaints thoroughly and impartially. To that extent, the IAG was housed at a location that was not part of the downtown Police Administration Building. This was done for several reasons, the most important one being that cops who investigated other cops needed to be housed in an environment where they could work without exposure to any form of peer pressure. The second major reason was more practical. There was a division within the IAG that conducted criminal investigations of suspected officers, and within that division was a top secret surveillance unit whose job it was to keep tabs on the investigative targets, and to do so effectively and safely, complete anonymity was absolutely essential. To house these spooks in the more public PAB would be to put them at risk of being recognized, and since their targets were assumed to be armed at most times, a chance meeting could lead to a deadly outcome that no one wanted to see.

For that reason, IAG's operational facility was a converted warehouse also on Grand Avenue, about two miles south of downtown Los Angeles.

Donahue had her Captain call ahead and she was booked in for a meeting with a Lieutenant named Andrew Magarian, the CO of the unit of super secret spooks.

She was greeted by a receptionist in a nondescript outer office who walked her through a secure door that led to a series of rooms filled with desks, file cabinets, and chairs. There were plenty of officers wandering around, many in suits, a few others in uniform. The number of people working there initially surprised her, but when she took a few moments to think it over, she realized that when you had an agency that was ten thousand officers strong, there was always going to be more than a few rotten apples. Hence, the need for more than a few to police the many.

Magarian was a good-looking man with dark hair, an olive complexion, and a soft spoken voice. His eyes were clear and sharp, and Donahue noted that he was quick to smile. He invited her into his private office and introduced her to his second in command, a Sergeant named John Homa, who was a little taller and thinner than Magarian, but certainly not as calm. Homa seemed a bit edgy to her, a guy whose mind was always racing; the kind of man who was always ready to lead others into action. His eyes never focused on any one thing for too long, but as she came to find out, in spite of what looked to her like an inability to concentrate, his mind was like a steel trap, and his penchant for details made him an indispensable part of the unit's most complex investigations.

They took seats around Magarian's desk, and Donahue explained to them the facts of the Petrovich bombing case. She talked about his matchmaking agency, eliciting a few chuckles when she mentioned the company's name; the visit paid to Petrovich before the bombing by Vlad Komarov; his believed links to Russian OC; and Komarov's telephone log and the calls made to the OC Intelligence Unit.

"Since we know the number he called, how can we determine who in OCI he was talking to?" she asked.

Magarian cleared his throat. "Just give me the number and I'll call it and see who answers."

Donahue's eyes went wide and she was just about to question the wisdom of that when Magarian broke into a smile.

"Just kidding," he told her.

Homa started to chuckle.

Magarian said, "It might take a few hours, but I can find out. However, if it turns out that there's any hint of impropriety, we're gonna have to open a full investigation."

Donahue nodded. "At the moment, I've got nothing that indicates any criminality, but if there is anything that doesn't seem right, I'll let you guys know right away."

"Fair enough," Magarian said. "Have you got the number?"

Donahue produced a piece of paper from her purse and handed it over to Magarian who looked it over, then placed the paper in his pocket.

"I can count on you guys keeping this under wraps, right?" she asked.

Homa smiled while Magarian's sweeping arm gesture took in the entire office complex.

"Welcome to the home of secrets."

*****

Back at her desk in the PAB, Donahue had a few minutes to ponder the imponderable. While she could make an argument that all three murders were somehow related, she could point to nothing that actually linked them together. If the bombing was an attempt to do a business takeover, then why kill Nika and Eliska? The who, what, and why's of this case was driving her crazy. There were too many loose ends and the fact that all the players had such foreign names made working the case that much more difficult.

What she needed was a night off and a few tequila shooters, but there was no chance of that until the case was solved.

She sighed slowly, then got to her feet and made her way to Captain Tom Elwood's office where she left him a note stating that she wanted to meet to discuss the idea of setting up a task force to work the three cases.

When she got back to her desk, she found Shari Thompson waiting for her.

"I spent most of the morning going through the files at Vice."

"Any luck?"

"Yep. I found her. The girl in the photo on Irina's marriage board is Katya Ivanova." She handed Donahue a booking photo and a copy of the rap sheet. "Katya had four arrests for prostitution. Her last bust was one and a half years ago."

"She cleaned up nice," Donahue said, comparing the old booking photo with the one from the marriage board. She carefully studied them both. "Looks like she was using when this picture was taken."

"She was seventeen in that photo," Thompson said. "And as I recall, her drug of preference was heroin."

Donahue nodded, then handed the photos back.

"Looks like someone got her off the drugs and gave her some grooming lessons."

"There's no current address on file for her, but that doesn't surprise me. It looks like she left the street life behind."

"Wonder if her husband knows about her past?" Donahue said.

"I doubt it. Anyway, while I was down in Vice, I looked up the names of a few of her associates, then I ran them through the system." She put the rap sheet and photos back down on her desk.

"One of them, Oksana Pashinka, is currently in custody over at the county jail. Wanna go with me to pay her a visit?"

*****

CHAPTER 26

October 25, 1:50 p.m.

The Century Regional Detention Facility (CRDF), formally a male facility, was now an all female jail that reopened as such in 2006. Located in the city of Lynwood, California, it was run by the Los Angeles County Sheriff's Office but served the as the holding center for female prisoners from throughout the entire county.

Thompson had called ahead, and after passing through several security checkpoints set up specifically for sworn personnel, they were taken to an interview room deep within the facility, one that offered secrecy for inmates being talked to by the police. This was done for the prisoner's safety, as well as for the security of the jail at large.

The Sheriff's had called Oksana Pashinka out of her module, and they escorted her to the interview room. She was told she was going to see the medical officer, a cover for her movement should anyone ask where she was taken. When she arrived at the interview room, she was cuffed behind her back and told to sit in a chair that was one of four that were grouped around a plain metal table. She was wearing a jail-issued jumpsuit, blue in color, that signified that she was part of the general population. They did not tell her why she was there, and Oksana was too savvy to ask. She figured she wasn't there to see anyone from the medical staff, so she kept her mouth shut, knowing that she would find out soon enough what it was all about.

Thompson and Donahue were let into the room, and the door was closed and locked behind them. Oksana, who looked sleepy, looked up when they entered, then returned her attention to her lap.

The two detectives pulled out chairs and sat down. Thompson was the first to speak.

"Oksana? Do you remember me?"

Oksana looked up slowly. Her skin was sallow and clammy looking, and her eyes, half-shut, were bloodshot.

Thompson looked over at Donahue, gave her a knowing look, then said, "What are you on?"

"I'm not," Oksana replied.

"Let me rephrase that. What are you trying to kick?"

Oksana sighed. She struggled to lock eyes with Thompson.

"I was using H."

"Are you getting treatment here?"

Oksana shook her head. "They don't give a shit about me."

Thompson knew that wasn't true. All inmates went through an initial assessment when they first came into the lockup. If Oksana wasn't receiving any treatment, then it was likely that she'd gotten high from drugs she'd taken while in the jail.

"I understand you're still working the streets," Donahue said, a reference to Oksana's current arrest for soliciting an act of prostitution. "You still going by the name of Chrissy?"

Chrissy had been the name that Oksana had used with her tricks. Many of the women who emigrated to the United States and found themselves working in prostitution often adopted names for use on the streets to help them conceal their true identities from both the customers as well as the police.

Oksana nodded. It was no use lying to these detectives. They knew all about her, of that she was sure.

She stared at Thompson for a while, then slowly the light went on.

"I remember you," she finally said. "You work Hollywood Vice. Right?"

"Used to," Thompson said. "How come you're still working the streets?"

She shrugged. "Gotta get by. You know what it's like."

"I do, and that's why I'm here. I'd like to help you out if you're in a position to give me some information?"

Oksana held her glance, clearly interested. She was no stranger to the game, and this looked to be an opportunity to get out of her current legal predicament. But in her experience, cops could be greedy with what they wanted, and she approached this offer with a measure of suspicion.

"What do you want to know?"

Thompson leaned back in her chair. "What can you tell us about Katya

Ivanova? She went by the street name of *Allia*."

Oksana laughed.

"What's funny?"

Donahue was easing into the role of bad cop to Thompson's good one.

"Nothing." Oksana suddenly worried that she wouldn't be getting any help.

"Good," said Donahue, "then tell us all about her."

Oksana looked back over at Thompson. "What's in it for me?"

"Tell me what you know, and if it helps, I'll get you out of your current beef."

That was enough for Oksana, but now she was worried that she didn't know enough.

"I haven't seen her in a year." She looked at Thompson for moral support. "She got off the streets. Went to work with an agency of some kind, dating old rich guys, I guess."

"How'd she get hooked up with that agency?" Donahue asked.

"A guy in a club told her about it."

"Who was the guy?"

"I don't know. All I know is that he was Russian."

"Did this guy have a name?"

Oksana looked hard at Donahue. "I said I don't know."

Thompson leaned forward, a move which recaptured Oksana's attention.

"So this guy tells her about this agency. How did it work?"

"He cleaned her up, got her off the drugs; nice clothes, a nice apartment." She shook her head, a gesture that revealed the depths of her jealousy.

"An apartment?" Donahue was relishing her role as the bully. "That's a lot of effort, wouldn't you say so Shari?"

"I would," Thompson agreed. She focused her stare on Osaka. "So why'd this guy go to all this effort?"

Oksana looked from one to the other, then shrugged. "How the hell would I know?"

"Was she being paid for turning tricks with these millionaires?" Donahue asked.

"She said she wasn't, but I didn't believe her. She said she was giving it away."

"And you expect us to believe that?" Donahue asked.

Oksana looked panicked. She was telling them the truth, but if they didn't believe her, they would walk away and leave her without a deal.

"I didn't believe it myself," she said, "but she was doing it to find a husband. That's all I know."

"Did you ever get approached with such an offer?" Donahue asked.

Oksana nodded.

"So? What happened?"

"I wasn't ready to give up the drugs."

Oksana's expression turned into a frown, and both detectives knew without a doubt that she'd regretted that decision from the moment it was made.

"You said you haven't seen her." Donahue leaned forward. "Have you talked with her in the past year?"

"A couple of months ago she called me on my cell, all upset. She'd gotten married, but she told me her husband got killed in a robbery somewhere in West LA."

Thompson flashed Donahue a surprised expression. Irina never mentioned that any of her so-called matches had ended so tragically.

"She was very upset," Oksana added. "I offered to help her, but... *you know...*"

"Yeah, we know," said Donahue. *"You were still on the drugs and not ready to give them up."*

Oksana shrugged. She'd been jealous of Katya and didn't really care at the time about her problems, but she wasn't about to admit that to the detectives.

"Do you know how we can reach her?" Thompson asked.

"Are you still going to help me?" Oksana asked.

Thompson's eyes narrowed.

"Do you know where she is?"

Oksana nodded. "Her number is in my cell phone. The Sheriff's took it away when they booked me in."

"We'll check it out of your property," Thompson said, "and if her contact information is there, I'll help you out."

Oksana smiled, but it only lasted for a moment, for her mind had already drifted to thoughts of where she was going to go to get her next fix.

"What was the husband's name?" Donahue asked.

Oksana shrugged. "I don't know the name, but she said he was shot in a parking garage. That's all I know."

The two detectives got to their feet and turned to go.

"Tell her I said hi," Oksana said, but neither detective bothered to respond.

CHAPTER 27

October 25, 3:00 p.m.

Donahue and Thompson entered the squad room amidst a flurry of activity, and it was Roberts who approached them with a smile on her face.

"We just got a hit on the Flower Street rapist," she said.

Donahue put her purse down on her desk to give Roberts her full attention. The Flower Street rapist had nineteen rapes and two homicides to his credit, all women who'd been attacked in the downtown metropolitan area. Some were prostitutes from the skid row scene, but others were women who worked in the hundreds of small businesses that made up the East side of downtown.

"His name is Rodrigo Castaneda. He did time at San Luis Obispo for burglary and assault."

"Is he in custody?" Thompson asked.

"No, he's been out for two years. His PO (probation officer) says he's working in a soup kitchen on Fourth Street." She looked around the room. "SIS is on him and they're putting together an arrest team. You want in?"

SIS or Special Investigations Section was an undercover surveillance group who often tailed identified suspects while the final arrest plans were put together.

"Can't go," Donahue said, "but it looks like you've got enough volunteers."

More than a dozen detectives were standing around, waiting for the Captain to decide who was going to take part in the arrest. With the Flower Street rapist, years had been spent trying to track him down, and it wasn't until his most recent victim that a DNA sample had been obtained. By running it through the statewide system, they'd gotten a hit from his past incarceration, and a lot of detectives who'd spent the better part of a decade trying to identify him wanted nothing more than to be in on the arrest. It was a way to help them put the case behind them, and mindful of that, it was likely that the Captain would let everyone go who wanted to go to witness the final act.

They checked Oksana's phone out of the jail's property division and discovered that Katya Ivanova's name and number were in there. Thompson wrote it down, and on the way back to the station, they'd called Mitzi Roberts. They gave her the name and number, and twenty minutes later, when Mitzi called back, they learned that the address for the phone came back to an account in the name of Philip Katz, her husband. Since the address was for a business that was centered in Brentwood, they concluded that it had to have been for his office.

Plan A was out the window, so it was time to implement Plan B.

"Is Jackson around somewhere?" Donahue said to no one in particular when they got back to the squad room. She carefully scanned the room and spotted him with a group of detectives standing over near Gibson's desk, so she and Thompson walked over to where he was.

Rick Jackson was a thirty-five year veteran of the department. He'd spent the last twenty years working homicides, and as the second most senior detective in the unit, right behind Ulysses Gibson, he was treasured as a living encyclopedia. His memory was incredible, and he tended to remember even the most obscure cases; not only the details of the crimes, but who the suspect was if a suspect was identified, and the names of the investigators who were handling the case.

So starting with Jackson was a no brainer for Donahue. It could save her many hours of tedious research if she were forced to look things up by herself.

"Hey Rick," she said, "you got a few moments?"

"Always for you, *Jenny from the hood.*" Jackson was a large man with a bald pate surrounded by closely cropped white hair and a thick white mustache that covered his upper lip.

"I'm trying to track down a WLA homicide. It occurred within the last year or so."

Jackson smiled. His mind was already going through a mental list of the possible cases.

"The victim was a wealthy male investment banker—"

"Solved or Unsolved?" Jackson asked.

"Unsolved," she replied.

"Katz. Philip Katz. Fifty-five years of age. He was shot to death arriving at his office at about 6 a.m. The apparent motive was robbery. His wallet was missing."

Donahue smiled. Jackson's memory was truly amazing.

"Do you remember who was handling the case?" she asked, already knowing the answer.

"Larry London," he said, a big smile on his face. "A good guy. I've worked with him once before."

"Thanks, Rick." She headed back to her desk.

It took a few minutes to track London down by phone, but when she did, he found that he was completely comfortable about sharing his case information.

"Have you got a home address for the victim's wife?" she asked.

He opened his file, then said, "It's a condo on Wilshire Boulevard. One of those expensive high-rise buildings." He read off the name and address of the building which she dutifully copied into her notebook.

"I don't know if it's still any good," he said. "I haven't talked to her recently."

"Can I come by and get a look at the file?"

"Sure, I don't see why not. If I'm not here, it'll be on my desk with a note." He paused for a moment. "Just don't lose it."

"I won't. Is the victim's wife named Katya?"

"It sure is," he said, and after a moment of silence, "Are you going to tell me what you've got?"

"Nothing yet, but as soon as I come up with something, I'll let you know."

London didn't like the answer. He knew she wouldn't be asking about the case if she didn't have some kind of a lead. He surmised that it was probably an informant, which made her reluctance to talk about it all the more understandable. Cops felt duty bound to protect their informants, so he didn't push the point.

"If you get a good lead, let me know," he said. "I'll be happy to follow it up."

"I will," she replied, then hung up the phone.

She turned to tell Thompson that she'd tracked down the WLA murder and that she planned to look over the location on her way home when her desk phone suddenly began to ring.

"This is Donahue," she said, picking it up.

"It's Andrew Magarian. Is this a secure line?"

"It's my separate line," she replied, looking around. "It doesn't ring on the other desks."

"Good. I got that info you requested."

She knew what he was talking about. The department phone assigned to OC Intelligence, the one that Vlad had called several times just before the bombing that killed Milan Petrovich.

He said, "It's assigned to a detective named Clay Young."

She wrote the name down. "I'll let you know what we find out."

She then gathered up Thompson and they headed for the nearest vacant interview room where they could speak without being overheard.

She told Thompson about the WLA murder case and how she was going to drive by the location on her way home.

"I think I'll stop by WLA after that and pick up the file."

Thompson nodded. "So what do you want me to do?"

"The phone that Vlad called comes back to someone named Clay Young, a detective in OC Intelligence. Maybe you can give Yuri a call and see what he knows about Young?"

"I'll do it right away," she said. She pulled out her cell phone and dialed Yuri's number, but the call went to his answering machine. She left a message for him to call her back, then said to Donahue, "I'm gonna take off. I need some time with my kids."

"Give 'em my best," Donahue said. "I'll see you in here tomorrow."

*****

Donahue left downtown during the height of the rush hour traffic. To call it a "rush hour" was a misnomer. From three-thirty p.m. until almost seven o'clock at night, the freeways going in and out of Los Angeles were always bumper to bumper. What could be a twenty minute drive at four in the morning was easily more than an hour, so Donahue had learned to kill time by listening to books on tape. She was deeply engrossed in a Daniel Silva novel, the *English Girl*, when she spotted the building that housed the residence of Katya Ivanova Katz, the wife of the WLA murder victim.

Katya lived in a thirty story high rise called the *Wilshire Tower* that was newly built, but which had an architectural style akin to the art deco period of the 1930s. It was beautifully designed, and boasted valet parking out in front with a subterranean garage that probably went a half dozen floors below ground.

Rather than stop to check the residence directory, she decided to press on to the WLA police station. It was likely that Detective London was already gone, but she wanted to get the file from off his desk so she'd have something to read before bed.

She parked in the secure lot behind the WLA station, then made her way through security and in through the back door. She had worked in this division before going to RHD, so she still knew a few of the people who were working there. She said a few hello's, listened to some small talk, and finally found herself in the homicide room.

London was still seated at his desk, so she walked over and introduced herself.

Larry London was a good looking man with gray hair and an easy-going smile. He was munching on a piece of *baklava,* and offered her one of the pastries from a tin box he kept on his desk.

"I'm watching my waistline," she said, initially turning it down. Then, on second thought, "But maybe I could take a piece with me?"

As he wrapped a piece for her in a napkin, he said, "I understand you used to work here?"

"Seems like a million years ago."

He invited her to take a seat, which she did, then he slid a thick, blue, three-ring binder across the desk.

All homicide case files were set up in the same format. There was an initial index page followed by twenty additional sections that covered everything from statements to crime scene photographs. There was also a section for a chronology that detailed all efforts to investigate. This one was thick, so Donahue suspected that London had put in a lot of time and effort, but that all of it had been to no avail.

"I looked over the file again after I spoke to you," he said. "Robbery is still our best working theory, although my boss always wondered about the wife."

Donahue held his glance. "Where was she at the time of the killing?"

"With girlfriends in San Diego."

"Was there corroboration of that?"

London nodded. "We pulled the video tapes from the hotel where she was staying. She was in her room by one a.m. and didn't come out until ten-fifteen."

"Does he think she might have had someone do it for her?"

"Not really, but he's just naturally suspicious." He folded his arms across his chest, then sighed. "I'm betting she didn't. I spoke to her when it happened. She was genuinely upset when she found out he was dead. The kind of upset that's hard to fake. She had me convinced, and I don't tend to get easily fooled."

"Did she ever take a poly?"

"She did, and she came out clean."

"How long were they married?" Donahue asked.

"Just under six months."

"That's a real shame. Poor girl."

London nodded. "We've exhausted all our leads. Robbery is still the working theory, but if you turn up anything at all, I'd really like to insist that you give me a call. The victim was a decent guy, and his wife seems pretty decent, too, so I'd really like to put this one to bed."

Donahue nodded. "You have my word."

CHAPTER 28

October 26, 8:00 a.m.

Donahue arrived at the squad room in a very upbeat mood. Getting off at her usual end-of-watch the day before had given her time to relax. She'd made it to an evening yoga class, had eaten a chicken caesar salad, and had drunk several glasses of wine while she read the file pertaining to the murder of Phillip Katz.

Katz had arrived at the parking lot of his office at just after six a.m. He'd been driving a Black Bentley coupe and had parked in a spot that was reserved for him. A security camera had noted his arrival, but there was no camera where he parked his car. The sound of gunshots had been heard inside the building by the guard on post in the reception area. He'd called it in, and the first units on the scene had arrived less than five minutes later.

Unfortunately, the lot had several separate entrances and exits, and a person on foot could easily get in and out without being seen. They'd checked all the cars that came and went on the security camera film, but nothing unusual stood out. Katz was known to come in early, as most of his associates were known to show up at closer to 6:30 a.m.

He'd been shot once in the chest and once in the head while he was lying on his back on the ground. His wallet was missing, and his two front pants pockets had been pulled out, indicative of a robbery. The only thing that seemed to go against the prevailing theory was the fact that the victim was wearing a watch that was valued at seven thousand dollars.

Few robbers would leave behind such a valuable piece of property...unless, of course, he'd panicked during the robbery and had run away before completing a thorough search.

The other big question mark for her was the insurance policy he carried. It had been taken out six months before his death, just about the time of his marriage to Katya. She had been the single beneficiary, and the insurance company had delayed payment for about four months before finally conceding

170

that they had no evidence that would enable them to refuse a payoff for the full amount.

London had pulled together all of the family's phone records, including Katya's cell phone and that of her husband, but an exhaustive search of all calls in and out since the time of the marriage had turned up nothing suspicious. The thought that she might have paid someone to do it was determined to be highly unlikely.

Donahue put the file on her desk, then made her way to the coffee room where she poured herself a cup of coffee.

Thompson walked in and joined her at the coffee machine.

"It was great to get home early for a change," Thompson said with a smile. "I took the boys out for pizza, and we had a good talk about the hours I have to work."

"How'd they react?" Donahue asked.

"I think they're okay with things. The older ones know I love the job and they seem to be happy that I work as a cop. The little one is too young to understand, but the older ones are okay with the babysitter setup, so I feel a tad better about the situation."

"So you plan to stay on?" Donahue asked hopefully.

"We'll see," Thompson said. "A lot is going to depend on the list of girls you gave me. If I can line up one or two that can help me out, then maybe it will work."

Donahue nodded. She could only hope that it did. She loved working with Thompson. They had each other's backs and they got along really well. It didn't get much better than that.

She filled Thompson in on the facts of the Phillip Katz homicide. "We need to talk to Katya, today if we can."

"Sure, why not? Let me get settled in and check my emails, then let's get out of here."

They walked back to the squad room where Thompson discovered that Yuri had called her back.

She listened to his message, then called him his phone, and was actually surprised when he answered it.

"Hey, Yuri, I need to ask you a question. Do you know a guy over there named Clay Young?"

There was a moment of complete silence, and for a second Thompson thought they'd been disconnected. She was about to speak again when he said, "Yeah, I know him. What's up?"

"Well, we ran the phone log from Vlad Komarov's phone and it turns out that he called Young's cell phone three separate times on the night that Milan Petrovich was killed." She leaned up and picked up a pen. "I just wanted to know what you can tell me about Young, and what, if anything, you think was going on?"

Yuri was silent again for a moment before finally saying, "Clay Young is my partner."

Thompson bit her lip.

Oh shit!

She had just made a huge tactical error, and for just a moment, she didn't know how to proceed. She should have talked with the Captain directly, learned what she could from him, then spoken to Yuri once she was sure that there was little chance that the inquiry would be compromised.

Yuri said, "Look. I think I can help you out here. I took the calls from Komarov that night."

"You were using your partner's phone?"

"No, I was using my phone. Here's what must have happened. When they gave out the phones, I probably grabbed the one assigned to Clay by mistake. I'm the one who took all three of those calls from Komarov that night, but I've had this phone ever since they handed 'em out."

Okay. That certainly sounds possible, but it doesn't explain why he would be talking with Komarov?

"But when you and I first talked, you said you didn't know him very well?"

"I don't. I said I met him a few times in the clubs." He sighed. "Man! What a fuckin' mess." He shifted the phone to his other ear. "Look, he knows I'm a cop. I've been working on building a relationship with him. I want to turn him into a confidential informant."

Thompson sighed. She'd already screwed this up, so she'd need to be cautious from this point forward.

"Okay, Yuri. Then tell me what those calls were all about?"

"Sure. He called me that night because one of his girls got picked up trying to score a buy of heroin for her personal use. He wanted to keep her out of jail. He asked me to see if the City Attorney would let her go into a rehab program, so I said I would. I made a few calls and the CA let her go into a rehab program, so now the guy owes me one. That's how we do it around here. That's what it was all about."

"Is your partner aware that you've got his phone?"

"I doubt it. Until you called, I wasn't aware there was a mistake. But it's too late to switch 'em back now because I've given out the number on my cell to people who don't know that I'm a cop, so I guess I'll have to talk to the Captain and let him know about the mistake. But it can't be a big deal. I'm sure we can just go back and write up a change to the equipment assignment log."

He was probably right. It sounded like a simple mistake, one that could easily be remedied.

She allowed herself a sigh of relief. Maybe this wasn't such a serious fuck-up after all.

"Does anyone know about your relationship with Komarov?" she asked.

"Relationship? I don't have a relationship with him, at least, not yet."

"Bad choice of words. Does your partner know that you're trying to recruit Komarov?"

"No, I didn't tell him We tend to keep our informants completely confidential, even from each other."

When Thompson started to speak, he added, "When you're dealing with these Russian mobsters, the less anyone knows, the better, and that includes other cops who might inadvertently let something slip."

"But what about your Captain? Don't you maintain an informant log?" It was a department-wide policy to do so, and one that brings about serious sanctions if it's not followed to the letter.

"Of course the Captain keeps the registration log, but I haven't registered Komarov because he hasn't given me anything yet."

Thompson was thinking that if she was running the OC Intelligence Division, she'd require a formal report of any contact made with a potential OC target.

She sighed again.

"Okay. Well, you've answered all my questions. I'll let you know if I have any others."

After a moment of silence, he said, "So? We're good, right?"

"Yeah, we're good."

She hung up the phone then spent a few moments considering what she'd just heard. His answers to her had been decisive and forthcoming without the hesitation so common when lying was involved. It was a strong indication that he was telling her the truth.

She walked over to Donahue's cubicle and quietly told her what had happened.

"Don't feel so bad," Donahue said. "I was the one who suggested that you run it by him in the first place. I guess the only thing we can do now is call his Captain and see if the guys who work in the unit are required to report their contacts?"

"Let's run it by Magarian first," Thompson said. "I'd hate for us to make another dumb mistake?"

"Yeah, you're right. I'll give him a call."

"Does it seem strange to you that Yuri doesn't tell his partner about his CI's?"

"Yeah, that seems a little strange to me, but we don't have to deal with these mob types very often, and I guess it makes good sense to keep an informant's identity completely confidential." She smiled. "You know how it goes around here. Nothing stays a secret for very long."

"You're right about that."

CHAPTER 29

October 26, 8:25 a.m.

Clay Young pulled into his driveway in a small, green Toyota four-door that he used as a run around car. He'd been on duty since ten p.m. the night before, and now that he'd finished the last of his paperwork, he was ready to catch a long nap.

He had stopped off on the way home at a *Pancake House* restaurant where he'd ordered the biggest meal on the menu. Three strips of bacon, three sausages, three pancakes, three eggs, and potatoes. He'd downed at least three cups of coffee, not worried that it might interfere with his nap. Coffee didn't do that to him. Once he walked into his bedroom, he knew he was gonna sleep like a rock.

He got out of the car and looked around. A large boat sat on a trailer in his driveway, a thirty-five footer for skiing and fishing. He checked the canvas cover, making sure it was tight, then made his way over to the front door.

Parked in the garage was his *Silverado*, a brand new Chevy truck that he used to tow the boat. He peeked in the side window of the garage and noted that his wife's Mercedes was gone. She had been a secretary for a plastic surgery firm, but once the four kids came along, she'd turned into a stay-at-home mom. He checked his watch. She was probably at an early morning yoga class...or was today her day for a tennis lesson?

His four kids were all in school, the youngest having just started kinder-garten. It always felt strange to come home to an empty house, but at the same time, he loved working nights because it meant that when he did come home in the mornings, he could get a little sleep without worrying about the kids, their extra-curricular activities, or their frequent bickering.

He stepped into the foyer of the six bedroom house in the Simi Valley and noted with satisfaction that his wife or maybe even the kids had cleaned it up. The bottom of the stairs seemed to be a collection point for school books, toys, and clothing. The constant mess was one of his pet peeves, so it was nice to know that someone had paid attention to his latest complaint.

He made his way to the kitchen, took a plastic bottle of water from the refrigerator, then headed upstairs to the master bedroom. Just as he arrived, his phone began to ring, and when he checked the incoming call log, he saw that it was Yuri on the line.

"What's up?" Fatigue was plainly evident in his voice.

"I just heard from RHD," Yuri said. "They checked the call log on Komarov's cell phone, and they found out that he called me three times on the night that Petrovich was killed."

"What'd you tell 'em?" Clay asked. He walked over and sat down on the side of the queen sized bed.

"I told them that I was working on Vlad to become an informant."

"Did they buy it?"

"Why wouldn't they?"

Clay rubbed a hand through his hair. It was a stupid mistake on Komarov's part. He should have deleted his call log.

"You think they're gonna follow up on that?" Clay asked.

"I'm sure of it," Yuri replied. "So right now you might want to think about what you're gonna say if they decide to talk to you."

Shit!

Clay slowly shook his head. *He hated to be drawn into something like this.*

"So what do I tell 'em?" he asked.

"You tell them that you don't know nothing about Komarov being an informant. That I never told you what I was doing."

"But I do know, so why would saying that cause any problems?"

"Look, Clay. The best thing for you is to keep out of this. If you say you know, then both of us have got to explain why we've never reported my contacts."

"You haven't been writing them up?"

"You know I haven't. That was part of my deal with Komarov. He gives me intel, but there's no mention of him anywhere."

"So what are you gonna say to the Captain?"

"I'll just tell him I've only talked to him twice, and I was holding off until I

176

had something to report."

"They might ding you for that," Clay said.

"He'll understand."

"You planning on saying anything to Komarov?"

"Yeah. I'll tell the stupid shit to start erasing his phone log."

"Be careful, Yuri. He's dangerous, and sometimes I think you forget that."

"I can handle Vlad," Yuri said. "Just make sure that you and I are on the same page."

Clay nodded to himself. Yuri was his partner. He'd cover for him. It was the least he could do.

"Vlad is not gonna take this well," he cautioned.

"That's his fuckin' problem. He's the one who made the mistake, so he'll just have to live with it."

"I don't trust the guy, Yuri. He could turn on you at any time."

"You let me worry about that, Clay."

"Whatever you say. I'll see you tonight."

*****

Outside Clay Young's house, in a car parked three doors down to the North, John Homa was seated in the passenger seat of a Ford Escort, busily snapping pictures of Young's house, his take-home UC car, and the boat in the driveway.

Magarian sat watching everything from behind the steering wheel.

"Nice boat," Magarian said. "I'd like one like that for the *River.*"

"You and me both," said Homa.

CHAPTER 30

October 26, 8:25 a.m.

Donahue leaned forward in her chair and rested her hands on the table top. She was in an interview room in the Internal Affairs facility, huddled together with Thompson, Magarian, and Homa.

"So Komarov's phone was used to call Yuri Pavienko's phone three times on the night of the murder?" Magarian looked up from his note taking. "And he said that his partner doesn't know that Komarov is one of his CI's?"

"That's right," Thompson replied.

Magarian looked over at Homa. "What do you think, John? Does that sound plausible?"

Homa shook his head. "It's bullshit. Guys tell their partners about their CI's. This guy Pavienko is lying."

"So what's in it for him?" Magarian asked. "Why lie about something like that?"

"Good question."

But Homa didn't bother to volunteer an answer. Unless and until they dug into the backgrounds of both of these guys, they wouldn't have a clue about what might be going on.

"I'm sorry I tipped off Pavienko," Thompson said. "I should have done it a different way."

"Nothing to worry about," Magarian told her. "His explanation sounds plausible, but we'll get to the bottom of it." He looked over at Homa. "What do you think, John? Should we have a talk with their Captain?"

Homa nodded. "I know Odom from the Academy. We were classmates. I can tell him that Vlad Komarov's name came up in RHD's homicide investigation, and the Chief wants to know if he's ever been an informant for the Department."

"That should work."

Magarian turned to Thompson. "If he tells us that Komarov's not registered as an informant, or that Pavienko has not reported his contacts with him, then Pavienko is gonna have a serious problem." He leaned back in his chair and smiled. "Not reporting a relationship with a known criminal is a violation of department policy, and that will obligate us to open a full investigation of his activities, and maybe that will help you with your case."

"There may be a little problem with that," said Donahue. When everyone looked her way, she added, "So far as we know, this guy Komarov doesn't have a criminal record."

"But you said—?" Magarian started.

"Pavienko called him a pimp and said he might be selling drugs, but Shari ran him..."

She looked over at Thompson who nodded and finished the statement.

"...and he doesn't have a rap sheet, so technically, it looks as though Komarov is not a known felon." She looked from one to the other. "I guess that means that under a strict reading of the department's regs, Pavienko has no duty to report his contacts with Komarov."

"Did you go to law school?" Magarian asked.

Thompson gave him a puzzled look.

He smiled. "'Cause if I ever get in trouble with the department, I want you to represent me."

Donahue smiled. "So does that mean you can't open a case if he didn't report his contacts?"

"I didn't say that. If we suspect wrongdoing, we can look into it." He looked back over at Thompson. "But you think like a defense attorney. You may have missed your calling."

"I just hate the fact that I might have tipped him off because of my call."

She was really disgusted with herself, but there was even a bigger problem at the core of the situation. Vlad Komarov was the only lead they had in their murder investigation, and after Thompson's talk with Yuri, they still had nothing to implicate Komarov except an unproven allegation by their now dead victim that Komarov was trying to muscle in on his business.

In effect, they were back at square one.

"For what it's worth," Thompson began, "I don't think we're going to get anywhere with an investigation of Yuri Pavienko. It makes sense that the fewer people who know the identity of an informant, the better it is for the informant's security. That resonates with me, and if I were working in their division, I'd probably keep everything to myself, too."

Donahue frowned. "You mean you wouldn't tell me?"

It was said as a joke, but Thompson could sense there was a hint of disappointment in her tone.

"Not even if you promised to watch my kids for a month," she replied.

"But if I plied you with tequila...?"

Thompson shrugged and smiled. She looked over at Magarian.

"Liquid truth serum. I'd probably spill my guts."

"Make a note of that, John," Magarian joked, "in case we ever have to open a case on Detective Thompson."

Donahue laughed. "Then you better put that down in my file, too."

Magarian leaned back in his chair. "Just so you know, we're going to take a closer look at his partner, Clay Young. I've got a team that's working up a financial profile on him, and if we find out anything unusual, we'll be putting him under full time surveillance."

"Was there something that caused you to go forward with that?" Donahue asked.

"Routine," he replied. "If a guy is working in an undercover unit, from time to time we audit his financial situation."

On their way out of the IA location, Thompson turned to Donahue.

"Those guys really scare me," she said, referring to Homa and Magarian. "They get a logical explanation from Yuri, and they decide to look into his partner's financials."

"I wouldn't want them pouring through my life," Donahue agreed.

"This case just keeps getting more and more complicated." Thompson tightened the scarf around her neck to ward off the morning chill. "I feel like we're pulling at threads. Something's unraveling, but I can't see the bigger picture."

"It's the universe, Shari. Second law of thermodynamics."

"Oh brother, here we go." Thompson rolled her eyes. "So what the hell are you talking about this time?"

"*Entropy*. It means that all order in the universe must eventually decrease."

"*What?*"

"In a given system, without an increase in energy, all order in that system will decay."

"You're scaring me, Jen. I have no idea what you're talking about?"

Donahue stopped walking.

"College chemistry."

"I never took it."

"It just means that the order that existed in the universe yesterday is far less ordered today. Society is decaying, Shari, and we're picking at the edges where it's falling apart."

Thompson studied her partner for a long, few moments.

"I think I just figured out why you have so much trouble holding on to a man."

*****

11:30 am

Donahue and Thompson drove past the valet stand in front of the *Wilshire Tower* Building and parked in front but off to the side. When the valet approached, Donahue flashed her badge and told him that they were going to go inside for a while and that they planned to leave the car where it was. The valet didn't complain, but he stared at her as though he expected a tip.

"I'm not going to give the guy a tip for doing nothing," Donahue said to Thompson as they entered the building.

"It's just *entropy*, Jen. The social norms are decaying."

Thompson checked the resident's directory, while Donahue flashed her badge to the security man behind the desk. They didn't bother to tell him where they were headed, in case he was required to announce to the resident that they were on their way.

They rode up in the elevator and Thompson noted, "The lobby in this place has better furniture than my home."

Donahue smiled. They got off on the twenty-first floor, looking for 2106. It was a corner unit with a view of Los Angeles, both south and west.

Thompson rang the doorbell, and they waited a few moments until the door was answered by a young Hispanic woman.

Donahue frowned, then checked the number on the wall next to the door.

"Hi. We're looking for Mrs. Katz? Have we got the right location?"

The young woman nodded.

"I'm Detective Donahue." She flashed her ID card. "Can you get Mrs. Katz for us, please?"

The young woman closed the door over, leaving it slightly ajar. She spoke broken English to someone who quickly arrived at the door.

"I'm Katya Katz," said a very young woman when the door was opened wide.

"I'm Detective Donahue, and this is my partner Detective Thompson." Donahue held up her ID card in one hand while she gestured towards Shari with the other. "Can we come in and talk to you?"

Katya nodded and stepped aside.

The two detectives entered the foyer and Katya led them into a contemporary living room that was furnished with modern leather chairs, a leather couch, and a large glass coffee table. One wall was glass from floor to ceiling, and the view stretched all the way to the ocean which was probably a good ten miles away.

"You've got a beautiful home," Thompson said to break the ice.

"Thank you."

They all took seats.

"How can I help you?" Katya asked.

"First of all, we want to extend our sympathies for the loss of your husband," Donahue said. "It's a tragedy that shouldn't have happened."

Katya teared up, then nodded. She'd been caught by surprise and didn't know how to respond.

"We're investigating a murder that might somehow be connected to the death of your husband," Donahue said, "so we thought we'd stop by and see if there's any way that you can help us out?"

"Who got killed?" Katya asked in a trembling voice.

"Nika Kaminski," Thompson said. They watched for her reaction. "But you might only remember her as *Sasha* from the days when both of you were working the streets."

The color drained from Katya's face, and both detectives knew it came from genuine surprise that Nika was dead, as well as the revelation that they already knew all about Katya's past life.

Katya inhaled deeply, then sat up a little straighter and locked eyes with Thompson.

"I knew her. Is she really dead?"

"Shot to death in her apartment," Donahue said.

Katya's face crumbled. The initial surprise turned to tears.

They watched her for a few moments, and Donahue was thinking that her reaction seemed genuine and appropriate for the moment.

"We'd like to know about your experience with the *Trophy-Wife Agency,*" said Thompson. "Like how you met your husband; the courtship; stuff like that?"

Katya was looking down at her lap. "You want to bring this all up again?"

"Yes, Katya," said Donahue softly. "It's important. There may be something that's been overlooked."

Katya sighed. "I was recruited to join the agency by a man I met at a club. He said his name was Milan. He told me I could date wealthy men, and I might find a good husband, so I agreed."

"You were turning tricks at the time?" Thompson asked.

A brief flash of anger crossed Katya's face, but it quickly disappeared.

"I got into it when I answered an ad for a position as a Nanny. I was in Saint Petersburg with my family. The job was supposed to be in Denmark. They held me prisoner there and forced me to sell my body. They hooked me on drugs, and I ended up here." She folded her arms across her chest. "I didn't ask for that kind of life. I got forced to do it."

Thompson nodded contritely. "I didn't mean to sound judgmental, Katya. I've dealt with lots of women who were victims just like you. I only ask the question because I think your situation had something to do with why you were recruited by this particular matchmaking service."

"If you're suggesting that I was supposed to fuck the customers, you're wrong. I was told that the agency was completely legit and if I broke the rules, I'd be back out on the street."

Donahue looked at her skeptically.

"I know you don't believe me, but it's true. They cleaned me up, got me an apartment, then set me up with gentlemen who were looking for a wife. It was the first real break I ever got in my life, so I did what they told me, and it worked."

"They set you up with your husband?"

She nodded.

"How long were you dating him?"

"Almost six months. He was kind to me, bought me things. He wanted to have children, too."

"Did he know about your other life?" Thompson asked.

Katya shook her head. "Philip would never have understood. I couldn't tell him the truth."

She started to cry, and they waited her out.

"Did your husband have insurance?" Donahue asked. She already knew the answer, but she wanted to see if Katya was going to tell them the truth.

"I know you already know this. The other officer asked me about that, too." She glanced from one to the other. "I'm not stupid, detective. I know the insurance makes me look like a suspect, but I had nothing to do with my husband's death. I was in love with him, and he loved me."

"I checked our file for the date on the insurance policy," Donahue said. "It was issued four days after the two of you were married."

"Philip said it was a wedding present. He wanted to make sure that I was taken care of in case something ever happened."

She started crying again, and once again they let her cry it all out.

"It usually takes a long time to get an insurance company to issue a policy," Thompson said. "Your husband would have had to undergo a complete physical exam, and even then there are no guarantees that the policy would be issued."

"Philip did all their medical tests. He was quite a bit older than me, so he said they were going to really check him out." She momentarily looked down at her lap. "It was like a wedding gift to us from the agency. It was supposed to eliminate any worries about the future."

Thompson looked over at Donahue, then back at Katya.

"What do you mean it was a gift from the agency? Did they pay the premiums?"

Katya shook her head.

"Milan told us he had a friend who worked for an insurance company, and if we wanted, he was sure that the friend would give us their best rate as a sort of gift from the agency." She looked over at Thompson and smiled. "My husband told me that he shopped around and discovered that the premium level they offered to us was a very good deal, much better than any of the other companies, so we went ahead and got the policy through Milan's friend."

She seemed nervous talking about the insurance, and Donahue chalked it up to the fact that it was the one glaring red flag in an otherwise tragic story and because she'd been aware of the fact that it made her a possible suspect, her anxiety was completely understandable.

"How much were the premiums?" Donahue asked.

"I don't remember exactly. Philip handled all of that. But I think it was something like twelve thousand a year, compared to fifteen thousand that the other companies wanted."

"That's a twenty percent savings," Thompson said to Donahue. "Not bad."

"But also not illegal," Donahue said. "That kind of a discount is within the norm."

"And you know that...*how?*" Thompson asked.

"I once dated an insurance agent."

"Oh? I see."

Katya looked from one to the other.

"Phillip was an exceptional businessman. He recognized a good deal, so he took it."

Donahue leaned forward.

"Let's talk about Nika Kaminski for a moment, the girl you knew as Sasha. Did you ever run into her after you got off the streets?"

"Not in person, but she called me once."

"Oh? And what did you two talk about?"

"How our lives had changed. She said she was working at a really good job and that she'd heard about the agency and how I'd found my husband. She wanted to know if it was on the up and up, so I told her it was; that the men were really decent."

She sniffed a few times and used the back of her hand in place of a tissue.

"You okay?" Thompson asked.

Katya nodded, then continued.

"She asked me if it was just a front for sex and I told her it wasn't. The men were looking for wives, not just a lay."

"Did she say anything to you about the agency? You know, like did she warn you about the people involved or anything like that?"

"No." She looked from one to the other. "I told her we should get together and meet for lunch, but she never got back to me."

"How long ago did you speak with her?"

"I don't know. A couple of months. I can't be sure. Everything since Philip's death has been a blur. I just don't know what more I can tell you."

"Where did your marriage take place?" Thompson asked. She was fishing around now, but she wanted to end things on a high note in case they had to come back and question her again.

"We got married in the Russian Orthodox church." She briefly smiled at the memory, then the mask completely cracked. The smile disappeared and was quickly replaced with a look that revealed the depth of her pain.

"My life was so good. It completely turned around. I was off the streets and with a man who really cared about me." She folded her arms across her chest and rocked back and forth in the seat.

"And then this had to happen..."

Her voice trailed off, and she began to cry again.

"What exactly happened?" Donahue asked, sure that Katya was on the verge of telling them something important.

But Katya quickly recaptured her composure.

"Philip's murder. It destroyed everything."

*****

The two detectives got back in their car.

"What'd you think about her apartment?" Donahue asked.

"The girl's got great taste," Thompson said.

"I know, and that's what bothers me."

"Oh?"

"I don't think she had him killed. In fact, I have the feeling that her husband was worth more to her alive than dead. A very expensive condo, fancy furnishings, a tony address… her husband was a very good provider. If I'm right, the insurance money she got for his death was small change."

Thompson nodded. "I'll ask Mitzi to get ahold of her financials. That should tell us whether or not you're right."

Donahue nodded. "I think she was just about to tell us something there at the end, but then I got the feeling that she changed her mind."

"I felt the same way, but this case has got way too many loose ends. I think it's time we pressed the Captain to get us more help. We're drowning in leads, Jen, and if we don't get a handle on things soon, we're gonna get lost in the minutia."

"Whoa!" said Donahue. "*Minutia*?"

"College English," Thompson replied while she studied her nails.

Donahue smiled.

"Now who's being scary?"

CHAPTER 31

October 26 afternoon

Back at the PAB, Donahue, Thompson, and Gibson spent the better part of an hour convincing their Captain, Tom Elwood, that it was time to set up a task force to deal with the complexities of their investigation. Most task force operations required a name, so after about ten minutes of humorous discussion, where names such as *Pay-for-Play* and *Arm-Candy Caper* were jokingly considered, Elwood put an end to the jocularity by announcing that *Operation Gulag* would be the simple *nom-de-guerre* or pseudonym for the combined investigation of the cases.

Donahue and Thompson were charged with preparing charts for a visual presentation, while Elwood scheduled a meeting for three p.m. that afternoon to bring everyone else on board.

After a quick lunch at the *Fireside Pizzeria* across the street from the PAB, the two detectives put together several flow charts and moved them into the large conference room on the fifth floor in preparation for the task force meeting.

Present for that presentation were Donahue, Thompson, Gibson, Roberts, Bengtson, Jackson, and Elwood from RHD; Magarian and Homa from Internal Affairs; Grayson and Tucker from Hollywood Division; Joel Price from West Valley Homicide; and Larry London from WLA.

Elwood opened the meeting by advising everyone that they were there to plan a strategy for moving forward with the investigation. He turned things over to Donahue who kicked things off by demonstrating the overlapping connections between the cases.

She discussed what was known about the killings of Nika Kaminski and Eliska Rodinova, the similarities between the method used to kill them, their relationship as lovers, and Nika's prior victimization at the hands of the Russian mob.

She progressed by going over the known facts surrounding the bombing death of Milan Petrovich; the use of a Russian-made explosive to blow him up, and the alleged attempt by Vlad Komarov to pressure Petrovich into turning over an ownership share of the *Trophy-Wife* agency. She concluded by discussing the death of Philip Katz, the husband of a former Russian prostitute; their meeting through the dating agency; and Nika Kaminski's discussion with Katya Katz several months before Nika's own shocking murder.

"Is there any hard evidence to connect the Katz killing with the murder of the two women?" Price asked. "I bring that up because it certainly looks to me like the Katz killing is a robbery gone bad."

"The murder of Katz might not be related," Donahue said. "The working theory is robbery, but I've included it in our presentation because it has the smell of amazing coincidence, and as we all know from our years of experience with these cases, there's no such thing as coincidence."

There was a mild acknowledgment of that sentiment among the assembled group.

Larry London leaned back in his chair. "It should be mentioned at this point that Katya Katz, the widow in my case, collected on a million dollar life insurance policy that covered her husband's death."

"Thanks for bringing that up, Larry," Donahue said. She shifted her gaze back to the others in the group.

"Shari and I interviewed Katya this morning, and both of us are convinced that she's holding something back as it relates to the agency. But concerning the insurance, she told us that Milan Petrovich referred them to a contact of his at an insurance company. She said that the referral was in the nature of a wedding present from the agency, in as much as the premiums to be paid on the policy were at a rate usually given to their best customers. I looked it up, and the rate they were charged was for a Triple-A insurance risk."

"Is that legal?" asked Magarian.

"It is," Thompson replied. "Her husband apparently went through the full physical exam before the marriage, and the policy was secured through entirely lawful means. The rate her husband was charged was legitimate, and considering her husband's health and financial situation, the rate he was given was completely appropriate."

Tucker asked, "If the Russian mob is somehow involved, shouldn't we get OC Intelligence involved in our task force?"

Gibson looked over at Elwood and said, "Let me handle that, Tom." He then turned his attention to Tucker.

"For the time being, we're going to leave OC out of the loop. It turns out that one of their officers might be using our current chief suspect as a confidential informant."

There was a low mumble throughout the room, so Elwood added, "That hasn't been confirmed yet, so we'll reassess our decision not to invite them on board until after we pull together all the facts. But for now, that subject is completely confidential and not to be mentioned outside of this room."

There were no more questions, so Donahue said, "I've started a detailed list of assignments intended to move all of the separate investigations forward." She looked over at Tucker and Grayson. "We'd like you guys to take over the analysis of Nika Kaminski's phone records. Mitzi was going to do it, but we need her for something else. Are you okay with that?"

"What exactly are you looking for?" Tucker asked.

"Shari will give you a list of the known phone numbers of everyone who might be connected with the various cases. We'll be referring to that as our master list. We'd like you to look for overlap, and to research any of the numbers from her phone records that don't appear on the master list."

"No problem. We'll do it."

She turned to Joel Price and Larry London. "Can you guys do the same for the phone records in your cases?"

Both men nodded. Price would go over Eliska's records, while London would do the same for Phillip Katz, the deceased, and Katya Katz, his widowed wife.

In an acknowledgment to London's still lingering concerns, she added, "To make sure that we've covered all our bases, Mitzi will begin a financial analysis of the assets of Katya Katz. She's probably not involved, and we don't want to waste too much time on this, but it won't hurt to work it up. I'm convinced that the million dollars she got for her husband's death were small change, which would eliminate the insurance policy as a motive for her to have him killed."

London nodded to Donahue and smiled with satisfaction. He was naturally suspicious by nature, and the idea that anyone would profit from a loved one's murder never seemed to sit well with him. And while the likelihood of finding anything to implicate Katya was incredibly slim—she had, after all, passed the polygraph—he'd settle for an exoneration if it would enable him to refocus his efforts on the case.

Donahue caught his smile and smiled back.

"And lastly," she said," Shari and I will focus on Irina Konstantinov, Milan's Petrovich's business partner, and what's going on with her dating business."

"Who's going to focus on Vlad Komarov?" Grayson asked.

"We will," Thompson added. "We'll be assisted by Jackson and Bengtson, so I think we can handle that part of it for now."

The meeting broke up, but Magarian and Homa waited behind. When the others were gone, they huddled with Donahue and Thompson.

"I spoke with the Captain at OC Intelligence," Homa said. "Vlad Komarov has never been registered as an informant by any of his people."

Thompson asked, "Does that mean you're gonna be looking at Yuri, too?"

Magarian nodded. "At this point, we have no choice. I discussed it with my Captain, and she wants us to do a full workup on both Young and Pavienko. We should have something for you in a couple of days. Let's meet again tomorrow at ten a.m. You can fill us in on any updates, and we'll let you know if we've managed to uncover anything of importance."

The two IA investigators then left the building while Donahue and Thompson returned to the squad room where Elwood was waiting to speak to them. They gathered at Donahue's desk, and were quickly joined by Gibson, Bengtson, and Jackson.

"I've given this a lot of thought," Elwood began, "and I think we should send someone into the agency to pose as a potential client. I think it might turn out to be important sometime later that we get the pitch first hand. Let's see what they're really telling their clients."

"We'll need to set up a solid cover," Thompson said. "I'm sure they're going to check him out."

"I think I know someone who can help us with that," Donahue said. "I've got a friend at Wells Fargo Bank. He's a VP in their Private Banking Department, and if we can get him to vouch for our UC as being an employee in his department, it should hold up to their inquiries."

"We'll need to put together a dummy credit report," Thompson added. "Who'd you have in mind for the job, boss?"

Elwood looked around.

"I'm volunteering," Bengtson said.

"Not good," said Jackson. "You're married, Rich, and I doubt that going into a dating agency would sit well with your wife." He looked over at the Captain. "I guess it falls to me."

"Hold on," said Bengtson. He was not going to roll over that easily. He caught the Captain's glance.

"He's too old to appeal to such young and beautiful women. I think I'm probably more along the lines of what the agency is used to dealing with."

"Russian women prefer older men," Jackson countered. "Remember? They're looking for security, not immaturity."

"Oh, my," said Thompson. "Male catfight!"

Everyone laughed.

"Well, I have to concede that you've got me there," Bengtson said evenly. "You're clearly much older than I am, and if they're really looking for the grandfather type, then you've got the job hands down. But if these ladies are looking for a guy who can give them children, I'm the much better choice." He smiled at Jackson. "And between the two of us, I look more like a guy who's financially secure. A young up-and-coming banker...I can pull that off."

"Have you taken a close look at his suits?" Jackson said to the group at large. "Shabby chic doesn't exactly radiate prosperity."

"At least my suits are fairly new," Bengtson countered. "Those wide lapels and shoulder pads that you're still sporting say *'stuck in the eighties'* to anyone who knows anything at all about fashion."

When the rest of the group stopped laughing, Elwood tapped Gibson on the shoulder.

"Get it worked out and let me know." He then headed back to his office.

As the group broke up, Bengtson took off his suit jacket, studied it, then said to himself, "My suits aren't shabby."

CHAPTER 32

October 27, 1:20 a.m.

Yuri Pavienko walked into the nightclub called *Blok* in Hollywood and began the slow process of searching the main room for Vlad Komarov. The *Blok* was a mainstay on the nightclub circuit, a location that attracted a large Russian following as well as the young and beautiful from the regular Hollywood scene.

The place was decorated like a vintage bordello with a party atmosphere that boasted well-known celebrity DJs (like Eli M and Igor 32), flashing colored lights, and a crew of female serving girls whose stunning beauty was their ticket to very big tips.

The dance floor was packed as usual with revelers, and the drinks flowed freely among the young women who graced the dance floor with sexual gyrations that matched the incessant throbbing of the amplified base that pounded in sync with their movements.

He made his way around the outside of the dance floor, knowing full well that Komarov was not the dancing kind. He finally spotted him seated in a booth, in the company of three beautiful girls. They were drinking champagne and vodka shooters, and the girls appeared to hang on his every word.

Yuri slowly walked over to the booth and came to a stop just short of it. He did not speak, waiting instead for Komarov to acknowledge his presence.

Komarov looked up, caught his glance, and gave him a welcoming smile, but Yuri didn't smile back, so Komarov must have sensed that something was wrong. He leaned over to speak to the girls sitting with him, and after telling them to give him five minutes alone, they scooted out of the booth, ignoring Yuri, and made their way out to the dance floor.

Komarov nodded to Yuri who quickly slipped into the booth. The lighting in the club tended to be darker off the dance floor, so Yuri was fairly sure that the meeting would go unnoticed if there were other mob members in the club.

Komarov frowned. "You look angry, my friend."

"It couldn't wait," Yuri said. He picked up a glass half full of alcohol that one of the girls had been drinking. He held it up in one hand while resting his elbow on the table. He would use it as a shield to conceal his face during their conversation. The fewer people who saw him here at the table, the better.

He leaned in and lowered his voice.

"The detectives who popped you the other day got a look at your cell phone log."

"So...?"

Yuri frowned. "They discovered that you called my cell phone three times on the night the bomb went off over at *Siberia.*"

Yuri thought that over for a few moments. "So what's the problem?"

"They want to know about our relationship."

"Relationship?" He stared at Yuri with hooded lids. "We don't have one."

Yuri pressed on, ignoring Komarov's denial.

"I told them that you've agreed to supply me with information and that you're going to become a confidential informant."

Komarov slammed down his drink glass, spilling a significant portion of what was left of the champagne.

"I'm not your informant, Yuri," he said evenly through clenched teeth.

"I told them that you haven't given me anything yet, so that's why I never logged you in as a contact."

Komarov shook his head. "You listen to me. That's your problem, not mine. We have an understanding." He pointed with his finger. "No one is to think that I'm an informant."

"I have no choice with this, Vlad. I have to report the fact that we've had contact. But the only one who'll get that information is my Captain, and trust me, he'll never say a word to anyone."

"What about the detectives who took me in? You planning on telling them?"

"I already told you, I told them you're not an informant yet, that I've been trying to work you, but so far you've given me nothing."

Komarov looked for any signs of deception, but Yuri held his stare and did not flinch. He suddenly broke out with a smile.

"So we have no choice about this?"

"None at all. You forced the issue when you neglected to erase your call register."

Komarov's expression suddenly changed, and Yuri could see that his eyes had grown dark.

"Make sure that I'm never listed as an informant," he said, "or I will hold you personally responsible."

Yuri held his glare, then lowered his voice.

"Are you threatening me?"

Komarov chose not to respond. Instead, he signaled to the girls who were out on the dance floor and waved them back over to the table.

Yuri put down the glass he'd been holding and slowly slid out of the booth.

Komarov watched him walk away, then poured himself another vodka which he drank in one gulp.

Outside, Yuri walked across the street to a parking lot and climbed into his undercover vehicle. Clay Young was seated in the passenger seat, smoking a cigarette, while he watched the crowd across the street who were lined up and waiting to get inside.

"Was he in there?" Clay asked.

Yuri nodded. He started up the engine.

"So what did he have to say?"

Yuri looked over his shoulder, then pulled out into traffic. "He doesn't like it, but he understands."

Clay shook his head. "Be careful with that guy, Yuri. He's a dangerous motherfucker, and he can't be trusted."

Yuri smiled.

"I'll keep that in mind."

*****

CHAPTER 33

October 27, 10:00 a.m.

At 8:00 a.m. the following day, Shari Thompson was already seated in her cubicle in the squad room, drinking coffee and surfing the internet. She'd come in earlier than usual to see if she could find an evening bag she liked to go with a new black cocktail dress that she'd purchased for an upcoming retirement party.

Her phone rang, and she grabbed it without looking at the screen to see who it was. To her surprise, it was Yuri Pavienko.

"I didn't think you came in this early," he said. "I was just going off duty so I thought I'd try and get back to you about those phone calls you asked me about."

Surprised, Thompson tried to recall the details of her conversation with him. He'd already admitted taking the calls from Komarov, so what could he possibly have to add?

"I'm all ears," she said.

"I guess you or someone spoke to my Captain because he came by and asked everyone if they were using Komarov as an informant. I told him I wasn't, for the benefit of the other guys in the unit, but I met with him privately right after that and explained to him that I was working on Komarov to get him to become a CI."

"And…?" she said after a few moments of uncomfortable silence.

He chuckled. "I got my ass chewed out for not reporting the contact, but I explained to him that Komarov said he'd never give me any info if anyone else knew that he was informing."

"How'd your Captain handle that?" she said, leaning back in her swivel chair.

"He said he'd consider my explanation, but I don't think I'm out of the woods."

Thompson sympathized with his position. On more than one occasion during her LAPD career, she'd said or done things that could have gotten her in potential trouble with her superiors. The fact that she'd avoided problems with the department was just a question of luck, and while she didn't condone his failure to report his dealings with a possible mob figure, she felt there was some merit to the reason why he hadn't.

"I don't know what to tell you, Yuri. That contact rule is there for your protection."

"I know," he said, sounding contrite. "The Captain made that perfectly clear."

"How about the cell phone mix-up?" she asked.

"I told him about it. He said it's no big deal. They're amending the assignment log so it will reflect that the phone was mine since it was first handed out."

Thompson decided that Yuri was smart the way he was handling the situation. By being completely up front, he was avoiding any inference of an attempted coverup. That would go a long way with the administration, and while he was still likely to face a short suspension, he could probably hold on to his job.

But there was something she'd thought about the night before, something that came to her while she was lying in bed. She racked her brain to remember what it was, thinking it had something to do with his story about the calls.

She suddenly remembered.

"Hey, Yuri. I just had a thought. You know that girl that Komarov asked you to help out? The one he wanted you to get into rehab?"

"Yeah. What about her?"

"Well, I was thinking I'd like to talk to her. We're still looking at him for the bombing, and getting close to people in his inner circle is probably not going to happen. I figure maybe I can talk to her, find out more about his associates, and if I get lucky, maybe we can find someone we can turn to help us with our case."

"I've got a problem with that," he said. "If you guys start talking to her, it'll get back to him, and if that happens, he'll know right away that I've been talking to you guys and that will end our chances of recruiting him."

"But he's a possible target, Yuri. He might be involved in a murder."

"I know you think that, but I'm not convinced you're right." He was silent for a moment. "Look. We need him to go up the chain. If he's really got connections within the SB as he claims, he can help us bring down the informal leadership. He could be a goldmine, Shari. A chance like this doesn't come around very often."

"I'm sure it doesn't, but we can't just ignore the fact that he might be responsible for the *Siberia* club bombing."

"I know that." His mind was racing. "Look. What if I talk to her? She's probably not ready to say anything yet. The girl had a pretty bad habit. But I can probably speak to her without his being any the wiser, and if I come up with anything useful, I'll be happy to pass it on."

Thompson gave it some thought. It was not ideal. She knew the direction she liked to go with her interviews, and while she assumed the girl would not know anything at all about the bombing, she might know other girls or people he dealt with who might know something that could be exploited.

On the other hand, Yuri was probably right. If she spoke to the girl, it would likely get back to Komarov, and she had no doubt that he'd quickly figure out that she'd been acting on information that only someone like Yuri could have told her. And if it turned out that he wasn't involved in the bombing, it could destroy any chance that OC Intel might have to get him on board.

"Okay, Yuri. I can live with that. I need you to ask the obvious questions about the bombing and about his relationship with Milan Petrovich. She might not know much, but if she does, it could be great."

"I'll take care of it," he told her.

"Wait," she said. "I also need you to talk to her about his associates. That's really important, Yuri. We need to find out who he trusts and who we might later be able to exploit."

"I'm with you, detective. That's stuff we should be gathering as part of our mission. I've got no problem with doing that for you. However, if I learn info that doesn't pertain to your case, I'll need to keep it confidential as part of our mandate to gather intelligence."

That was not something she felt comfortable with, for it meant that Yuri would be the arbitrator of what was important to her case and what wasn't. It was certainly less than ideal, but what choice did she have? She could run the situation up her chain of command, but in the end, too many people would know about Komarov's possible recruitment, and that could kill everything that all of them wanted to accomplish.

She sighed. "I guess that sounds okay. Let me know when you're ready to talk to her."

"And you'll keep this just between us?" he asked.

"Yeah. I will."

"I'm just glad we got that straightened out." There was a moment of awkward silence before Yuri added, "Say, listen. I don't suppose I could persuade you to meet me for a drink sometime?"

She slowly shook her head. The guy was a player; a self-centered narcissist who was exactly what she was attracted to and precisely the kind she should avoid. She thought about how good looking he was; how he seemed to be genuinely interested in her; and how her having three young boys at home had not deterred his interest.

She supposed that a drink wouldn't hurt.

"I guess I could," she said.

"Great! How about this evening?"

"Do you have a place in mind?"

He mentioned a place, she countered with one that was closer to her home, and he quickly agreed.

"About eight?" he asked.

"Eight's a little early," she said. "Bedtimes and all for my kids. Can we make it closer to nine?"

"Sure. That'll work."

*****

At roughly ten-thirty a.m., Magarian and Homa showed up for their briefing with Donahue and Thompson. They went to the coffee room first, and after Donahue had dropped a dollar in the can that held the coffee club fund, she poured four fresh cups from their coffee maker, then led everyone down the hall to the privacy of an interview room.

Homa began by telling them that Captain Odom had called him back to say that one of his guys had reported that he'd had contact with Komarov, but that it hadn't yet amounted to the status of informant. He said he thought the guy might have been in violation of the contact reporting rules, and that he'd set him straight, but that as far as his unit was concerned, Komarov was not a confidential informant.

Thompson did not volunteer what she knew. She decided she'd fill Donahue in after the meeting, but Yuri had asked that parts of their conversation remain confidential, and she was gonna have to give that some serious thought.

Magarian said, "Let's talk for a few moments about Officer Clay Young." He turned to Homa.

"You wanna fill them in, John?"

Homa nodded and leaned forward in his chair.

"Young was born in Norman, Oklahoma, where he lived until he was eighteen. Both parents are still alive. His mom is a homemaker, a former saleswoman, and his father works for an auto parts wholesaler. He's got two brothers, both of whom still live in the Midwest.

"He went to Oklahoma State University in Stillwater, Oklahoma, where he studied Nutritional Science and played football for the OSU Cowboys."

"What position?" Donahue asked.

"A wide receiver." Homa looked down at his notes. "Blew out a knee during his junior year and it ended his career."

He flipped to the next page in his notebook.

"He came out to LA, took a job at a health club as a nutritionist, applied to LAPD, met his wife—Denise Chapman, a secretary at a Plastic Surgery Center in Torrance—tied the knot eight years ago, and bought a house in Simi Valley when the first of their four children arrived."

"Sounds pretty normal," Donahue said.

Homa locked eyes with Donahue. "Here's the interesting part. He worked for three years in patrol out in North Hollywood, then transferred into OC Intelligence. He has to file a copy of his tax returns to work in the Intelligence Division, so I got my hands on 'em, and it looks as though he's living well beyond his means."

Donahue shared a quick glance with Thompson, then shifted her gaze back to Homa.

"Is he in debt?" she asked.

Serious debt was a reason to keep an officer out of a specialized division. The reason behind it was sound. Officers who find themselves in debt are susceptible to bribery, so they are moved out of sensitive positions to minimize the risk of their being compromised.

"Just the opposite," Homa said, "and this is what has us concerned."

He looked over at Magarian who gave him a barely perceptible affirmative nod.

"We checked his credit reports, his DMV registrations, and reviewed his spending habits. In the last two years, Officer Young has spent almost a quarter of a million dollars on such luxuries as a *Mainship 30* for $98,500., a brand new Chevy Silverado, as well as an assortment of jet skies, golf clubs, and expensive bicycles for his entire family." He looked up from his list. "In short, we have no idea where he got the money to pay for all these items."

"Do I take it that the *Mainship 30* is a boat of some kind?" Donahue asked.

"A thirty-foot power boat; good for ocean fishing," Magarian replied.

"And you said his wife doesn't work?"

"That's right, she doesn't."

"That's a lot of money to account for," said Donahue, and then, in a mock Cuban accent, she added, "*Lucy's got some 'splainin' to do.*"

"Pardon?" said Homa.

"Lucille Ball. Ricky Ricardo. Didn't you ever watch *I Love Lucy?*"

When Homa frowned, she sighed.

"Never mind. It was just a line from a TV show." She looked over at Thompson. "That puts Officer Young back on our radar."

Thompson nodded.

"We've brought this to you just to let you know where our investigation will be directed," Magarian said, "but this is strictly confidential for the moment. As I said, we have no idea where the money came from, and until we do, the guy has the presumption of innocence until we find evidence to the contrary."

"What about Pavienko?" Donahue asked. "What's his background like?"

Magarian opened his notebook.

"Yuri Pavienko was born in Zvenigorod, a little town near Moscow in Russia. Educated in public schools; he worked after high school in construction. He emigrated to Stockholm, Sweden, at the age of twenty-two. He lived there with an uncle, the brother of his mother, and worked in the uncle's sundry store for three years while he obtained his Swedish citizenship. After he got it, he applied for a visa to travel to the USA where he signed up for the Marines—"

"Hold on," Donahue said, interrupting the recitation. "How'd he get citizenship so quickly in Sweden?"

Magarian looked up from his notes.

"Apparently, he was there for a year when he married a Swedish citizen, a woman named Anika Engstrom, and under Swedish law, if you are married to a Swedish citizen for at least two years, and if you've resided in the country for three years, you can become a citizen."

"So he's married?" said Thompson. The disappointment in her voice was obvious to Donahue whose first thought to herself was... *Oh, no.*

"Divorced," Magarian responded. "When he arrived in the USA, she filed for and received a divorce. No children involved."

"You said he joined the Marines?" Donahue asked.

"That's correct. He did two tours in Iraq, then applied for USA citizenship, and because of his service, he got it right away. After that, he came to LA, settled in the North Hollywood area with other Russian expats, and applied for a job with LAPD. Because of his language skills, both Russian and Swedish, and because of his distinguished service in Iraq, he was sent through the Academy and sworn in six years ago."

"Tell me about his service in Iraq?" Thompson asked. "You said it was distinguished?"

"Marine sniper," said Magarian. "Twenty-three confirmed kills. A Silver Star and a Purple Heart. The Silver Star was for gallantry displayed during combat. I read his citation. He was on overwatch when a group of Marines was attacked by an overwhelmingly superior force of insurgent fighters in an operation to clear the city of Ramada. He killed sixteen of the enemy during a battle that lasted six hours. A grenade was tossed into his overwatch position, and he caught a single piece of shrapnel in his right calf; hence the Purple Heart. He managed to kill the grenade thrower, then returned to his overwatch position and killed another two enemy combatants."

Thompson was speechless, but Donahue said, "The guy's a legitimate hero. No wonder we took him on."

"We haven't had a chance to review his finances or his current living situation, but we hope to get started on that later this evening."

"Well, it appears as though you're going to have your hands full with his partner, but it sounds like Yuri's okay."

"We still have to check him out," said Magarian. "If his partner's a rotten apple, we need to determine if he's been infected."

"You guys are so cynical," said Donahue evenly.

"You have to be to work in IA," Magarian replied.

"I suppose. So while you're checking up on Clay Young, we're going to reinterview everyone connected to Nika Kaminski and Eliska Rodinova. We didn't know anything about the dating service when we did the first interviews, so we're hoping that a follow-up will give us something new."

The conversation then drifted off to more mundane topics while they finished their coffees, and after that, the meeting broke up.

When Magarian and Homa were gone, Donahue and Thompson located Gibson who was talking to Jackson and Bengtson.

Gibson said, "I was just telling these two that your source over at the Wells Fargo Private Banking Department has agreed to provide a plausible cover for Jackson to go in as a potential client at the *Trophy-Wife Agency*."

"*Yes!*" said Jackson. He fist pumped the air. In his mind, he'd all but conceded the assignment to his partner, the younger Bengtson, so it came as a total surprise.

Gibson turned to a now frowning Bengtson.

"The Captain felt that Jackson was more suitable for the role of *a horny old man looking for a little arm candy*." He then shifted his gaze over to Jackson. "He said you had a more *desperate* look."

"*Horny and desperate.*" Bengtson was now smiling broadly. "The Captain is certainly perceptive."

Jackson looked at Bengtson over the top of his reading glasses. "Is that the green monster of jealousy I hear popping up?" He shifted his glance back to Gibson. "And this from a health food fanatic who supplements his diet with little blue pills."

"Oh my," said Donahue, feigning shocked surprise, and to Bengtson, she asked, "You really use that stuff?"

"Hell no," he replied, just a little too quickly. He looked over at Jackson who was grinning like the Cheshire Cat.

"Let me give you a little advice," he said to Jackson. "If you don't want to come off as a man of your real chronological age, don't start talking about fiber in your diet, constipation, bunions, or the pain you endured while recovering from your hernia surgery."

His glance shifted to the rest of the group who were now all smiles. Then added, "Five bucks says he doesn't last ten minutes into their interview without mentioning at least one of those topics."

"And on that note..." said Donahue with a laugh. She turned her attention back to Jackson.

"I'd suggest you call up their website and pour through what's on there. When you go into their office, they're gonna ask you questions about how you heard about them and what type of woman you're interested in?"

"That's easy," said Jackson, still smarting from Bengtson's good natured kidding. "I like my women to be...?"

He was suddenly at a loss for words.

"A senior moment?" said Bengtson flatly. "I rest my case."

"Not at all," Jackson replied. "I just realize that I like *all* women. I've never been able to narrow things down to a certain type."

"Just check out their website," Donahue repeated. "Focus on one or two, and use their attributes as a blueprint for what you're supposedly looking for." She gave Jackson a smile. "It's not for real, Rick. You're just playing a role."

Bengtson, who'd moved over to his desk, had already called up the website. He started going through the photo gallery that showed many of the women who the site proudly said were ready to meet the male clients.

"Here," he said to Jackson. "I've got it up. Check this out."

Jackson made his way over to Bengtson's cubical and Thompson was close behind.

Bengtson flipped from picture to picture. Each successive woman's photo seeming to look prettier and more exotic than the one that preceded it.

Bengtson and Jackson were discussing the obvious attributes of the young women connected to the agency, with Bengtson making suggestions as to which ones Jackson should show interest in when Thompson told the two of them to quiet down. She had Bengtson flip back several photos, then told him to freeze the screen.

"Hey, Jen," she yelled out to Donahue. "Come over here and look at this."

Donahue walked over and examined the screen.

"Know her?" asked Thompson, pointing to the photo on the screen.

Donahue studied the photo. It was a stunning brunette, mid-twenties, who looked like the all-American girl next door.

"Can't say as I do," Donahue replied. "Should I?"

"I'm pretty sure I ran across her once when I was working in sex crimes. Her street name was Lana."

"She's gorgeous," Bengtson said.

"Yeah, she looks great in that photo, but you wouldn't think she was all that hot if you saw her when she was working the streets."

"Photoshop," said Donahue. "That's what they do to those girls in the fashion magazines who make us all feel insecure about ourselves."

"I couldn't agree more," Thompson said, "but what interests me now is the fact that she's the second Russian hooker in the agency's hit parade."

She looked over at Donahue and cocked her head to the side. "There's no way these guys are legit. This has got to be a money-for-sex operation."

Donahue walked over to Jackson who'd taken a chair next to Bengtson. She stood behind him, put her hands on his shoulders, and massaged them gently.

"That's why we're sending this horny, old, desperate guy in. To get to the bottom of what's going on."

Jackson looked back over his shoulder and smiled.

"I just may have to go out with a few of these women to make sure I get the full story."

Donahue laughed. "In your dreams, old man. In your horny, desperate dreams."

*****

"Can I speak to Director Flynn, please?"

Donahue held the phone to her ear and waited while the secretary spoke to her boss.

Donald Flynn was an Assistant Director of the United States Secret Service

Flynn first met Gibson when he was assigned to the Los Angeles Field Office as a criminal investigator, and after he promoted and returned to Washington, Gibson had stayed in contact, and the two of them had remained good friends. Gibson had called Flynn on several occasions for the kind of information that wasn't easily forthcoming from certain other Federal Agencies—the one's who considered themselves a cut above the rest of law enforcement—and Flynn had encouraged him to call anytime. From that moment on, it became a two-way street, with Gibson checking things out for Flynn or for other guys from the Secret Service who needed a contact within LAPD.

Gibson, in turn, introduced Donahue to Flynn, and at Flynn's suggestion, she had developed a similar type of relationship with him, so much so, that she had no reservations about calling him on this particular case.

Flynn, who was seated at his desk in a window office that overlooked the Potomac River in Washington, D.C., came on the line a few moment later.

"Jennifer Donahue! How's it going?"

"Just fine, Don."

They spent a couple of minutes catching up on Flynn's family life and Donahue's lack of a social one.

"So, how can I help you out?" he finally asked.

"Well, we've got a bombing case that we're working. It involves the Russian mob, and a particular name has surfaced. Vladimir Komarov, a male Russian, age thirty-nine. We just picked him up for questioning, but we've got nothing on record for this guy. He's believed to be connected to a group that calls itself *Solntsevskaya Bratva.* This guy must have a record somewhere, Don, so we were wondering if you can steer us to a contact in Russia or maybe with the FSB…someone that we can talk to about this guy?"

"I can try, but since Putin got his panties in a knot, things have been a little strained with the FSB. Have you got a description and a date of birth?" Donahue read off the info they'd developed on the booking sheet for Komarov's recent arrest which matched his DMV printout.

Flynn said, "I think the FBI has a liaison agent assigned in Moscow to work exclusively with the Russian FSB. How quickly do you need the info?"

"It's not a super rush, but the sooner, the better."

Flynn laughed. "I don't know why I even bother to ask that question. Okay, Jen, I'll see what I can do."

*****

CHAPTER 34

October 27, 3:00 p.m.

Rick Jackson rode the elevator up to the penthouse floor of the building in Brentwood that was the home of *Trophy-Wife Match*. He was wearing a pale gray suit, black lace shoes, a white shirt, and a light pink necktie. The necktie was one of his favorites, one that he'd owned since the early 1990s. He often explained to anyone who asked that the color went well with the complexion of his skin.

His partner, Rich Bengtson, was parked at a spot on a side street just around the corner. He was running the receiver on Jackson's body wire, and could hear everything going on in the office through the microphone that was taped to Jackson's chest. The receiver was a pocket-sized, portable digital unit, and the entire conversation was being recorded.

Still betting that Jackson would somehow blow it, he left the car and scoped out the building. He knew exactly where to go to get to the office and how to get there quickly should Jackson need backup for an unforeseen event.

Jackson had spoken with Donahue's contact at Wells Fargo, an executive Vice-President named Robert Meeks. Meeks was an affable fellow with a gregarious personality who loved to talk. They had discussed a few things that Jackson could say about his line of work as a banker, and they'd settled on a name that he could use in place of his own. For this operation, the name they had decided on was James Winston.

Meeks had his secretary call and make the appointment with the agency. Jackson had suggested that they do it this way to give credibility to his portrayal as a banker, and to give the agency a number they could use to make a callback in case they intended to verify his employment.

Jackson approached the door and pushed the buzzer. A pleasant female voice quickly answered, and when he identified himself as James Winston, the electronic buzzer clicked on the door and he immediately went inside.

"Hello, Mr. Winston," the young woman said. She extended her hand and gave him a smile. "Can I get you a coffee or something to drink?"

"Coffee would be nice," he said.

She led him over to a couch in the VIP waiting room, but before he could sit down, Irina Konstantinov stepped out of her office and walked over to meet him.

She led him into her office and closed the door behind them. When he was seated in front of her desk, he handed her a Wells Fargo business card that he'd printed up at *Kinko's* on his way over. She accepted the card, looked it over, then started things off with a series of innocuous questions designed to discover more about him and his lifestyle.

They were briefly interrupted when Irina's assistant came in with Jackson's black coffee. It was served in a china cup with a saucer, and since he was only used to styrofoam cups, he had an awkward time trying to hold it in his lap.

But in spite of that minor tell, he had his cover story down. He told Irina that he was a Senior Vice President in the Wealth Management Department of the bank. He'd been married once when he was much younger, but for unstated reasons, it hadn't worked out. He'd been dating for the last ten years, but he no longer felt that he had the time to get out and meet the kind of women he was interested in. He was looking for someone to share his life, and he thought that her agency could possibly help.

Irina smiled broadly. To her, he sounded perfect. She told him she was sure that they could fix him up with someone for a long term relationship, and she wanted to know if he had any questions?

Jackson was relishing his role as a wealthy bachelor, so he started off with questions about the girls.

"I had a chance to look over the photos on your website, and I must admit, the women are absolutely beautiful."

Irina smiled. "We search extensively for the right young women. I'm glad you like them."

"But one thing troubles me," he said. "They seem awfully young." He shook his head. "I can't imagine that these beautiful young women would be interested in an older guy like me."

"Don't worry about that, Mr. Winston. European women prefer older men. They see them as stable, reliable and financially secure; virtues that to them are extremely attractive." She leaned forward in her chair and said, "Unlike most young American women who seem to be interested only in young, attractive men, European women—particularly those from Russia and the Eastern Bloc nations—see older gentlemen with your attributes as sexy." She smiled. "I can tell just by looking at you that you'll have no difficulty attracting the woman of your choice."

"That's great to hear," Jackson said with a smile. "Now, your website didn't mention price, so how much is this gonna cost me?"

Irina leaned back in her chair. This was always the most difficult moment. Two out of every three men who went through the interview process walked out at this point after hearing the cost involved. Irina suspected that Jackson might be one of those, but that was the nature of the business, and she might as well get it over with, rather than wasting any more of her time.

"We have several different levels of involvement, Mr. Winston. Our entry price is ten thousand dollars. For that, we will introduce you to a new girl every month. To make sure that the dates are to your liking, we will have you answer a questionnaire after each date to enable us to refine our search for the perfect woman. We will also meet with you after your first two dates to discuss the young women you've met, to enable us to get a firsthand impression of what we might not be doing right."

"You mentioned other levels of involvement," Jackson asked. He tried to act as though the money would not be an issue.

Irina smiled. "The first plan I mentioned was the price for a dozen different introductions. We also have a program that enables you to have more than one new introduction each month. In fact, you could go out with a different woman every night if you wished. You would also fill out a questionnaire after each introduction... again, to enable us to better refine our search." She leaned up again, and lowered her voice. "The idea is to find you a partner for marriage, Mr. Winston. We are absolutely sincere when we say your happiness is our primary goal."

"How much?" he asked.

"Twenty-five thousand."

"Would that plan be good until I actually find a woman to marry?"

Irina smiled. His question had just convinced her that the cost of this particular option was clearly beyond his reach.

"It's for one year, Mr. Winston, but if you meet someone early in the process, we can put the others on hold, and if we do that, you'll still be guaranteed a full twelve months of introductions if things don't work out."

When he didn't immediately balk, she said, "Would you like to look over our current photographs of the women you're going to be choosing from?"

"Absolutely," he said. "That's why I'm here."

"Good."

She got to her feet, walked over to a sideboard and picked up a photo album which she placed in his hands.

"I'll let you look this over for a few moments while I take care of something out in the front office," she said.

Irina left him sitting in her office pouring through the book while she went out to the front reception desk.

"Did you check him out?" she said to the receptionist.

The young woman nodded. "I spoke with an Executive Vice-President named Robert Meeks. He confirmed that Mr. Winston has been employed there for more than ten years and that he's a very successful money manager."

Irina nodded. A pleasant surprise.

Martun Hagopian came out of an office that had once been used by Milan Petrovich, but which he was now busy redecorating for his personal use. Apparently, he'd gotten the message from Vlad Komarov, because his hair was neatly cut, his face cleanly shaven, and his dark blue suit was a beautifully tailored, three button, worsted wool from the house of *Giorgio Armani.*

"Did you close the deal with him?" he asked.

Irina shivered. His dark eyes were cold and lifeless. She hated being anywhere close to this man.

"Not yet. He's looking over the photographs."

"Perhaps I should have a talk with him," he told her in a tone of voice that brooked no dissent. "You stay here and I'll see what I can do."

Before she could stop him, he headed off to her office with one of the other photo albums under his arm.

He walked right in and introduced himself. His English was less articulate than Irina's, and he appeared to have trouble with the letter W sound. He pronounced the name Winston as *Vinston*.

"Mr. Vinston. My name is Martun Hagopian."

He handed Jackson a business card which Jackson held on the edges while he slowly looked it over.

"Nice to meet you, Mr. Hagopian."

"I see you are looking over the young women." Hagopian nodded towards the album that was open in Jackson's lap. "Did you find someone that you're interested in?"

"They're all so attractive, I just can't make up my mind."

"Well, perhaps I can help you? What exactly are you looking for?"

Jackson appeared to give it some thought.

"Since they're all so good looking, I suppose I want someone with a good personality; and a sense of humor would be nice—"

"Yes, yes. Of course, but let's start with the basics, man to man. Do you prefer big breasts?"

Jackson was momentarily taken aback. What had been a professional pitch up to this point had suddenly gotten very interesting.

"I sure do," Jackson said, holding Hagopian's stare.

"And you like them young?"

"Well, not too young," Jackson quipped.

Hagopian smiled.

"Shall we say…eighteen to twenty-two?"

"I guess so."

Jackson felt he had no choice but to play along and see where Hagopian was going to guide him.

"I thought so. You look like a man who knows what he wants."

Hagopian reached down and took the album from Jackson's hands and presented him with the one that he'd carried into their meeting.

"These are the women we usually make available to our special clients," he said. "Perhaps one of these would be more to your liking?"

Jackson took the book and opened it up. He had no idea what to expect, but quickly realized that these were the youngest of the ones he'd seen and that some of them, but not all, were in the book he'd already looked at."

The book was smaller than the other one he'd been reviewing, and if he had to guess, he decided that there were more than twenty different girls available for the *special clients.*

He looked up after flipping through a couple of pages. "I saw some of these same girls in the other book," he said. "What's the difference?"

"These young ladies are special. As I said, they are usually reserved for our premium clients. They are women who really like to please the men they are courting." He gave Jackson a wink. "You can choose women from any of the books, but these women tend to get the most favorable ratings among our discerning clientele."

Hagopian smiled, and Jackson was struck by how crooked Hagopian's teeth appeared.

Hagopian moved over to stand behind him.

"Are there any that you'd like to start dating?" he asked.

Jackson said, "Let me look a little longer."

Hagopian smiled.

Jackson flipped through the pages of the *special* book, then stopped when he spotted a particular photo. He looked up over his shoulder. Hagopian was standing too close, and it made him very uncomfortable.

"I like this young woman," he said. "What can you tell me about her?"

The photograph that Jackson was referring to was the one he'd seen on the internet, the one that Thompson had told him was of Katya Katz, the girl who's husband had died in the WLA robbery.

"An excellent choice. I've been told that she's a young widow. Very personable and kind." He leaned over and whispered. "Are you looking for a woman who'd like to have a family?"

Jackson nodded. "I think kids would be great."

"Then she's perfect for you. She'd love to have children right away."

"You said she's a widow?" Jackson asked.

Hagopian nodded. "Tragic situation. Her husband died about a year ago in an unfortunate accident. But she wants to get married again, and I can assure you, she is well worth your time and attention."

He said it in such a way that Jackson felt the hair go up on his neck. This guy was clearly pimping out these very young woman, and this whole operation was starting to feel like a scam.

He'd seen enough, and he was tired of Hagopian breathing down his neck, so he got to his feet, turned to Hagopian, and handed the album back.

"I've stayed longer than I intended, Mr. Hagopian. I need to get back to the bank. Thanks for your time and all the information. I'll give it some serious thought tonight, and I'll try to get back to you later this week."

"Before you go," Hagopian said, "I suspect you were quoted a price of twenty-five thousand for our VIP clients. Since I feel you're a man who knows what he wants, I'm willing to negotiate a better price with you, one that I think you'll find more than generous."

He came around from behind the chair and stood directly in front of Jackson.

"If you pay the full amount in cash by the end of this week, I'll let you have our premium, unlimited package for just fifteen thousand dollars." He smiled a toothy grin. "And I'm quite sure that I can arrange for your first date to be with the lovely Katya, the young widow you took such a liking to."

Jackson smiled. "That's a very generous offer. I'll certainly give it some serious thought. All cash, correct?"

"That's right."

Hagopian studied him carefully as if considering whether or not to push him harder.

"Allow me to let you in on a little secret, Mr. Winston. Russian women— particularly the younger ones—have few inhibitions. They love men, particularly older, successful men such as yourself. When you sign up with us, I can guarantee that none of our young women will ever disappoint you."

"I'm sure they won't," Jackson said.

*****

Jackson arrived at the car, opened the passenger door, and slipped into the

215

front seat.

Bengtson held out a five dollar bill.

"What's that for?" Jackson asked.

"The bet. You didn't bring up any of that old man ache-and-pain shit. You win."

"Thanks." Jackson grabbed the fiver and slipped it into his suit pocket. "Did it come through okay?"

"Loud and clear. Who the hell was that guy you were talking to?"

"He said his name was Martun Hagopian. I've got his card in my pocket. His prints are all over it so I won't show it to you now, but let me tell you, that guy's a real asshole, and for my money, he's pimping out the girls."

"It sounded like he was making specific guarantees. Who was that girl you were talking about? The one he wants to fix you up with?"

Jackson frowned.

"Let's get going first, in case he comes out of the building and looks around."

Bengtson started up the car and pulled away from the curb.

"The woman we were talking about was Katya Katz. She's the one whose husband was shot to death in the robbery out in WLA."

"No shit?" Bengtson scratched at his chin. "And she's in the book for another setup?"

Jackson shifted in his seat and loosened his tie.

"So much for grief." He turned to look at Bengtson and lowered his voice. "There's something else, but you've got to promise you won't say anything to anyone."

Bengtson looked over.

"There was another woman in the book that I recognized. It was our Jen Donahue."

"*What*?" Bengtson nearly sideswiped a car in the adjacent lane. "Are you shitting me?" He looked over at Jackson's serious face. "You mean *our* Jen Donahue?"

Jackson smiled. "Had you going, didn't I?"

"You shit," Bengtson said, returning his attention to the road. "I almost got us into a wreck."

Jackson laughed.

"So, I really did recognize a second girl. It was the one that Thompson said she knows, the one she called Lana. Both she and Katya were in his special book…girls who *'know how to please their men'*."

"So they bring in street hookers, clean them up, then pimp them out on a matchmaking site." Bengtson who was thinking out loud looked over at Jackson and smiled.

"Pretty neat scam. I wonder if it's legal?"

"Pimping is pimping," Jackson said. "The clients are paying for what's being promised—a *guaranteed* lay. That's money for sex, *grasshopper,* and these leeches are living off the misery of others."

CHAPTER 35

October 27, 9:00 p.m.

Shari Thompson sat down on a couch in one of the relaxed conversation groupings set up in the lobby bar of the Miramar Hotel in the city of Santa Monica. She had expected Yuri to be there, but when she didn't see him anywhere in the lobby, she decided to make herself comfortable and have a glass of wine.

She ordered from a young waitress who presented her with a menu, but she didn't bother to read it. She wasn't hungry, having had a BigMac and fries with her kids before the new sitter showed up for a tryout.

The young woman watching her boys seemed nice enough, and she claimed to have experience with babysitting multiple children, but Thompson couldn't help but be worried. Her three, when together, were hellions on wheels, and she'd cornered them individually before leaving the house and warned them in no uncertain terms that if the sitter had even one complaint about their behavior, they would be dropped from their afternoon sports activities and confined to their rooms for the next six weeks. The speech had no effect on the youngest one, but he did have a favorite stuffed animal named *Louie,* a toy he slept with every night, and she had threatened to see to it that Louie would go on a vacation without him for several days, and that seemed to have the desired result.

Her wine arrived, and after checking her watch, she took a large gulp. She was really attracted to this Russian man, but she wasn't sure she was doing the right thing. She'd been with his type before, and while guys like him could be really exciting, they were never any good for anything more than a one night stand or a passionate affair.

She was looking to meet someone more stable, someone who wanted to be involved in a real relationship, but guys like that were few and far between, and the odds of finding one who wanted to be with a woman who already had three kids under the age of ten was slim to none. So being the practical woman that she was, she would take advantage of what was available, and not worry about what she couldn't control.

She was beginning to wonder if he was going to show up when he suddenly arrived. He noticed her right away and quickly made his way over.

"I'm sorry I'm late," he told her. "Accident on the freeway. I got caught in the backup."

"Not a problem," she said.

He sat down next to her on the couch and waved to the waitress who hovered nearby. When she came over, he ordered a couple of shots of vodka.

"You off duty tonight?" Thompson asked.

"No, I'm on, but I thought you might join me for a Russian toast."

She liked his confidence, and let him know she would with a smile, so when the vodka arrived, he handed her one, then raised his glass and said, "Чтобы столы ломались от изобилия, а кровати – от любви!"

"What in the world does that mean?" she asked.

He smiled. "Let the tables break from abundance, and the beds break from love!"

"Nice," she said smiling back. "I'll definitely drink to that."

They downed two shots of vodka apiece, and Yuri smiled broadly when he signaled to the waitress to bring them another round.

Over thirty minutes of conversation, he revealed a bit about his background, telling her that he had lived for a while in Saint Petersburg as a young man, but that he had emigrated to Sweden as a teen when his parents were killed in an automobile accident. He'd lived with an uncle, his mother's brother, and worked in his family's convenience store.

Thompson was already aware of most of these facts from the briefing she'd been given by Magarian, but her efforts to tease further details out of him had mixed results. He told her that his marriage to a Swedish girl had fallen apart when the two of them realized that they had very different views about having children. She had wanted them right away, but he had wanted to wait until his life was more settled.

He gave her a shrug and rolled his eyes. "We were too young. What more can I say?"

He told her about coming to the United States, and how he signed up for the military, but he never mentioned any details about his heroics, and she admired him for that. She was used to guys who liked to talk about how important they were, and she found Yuri's modesty to be very refreshing.

"Enough about me," he said, as he ordered them another round. "What about you?

"Are you trying to get me drunk?" she asked with a smile.

"You're a beautiful woman, so of course I'm going to try and get you drunk."

She laughed at his directness. She was beginning to feel a decent buzz coming on and that heightened the experience of being with a strong and very likable man.

"I forgot what you asked me?" she said.

"I want to know about your life?"

"That's right. My life." She started to laugh. "What life? I've got three little boys to take care of. That's it in a nutshell."

"What happened to your husband? Doesn't he help you out?"

"We don't get along. He was angry when I divorced him, so he pays the alimony, but he doesn't have much to do with the boys." She downed her vodka which had just arrived, then looked up at Yuri who gave her a smile.

"That's his loss," he said.

She nodded. "He might figure that out someday, but in the meantime, the boys seem to miss him..."

Her voice trailed off as she thought about how unfair it was for her kids, but Yuri was quick to bring her back into the moment.

"At least they have you," he said. "I'm sure you're a great mother, and that is all they really need to become strong, young men."

She smiled at him, her eyes twinkling. The vodka was warm in her stomach, and she had reached the stage of intoxication where she was feeling really good and throwing caution to the wind.

"Why don't we go out into the garden and walk around?" she told him. "I need to get a little fresh air."

Yuri nodded. He pulled out a sizable roll of bills and paid the check while leaving a generous tip.

After a quick stop at the restrooms for both of them, they made their way out into the central courtyard that was dimly lighted and filled with palm trees and tropical plants, many of which were over ten feet tall. Yuri had taken her hand, and when they were seemingly alone and out of view, he turned her towards him and gave her a kiss.

She kissed him back, softly at first, but then passion took over, and the intensity grew. He held her tight, and she began to rub her breasts back and forth across his chest.

He broke off the kiss, held her glance, and gave her a small smile.

"Would you like me to get us a room?"

She laughed. "Too soon for that, Yuri. Besides, I've got to get home to my kids. I've got a new babysitter tonight, and I don't want to be away too long in case the boys start to drive her crazy."

He nodded, seeming to understand.

"Another time then," he said.

She nodded, then kissed him briefly on the lips.

They walked back through the lobby of the hotel, then out the front door where the valet parking was located.

"Do you have your ticket?" he said, intending to pay the fee for her.

"Actually, I came in a cab."

"Really?" He seemed to give that some thought. "Then I insist on driving you home."

"It'll be out of your way, Yuri."

"No problem. I was just going to head into work. My car is parked out on the street. I'll give you a lift."

She knew she should probably say no, but she had enjoyed his kiss, and if things went right, they might do a little more before she reached her front door.

He took her hand and led her down the path that paralleled the long driveway that traversed the hotel grounds on its way to the street. When they reached the front gate, he led her around the corner to his undercover unit, a dark blue Crown Vic that gave no indication that it was anything but a civilian vehicle.

Ocean Avenue, the street they were on, was nearly deserted. It was just after ten p.m., on a weekday night, and the temperature was growing colder as an overcast layer made its way in from the ocean.

He put his arms around her and leaned over to kiss her. It hadn't come as a surprise, she knew that he wanted her, and the way she was feeling she really wanted him, too.

But getting laid in the back of a city car was not something she had any intention of doing. And she was serious about getting home to her kids, but that started to fade when his hand slipped into her coat and began to fondle her breasts.

She broke off the kiss, then gave him a smile.

"Tell you what," she whispered. "I'm in a real rush tonight, but maybe there's time enough to give you a little something to make the night memorable."

"I'm all ears," he said. A big smile crossed his face. "What do you have in mind?"

She slowly looked around, careful to confirm that there was no one nearby before she reached down and found the zipper on his pants.

"Backseat," she said as she unzipped him. "But we have to make this quick."

CHAPTER 36

October 27, 11:50 p.m.

Clay Young pulled into the gated parking lot behind the OC Intelligence Unit facility and parked his run-around car in a spot that was close to being the farthest from the rear of the building. He quickly made his way into the back of the station and walked directly over to Yuri's desk where his partner was sitting with his feet up, reading over a report he'd written about the money he'd spent on drinks while he worked undercover on the job.

"We need to talk," Clay said.

"Take a seat," Yuri told him.

"Outside."

Clay pointed to the back of the building, then spun on his heels and led the way towards the outside door.

Yuri got to his feet, slid a 9 mm Sig Sauer out of his desk drawer, tucked it into the waistband on his back, then followed Clay out into the parking lot.

Clay led him to a spot that was dark and untouched by the high-intensity lights that flooded the rest of the area from dusk until dawn. When he was sure they were out of earshot of any of the employees arriving for the change of shift, he stopped walking and turned around.

"I'm pretty sure I'm being followed." His eyes met Yuri's stare. "On the way over here, I spotted the same car twice; a black Chrysler four-door. I don't know who they are, but they're good. I couldn't shake 'em."

A cold breeze suddenly kicked up, so he plunged his hands into his front pants pockets. He'd been so concerned about what he thought was going on that he'd forgotten to remove his jacket from his car.

Yuri studied him intently. Clay was clearly rattled, and he would need to calm him down.

"Who would have any reason to follow you?" he asked.

"I don't know, man. Maybe this is related to those stupid phone calls."

Yuri shook his head. "The department has no reason to be looking at you, and unless you know something that I don't, I just don't see it."

"Then who could it be?" Clay looked nervously around the lot. "You think it might be that *asshole* Komarov or someone from his crew?"

"Again, why? He doesn't know you from shit."

"Then you tell me, Yuri. Why am I suddenly being followed?"

"Maybe you're not being followed at all. Maybe you're just mistaken."

"No, man. I know what I saw."

Yuri knew from experience that Clay was a very perceptive cop, always on and always aware when he was out on the streets. If he was convinced that he was being followed, then he probably was, and that was something they needed to take seriously.

"I suppose it's always possible that those calls that Komarov made to your phone might have triggered an investigation."

"My phone? You're the one who was using that phone, not me."

"I didn't mean it that way. Chill out, man." He squared himself up to Clay and met his glare. "If it is IA, things will blow over quickly. They haven't got shit on either one of us."

Clay took another quick look around the lot.

"I don't need this, Yuri."

"Relax, Clay." Yuri gave him a pat on the shoulder. "They got nothing on you. I told 'em what's up with the calls, and Komarov's on board with it, so there's nothing to worry about. They'll follow you around for a while, maybe call you in for an interview, but what can they do? It'll all blow over. You'll see." He tried to sound positive. "You worry too much."

"It's kinda hard not to worry when it's my career that might be on the line."

"Your career's not on the line, you haven't done shit. But in the meantime, as I mentioned before, we stay clear of Komarov for the time being…let things settle out."

Yuri took a few moments to scan the lot for himself. He then said, "Just to make things easier, we'll stay low key tonight. Maybe drive around a bit, see if we can spot 'em again. Okay?"

"Yeah, I guess."

They went back into the station, got themselves organized, then walked back outside about an hour later. They climbed into their gray Crown Vic and left the lot, heading slowly towards a club on the far east side of Hollywood.

*****

Down the street from the OC Intelligence unit building, in a black Chrysler that was parked in a laundromat parking lot, sat the boys from Internal Affairs. Andrew Magarian was behind the wheel, with John Homa riding shotgun in the passenger seat.

On the floor behind the seat were the remnants of a box of tacos that they'd been munching on for almost forty-five minutes.

Homa had an *AirMac* computer in his lap, and displayed on the screen was a map of the city streets. A small blue dot was making its way from the OC Intelligence parking lot, headed directly to the East.

"You can go anytime?" Homa said, looking over at Magarian.

"Let's let 'em get a little farther ahead. No need to risk being spotted. This tracker's got a range of about five miles, so there's no way they're going to shake us."

"Whatever you say, boss."

Homa then settled back in his seat, and after a few more minutes of watching the screen, he said, "If we get a chance, let's stop and get some coffee. I'm startin' to fall asleep."

CHAPTER 37

October 28, 9:00 a.m.

Donahue was driving the take-home Crown Vic when she noticed that Thompson, who was seated in the passenger seat, was staring out the front windshield with a big smile on her face.

"Somebody's in a good mood this morning," she said.

Thompson looked over, the smile still glued to her face. "I tried out a babysitter on the list last night."

"Oh? How'd it go?"

"Perfect. Just perfect. The boys were well behaved, and all three were in bed by nine-thirty."

"No kidding? That's great! A little late for them though, don't you think?"

"Last night was the exception to the rule. The two older ones both fell asleep after soccer practice, so it would have been useless to put them down at their regular time. And my little one is a night owl. He takes his nap in the afternoon and usually stays up with the older ones until they go to bed at eight p.m."

"Did you save any money with this new girl?"

"A little, but at least it didn't feel like extortion."

Donahue waited for more, figuring that Thompson would tell her the details of her night out, but when it wasn't forthcoming, she said, "So, are you gonna tell me what you did last night?"

Thompson kept the smile on her face as she mulled over what to say.

"I met Yuri for a drink last night?"

Donahue shot her a glance.

"You didn't?"

"Yes, I did, and it was lots of fun."

"But I thought we decided that this guy was not the relationship type? In fact, he sort of matches the profile of everyone else you've been out with since your divorce."

"He does, doesn't he?" she responded. "But this is going nowhere, and

I wouldn't want it to. He's a really great guy; he's fun and understanding, and he's really a damn fine kisser."

"*You didn't?*"

"Don't sound so disapproving. He's just a boy-toy, Jen. It's nothing serious." She met Donahue's critical glance, then added, "You should try it sometime, girlfriend. It would be good for you to let your hair down once in a while."

"I do just fine," Donahue replied.

"I can always ask Yuri if he's got a friend—"

"No, Shari, we have to work with that guy. How could you?"

"Well, for one thing, we don't work with him, we consult him, that's all. And it seems to me that you've had one or two boyfriends that you've consulted with."

"That's not the same," Donahue replied. "They didn't work for LAPD."

"So what? I'm not worried about it, Jen. I don't get the feeling that he's a locker room talker, so I'm not concerned about my reputation."

Donahue shook her head. "You slept with him, didn't you?"

"Of course not." There was a long silence. "But he went away a happy camper."

"Oh, my God, Shari! You just burned an image into my brain that's gonna rear its ugly head if he ever comes around."

"Good! Maybe that will get you off that big butt of yours and back out into the dating world."

"My butt is not big."

They pulled up at the American Standard Life Insurance Company and made their way to the conference room on the fifth floor where Leigh Cherlina was already seated, awaiting their arrival.

"Ms. Cherlina," said Donahue, "thanks again for making the time to see us."

"Whatever I can do to help. Nika was a sweet girl and whoever killed her should have to pay."

The detectives took seats at the table, then Donahue began the questioning.

"Since we last spoke with you, we've interviewed a lot of different people, and there are a few new areas of interest that we'd like to discuss with you."

"Certainly."

"Did Nika ever mention anything about a dating agency called Trophy-Wife Match?"

Cherlina smiled. "Pretty cheesy name isn't it." She folded her hands in her lap. "As a matter of fact, Nika did mention that agency."

"In what context?" Donahue asked.

"She told me that during a six-month period that two separate files came across her desk for preparation, and both files were for claims made for the death of husbands of Russian women who had met their husbands through that particular agency."

Donahue waited for more, but it wasn't immediately forthcoming. Leigh Cherlina appeared to be focused on the questions she'd been asked, and she only gave the answer asked for without volunteering any further information. She was the kind who would make an excellent witness in court, and Donahue began to wonder if testifying as a witness was part of her duties for the insurance company?

Thompson looked up from her notepad. "Did she say anything else about the agency?"

"Not that I recall, but she did say that she knew both of the women personally. I found that rather surprising."

So did Donahue and Thompson. They exchanged a knowing look that signified to both that they were clearly on to something.

"What happened to the cases?" Donahue asked.

"I don't really know. They were processed for payment, and I assume that's what happened."

She leaned forward in her chair.

"You might want to talk with Mr. Grushik. Nika said she was going to mention it to him."

They asked another dozen questions but learned nothing new, so Donahue finally asked her for the names of the two mentioned cases.

Cherlina excused herself, then made her way out of the room to track down what she had on the two paid out files.

Thompson whispered, "Maybe this is what she wanted to talk to you about?"

"Maybe," replied Donahue. "I don't remember the name of the insurance company involved in the Katz case, but I'm pretty sure it wasn't American Standard Life."

"We can check it out when we get back."

Nicholi Grushik walked into the conference room and made his way over to where they were sitting.

"I was told you were down here. How are you, detectives?"

Donahue smiled. Grushik was an absolute fashion plate in his dark brown suit from *John Varvatos,* and his chocolate *Scarab Sloane loafers* from *Jimmy Choo. S*he quickly concluded that he must have a fashion consultant and a very big bank account.

"We're doing fine, Nicholi," Donahue told him.

He smiled broadly. "I just ran into Leigh Cherlina and she said you might have a question or two for me?"

"Actually, we were going to come by and speak with you after Ms. Cherlina got back, but as long as you're here, I guess we can do this now."

"Excellent," he said, pulling out a chair. "We all feel so sad about Nika's death. It's just terrible."

Donahue cleared her throat. "We're trying to run down dozens of leads, Nicholi, and one of the things that came up during our investigation was that Nika discovered a couple of claims that were filed on behalf of two separate Russian women. Both of them just happened to have met their husbands at a match making agency called *Trophy-Wife Matchmaking.* Did she ever mention anything like that to you?"

Grushik was silent, but he slowly shook his head.

"No, I can't say I remember any such conversation. Was there anything else you can tell me about the cases?"

Thompson started to speak. She was going to mention to him that Nika knew both of the widows involved, but Donahue quickly silenced her with a hand on her arm.

"That's all we know," Donahue said. "We thought it might be something, but if she never mentioned anything to you, then I'm sure it's nothing at all."

"We sell a lot of policies, Jennifer. It's entirely possible that something like that would happen, but if the claims were legitimate, we'd certainly pay them without delay."

"Does the fact that the two couples involved may have met at the same matchmaking agency have any bearing on whether or not you'd pay the claim?"

"Certainly not. Let me give you an example. We have a program set up with the Los Angeles County Sheriff's Department where we offer life insurance policies to their deputies. In any given year, we probably process a dozen or two claims for insurance payouts from that agency alone."

Off Thompson's incredulous look, he added, "Mostly retirees, but you can see that two claims connected in a singular way would not raise any concerns."

Thompson nodded her understanding.

Donahue asked, "Is there any way you can determine for us how many cases you processed last year that were the direct result of death by homicide?"

"That would be relatively easy to determine."

"Could it be further refined to list how many of those cases involved widows of Russian descent?"

"A lot more difficult. The beneficiaries ethnicity is not a statistic that we keep. I'm just thinking out loud here, but I guess we'd have to do a search by names that sounded like they are Russian, but even that would be inaccurate."

"How so?" asked Thompson.

"If the beneficiaries were Russian women, their married last names might be anglicized."

When Thompson nodded, he said to Donahue, "There's also another problem. You'd need to get a search warrant for that kind of information since our files are all confidential."

Donahue nodded. There was no way they'd be able to get a warrant, at least not yet. Two cases, while suspicious on the face of it, did not seem to raise any concerns within the industry, so they were probably barking up the wrong tree. Still, it was the best lead they'd had since getting the case, so they'd have to pursue it, even if it led them nowhere.

"Well, thanks for your help," Donahue said. "We won't take up any more of your time."

"Anytime, detectives." Grushik got to his feet, then gave them a smile. "You're always welcome around here."

He started for the door, then turned back for a moment.

"Are you all finished up? I don't want to rush you, but the room was reserved for a meeting with our legal department."

"Of course." Donahue got to her feet. "We'll just gather up our things and get out of here."

Grushik nodded, then left the room.

"I still think we're on to something," Thompson whispered as she hung her purse over her shoulder.

"Me, too," replied Donahue, "but given the roadblocks that Nicholi has mentioned, we may have a difficult time working it through."

Thompson was focused on the door. She reached over and tapped Donahue on the arm. Leigh Cherlina had just walked in.

"Found it," she said. She was carrying a piece of paper.

Donahue smiled. Apparently, she did not run into Grushik, who certainly would have told her that the information they were seeking was confidential.

"The two are Philip Katz, deceased, and William Baker, deceased. This printout has the case number and the names of the beneficiaries.

"Thanks," said Donahue. She quickly scanned the paper. "It says here that the Baker case is *American Standard*, but the Katz case is from a company called *Rocky Mountain Life*?"

"American Standard is the parent company of half a dozen insurance companies," Cherlina told her. "*The Rocky Mountain Life and Casualty Insurance Company* is a subsidiary of American Standard Life."

"So you process their claims here?"

"When the policyholder and beneficiary live here in this region, we take over the claims. It makes things easier for the beneficiary, and it's less expensive for us if we have to conduct a major investigation."

Donahue was dying to look at the other case, but she had what she needed to look it up without Cherlina's help. The important thing now was to get out of the building before Grushik, or anyone else alerted Cherlina that the information she provided them might be confidential.

Donahue stuffed the paper into her purse, then signaled to Thompson it was time to go.

She gave Cherlina a smile. "Thanks for your help. We'll be in touch."

CHAPTER 38

October 28, 10:30 a.m.

When Donahue and Thompson arrived back at their squad room in the PAB building, they found Jackson and Bengtson huddled together discussing the undercover visit the day before to the *Trophy-Wife Matchmaking* offices.

Donahue walked over to join them while Thompson decided to review the information they'd gotten from Leigh Cherlina.

"How'd it go yesterday, old man?" she said to Jackson.

"I won the bet," he said with a smile.

She looked over at Bengtson, who nodded.

She sighed. "I meant how'd it go for the case?"

"I think you'll be pleased," Jackson said, warming up to having the floor. "First of all, I think there's a new player in the game." He held up a clear plastic bag containing Hagopian's business card.

"He says his name is Martun Hagopian. He's short, maybe five-nine, dark skin, long dark hair, but he appeared well groomed; expensive suit. Went with the appearance of the place."

"I thought you were going to meet with Irina?" She was holding up the plastic bag and looking at the business card.

"He handed me the card, so I know his prints are on it," Jackson said. "I held it by the edges."

She nodded, then put the envelope back down on Jackson's desk.

"I spoke with Irina when I first got there. She gave me the pitch. Ten thosand dollars for one introduction a month for a year. It's all on tape. No hint from her that there was prostitution involved, but while I was going through the photo books, she left the room, and he took over."

"The Closer," Bengtson volunteered. "Good name for a TV show."

Jackson said, "Hagopian showed me a second book. Mostly beautiful, very young women. He told me that they were 'special' and that they 'knew how to please their dates.'"

"So you think they're running a high-end escort operation?" she asked.

"Not exactly. He said access to those girls was at the twenty-five thousand dollar level. Unlimited introductions for a full year."

"Interesting. Pay a flat fee, and the girls are on call."

"He offered me the premium package deal for fifteen thousand in cash."

"You must have impressed him," Donahue said.

Jackson laughed. "He said…and I quote, '*because I'm a man who knows what I want.*'"

Bengtson started to laugh and shook his head. When Donahue looked over to find out why, he said, "I just figured out why they offered him a discount."

"I'm all ears," she said.

"They sized him up and realized that he could never fully exploit the deal. A once a month guy at most, so the wear and tear on the girls would be practically nothing. Easy money."

Donahue smiled. "Still waters run deep, Bengtson. I talked to one of Jackson's recent girlfriends, and based on what she told me, I have absolutely no doubt that his performance would put guys half his age to shame." She gave him a wink. "If you're lucky, maybe he'll give you some of his pointers."

She turned back to Jackson who overheard her remarks and was now sporting a blush and a smile from ear to ear.

"Book in the business card, and have the lab print it using ninhydrin," she told him. "If they bring up some usable prints, we'll run them through CII, and we'll see if we can get a handle on what this guy is all about."

"I'll take care of it, but there's more."

"Oh?"

"I recognized two of the girls on display in the special book. One was Katya Katz, the widow you've been talking about. He promised me a date with her as soon as I signed up."

"No kidding?" Donahue was really surprised.

"The other girl I recognized was the one that Shari was talking about; the one she spotted on the internet. She was in the high rollers book, too."

"So you're saying that it looks like the girls are all in the main photo book, but certain ones—in this case, two former street walkers—are in the book of special girls?"

"That's right," he said.

She turned to Bengtson. "Is there a copy yet of the audio tape?"

He nodded. "I had it put on a CD for you."

"Let me have it. I want to listen to it on my way home in the car." She walked over to Bengtson and took possession of the CD. "See what you can find out about this guy Hagopian. Run him by name through Immigration and DMV. We need to know more about him."

Thompson walked up and tapped her on the arm.

"Got something here."

"So quickly?"

"It's all in where you look. That second insurance policy case? The widow was named Maryna Baker. The name Maryna is Russian, so I ran the name Maryna Baker with DMV and got a photo. I remembered her as *Lana*, the girl I recognized on the Internet. Her true name is Maryna Dragnov, and I got an address for her from the DMV. It matches the address on the insurance printout."

She looked up at Donahue. "The policy payoff was one point five million, Jen."

"Death by natural causes?"

"Doesn't say," Thompson replied.

"Let's put it to the *Zen Master.*"

She turned to Jackson who was still sitting in his chair. He was filling out the paperwork to book in the business card.

"Rick," she said when he looked up. "Does the name William Baker ring any bells?"

Jackson gave it some thought.

"Not off hand. Did you run the name on the case index."

"Not yet," she told him.

"Found it," said Thompson. Donahue spun around. Thompson was standing at the computer in her cubicle. She began to read the information off.

"William Baker. The case number shows it's a Hollywood case." She looked up and smiled. "It's a 187."

187 was the California Penal Code section for murder.

"Unbelievable!" said Donahue. "Both husbands murdered. Another fuckin' coincidence?"

"And as we all know—" Thompson chanted," —there's no such thing as a coincidence."

Donahue walked back over to her desk. "I'll give *Frick and Frack* at Hollywood a call. Maybe they can track down the file."

"Frick and Frack? Who's that?" asked Jackson.

"Grayson and Tucker."

He smiled. "That fits."

*****

Thirty minutes later, Thompson received a document on her computer that she forwarded on to one of the squad printers. It was a six-month follow-up report on the William Baker case.

Thompson spent the next thirty minutes reading over the known facts surrounding the homicide. She picked up her coffee cup, got a refill in the coffee room then tracked down Donahue who was meeting with Gibson.

"Want the *Reader's Digest* version?" she asked.

Donahue nodded.

"Okay. Here goes. William Baker, age fifty-seven. He was killed during a street robbery while on a business trip to London. He was beaten to death on his way back to his hotel room in the district of Kensington. The weapon used was believed to be consistent with a piece of pipe. Robbery was the suspected motive. The case is currently unsolved."

"London? What the hell? There goes our theory that the cases are related."

"What kind of business was he in?" Gibson asked.

"Manufacturing. Apparently, his company makes parts for commercial aircraft."

"Is Hollywood handling the case?" Donahue asked.

Thompson shook her head.

"The Metropolitan Police in London have it. Their progress report is attached to a dummy file that Hollywood put together. Apparently, Hollywood was only involved peripherally. They were providing background and a few initial interviews with the wife and some of her husband's associates."

"Any possible suspects listed in the report?" Gibson asked.

Thompson glanced up. "No. It looks like what it is, a straight street robbery." She took a seat at her desk. "Pretty strange though. Both wives met their husbands through the agency."

"We don't know that for sure," Donahue cautioned. "We still need to confirm that with the widow."

Thompson nodded. "Even so, you've got two former streetwalkers whose older husbands get murdered during the course of separate robberies, and both widows are the beneficiaries of large insurance payouts from the same group of insurance companies." She crinkled her nose. "This whole thing smells."

"I'll give you that," said Donahue. "See if you can confirm that address for Maryna Dragnov Baker. We need to talk with her right away."

"What'll you be doing?" Thompson asked.

"I'm gonna give Don Flynn another call. Maybe he can give us some help."

*****

Don Flynn was sitting at his desk in the Headquarters Building in Washington, DC. His coat was hung neatly on a nearby wooden coat rack, and in keeping with Secret Service protocol, his shirt was still buttoned and his tie still neatly tied.

When his secretary told him who was on the phone, he picked it up and said, "It has only been twenty-four hours, Jen. I'm still waiting to hear back from the Bureau about who they've got working with the FSB."

"I'm not calling to nag you about that, Don. I've got another question."

"Fire away," he said, leaning back in his chair. "The great and powerful Karnak is ready to answer all questions."

Donahue smiled at the reference to the Johnny Carson routine.

"Okay. Here goes. An American citizen got murdered in London about eight months ago. His death might be tangentially connected to my bombing case. Is there any way to determine if my possible suspect, Vlad Komarov, was in London during the time of the commission of the murder?"

Flynn gave it some thought.

"I can probably call a guy I know over at Customs and Immigration. When was the murder?"

She gave him the date.

"We talking about the same Vladimir Komarov you asked me about before?"

"Same one."

"Anything else?"

"No. I guess not."

"I'll follow up with the Bureau this afternoon about their liaison with the FSB." He looked at his watch. "It might take a day or so to connect with my connection at Customs and Immigration, but I'll call you back just as soon as I know something."

"I appreciate this, Don. I hope I'm not putting you out?"

"You are," he said, half seriously, "but I know you'd do the same for me."

She smiled. He was right about that.

"Next time you're in LA, the dinner is on me."

"I'll have my wife and kids with me," he warned her.

"That's fine. I'll pay for everyone. There's an *In-and-Out* burger restaurant close to the airport—"

She heard him laughing as he hung up the phone.

****

3:45 p.m.

Captain Tommy Elwood entered the conference room and looked around, noting with satisfaction that everyone was there. He took his place at the head of the table and cleared his throat.

"I heard from the Chief this afternoon. He wants to know what's going on with the bombing case?"

Donahue, Thompson, and Gibson were seated to his immediate left, while

Roberts, Bengtson, and Jackson were to his right. He looked directly at Donahue and waited for a response.

Donahue sighed. "Well, my source in the Secret Service is still attempting to make contact with the FBI liaison in Moscow. The contact has agreed to speak to his counterpart in the FSB to determine what we can about Vlad Komarov's background."

Elwood waited for more, but when it wasn't forthcoming, he said, "And...?"

Donahue shrugged.

Elwood looked around, but no one made eye contact. He leaned forward in his chair.

"What about the undercover operation? Anything come of that?" He looked over at Jackson.

"Rick?" he said.

Jackson folded his hands together on the table. He told Elwood what happened at the agency, about the fees, the two books full of young women, and about the implied promises made to him by Martin Hagopian.

"So it's a high-end pay-for-play operation?"

"It looks that way," said Gibson, "but we don't have any actual proof that the women are paid anything for putting out."

"Seems to me the pimp is getting paid, so the women must be getting something?"

"Not necessarily," Donahue said. "We interviewed one of the women who dated through the agency. She was a former streetwalker, but Petrovich cleaned her up and set her up with introductions. She went out with one of the customers, fell in love, and married him."

"Where is this going?" Elwood scratched his head. "Either they're running a high-end prostitution service, or they're not. Which is it?"

"We don't know yet," Donahue replied, "but it gets even stranger. Her husband was murdered six months after the wedding. Shot to death in an apparent robbery in the parking lot of his office in WLA—"

Elwood's eyes went wide with surprise.

"...and according to Rick, she's back in the book, and this Hagopian guy offered to set Rick up with her as his first introduction."

"This is a can of worms," Elwood said as he leaned back in his chair and began running his hand through his hair.

"She was in the second book of women, the special book, according to Hagopian," Jackson told him. "And I spotted a second woman in that book, a young female that Shari recognized from their on-line website."

Elwood glance over at Thompson, who added, "Her street name was Lana, but her true name is Maryna Dragnov Baker. Her husband, Philip Baker, also died, an apparent victim of a street robbery."

Elwood brightened up.

"Now we're getting somewhere. Two escorts, both of whom had husbands who died in street robberies. There has to be a connection with the agency."

"We can't say that for sure," said Thompson. "We haven't talked with the widow Baker yet, so we still haven't confirmed that she met her husband there. On top of that, the husband was killed in London, and the wife was here in LA at the time."

Elwood shook his head in frustration.

"Am I the only one, or does this case resemble a yo-yo? First it looks like a connection, then it isn't. What the hell is going on?"

"Both of the widows collected on their husband's life insurance," Donahue told him. "That may have something to do with it, but we're just not sure about anything yet."

"Do you want to mention that little thing we learned about Nika?" Thompson asked.

"Should I?" said Donahue with a smile.

"I think it might be appropriate," Thompson said with a grin.

"Out with it," said Elwood.

"Well, according to Nika's supervisor over at the insurance company, Nika said that she knew both of the victim's wives."

"No kidding?" Elwood slipped into thought to consider everything.

No one spoke. They knew from experience to wait him out.

He finally said, "So, we've uncovered two murders possibly connected to the agency, possibly for the insurance payouts, and two murders of women who may or may not have been killed because they knew something about the agency, and we've got a bombing murder of one of the principals connected to the agency." His eyes came back to life and moved from one to the other.

"To me, this has all the hallmarks of organized crime."

There were nods of agreement from everyone at the table.

"At the moment, Komarov is our only possible lead in the bombing case," Donahue told him, "so until we discover something to the contrary, I'd have to say I think it's Russian OC, but I don't want to rule out anything else."

"As well we shouldn't," Elwood replied. "What's the story on this guy Hagopian?"

"We've got the lab trying to lift his prints off a business card," Jackson said. "And once we get those, we'll do a full background."

Elwood nodded. "Any idea how long he's been working at the agency?"

"No idea," Thompson replied, "but if I remember correctly, Irina told us that Petrovich recruited the women and that she used women in the office to close the deals with the male clients, so perhaps he's new to the operation."

"Find out what you can," Elwood said to Donahue.

She nodded.

He looked over at Gibson. "Get someone to focus on the insurance angle. We need to resolve that if we can."

"Jen, Shari and Mitzi are already looking into it," Gibson replied.

"Good!" He looked back over at Donahue. "You've done quite a bit in a very short time. Keep it up. Somewhere, somehow, you're gonna catch a break, and as complex as this appears to be, that very complexity will turn out to be their Achilles heel."

"Yes, sir."

Elwood got to his feet. "I'll brief the Chief." He glanced over at Gibson. "Keep me up to speed, Gibby, and let me know if you need more bodies."

When Elwood was gone, Gibson stood up.

"Let's meet again tomorrow afternoon and see where we're at."

*****

CHAPTER 39

October 29, 1:00 a.m.

Yuri Pavienko made a slow turn off Sunset Boulevard and drove south to Santa Monica Boulevard where he made another turn before heading east. He drove in the lane closest to the curb at a speed of no more than twenty-five miles an hour.

His partner, Clay Young, was seated low in the front passenger seat, eyes closed, his head against the seat back. He was doing what he liked to call...*resting his eyes*. One of his sons had been home sick all day from school, so his usual sleep pattern had been broken up while he tended to the child's needs.

They'd been driving around for a couple of hours, making the rounds at Russian clubs, just looking around, noting who was with whom, and hitting up informants if they happened to come across them, hoping to pick up little snippets of intelligence to keep the shift from being a total waste of time.

Yuri reached over and tapped Clay on the arm.

"It's one a.m., *Sunshine*."

"I'm awake." Clay opened his eyes, sat up straight, looked around to get his bearings, then yawned.

"Wanna stop by the *Musso and Frank Grill*; get something to eat?"

Clay shook his head. "I'm not hungry yet, but we can go there if you can't wait."

He looked back over his shoulder and stared out the rear window.

"Any sign of 'em?" he asked.

"No one's following us," Yuri replied.

"You sure?"

"Absolutely! Whatever you think you saw the other night, it's not happening tonight."

Clay turned back in his seat.

"Maybe I made a mistake."

"Maybe so," said Yuri, glad to see that his partner was coming around.

He'd been concerned with Clay's first report that he was being followed, but after driving around for the past two hours, using counter-surveillance techniques like doubling back, speed changes, and park-and-watch surveillance, he was pretty sure that there was no one on their tale.

"We going to eat?" Clay asked.

"Yeah, I'm starved."

Yuri turned on Vine and headed up towards Hollywood Boulevard while Clay settled back in his seat and studied the crowd still out on the street.

"Don't these people ever go home?" he said, referring to the mixture of tourists, teens and the homeless who walked up and down the boulevards all night long.

He looked over at Yuri.

"You hear anything from your lady detective about how the bombing investigation is going?"

Yuri looked over. "Not a word. Why?"

"Just wondered. They turned Vlad loose, so I'm assuming they didn't have enough to charge him."

"I heard they didn't get any physical evidence during the searches, so without it, I guess there's nothing to connect him."

"They gonna keep working him?"

"I don't know. Probably."

Yuri glanced over and watched as his partner's eyes closed again.

*****

At just after three a.m., Yuri pulled into the OCI parking lot and woke up his partner again before the two of them headed into the building. Once they were inside, Clay went to the head while Yuri took a seat at his desk.

When Clay came out of the restroom, Yuri said, "You know, it just occurred to me that if it is Internal Affairs that are trying to follow you around, they might be using a vehicle tracker."

Clay sat on the side of his desk.

"I thought about that, too. They could also be tracking my iPhone, so I turned it off and took out the SIM chip."

"That's smart," Yuri told him. "Look, if they're gonna fuck with you, then maybe we should fuck with them, too. You know, show 'em that we're on to their game. You up for something like that?"

"Won't that just make things worse?" he asked.

"Not if we're smart about it."

Clay smiled. "What'd you have in mind?"

"You bring your truck tonight?"

"You think they've got a tracker on it, too?"

"Maybe. I think we have to assume that they've got all of our rides wired up. Let's leave our cars here tonight and take home a couple of the UC cars that we haven't been using in a while."

Clay smiled again.

"They'll be sitting out here for the rest of the night, wondering what the hell is going on." He thought it over. "I like it."

"And if they ever figure it out, we just say the vehicle switch was just a standard precaution. We had no idea they were following us."

"Sure, fuck 'em! If they're gonna follow me around for no good reason, we can make it a practice exercise in counter surveillance and evasion."

"My thoughts exactly," Yuri said. "Look, why don't you go on home? I'll handle the paperwork, and you can get some sleep."

"You sure?"

"Yeah, I know you're dog tired. No sense you sleeping here in your chair."

"You sure you don't need me for anything?"

"No, I'm good."

Clay nodded. He made his way over to the vehicle key locker where the keys were kept for more than a dozen vehicles that were used by the squad for undercover operations. He selected the keys for a BMW, then headed for the exit door, stopping on his way to fist bump Yuri before making his way out to the parking lot and over to the BMW.

Once he was gone, Yuri gathered up his things and made his way to the vehicle key locker. He put the keys for the vehicle they'd been using all night on one of the hooks, then removed a set for a Prius.

He went back to his desk, composed a little note for the Captain, describing their change of vehicles as a routine security measure, then placed the note in his outbox where a day watch secretary would find it in the morning and forward it on to the Captain's office.

He then made his way out to the lot, located the Prius, then drove away from the station.

*****

Magarian and Homa were parked next to the curb between two cars. They were a block to the east of the OCI building, and Homa had his *MacBook Air* open and resting in his lap.

He was focused on the screen, a blue dot silently blinking in the Google map overlay that showed the OCI building and the adjacent parking lot. The tracking device they were using was attached to the car that Pavienko and Young had been cruising around in for the majority of their shift.

He checked his watch, noted the time, then made an hourly notation that the car remained parked in the police lot at 3:30 am.

"You about ready to call it a night?" he said to Magarian. "These guys aren't going anywhere now. It's almost their end of watch."

Magarian shifted in his seat, then yawned.

"We'll stick it out. If you want to catch some Z's, go ahead. I had my cat-nap, so I'll take the next watch."

Homa nodded. He placed the laptop on the center console, then opened the front passenger door.

"Where you going?" Magarian asked. The dome light was permanently disabled so as not to light up when the door was open.

"I need to take a leak," Homa said.

He wandered off to find a private spot while Magarian positioned the computer so that he could watch the blue dot on the screen.

Neither detective had any idea that both Pavienko and Young had left the facility in cars that were not being tracked.

CHAPTER 40

October 29, 6:00 a.m.

Shari Thompson arrived at the PAB at just after six a.m. Her mother had spent the night at her house, and she was willing to stay there to see that the boys got breakfast and off to school on time. This act of kindness by her mother allowed Shari to go in very early for a workout in the basement gym of the PAB building. But before she went into the locker room to get ready to hit the machines, she made a stop at the fifth-floor squad room to have a look around.

No one else had come in yet, a fact that made her smile.

She had with her a purse and a workout bag, so she set them both down on the top of her desk, and with one final look around to make sure that no one could see her, she unzipped her workout bag and removed a small package.

It was cold to the touch, but not frozen, and it was double wrapped in layers of aluminum foil. She then pulled out a roll of duct tape, tore off a piece about a foot long, then stuck one edge to the corner of her desk, while letting the rest hang freely. She would need it in a moment, and there was no time to waste if she wanted to get this done before being discovered.

She opened the package, grabbed the strip of duct tape, stepped around the wall of the cubical and quickly moved over to the desk that belonged to her partner. Thirty-seconds later, when she had accomplished what she set out to do, she placed the aluminum foil minus its treasure back into her workout bag, took a quick look around to make sure that all traces of her handiwork were concealed, then made her way out of the squad and down to the gym with a smile as big as the state of Texas.

*****

Jennifer Donahue arrived at the squad as just after eight-thirty. After settling in at her desk, she started writing up the investigation log for the Pavienko murder book.

246

Thompson arrived twenty minutes later, and Donahue noted that she appeared to be in an awfully good mood.

"What's up?" she asked.

"Not much," Thompson replied. "I got my mom staying at the house, so I came in early and got in a workout." She studied Donahue's face. "How are things with you?"

"Good! I've been working on the follow-up report." She studied her friend. "You seem awfully chipper today?"

Thompson smiled. "It's just nice, for a change, to get a chance to workout. I feel like a brand new woman."

After a quick trip to the coffee room and a few idle conversations with other detectives who were beginning to arrive, Donahue returned to her cubicle and got back to work.

Thompson, for her part, was too excited to work. Patience was usually her long suit, but she was starting to wonder if her little project was actually going to pay off.

Two hours later, Donahue was still seated at her desk. She had the case file now up to date, and she was reviewing her emails and watching the clock. She was considering what to eat for lunch—knowing that she would need to load up on carbs to go for a long run later that afternoon—when her phone began to ring.

She immediately recognized the number that appeared on the screen. It belonged to Donald Flynn.

She checked her watch as she picked it up, computing the hour in DC as just after two p.m.

"You're working late," she said. "I thought you government suits liked to take lunch from noon until four p.m.?"

"Please hold for Assistant Director Flynn," said a pleasant female voice. *Oops...*

When Flynn got on the line, he wasted no time.

"Hey, Jen. I've made contact with the Bureau representative to the Federal Security Service of the Russian Federation. His name is Charlie Crawford. I told him about you, but he said he'd rather deal directly with me, so I gave him the info you provided, and he said he'll get back to me after he meets in Moscow with his counterpart."

"Why wouldn't he deal with me?" she asked, a little hurt.

"He says his role is to process Bureau requests, not the requests from local police agencies. If you wanted to deal with him directly, you'd have to work through the Los Angeles FBI field office."

"But---?"

"On the other hand, he does process requests directly from the Secret Service, so since it's coming from me, he says to stay within the guidelines, he'll have to respond to me directly."

"Oh, man!" The exasperation in her voice was plainly evident. "I didn't mean to get you involved in this, Don. If you want me to go to the local Bureau office here in West LA, I can do that without any problem."

"Don't be silly. I still haven't heard back from my contact at Homeland regarding the passport info you wanted, but we should hear back from the FSB on Komarov within a few days."

"That's great, Don! Thanks so much."

"And since we government suits usually take lunch from noon until four, I guess I'll just have to wait until tomorrow to do the follow-up with Homeland."

Oh, God...

She blushed. "I didn't know your secretary was the one making the call."

"She had a good laugh," he said as he looked at his watch. "I've got to run, Jen. I've got a meeting in ten minutes. I'll get back to you as soon as I've got something to pass on."

"Thanks, Don. I'll talk to you later."

*****

1:00 pm

At Thompson's suggestion, she and Donahue had lunch together at the Ocean Fish Market in downtown Los Angeles; an open air restaurant that fed many hundreds of people on patio tables during the busy lunch hours. It was famous for serving large slabs of grilled fish with crispy, golden fries and a large pile of slaw.

When they returned to the office, it was just after two p.m. They made their way to their respective cubicles, and once Thompson was seated, she could hear Donahue sniffing the air.

Thompson smiled to herself. For this to work, it was incumbent upon her to keep a straight face.

"What the hell?" said Donahue from her side of the partition. "It smells like rotten fish around here."

"Did you step in something back at the restaurant?" Thompson asked. She refused to look up, afraid that she was going to smile.

Donahue checked her shoes.

"Nope."

She stood up and took off her jacket, examined it, then tried to determine if she might have gotten something greasy or rotten on her pants.

She came around the partition and turned around so that her back was facing Thompson. She looked over her shoulder.

"Anything on my butt?"

"No," said Thompson with a straight face. "But I don't smell anything."

"Oh, God!" said Donahue. "Maybe it's my breath?"

Donahue breathed into her hand then sniffed. Realizing that it wasn't, she returned to her cubicle and began a quick search, beginning with her wastebasket.

"Oh, man," she said. "Here it is." She picked up the wastebasket, then looked over at Shari.

"Someone put a piece of rotten fish in my wastebasket." She held her nose with one hand, then carried the basket away from her desk, going all the way out to the central corridor where she placed it down in the hallway next to the door to the men's room.

She came back in and walked back to her desk, quickly sitting down in her chair.

Thompson, who was seated at her desk, kept her head turned away from Donahue's possible line of sight. She was unable to keep from smiling.

"God damn it!" she heard Donahue say. "It still stinks over here."

Thompson could hear her opening and closing her desk drawers as she conducted a search for the offending source of the odor. But after a minute, she gave up.

"What the hell is causing that smell?" she muttered.

Gibson, who happened to be passing by, quickly stopped in his tracks.

"What is that smell?"

"Rotten fish," said Donahue. "There was some in my trash can, but there must be more. It seems to be getting stronger."

Gibson covered his mouth and nose with his hand.

"You've got to do something about that, Jen. It's gonna make people sick."

Donahue was growing angrier by the moment.

"I looked everywhere," she said. "You find it."

It suddenly occurred to her that Gibson might somehow be connected to the smell. She looked at him with a questioning stare, then said, "Did you put that stuff in my wastebasket?"

"Me? God, no!"

Donahue looked over at Thompson but immediately discounted her as a suspect. They'd been together since early morning, and whoever had done this must have done so while she and Shari were having lunch.

She began sniffing around her desk, this time opening drawers again and sniffing in each one.

Then, in a moment of inspiration, she got out of her chair and down on her knees and peered around under the desk.

"God damn it!" she said. "Here it is."

A large piece of raw fish had been duct taped to the bottom of her desk. Donahue peeled the tape off and got to her feet holding the fish that was still stuck to the tape.

"Who did this?" she yelled out to the room at large.

She was greeted by surprised stares, but as word spread about what it was, those who were present began to laugh.

Donahue was tempted to throw the rotten fish at someone…anyone, but instead, she walked up and down the aisle, carrying it with her, stopping at each desk to ask the detectives individually if they were responsible. And while everyone denied it, the act of confronting them individually ensured that each one would get a whiff of the rotten smell.

But she didn't stop at Thompson's desk, and that was just fine with Shari. She was pretty sure she'd figure it out later: that the fish had been cold when brought in to delay the stench of decomposition until after the two of them were out to lunch. She might also come to realize that the fish in the wastebasket had been a diversion, one designed to prolong the experience, so that once she got rid of what was in the wastebasket, she would be falsely lulled into thinking that the smell would be gone, only to discover very quickly that she was fated to be tormented until she discovered the one that was taped to the underside of her desk.

Donahue dumped the last of the rotten fish in the wastebasket out in the hallway before returning to her desk and the snickering that was pervasive throughout the squad room.

Thompson, still smiling inwardly, was now satisfied that she'd gotten even for Donahue's having set her up with the burned body autopsy.

*****

Donahue's phone rang just as she returned to her desk. "Hey Don," she said. "I didn't expect you to call back so soon."

"I just heard from my friend at Customs and Immigration. I gave him the info on Vlad Komarov, and he ran him for me while I waited. Turns out he has a Russian passport, but they've got no record of him using it recently or being out of the United States at the time of your murder in London."

Donahue gave that some thought. "Would Customs know if he'd gone there on a forged passport?"

"Not without knowing what name he was using." Flynn lowered his voice. "Look, Jen, it's always possible that this guy has obtained a second passport. It could be a forgery, or a legitimate one he picked up from God knows where. You said this guy might be connected to organized crime?"

"Uh, huh."

"The Russian mob is international and they're into everything. I'd say it's absolutely possible for a guy like him to have bribed someone in the Russian

Federation to issue him one in a different name. Either that or maybe he worked with a good forger who made him a new one."

"So I really can't rule out his being in London at the time of the murder. Is that what you're telling me?"

"Yeah, and unless he has an iron clad alibi placing him here in the States at the time of the murder, I'm afraid that's the case."

Donahue was bummed. It seemed to her that it was going to be easy to determine if Komarov had been in London during the time of the murder. But because he was possibly connected to Russian organized crime, he might be using a false or stolen passport to fly in and out of the country. She was back to square zero, and for all her work, there were now more questions than answers.

She wanted to ask for another favor but didn't want to burn her bridges with Flynn by asking for too much. After all, he was second-in-charge of the Secret Service, hardly a person she could expect to do her bidding.

"We've got another possible suspect, Don. A guy named Martun Hagopian. The lab is lifting his prints off a business card right now, so I was wondering if I could send what I have on him over to your friend at Homeland so that we can see if there's any chance that he was in London during the murder?"

Flynn chuckled. "I can see what's going on here. Bit by bit, one at a time, you're going to ask about every Russian living in the LA area."

Donahue held her breath. He hadn't said no, and he didn't sound angry, so maybe she hadn't asked for one favor too many.

"You might have to babysit my kids one evening when Cami and I get to LA...in addition, of course, to that promised feast at *In-and-Out*."

Donahue smiled. "You got it, Don, and thanks so much. I'll send you Hagopian's prints just as soon as I hear from the lab."

She hung up the phone, then turned to Thompson.

"Flynn says that Vlad Komarov has a valid Russian passport, but he didn't travel on it during the time of the London murder."

"So he wasn't involved?"

Donahue shook her head. "All we know for sure is that he didn't use his own passport to leave the country. Don says if he's mobbed up, he could have bribed someone in the Russian Federation to issue him a second one under a different name. Or...he could have had a good forgery made under a different name. Either way, we can't know for sure."

"Well, that sucks."

Thompson stretched out in her swivel chair, rocking slowly from side to side. It had been a long day, and this was just another possible investigative lead that had gone south.

"I asked him to check on Hagopian," Donahue added, "and that reminds me. I need to go down to the lab and get his prints. Flynn wants a copy to send to his guy in Homeland Security."

"I can get 'em for you," Thompson said. "I'm tired of sitting around."

"You and me both. I think I'm going to get out of here a little early and go for a run. I need to clear my head and breathe in a little air that doesn't smell like rotten fish."

Thompson was about to snicker when Gibson came out of the Captain's office and walked hurriedly over to where they were sitting.

"What's up?" Donahue asked. She got to her feet. She could see the concern on his face.

"They just found a body up in the Hollywood Hills. I want the two of you to go up there and check it out."

Donahue knew that he wouldn't be asking them to take a new case, not when they were so deeply involved in the bombing and related homicides. So there had to be some other reason.

"You think it's related to our case?" she asked.

Gibson nodded. "Hollywood Homicide is handling it. The victim is a male, probably Russian. No ID, but they're saying he's got a lot of very stylized tattoos."

Donahue nodded. "You ready?" she said to Thompson.

"Let me make a few calls," and for Gibson's benefit, she added, "My kids. I need to set up a sitter."

Donahue opened her desk and removed her weapon which she quickly belted around her waist.

But while she was all business on the outside, her stomach was starting to churn.

Too many bodies. What the hell is going on?

*****

CHAPTER 41

October 29, 4:00 p.m.

Laurel Canyon runs from the San Fernando Valley into the city of Holly-wood, and unlike other nearby canyon neighborhoods, it has houses lining one side of the main street almost all the way up to Mulholland Drive, a street at the top of the mountain range that effectively separates the Valley from the West side of Los Angeles.

Several hundred yards from the intersection of Laurel and Mulholland, on the western side of Mulholland, was a small dirt turnout leading to a lot that was occasionally used as a lover's lane. The nearest nearby residence was almost a quarter of a mile away, and the area was full of waist high weeds, pine trees, and pull outs along the side of the road that sometimes capped a drop-off of more than a thousand feet.

It took Donahue and Thompson almost forty minutes fighting through traf-fic to make it from the PAB to the top of Laurel and Mulholland Drive. Traffic moved slowly through the canyon as a result of the closure of Mulholland and the obvious signs of police activity.

The area had been used as a body dumping ground in the past, so those dri-ving by assumed that the closure was the result of a fatal traffic accident or the discovery of a body. In this case, the latter had been the truth.

Donahue parked along the side of the road about fifty yards from the turnout. She and Thompson made their way on foot to the officer charged with logging in everyone who entered the restricted crime scene area. Once they'd complied with the sign-in requirements, they made their way to the lot where they could see a group of detectives from Hollywood who were gathered near the edge of the drop-off.

Donahue recognized the lead detective and walked directly over to where he was standing.

"Hey, Red," she said. "How you been?"

Johnny "Red" MacLean was a large man of Scottish heritage, with a thick head of red hair that was slowly turning gray. He looked over at Donahue and smiled.

"Jennifer D." He gave her a wink. "I was told you might be coming out here. How's it going?"

"You know, same old stuff, Red. This is my partner Shari Thompson."

MacLean gave Thompson a smile. "I hear you two picked up the bombing case."

"Unfortunately. We hear you may have a Russian victim?"

"Looks like it. We've taken prints, so hopefully, we'll know who he is in a couple of hours."

"No ID on the body?"

"Not yet."

She could see the body lying thirty feet away, covered by a white sheet.

"Cause of death?" Thompson asked.

MacLean held her glance. "Gunshot to the back of the head. You wanna take a look?"

"Yeah."

She and Thompson then followed him on a marked out path to a spot a few feet away from the corpse.

The body was lying in a clump of low weeds. There was soft dirt surrounding the immediate area, and small white numbered cards were set out to identify what was perceived to be possible evidence in the case.

"We've got some shoe prints and a tire tread design that we're going to cast once the crime scene techs arrive, so we'll have to do this carefully. Okay?"

Donahue nodded.

MacLean then led them over the last of the pathway to the body. He squatted down and peeled back the sheet where it covered the victim's face.

Both Donahue and Thompson were momentarily stunned.

"Is that Komarov?" Donahue asked, looking over at Thompson.

"No shit!" Thompson leaned in to get a better look. "It sure looks like him." She glanced over at Red MacLean. "Any chance I can get a look at the tattoos on his chest?"

"I can't really mess with the clothing until the Coroner's investigator gets here," he said, "but he's wearing a short-sleeved button down shirt, and you can see the ones on his arms and part of one on his upper chest.

He pulled the sheet farther down the body, exposing the victim from the waist up.

Thompson leaned over and looked at the arms, then studied what little was showing of the upper chest; a Russian church steeple coming off an onion dome.

"That's Komarov," Thompson said. "I'm sure of it."

MacLean looked up from his squatting position.

"So who is this Komarov guy?"

"He was our primary suspect in the bombing case," Donahue answered.

"*Really?*" MacLean stood up, then smiled. "Does that mean you're gonna take this one over?"

"Not a chance," Donahue said with a chuckle. "We're already looking at two to four other killings that might be related, so thanks, but no thanks. However, on the brighter side, I think this assures you a spot on our task force." She reached over and patted him on the arm. "Welcome aboard."

"Just what I need. A cluster-fuck case."

He asked for an overview, and Donahue gave him a quick version while Thompson notified Gibson by phone that Vlad Komarov appeared to be their murder victim.

When Donahue had finished her overview, MacLean simply shook his head.

"Hell of a mess, Jen. What more do you need to know about this one?"

"Any shell casings located?"

"No."

"You think he was killed up here?"

"Looks like it. There's a small puddle of blood behind the head, so I'd say it's likely that he was shot up here."

She looked around. "Did you locate a vehicle?"

"No again."

"So he rides up here with someone, gets out of the car, then takes a shot to the back of the head?"

"That's the most likely scenario. From the shoe prints in the dirt, it looks like only our victim and one other guy, so that scenario tends to make sense. However, there could have been others involved. Maybe a driver who didn't get out of the car."

MacLean looked down at Komarov's body.

"The victim looks like a guy who could handle himself, so if he weren't up here voluntarily, it would have taken two or more to get him to walk out here."

Donahue nodded ever so subtly. "He's not wearing a jacket, Red. It was cold last night, too."

"He might have taken it off when he got in the car," Red speculated. "Maybe the heater was on?"

"Any signs he was tied or taped up?"

"No, which is all the more reason to believe he was up here voluntarily with someone who used the opportunity to cap him from behind."

"Maybe it was a meet?"

"Maybe…"

"Who found the body?" she asked.

"A UPS driver, about an hour and a half ago. He pulled over in the turnout to organize some of his packages, and from that high-up seat of his, he was able to spot what looked to him like a body in the weeds."

"Did you check that out from his cab?" Donahue asked.

MacLean gave her a look that said...*how can you even ask such a ridiculous question*?

"Of course you did," she said not waiting for his answer. "Any neighbors hear a shot or anything going on?"

"Not that we know of. No one called it in. However, I've got uniformed guys checking out all the nearby residences, as well as those within view on the other side of the canyon, but unless someone comes up with a reliable eye witness, I won't hear anything directly. But I'll check out all the contact sheets later tonight when I get back to the station."

"You'll let me know if something pops up?"

He smiled. "You mean you're not going to hang out here with me until the scene is worked up?"

"Not a chance. I need a break. My brain is spinning, and I need a little time to process what we've got already."

"I've been there." He was looking past her, and she turned around to see that the crime scene team and the coroner's investigator had just arrived in their separate vehicles.

"In fact, I think Shari and I have seen enough, and with you in charge up here, I feel comfortable leaving the scene in your capable hands."

MacLean nodded. "Let me know if your Captain wants me on the task force."

"I will," she replied.

*****

The two women sat in silence in the car for most of the way back to the squad room. Both were deep in thought, trying to get their heads around this latest turn in their case.

Donahue was the first to break the silence.

"I'm completely stumped." She briefly looked over at Thompson. "It feels like we're no closer to solving our bombing case then we were when we first picked it up."

"I still think that Vlad was involved in the bombing," Thompson said. "He's the logical suspect... in fact, he's the only suspect we ever had."

"You think his death is related to all the others?"

"Don't you?"

"I don't know. I suppose it's possible, but the guy was a low life scum. He probably had enemies coming out of the woodwork."

"So then you're also thinking that maybe his death has nothing to do with our case or any of the others?"

Donahue shrugged. "I honestly don't know. Something's going on here, Shari, and all of these killings just have to be related."

"But that would be the crux of the problem, Jen. We still have no idea what the end game is, and until we do, how the hell are we ever going to be able to tie these things altogether?"

Donahue started thinking out loud.

"Who stands to profit from Komarov's death?"

"Maybe the guy at the agency. What's his name? Hag-something?"

"Martun Hagopian?"

"Yeah, that's it." Thompson shook her head. "He certainly seems to have profited from Petrovich's death."

Donahue suddenly brightened. "You may be on to something, Shari. We need to take a hard look him."

"I'm having dinner with Yuri tonight. Want me to fill him in and get his take on Hagopian?"

Donahue gave her a quick look.

"Moving kinda fast with him, aren't you?"

"It's just for fun, nothing serious."

Donahue didn't like seeing her friend go down this path, but she wasn't her partner's keeper, and if Shari wanted to set herself up *again* for a load of romantic grief, then so be it. The best way to screw up a friendship would be to start voicing an opinion that might force Shari to go into a defensive posture, and that was not at all what she wanted to do.

And besides, she'd never even met this guy, so she decided that she should probably just back off a bit and reserve an opinion, at least until she had a chance to meet him.

"Well, if you're gonna see him tonight, you might as well go ahead and pick his brain. See if he has any ideas about what might be going on or who we should focus on?"

"You suggesting a little pillow talk discussion?" Thompson said with a smile. She enjoyed making Donahue uncomfortable by talking openly about sex.

Donahue rolled her eyes.

"I don't mind taking one for the team," Thompson said.

"*Jesus, Shari, y*ou're incorrigible."

CHAPTER 42

October 29, 9:45 p.m.

Shari Thompson sat across the table for two from Yuri Pavienko who was just finishing an after-dinner cup of coffee. They were at a popular Beverly Hills restaurant called the *Cheesecake Factory*, an upscale chain restaurant that served large portions and decadent deserts. The lighting inside was dim, the atmosphere noisy and busy. All in all, it was decidedly unromantic.

They'd spent the past hour eating their meals while discussing such mundane subjects as the latest movies, the Clippers previous season, and the most interesting vacations they'd ever taken.

Shari was beginning to get a little bored with the conversation. It seemed completely shallow...and frankly, uninteresting. She had hoped he'd be slightly more forthcoming about his life, but whenever she tried to get him to open up, he would deflect her questions with a smile, then turn the conversation towards some insignificant topic, something she had no interest in.

It appeared as though they had virtually nothing in common, and she was beginning to realize that other than a possible roll in the hay with a good looking bad boy who carried a badge, there was little else about him to hold her interest.

She studied her watch. They'd gotten a late start, and her babysitter was only available until eleven, so it was highly unlikely that they were going to be getting together for sex this evening. Rather than waste what was left of their time together, she decided to bring up Vlad Komarov's murder to get his thoughts on who might possibly be involved?

She took a sip of her coffee, set down the cup, then slowly leaned back in her chair.

"Is there any talk on the streets about who might have pulled the trigger on Vlad Komarov?"

Yuri looked at her in disbelief.

"I'm sorry. Did you say Vlad Komarov?"

Shari held his stare. "You didn't know?"

"No! What happened? Is he okay?"

"Vlad's dead, Yuri." She shook her head, surprised by his reaction. "Someone shot him in the head up on Mulholland Drive."

There was a long pause, then, "When did this happen?"

"Sometime last night. When they found him, he was in full rigor, so the Coroner says he was killed sometime close to three or four a.m."

"He would have been a good informant." Yuri shook his head and wiped his mouth with his napkin, then threw it down on the table. "All those hours of trying to get him on board...what a fucking waste!"

"Yeah, well, we still need to sort out if he was involved in the bombing or any of the other killings."

"Good luck with that."

She had been taken aback by his initial response upon learning about Komarov's death, but his apparent dismissal of her efforts to investigate the case was starting to piss her off.

"Oh?" She didn't need to add *what do you mean by that?*

Yuri sensed the anger in her challenge and it surprised him.

"What I meant was that without him, and without any physical evidence from your search, it's going to be all but impossible to connect him to any of the crimes." He studied her face. "I didn't mean to offend you."

She produced a half-hearted smile.

"Look, I'm not offended, Yuri. Just a little disappointed. So far you haven't given us a whole lot of help with our case. I've asked you several times to help us out, but each time I do, you give me some bullshit line about you'll see what you can find out, but then you never get back to me."

He frowned. "I get back to you, Shari. I've told you everything I know." But when she didn't respond, he said, "What exactly are you asking about?"

"Okay. You remember when I sent you that copy of a piece of paper we found in Komarov's wallet when we took him into custody? The one with the Cyrillic writing on it? You were going to look it over and get right back to me with a translation."

He frowned again. "I guess I forgot to get back to you." He gave her an embarrassed smile. "There were three letters, followed by eight numbers. Off the top of my head, I think the letters were FCI. When I get back to the office tonight, I'll get the exact information to you. Okay?"

"So what does it mean?" she asked.

"I don't know. It could be anything. The initials could be for someone he's working with, for a name of some kind, or possibly a code of some type. The eight numbers...possibly a phone number, although I don't think so. The first two numbers were separated by a dash, which suggests that they might be an international calling code, but the six numbers that follow it are too few for a phone, so I really don't have any idea." He leaned forward in his chair.

"Was there anything else I failed to get back on?"

"Yeah. What's the word on the street about the bombing? There must be some intelligence floating around about who did it?"

"Nothing. Clay and I made the rounds of the clubs last night, but no one has any idea about who did it."

"So, what about the killing of Nika Kaminski? Is there anything at all about that?"

"Again, same answer. No one is even speculating about her death. In fact, no one I've talked to even knows her or anything about her."

Thompson shook her head. "I just don't get it, Yuri. You guys are supposed to be gathering intelligence on the Russian mob, but you don't seem to be able to come up with anything that can help us. All these murders in the Russian community and no one's talking? I find that hard to believe?"

"*All these murders*...what are you talking about? You've got a couple of dead prostitutes and a street pimp that could have pissed off any number of people." He leaned forward and pursed his lips. "Look, Shari. There are several hundred Russian gangsters in the greater LA area. They're into all kinds of rackets, and none of them are snitches. The only way to get information from these guys is to cultivate an informant, which is not easy to do. Komarov was my best shot in the last two years at getting someone within the organization."

He looked around the room, then lowered his voice. "I'm sorry I haven't uncovered anything to solve your case, but it takes a long time to develop good sources, and at the moment, I've got no one positioned on the inside who can give me the answers you want to hear."

He wiped his mouth with his napkin. "Besides, these killings you've been asking about…they might not be connected at all."

"What makes you say that?"

"Well, for one thing, someone might have discovered that Komarov was a possible informant. How that would be known, I don't know. But once the SB even thinks that someone is informing, his death warrant is signed."

"You think that's what happened to Vlad?"

"I don't know. But let me ask you this? How many people inside your unit know that I was working on Vlad?"

Thompson winced. Was he suggesting that they had a leak within the task force?

"I'm not pointing fingers," he said, "but once the cat is out of the bag, someone could innocently say something that gets overheard and just like that the secret is out."

He was right, of course. Maybe they had been a little careless with the number of people who knew about Yuri's efforts to recruit Komarov. Maybe his killing wasn't connected.

"Then again, maybe it's something else entirely. Who knows? And those two women who got killed? They were lovers, right? Well, you and I both know that cases like that usually involve a love triangle." His eyes narrowed. "If I were running your investigation, I'd be looking at which of them had an ex-girlfriend who might have harbored a jealous grudge."

She had been just about to mention that there were two more deaths that were seemingly connected to the Russian community; the robbery deaths of the husbands of two women who had used the same matchmaking agency. But when she put it that way, without any real proof, he would likely start laughing, countering her assertion by stating that just because someone is married to a Russian doesn't make the cases related, and that would really piss her off while accomplishing nothing. It wasn't that he was intentionally obstructing her investigation, he just didn't seem willing to acknowledge her role and skill as a homicide detective.

And to top it off, even more galling, was the fact that he just might be right.

She sighed. He was really a hot looking guy, but he seemed to be a tad short when it came to gray matter. He was just too easy going and too cavalier to care about doing the work in the trenches. He should be out there beating the bushes, trying to get leads to help her out. Someone had to know something, but apparently, he wasn't a real a go-getter, and berating him about it would likely do no good. No, she quickly decided that it was better to drop it now and move on to her newest request for help.

She locked eyes with him and held his stare.

"You may be right, Yuri. Maybe they aren't all connected. But let me ask you this. Have you come across a guy named Martun Hagopian?"

"Yeah, I did. I met him once at the club *Siberia*. Komarov introduced him to me. Why? You got something going on that guy?"

"Apparently he's working at *Trophy-Wife*, Milan Pavienko's dating agency. He seems to have taken Pavienko's place as the deal closer. What can you tell me about him?"

"At the risk of sounding like a broken record, not a lot. When Vlad Komarov introduced him to me, he said he was an old friend from *Dagestan*. He was going to help the guy get set up running a few girls or maybe selling coke or grass in some of the clubs. The guy was pretty ragged looking, so I can't imagine him fitting in with a high-end dating operation."

"He's cleaned up now," Thompson said, "and he's clearly working there in a management capacity." She sighed heavily. "So please, let me know if you come up with anything. With Komarov now out of the picture, Hagopian has risen to the top of our suspect heap."

Yuri leaned in and lowered his voice again. "I had my partner check him out with the FSB. You know who they are?"

Thompson was surprised. She didn't know that the LAPD had a source within the Russian Security Service and considering all the hoops that Donahue was going through to get information on Komarov, maybe Yuri or his partner could hook them up with their source to speed up the background process.

"I know who they are. So what'd you come up with?" she asked.

"He's got no record in Russia."

"Really? If the guy runs with Russian mobsters, I find it hard to believe that he doesn't have a beef somewhere?"

"Two things, Shari. First, he's supposedly from *The Republic of Dagestan.* That's in the North Caucasus region, and they may not be too good at sharing information with their counterparts back in Moscow. And secondly, the level of corruption among law enforcement officers in the Russian Federation is quite high. With money, you can often buy your way out of an arrest, even for very serious offenses."

"So we can't trust what they tell us?"

"Who knows?"

He could tell that she was getting ready to go, so he reached for the check, pulled out his wallet, and removed a few twenties to cover their tab.

"Thanks for dinner," she said, "and for the info about the FSB. I'll pass that on to my partner."

He reached over and put his hand on hers.

"Would you like to come back to my place for a while?"

Thompson smiled. "As enticing an offer as that is, I've got to turn it down. I promised my babysitter I'd be home by eleven, and if I leave now, I might just make it."

"Another time then," he said, getting to his feet.

He walked her out to the street and waited while one of the valets ran off in search of her car.

"Thanks again for dinner," she told him. "I had a nice time."

He leaned over and gave her a kiss.

"I'll give you a call tomorrow," he said. "Maybe we can get together some-time later this week?"

"If I can," she said.

Her car arrived, and after another kiss, he waited and watched while she disappeared in traffic before he took off down the street to a curbside meter where he'd left his undercover car.

CHAPTER 43

October 30, 10:00 am

Shari Thompson sat at her desk in the squad with a cup of coffee and a power bar. Her mother came over at the crack of dawn, so the kids were taken care of, and this enabled her to come in early again to get in a workout in the basement gym. What no one knew was that she had also stopped off for an early morning visit to the Coroner's Office where she left a little surprise for Dr. Annabel "the Cannibal" Corrander.

She had her desk phone up to her ear where it had been pressed for the last five minutes while someone was trying to track down Ulyana Chirkoff for her. Chirkoff was a professor of Russian languages at the University of Southern California. Thompson had gotten her office number by calling the University directly and asking for her by name.

"Good morning, Detective Thompson. Sorry you had to wait so long on hold. I was just finishing up one of my classes. How can I help you?"

"Thanks for taking my call, professor. I got your name from the FBI. They said you were an expert on all things Russian."

Chirkoff laughed. She was in her early fifties, a tall woman with unremarkable features; a full head of gray hair, and a personality that was dominated by a deep, resonating laugh and a quick sense of humor.

"Russian languages, customs, and food, but when it comes to Russian men, I'm certainly no expert."

Thompson smiled. Nice sense of humor. She liked her already.

"I've got some photographs of a Russian male who's adorned with tattoos, and I was wondering if you could look at them and maybe tell me what some or all of them mean?"

"I suppose I could," Chirkoff replied, "but while some have a universal meaning, others may be nothing more than the personal preference of the wearer or the lack of imagination on the part of the artist."

Thompson said, "If you give me your email address, I can send them over.

Are you near your computer."

"Sure. You've caught me at a good time." She gave Thompson her email address and Thompson, who had already scanned Komarov's booking photos into her computer, sent them as an attachment to Chirkoff's email address.

"Got 'em," said Chirkoff a few moments later. "Let's see what we've got."

She studied the photographs for an extended period.

"Any tattoo's on his lower body?" she asked.

"We never checked," said Thompson. The photos of his chest, arms and back were complete, but they'd neglected to check the rest of his body at the time of his initial arrest. She made a note to herself to get the body examined during the autopsy and have any other tattoo's photographed for her case file.

"Well, right off the bat I can tell you that this man is *Vor v Zakone.*"

"What does that mean?" Thompson asked.

Chirkoff chuckled. "I thought you'd never ask. You ready for a little history lesson?"

"Sure."

Thompson opened up a blank page on her computer and was already typing. Chirkoff said, "Organized crime has existed in Russia since the time of the czars. Mostly it was in the form of petty theft and burglary. But later, when the Soviet Union emerged from the czarist era, so did a band of criminals who called themselves the *Vor v Zakone,* or *Thieves in Law.* After the breakup of the Soviet Union in 1990, the Vor began to play an important role in the criminal hierarchy of Russia. They consider prison to be their true home. Their rules forbid members to cooperate with the authorities. Additionally, under the code of the Vor, the members must have no emotions; must forsake all family members; must have no wives or children; and they must never deny their *Vor v Zakone* status among others."

"And you can tell all this about this particular man from what, exactly?" said Thompson whose hands were flying across the keyboard.

"The eight-point stars on his shoulders. They signify *Otritsala.* That means that this man does not work for the administration of the prison, and he does not comply with their laws. Some experts also believe that it signifies the rank of a Captain in the mafia."

No shit!

Chirkoff scrolled through the photos that Thompson had sent her. "You're going to want to check his lower body and see if he's got tattoos down there."

"I'll do that first chance I get," she said.

Thompson sighed. She should have checked with an expert before her interview with Komarov. There was so much more she could have asked him if she hadn't been so ignorant about the Russian criminal culture.

"Prison tattoos are often seen as a rite of passage for the criminals," said Chirkoff. "Many are often tattooed before they are even sentenced to prison. In the Russian prison system, tattoos tell a prisoner's life story. Without tattoos, you do not exist. A lot of the tattoos have multiple meanings, but to the Vor, they tell the number of times a man has been incarcerated, where he's been, the crimes he's committed, his status, and more."

Thompson leaned back and stretched her tired fingers. She'd been typing like a crazy woman and needed a moment to refocus.

"So what about the rest of his tattoo's?" she asked.

"They tell his story," said Chirkoff. "For example, the cathedral with the onion-shaped cupolas? That may look like a religious tattoo, but the number of cupolas represents the number of times this man was incarcerated or the number of years in his sentence. In this case, because there's so many, I'd say he spent eight years in custody."

That liar said he did eight months in prison, thought Thompson. *He was playing me the whole time.*

Chirkoff continued. "The Madonna and Child on his back means he's been a thief since childhood, and the tiger? Now that's one you want to pay particular attention to. A tiger tattoo, often placed on the arms, neck or back, means that this member has harmed or killed a police officer, a prison guard, or other members of law enforcement."

Oh my God!

The tattoos were proving to be a coded rap sheet for these guys. She'd had no idea that the stylized artwork on Komarov's body had been so revealing. The man had certainly been dangerous and clearly connected to organized crime.

"What about the soldier on his stomach?" she asked.

"That's a Knight or sometimes referred to as a Crusader. It means that this man was known as a sadist, and it is often used to designate a prison enforcer."

Wow! But for the tattoos, they never would have known.

It occurred to her that Yuri had been less than candid when he'd told her that Komarov was just a low-level soldier, and while he might have done that to conceal the man's importance to him as a possible informant, it was one more mark against him as far as his level of cooperation with her investigation or his actual qualifications as an expert on Russian OC.

Now over the initial shock of the revelation of the meaning of the tiger, she said, "How about the bells on his back, professor? He told me that the ringing of the bells meant he'd found God or something like that."

Chirkoff laughed.

"He was handing you a load of horse manure. Bells usually mean that an inmate is willing to do his full sentence. That is usually signified by bells on one's hands or feet. But the ringing of two bells can often mean that the subject expects to serve a life sentence in prison."

There was a moment of silence while Chirkoff gathered her thoughts.

"I can't see him getting that tattoo unless he was already sentenced. Do you know much about his background, because I'm wondering if he had a life sentence somewhere? If so, was he released early, or did he escape?"

"I honestly don't know," Thompson said. This was coming too fast and there were too many unknowns.

What the hell were they dealing with?

"Then again, it may be that *'if he ever was to get a life sentence'* he would be prepared to serve it in its entirety."

Ambiguous, she thought, but nonetheless, it pointed out how completely antisocial this mobster really was.

"That's about all I can tell you now from these photographs," Chirkoff said. "If the man has additional tattoo's on his lower body, I might be able to tell you more."

"I'll be checking for that at the autopsy," Thompson said.

There was a momentary silence on the other end of the line.

"You mean he's dead?"

"Very dead," Thompson replied.

Chirkoff was silent again, then said, "I don't envy you, detective. Having to deal with these criminals. These mafia types are very dangerous people. When I told you about the Vor rules, I probably should have stressed how seriously these rules are taken. At last count, just before the fall of the Soviet Union, there were more than 8,000 known criminal organizations affiliated with the Vor, and these men take their oaths to the group very seriously. If you are investigating the Russian mafia, then you must watch your back. Most of these animals would have no compunction about killing you if you presented yourself as a threat."

Thompson sighed deeply. She was only now beginning to realize the seriousness of dealing with these individuals, and just how dangerous they really were.

"Thank you, professor, for your time, and more importantly, your information. I will be very careful when I deal with these people, and if it's okay with you, I'd like to be able to call you again if my partner or I have any further questions about the Vor or their tattoo's?"

"Call anytime," Chirkoff said. "You sound like a nice person. Please be careful."

*****

Donahue arrived at the squad room a little after ten. She went straight to her desk, locked up her gun, then sat in her chair and stared off into space.

Thompson stood up from her desk and leaned over the partition that separated their cubicles.

"Turns out that Vlad Komarov was heavily involved in the *Vor*," she said, but Donahue wasn't paying any attention.

Thompson noticed the apparent disinterest. "What's up?" she asked.

When Donahue turned to face her, Thompson could see that her eyes were welling up with tears.

"Let's go," she said to Donahue. "Room number two."

She marched Donahue out of the squad, through the hallway, and into the interview room.

When the door was closed, she said, "Okay, what's happened?"

Donahue sat down in a high back swivel chair and her head flopped back against the headrest.

"I got a call from my doctor this morning. The radiologist says I've got a lump in my right breast."

"Cancer?" Thompson hadn't meant to be so direct, but the word had just popped out.

"They don't know, yet. I'm scheduled for a biopsy at UCLA right after lunch."

"Oh, God, Jen!" Thompson didn't know what to say. "Is there a family history?"

Donahue shook her head.

"You're too young to have cancer. This is probably just a cyst or something like that."

Donahue had folded her arms across her chest. She started to cry.

Thompson got down on her knees and gave her a long hug.

"It's gonna be all right, Jen. You'll see. This is early detection, and if it turns out to be cancer, the chances of a cure are very high."

Donahue continued to sob, so Thompson let her cry it out.

"Want me to go over to UCLA with you?"

"No. I'll take care of it." She looked up and held Thompson's eyes. "It's just such a shock. I can't believe this is happening to me."

"I know, honey. I know. But like I said, it might be nothing at all. So don't make yourself sick worrying about something that might not be the case. Okay?"

Donahue smiled tightly and nodded.

"Thanks, Shari. I just needed to vent to someone."

"Anytime, Jen. You know I've got your back."

*****

Back in the squad room, Gibson walked over to Donahue's desk and asked,

"Are you all right?"

She swung her chair around and told him, "I'm fine."

"Okay, then. I've managed to get the autopsy for Vlad Komarov bumped up to one p.m., and since Shari did the last one, I'd like you to handle it."

"But—" she started.

"I'll cover it," Thompson said. She got out of her chair and joined them.

"You sure?" he said.

"Yeah, no problem. I've got it covered. Jen's already scheduled an interview for this afternoon, so I'll take the autopsy."

Gibson could tell that something was wrong, but it was clear that Donahue had no intention of taking him into her confidence. And with Thompson seemingly hellbent on covering the autopsy for her, he was in no position to question either one of them further.

"Okay," he said. You take the autopsy and Jen can do the interview."

He turned and walked back towards his cubicle.

Donahue looked over at Thompson and mouthed the word, "Thanks."

Thompson smiled, then returned to her computer screen to finish up some of her paperwork.

*****

Twenty minutes later, when Donahue's landline rang, she noted the caller ID, then picked it up.

"Hi, Don," she said. "I didn't expect to hear back from you so quickly."

"Hey, Jen," he began. "No news yet. Just wanted you to know that I forwarded the prints, booking photo, and description info on Komarov, as well as the prints on Hagopian to the Bureau representative with the FSB. It might take a few days, but the Bureau guy assures me that the FSB will be cooperative."

"That's great, Don! Thanks, but there's been an incident here. I was planning on calling you later this morning." She leaned back in her chair. "Vlad Komarov is dead. Shot to death early yesterday morning. They found his body up in the Hollywood Hills."

"Well, that's interesting. You think it might be connected to your bombing case?"

"It's certainly possible, but to be honest, we've had so many killings of Russian expats in the last few days that no one seems to know what the hell is going on."

"Well, if they are related, then it's likely one of two scenarios. A personal vendetta by someone who's got a serious grudge to avenge, in which case you might never figure things out, or internecine warfare of some kind, in which case you're going to need all the luck in the world to unravel who's involved and why."

"Gee, thanks," she said facetiously. "Your words of encouragement are most appreciated."

"Then again, it could be a combination of both, in which case, you're really screwed."

"Even better. So glad you called."

Flynn was laughing as she hung up the phone.

*****

Donahue cleared off her desk and made her preparations to go. She removed her gun from her desk and strapped it to her waist.

"You leaving?" Thompson asked from her side of the cubicle wall.

"I can't just sit around thinking about the test. I've got to get moving."

"I know what you mean." Thompson got to her feet and came around the partition. "If you need anything, or just want to talk, give me a call. Okay?"

"I will," Donahue said. The two women hugged each other.

"Thanks for taking the autopsy for me. I don't think I could've handled it today."

"I've got your back, remember?"

Donahue smiled sheepishly. "And I'm sorry we set you up for the Petrovich post. It seemed funny at the time, but I know it wasn't funny for you."

Thompson smiled.

"Well, since we're in a confessing mood, I suppose I should tell you that I'm the one who planted the fish."

Donahue's eyes went wide. "But how? You were with me having lunch when the fish got planted?"

Thompson shook her head. She couldn't resist a smile.

"I came in early before anyone got here. The fish was only half thawed so that it wouldn't start smelling until later in the day."

"You're genuinely pleased with yourself, aren't you?" Donahue said with a smile.

"Yes, I am. So, I guess…this makes us even?"

"Not a chance."

"Right. I didn't think so."

They hugged again, and Thompson watched as Donahue walked out of the squad room, a big smile on her face.

Gibson, who'd been watching them, walked over to Thompson's desk.

"You gonna tell me what's going on?"

"Nope."

He sighed. "Well, if it's serious or if there's something I can do to help her out, you'll let me know, right?"

"You'll be the first, Papa. I promise."

*****

Donahue arrived at the UCLA Medical Center twenty minutes before her appointment. She entered the basement corridor of the old hospital building, found her way to the reception desk, and after changing into a hospital gown, she was led to an examination room where a female radiologist explained in detail the procedure they were going to perform.

She was nervous about undergoing the biopsy, but the doctor calmed her nerves by telling her that because of her age and the lack of a history of breast cancer in her family, it was probably nothing more than a fibroadenoma, a non-malignant mass quite common in the general population. If that was the finding, it was likely that her doctor would recommend a *watch and wait* course of action, with removal or freezing of the mass only if it showed any signs of growing.

An ultrasound machine was used to locate the abnormal lump, and a needle was used to secure several tissue samples. Donahue felt no pain from the procedure, thanks to the injection of a numbing medication. Once the samples were taken, ice and pressure were applied to stop any bleeding and to minimize her bruising. A small bandage was applied to the site of the procedure, and within less than an hour, she found herself outside walking back to her car.

Once in the front seat, alone, Donahue had a good cry, more out of relief than from fear. In a day or two she would know the results, and until then, there was nothing she could do about her situation, so she made up her mind that she was not going to waste another single minute worrying about something she couldn't control.

To celebrate this newfound change of attitude, she stopped off on her way home at a *Baskin-Robbins* ice cream parlor and splurged on a three scoop banana split.

CHAPTER 44

October 31, 8:00 a.m.

Jennifer Donahue picked up the phone and punched in the number for Andrew Magarian at Internal Affairs.

She was seated at her desk, sipping on a latte from Starbucks and nibbling on a pastry she'd brought from home. As part of her reaction to the possibility of cancer, she had decided to embrace life and indulge herself with all the things she often passed up in order to keep herself fit and in top physical shape. Her reasoning was obscured by emotion, but completely understandable. If the results were good, she planned to get back on track, but she would never deprive herself again as completely as she had in the past.

If the results were bad, then what the hell difference did it make anyway?

When Magarian picked up the phone, he sounded sleepy.

"Yes."

"Lieutenant? It's Jennifer Donahue. Were you asleep?"

"Uh, huh,."

"Oh, God! I'm sorry. I can call back later—"

"I'm awake now," he mumbled. "What's happened?"

"I don't know if you heard, but Vlad Komarov was shot to death about twenty-eight hours ago. They found his body in a pullout off Mulholland in the Hollywood Hills."

Magarian, now wide awake, sat up in his bed.

"Any suspects?" he asked, now all business.

"Not really, but we're gonna take a long look at a guy named Martun Hagopian. He was an associate of Komarov's, and it turns out he took over for Petrovich, our bombing victim, at the *Trophy-Wife Agency*."

"No honor among thieves, eh?"

"There never is."

Magarian yawned.

"Sorry about that. We were up all night tailing Pavienko and Young."

"Oh? Anything interesting?"

"Not really. They hit a few clubs early in the evening, but they settled in at the barn at just after three and stayed in until their end of watch at six a.m."

"They work pretty long shifts," Donahue said.

"I think they're on the four-forty program," Magarian told her.

Donahue knew that the four-forty program allowed officers to work four ten hour days with three days off per week. It was a popular program, one that she wished would apply to her unit, but it was usually only available to patrol divisions and certain specialized units, like OCI, whose personnel were not needed on a daily basis.

"So what should we do about officer Young?" Magarian said. "We've turned up nothing unusual with our hit-or-miss surveillance, so I'd really like to haul him in and question him about his finances."

"I'd rather you didn't," Donahue said. "If he's doing something illegal with the Russians, I'd hate to risk tipping them off. Any chance you can hold off for a while until we have a better handle on Hagopian?"

"Yeah. Okay. Let me think about things." He yawned again. "I need to get some sleep, detective. I'll get back to you later."

Magarian rang off, and Donahue took another bite of pastry.

The squad began to fill up as the rest of the unit began to show up for their shifts. Thompson arrived, and when she set her purse down, she looked over at Donahue and said, "How'd it go?"

"It went," she replied.

Thompson knew that Donahue didn't want to talk about things in front of the others, so she said, "I'm gonna get a cup. Let's meet at the outdoor conference room in about five. Okay?"

Donahue nodded, and five minutes later, when she arrived in the courtyard in front of the building, she found Thompson seated on a small retaining wall, lighting up a cigarette.

"Want one?" Thompson said, offering her the pack.

"Really?"

Thompson suddenly realized that given what Donahue was going through, this particular type of self-destructive behavior was not only stupid but insensitive as well.

She crushed out the cigarette she'd just lit up, then walked over to a nearby trash can and threw away the rest of the pack.

When she returned to the wall, she said, "I'm sorry about that, Jen. I don't know what I was thinking. I started lighting up about a week ago. And, yeah, it's just dumb." She exhaled heavily. "Don't worry, I'm done with it."

She looked up and tried to smile while holding on to Donahue's disapproving glance.

"So?" she asked. "What'd they say?"

Donahue sighed. "They won't have the results until later today or tomorrow."

"What a load of crap!" said Thompson. "They should have looked at it right away instead of keeping us hanging like this."

Donahue smiled. The use of the word *us* said a lot about Thompson and how she was dealing with Donahue's situation.

"They've got lots of other people to get to first," Donahue said.

"Well, you're handling it well."

"I can't worry about what I can't control. Besides, according to the doctor, the odds of it being cancer are slim, so I'm just going to hold on to that thought and move on until they tell me something that changes my outlook."

"Fair enough." Thompson took a sip of her coffee. "I had dinner with Yuri last night."

"Oh? And did you guys hook up?"

"No. I made an excuse and went home."

"Why?" Donahue was secretly pleased. "What happened to 'taking one for the team'?"

"There's no spark with that guy. He's good looking, that's not the problem. It's just…" She paused for a moment to gather her thoughts. "There's nothing else about him that turns me on."

"What happened to 'nothing serious, just a little fun'?"

"I can do better than that."

Donahue smiled.

"Yes, you can."

When Thompson smiled back, Donahue said, "Did you talk with him about our case?"

"He told me a lot about the Russian mob. He said that he and his partner checked Komarov out with the FSB and that they said he had no record."

"What? They have a source in the FSB?"

"That's what he said."

"Dammit."

Donahue what thinking she'd imposed upon Flynn for a big deal favor and the OIC guys were already privy to what they wanted to know.

"Wish I'd known that before I asked Flynn to get involved."

"Can't hurt to have him get corroboration of what OIC was told. Yuri says there's a lot of corruption over there." She shrugged. "Just sayin'?"

"Yeah, you're right."

Donahue looked around. They were seated about thirty feet from the front door and a lot of officers and civilians were going in and out. She saw their Captain, Tommy Elwood, walk out of the building, headed in the direction of the nearest *Coffee Bean and Tea*. It was a daily routine for him, one you could almost set your watch by.

She turned back to Thompson. "Did you ask him about Hagopian?"

"Yeah, I did. He said he met him once at the *Siberia*. Vlad introduced him, and said he might let him run a few girls or some drugs out of the clubs, but other than that, there was nothing else."

"Well, at least we can connect Hagopian with Komarov. That says a lot right there."

Thompson nodded. "At the post yesterday, I got a chance to look at Komarov's tattoo's again."

She then proceeded to fill Donahue in on exactly what she'd learned about Vlad's tattoos from the professor at USC. It took almost five minutes, but she covered it all, including the steeples that indicated that he'd done eight years in prison, and the tiger that was indicative of a killing or attacking someone in law enforcement.

"The expert at USC told me the stars on his shoulders likely meant that he was a Captain in the Vor."

"No kidding? And to think we almost accepted what Vlad told you on face value. *'Made of Stardust?'* What a lying scumbag!"

"Can you believe that?" Thompson laughed. "Even I wasn't biting on that one."

"So he was a Captain in the Russian mob?"

"Apparently so, but don't forget, it's more a status thing with the Russians. It's not like the Italian mob which is highly structured."

"That may be, but it begs the question of why the FSB tells our OIC that Komarov has no prior record?" She locked eyes with Shari. "What does that tell us?"

"It means that we need to forget getting help from the FSB. The corruption in their system makes everything they tell us completely worthless."

Donahue shivered, stood up, and pulled her jacket tighter.

"You ready to go back up? I'm getting cold out here."

"Sure." Thompson got to her feet. "You feeling any residual effects from the biopsy?"

"A little bruising, that's all." Donahue reached out and put her hand on Thompson's arm. "I know they found this fucking tumor early, and I know it's probably not cancer, but what if it is, Shari? What if I have to lose one or both of my breasts?" Her eyes had started to tear up and she began to shake. "No man is gonna take a second look at me—"

Oh, God, thought Thompson. Jen's facade is finally cracking.

She put her arm around Donahue and held her tight.

"You said it yourself. It's too soon to worry about that, Jen." She pulled back and looked her in the eye, face to face.

"What's the worst that could happen? You know they found it early, so if worst comes to worst, you do an Angelina Jolie and get rid of the old ones." She gave her a smile. "You can get a new set of twins, any size you want. And if I know you, you'll settle for a set of bolt on's that will put those preteen boobies of yours to shame."

A look of shock quickly passed over Donahue's face, then she started to laugh.

Thompson, now aware that she had Donahue no longer feeling sorry for herself, started to jiggle her own breasts.

A uniformed officer who was entering the building flashed her a quick thumbs up.

"Men are so simple," she said to Donahue under her breath, her eyes now back on Jennifer's face. "You've got nothing to worry about, sweetie. With that face and smile, you'll have no trouble attracting men, and with a set like these, you'll be beating them off with a stick."

Donahue had tears pouring out of her eyes, but they were tears of laughter. It was just what she needed to get through the day.

*****

At four in the afternoon, back in the squad room, Elwood called for a meeting. Since Bengtson and Jackson were over at the courthouse on another case, he gathered Donahue, Thompson, and Gibson in his office to get an update on what was going on.

The three of them sat in hard chairs lined up in a row in front of Elwood's desk while Elwood leaned back in his leather office chair, feet up on his desk.

"I hear you attended the post?" he said to Thompson. "What'd the Coroner have to say?"

"Komarov died from a single gunshot to the back of the head. Dr. Corrander said there were no defensive wounds, and the slug they removed was a thirty-eight."

"Good enough for comparison?" Elwood asked.

"It bounced around in the skull," Thompson said. "Too damaged for comparison."

"So it might be a different killer? Unrelated to the shootings of the girls?"

"That's possible," said Donahue. "I've asked Don Flynn from the Secret Service to help us out, and he's sent the identifiers for Komarov and Hagopian to the FSB, so we'll see if anything turns up."

"Any other physical evidence from the scene of Komarov's killing?" Elwood asked.

"I heard from MacLean this morning," said Donahue. "They've got a shoe print and tire tread plaster casts, so that might help us out if we can identify a suspect or a vehicle."

"How about the neighbors?" Gibson asked.

"According to MacLean, the nearest neighbors were out of town that night, but one guy about a quarter mile away heard what sounded like a shot. But there was only one, and they get shots fired off up there every few months, so he didn't think too much about it."

"Not enough to call the police," said Elwood in disgust.

"Exactly," replied Donahue. "MacLean says they canvassed the area for CCTV, but no one up there had one set up that could catch vehicles out on the highway."

"Considering how many times people get killed or bodies get dumped up there, maybe the city should put some camera's in," said Thompson.

"That's too good a suggestion," Elwood replied. "Anything else?"

Thompson nodded.

"I had a conversation with a Professor of Russian Languages over at USC." She proceeded to tell them what Ulyana Chirkoff had said about Komarov's tattoo's and what they meant.

Elwood was livid. "How the hell does a guy like that get into this country?"

"Beats me," Thompson said.

"So what's next?"

"I want to bring the two widows in and talk to them again," said Donahue. "And I'd like to reinterview Irina Konstantinov, the owner of the dating service. I think she knows a lot more than she's saying."

"Okay. Get it done and keep me in the loop."

As they walked back towards their desks, Thompson said, "You wanna get some lunch?"

Donahue turned her down. "I'm not hungry. Nerves I think. Instead, I'm going to head on home and go over what we have so far." She looked around the room. "There are too many distractions here."

"Sounds like a plan. I'll hold the fort down while you're gone. I'm thinking of leaving early, too. It's Halloween, so I've got to get the boys ready to go trick-or-treating."

"You going to wear a costume?"

"Naw, I was slutty-girl last year and it didn't go over too well with the kids, so this year I'm going to go out as me."

"But costume or not, you're still slutty-girl," said Donahue with a smile.

Thompson shrugged. "What can I say? I'm just a good time girl who likes to... have a little fun."

Donahue laughed. "You cleaned that up, didn't you?"

"Takes one to know one."

"Have fun tonight, Shari. I'll see you tomorrow."

Thompson nodded, then lowered her voice. "You will let me know if you hear anything about the results?"

"I will."

"Good." said Thompson, then almost as an afterthought, "By the way, if you hear anything about Annabel the Cannibal finding a fish in her office, don't mention my name. Okay?"

"You didn't?" Donahue couldn't stop smiling.

"That's right. *I didn't.*"

Thompson gave her a wink.

Donahue headed for home thinking how lucky she was to have Shari Thompson for a friend.

CHAPTER 45

October 31, 6:00 p.m.

Jennifer Donahue stepped out of the shower, dried off, put on a robe, and walked into the kitchen of her triplex unit. She still had not received any word from her doctor, so she'd been doing what she usually did when she wanted to shut things out of her mind. She went for a run, a technique she'd developed over the years to rid her mind of the horrors of the job. She had a course blocked out, just over five miles, and she managed to run it in under forty minutes.

She started a pot of water for the capellini, retrieved a left over roasted chicken breast from the refrigerator, and was just about to fix herself a glass of merlot when her cell phone rang. She scrambled to find her purse, thinking it might be the doctor, but when she finally retrieved it, she discovered it was Don Flynn on the line.

"Hi, Don," she said. "Happy Halloween. You're working late?"

"I was at home, watching a hockey game with Cami and the boys when I got a call from my contact with the FSB. "

Donahue sat down at her kitchen table. "Let me guess. Vlad Komarov has no record."

"How'd you know?" he asked.

"'Cause it turns out our OIC intelligence division previously ran him with one of their contacts at FSB. In fairness, I just learned about that, so I didn't have a chance to pass that on to you."

"Did anyone at your OIC happen to figure out why he had no record?"

"Not so far as I know, but it does seem a little weird, considering his connection to the Vor."

"It turns out, based on the prints you sent me, that Vlad Komarov is really a guy named *Anton Sorokin*. The FSB says he's got an extensive record, and they've sent me their equivalent of a rap sheet which the FBI is working to translate now."

"That could explain how he got into the country. The passport he had as Komarov must be a forgery."

"Maybe not," Flynn said. "The Bureau says the Vor have people like wives or girlfriends working in their passport office. If you have the passport, we'd like to see it, but likely it's one that was actually physically issued by the Russian government, even though it's under an alias."

"Is this a big problem?" Donahue asked.

"I suspect it goes on more than they're willing to admit."

"So once we get his rap sheet translated, we'll know about his prison record, but what about his background? I'd like to know where he comes from and stuff like that?"

"I've been told they have a file on him which our guy at the Bureau has requested, but we'll just have to wait and see if they're gonna turn it over to us."

"Should we let them know that he's deceased?"

"I wouldn't," Flynn advised. "They might decide it doesn't matter and close down our inquiry if they know he's dead."

Donahue was okay with that decision. Flynn was obviously more knowledgeable about dealing with foreign intelligence services. She would be guided by his recommendation.

"Any word on Hagopian?" she asked.

"Not yet." He started to laugh. "My guy explained to me that the Russians are consummate *apparatchiks* when it comes to dealing with the West. They are by-the-book detail men, and if the clock says it's quitting time, they quit, no overtime, and my guess would be that it was time to punch out before they had a chance to run Hagopian. So I wouldn't think we'd hear anything until sometime later, hopefully tomorrow."

"Well, I appreciate you're getting back to me, Don. It's pretty clear you're not an *apparatchik.*"

Flynn chuckled. "Actually, technically, they'd call me a *nomenklatura.*"

"A what?"

"A *nomenklatura* is someone who holds a key administrative position in government."

"You'll have to put that after your name on your business card," she said.

CHAPTER 46

November 1,   9:45 am

The squad room was a beehive of activity as Donahue and Thompson arrived with Irina Konstantinov in tow. Irina had not been happy to see them, especially at nine a.m. which was the start of the workday at her office, but given the insistence of the detectives, and the prospect of being booked as an aider and abetter in a homicide, Irina felt she had no choice. An arrest like that, even if she was later released—which Irina was sure she would be—could spell the end of the agency and her livelihood. So as much as she resented their rather forceful persuasion, she accompanied them to the PAB without any further objection.

Five minutes before Donahue and Thompson arrived, Bengtson and Jackson showed up with Katya Ivanova Katz, the widow of Philip Katz. To keep her from seeing any of the other arrivals, they parked her in an interview room, provided her with coffee and a pastry from a nearby Japanese bakery, and they gave her a copy of the *Los Angeles Times* to keep her occupied until Donahue and Thompson were ready to do their interview.

Shortly after Irina was guided into an interview room, Mitzi Roberts poked her head in and gave Donahue a thumbs-up which signified that she and Gibson had arrived with Maryna Dragnov Baker, the widow of William Baker.

"Thanks, Mitz," Donahue said. "Put her in Room 3, and get her some coffee and a paper. Tell her we'll get to her as soon as we can."

Roberts nodded and left the room while Donahue took a seat next to Thompson, directly across the table from Irina.

"Tell us about Martun Hagopian," Donahue said.

Irina's eyes went wide.

"We understand that he recently started working for you?" said Thompson. It was a calculated guess, based solely on Jackson's undercover visit, but Irina had no clue as to the source of their information.

"He started working for me about a week ago," she said, looking down at the table. "He handles the male clientele."

"What's his connection to Vlad Komarov?" Thompson asked.

Irina looked from one to the other. "I told you before, I don't know that person."

Thompson rolled her eyes.

"Irina, you do realize that we're taping this conversation. Right?" Then, off Irina's worried look, "And lying to us during the course of a homicide investigation is felony obstruction of justice. Are you aware of that?"

Irina didn't answer. She suddenly felt trapped and didn't know what to do.

"Shari," said Donahue in a soothing voice. She was sliding into the role of good cop, a role she'd played many times before. "I'm sure Irina was just confused. She's not trying to obstruct our investigation. She's just afraid of these people." She looked directly at Irina who caught her glance.

"Is that right, Irina?" Thompson said.

Irina nodded, and both Donahue and Thompson now smiled inwardly. Irina had cracked; it would now be all downhill.

"Komarov was pressuring Milan to turn over a share of the business, wasn't he?" Donahue said.

Irina sighed. Her hands were clutched together on the table, and she was squeezing them so tightly that her knuckles were white from the lack of blood flow.

"I didn't want to say anything because he's a very dangerous man."

"Did he threaten Milan?" Thompson asked.

"He wanted fifty-percent of the business. Milan told him no, and a few days later, Milan was dead." Her eyes flitted from one to the other. "He has to be the one who killed Milan. He has to be."

Donahue was silently nodding her assent.

"So when he came to see me at my house about a week or so ago, I kept my mouth shut and listened to what he had to say."

"What did he say, Irina?" Thompson asked.

"He told me he was my new partner. He said that Milan owed him money, so he was entitled to a share of the business. He said he'd keep the competition at bay and would be responsible for supplying the agency with qualified women."

"Did Milan borrow money from him?" Donahue asked.

Irina shook her head.

"Milan didn't borrow any money from him. I know that for sure. He had a lot of money saved up which he used to get our partnership started." Irina sniffed. "Komarov was lying when he said that Milan owed him money. I know that for sure, but what could I do?"

Thompson looked over at Donahue, who asked, "What was Komarov getting in return?"

"He said our partnership would be sixty-forty. He'd take fifty for himself, I'd get forty, and *his* partner that pig Hagopian was going to get the ten percent since he'd be taking over some of my duties in the office."

"So Hagopian was his partner?"

Irina looked from one to the other. "That's what he said."

"And you were okay with that kind of a split?" Thompson asked.

"What choice did I have?" Irina's eyes were unwavering. "I knew what would happen if I said no." She started to tear up.

"You could have come to us," Thompson chided.

"And why would I do that?" Irina had said it with a challenge in her voice. "You people didn't exactly protect Milan when he first came to you with what was going on."

Donahue nodded. She had a point.

"By the time he came to us, it was too late," she said, "but it won't be the same for you."

Irina rolled her eyes. "Words are cheap."

"So what's the situation now?" Thompson asked.

"What do you mean?"

"I'm talking about Hagopian? Does he get the full sixty percent?"

Irina looked confused, and Donahue realized that she didn't know that Komarov was dead.

She leaned forward in her chair.

"Vlad Komarov was killed four days ago."

Irina was unable to hide the surprise on her face, but the moment quickly passed and a small smile suddenly appeared.

"He's dead?" she asked as if she couldn't believe what she was hearing.

"That's right. Did Martun say anything about it to you?"

"I haven't seen him for the last few days." She slid her folded hands from the table into her lap. Her eyes went downward. "He's been slowly taking over the office, so I don't like to go in there if I don't have to."

Her momentary elation at hearing the news of Komarov's demise suddenly changed, and a look of fear replaced it.

"What's the matter?" Thompson asked.

"What's going to happen now?"

Thompson reached out and touched her hand, a gesture designed to comfort her.

"We'll track down whoever is doing all this killing—"

"Not that," Irina said. "I mean Hagopian. How do I deal with him?"

Good question thought Donahue, and she quickly decided that it wasn't likely that Hagopian would simply go away. In fact, based on the way these mobsters seemed to work, it was almost a certainty that Hagopian would move up the food chain by assuming Komarov's role as well as his share. This wouldn't bode well for Irina, for it was very likely that once he got the hang of things, he would certainly force her out, one way or another.

Donahue thought that they might have enough for an extortion case, but that was gonna have to wait. They had too much on their plate already, so Irina's mess would just have to go on for a while longer.

"Tell you what, Irina. Once we get a little time, we'll see what we can do about Mr. Hagopian. But for the moment, you just sit tight in here. We have to talk to a couple of other people, then we'll be back, and if we have no more questions, we'll get you home."

She and Thompson got to their feet.

"Would you like another cup of coffee?" Thompson asked.

Irina shook her head. "I just want this nightmare to be over."

*****

"Got a few minutes, Jen?" Mitzi Roberts asked. They were standing in the hallway outside the interview rooms.

"I'll get a cup of coffee," Thompson said. She wandered off.

"I did the financial workup on Katya Katz, like you asked," Roberts said, "and I've discovered something important."

"Oh? Let's go over to the conference room." A few minutes later they were seated at a large oblong table.

Roberts opened up a file.

"I got a credit report on her and discovered where she does her banking. I served her branch with a telephonic warrant, and with the assistance of a contact of mine at the bank's Corporate Security office, I managed to get a computerized printout of her savings and checking accounts."

Roberts laid a several printed pages on the table in front of Donahue.

"She received a one million dollar check from her insurance company that she deposited directly into her savings account."

Donahue looked up from the page at Roberts. "That was the amount of the life insurance policy her husband took out. Right?"

"That's right, but check this out. Since the date of that deposit, she's made four separate withdrawals of one hundred thousand dollars from the savings account. Equal withdrawals spread out over a four-month period."

"One withdrawal a month?" asked Donahue.

"Correct. And here's the interesting part. All four checks were made out to *SB Trucking.*" She looked over at Donahue. "Wasn't that the name on that warehouse we searched when we were looking for explosives linking Komarov to the bombing?"

Donahue's eyes went wide.

"No kidding?" Her mind was spinning. While she had no idea what it meant, it seemed to be a connection between Komarov and some of the money that came from the insurance policy paid out after the murder of Philip Katz.

Donahue looked up from the bank printout. "You think that Katya was being blackmailed or extorted by Komarov?"

"That seems the most logical explanation," Roberts replied.

"Good point." Donahue took the bank printouts from Roberts and studied them carefully.

"Can I hang on to these, Mitz?"

"Of course."

"Any information on her total financial worth?"

"Not yet," said Roberts, "but I might be able to dig up more a little later."

"Stay on it."

"You gonna talk with her about it?"

"Darn right I am."

*****

Out in the hallway, Donahue briefed Thompson and Roberts on what she had learned from Don Flynn about Komarov's true identity. The two detectives could only shake their heads in disbelief.

"Anton Sorokin?" Thompson frowned. "Do we know for sure that's his real name?"

"That's who the FSB says he is," Donahue replied. "This whole thing reminds me of the Russian *Matryoshka dolls*."

"*Matryoshka?*" Thompson asked.

"You know, those painted wooden nesting dolls. You open one up, and there's another one inside; then another one...and you keep on going until they get really tiny."

"Nice analogy, Jen," Thompson said. "So we keep digging deeper with all of these people until we know exactly who we're dealing with."

"This could explain why I didn't get any hits when I tried to get background on Hagopian," Roberts said.

"It could explain a lot." Donahue agreed. She gave Roberts a smile. "I'll let you know what Don Flynn has to say when he hears back from the FSB, but I'll bet you're right."

While Roberts took off to head for the room where a monitor had been set up to record in real time the full interview with Katya Katz, Donahue filled Thompson in on the cash withdrawals that Katya had made from the payout she received from the insurance company.

"What the hell?" Thompson said. "You think it's blackmail?"

Donahue shrugged. "Maybe she paid to have him killed. Let's see what she has to say."

They entered the room and found Katya in a metal chair with her head and arms resting on the table. She sat up quickly as they took the two seats that faced her.

"Hello Katya," said Donahue. "Thanks for coming down here to talk to us."

Katya nodded nonchalantly. She hadn't wanted to talk to the detectives, a natural reluctance brought about by her ingrained distrust of authority during her childhood in Moscow and her dealings with the Los Angeles police during her time in the life.

"Since the last time we talked, we've learned a lot about our case and we've uncovered a few things about you that need to be clarified."

She now had Katya's complete attention.

"You've been writing some interesting checks," Thompson said, holding Katya's stare with her own. "Why don't you start by telling us what's going on?"

Katya's face revealed confusion. She believed she knew what checks the detective was talking about, but how to explain them without creating more problems for herself was her dominant thought.

"No response?" Thompson looked over at Donahue. "Maybe she thinks we're talking about her checks to the supermarket or the dry cleaners?"

Donahue shook her head.

"I think she knows exactly what checks we're talking about. *SB Trucking*. I bet that rings a few bells?"

For her part, Katya was completely stunned. She couldn't imagine how they learned about the checks. She was sure that Komarov would never say anything to the police, but somehow they knew, and it was pretty clear that they were not going to let her go without getting some answers.

"I'll ask you again, Katya," said Thompson. "What's going on with the checks?"

Katya bit her lip. Her arms were tight against her chest, and she hugged herself while she tried to muster up a plausible answer.

As the silence stretched on, Donahue was losing patience.

"Listen, Katya. We know about the four checks totaling four hundred thousand dollars, and we are aware you wrote them to SB Trucking, which was Vlad Komarov's phony company." She leaned forward in her chair. "Now, I'm sure there can be several explanations for giving Komarov that much money, but the only one that makes any sense to us is that you paid Komarov to kill your husband so that you could collect the insurance money."

She let her statement settle in for a moment, then noticed that tears had formed in the corners of Katya's eyes.

"Did you pay him to kill your husband?" Thompson asked.

Katya vehemently shook her head. "I loved my husband. I had nothing to do with his death."

"Then what's going on?" Donahue softened her voice. "Why did you give him so much money?"

Katya knew that she was cornered. She had no choice. They knew too much. She'd have to tell them.

She sighed heavily.

"After my husband's death, before the funeral, Komarov paid me a visit. He made a point of letting me know that he was from the Vor. He said that they were there to collect a share of my good fortune."

She looked from one to the other.

"*My good fortune*? Can you imagine that? My husband was dead, and he called it 'my good fortune.'"

She started to cry, and Thompson was about to comfort her, but Donahue stopped her with a small shake of her head. She was giving them what they needed to know, and Donahue felt this was not the right moment for them to interrupt.

A few moments later, Katya resumed speaking.

"He told me that his share was forty percent. He wanted one hundred thousand in four monthly payments. When I tried to protest, he informed me that I was lucky that he was feeling generous and allowing me to keep the rest."

She paused a moment, and Donahue had the feeling that she was reliving the conversation.

"He warned me that if I didn't do exactly what he said, I would be joining my husband in the ground."

Donahue sighed. Katya was describing an extortion under threat of death, but she still wasn't convinced that Katya was telling them the truth. And even though she'd passed the polygraph that was given to her during the initial investigation, she might have found a way to beat it with drugs. It was still very possible that she contracted out the killing of her husband to Komarov or someone else, in which case the payouts might be part of the deal or even the core of the blackmail.

"Did you have anything to do with your husband's death?" Donahue asked.

"Absolutely not!" Katya was adamant in her denial. "I loved my husband. He's the only man who ever treated me as a person and not an object." She held Donahue's stare without blinking. "I have no idea who killed my husband or why, but if I did, I'd kill them myself."

"Do you think Vlad was involved in the killing?" Thompson asked.

Katya shifted her eyes to Thompson and nodded.

"He knew about the insurance before my husband was even buried." Her eyes narrowed. "You tell me? How did he know?"

Thompson looked over at Donahue.

"Someone at the agency might have told him about the insurance," Donahue said to Thompson.

"You thinking Petrovich?"

"Possibly? Or it could have been a one-off remark."

Donahue returned her attention to Katya. "Why didn't you come directly to the police?"

"You don't know these people. They're *Vor*. Do you know what that means?"

"We're familiar with the Vor."

"Do you know how they work?"

When Donahue didn't answer, Katya said, "They'll make a demand, and if you don't do what they say, they'll kill your family, your friends...anyone you care about. And if you still resist, they'll kill you slowly and painfully." She shifted her glance to Thompson. "There's nowhere to run. They're everywhere, and killing means nothing to them."

Donahue leaned forward.

"We're gonna need you to take a polygraph examination. Do you know what that is?"

"Of course," she said. "I took one before. Didn't they tell you that?"

"Will you take another one today?" Thompson asked.

"Yes. I wasn't involved in my husband's death, so I have nothing to fear."

Donahue and Thompson got to their feet and told her to sit tight while they arranged for the poly. Then they left the room where they were immediately joined by Mitzi in the hallway.

"You believe her?" Thompson asked.

"For the moment," said Donahue. "She doesn't seem to know that Komarov is dead, so that gives her a bit more credibility. What we need to do now is talk to Maryna. We need to determine if she was approached by Vlad Komarov or anyone else?"

She turned to Roberts. "Can you get a poly set up for Katya?"

Roberts nodded.

"And get a blood sample from her, too. I want to make sure that if she passes the poly that she isn't using drugs to beat the test."

"Good idea," said Roberts. "And just so you know, I put in a call to Maryna's bank. I've asked them to pull her records. It's completely off the books, a favor from a friend, but I'll see if she can speed up the process."

Roberts quickly walked off to arrange for the blood sample to be taken and for the polygraph to be given to Katya while Donahue and Thompson found their way into the interview room where Maryna was cooling her heels at a small metal table.

"Hello, Maryna," said Donahue. "Thanks for your patience."

They took seats at the table across from her. Donahue introduced herself and Thompson, then said, "We've learned a few things this week that we want to talk to you about."

Maryna looked from one to the other.

"Did you find out who killed my husband?"

"No, but we learned that a man named Vladimir Komarov might be involved. Do you know Mr. Komarov?

"No. I have no idea who that is," but she looked away when she spoke, a telltale sign that she was lying.

"Mr. Komarov was connected to the Trophy-Wife Agency," Thompson prodded. "Does that ring any bells?"

Maryna shook her head. "I never met such a person."

This was going nowhere fast, so Donahue decided to cut to the chase.

"We're pulling all of your financial records, Maryna. We want to see if you've turned any of the insurance money over to Mr. Komarov."

When a surprised look appeared on her face, Donahue knew she had her. She said, "Did he have you make the checks out to SB Trucking?"

Maryna looked over at Thompson, then back at Donahue. She was clearly rattled, and from all indications, they appeared to have backed her into a corner.

"Now's your chance to tell us your side of it, Maryna," Thompson said, "but if you don't tell us the truth, you're going to make us believe you had something to do with the death of your husband."

Maryna's eyes went wide.

"But I'm not involved in his murder. I loved my husband."

"I'm sure you loved him," Donahue said softly, "but we need you to tell us the truth about your dealings with Komarov."

She folded her arms across her chest, then leaned back gently in her chair.

"This is your last chance, Maryna. Either you tell us what's going on right now or I'll charge you with conspiracy relating to the murder of your husband. Your choice, but you need to do it right now."

Maryna slowly shook her head, then closed her eyes tightly as she exhaled deeply.

"Komarov came to see me after my husband died. He knew about the insurance, and he demanded most of it."

"How did he know about the insurance?" Thompson asked.

"I don't know, but he did."

For the next five minutes, she described a meeting that was eerily similar to the one that Katya had experienced. Threats were made to her and her family back in Russia, and in the end, she agreed to give him the money in exchange for her life. He'd used his connection to the Vor to persuade her, and she'd made out the checks, four of them, for one hundred and twenty-five thousand dollars each.

"This is important, Maryna. Who knew about the life insurance policy?"

"I don't know. I didn't tell anyone, and William would have no reason to say anything to anyone, except maybe to his accountant or his lawyer."

"His lawyer?" Thompson asked.

"The one who handles his will and estate planning."

"What about the people who sold him the policy?"

"I don't know anything about that. Everything went through Mr. Petrovich's friend."

"Do you know the name of that friend?" Donahue asked.

"Mr. Grushik," she said with a nod. "He worked for the insurance company, but he wasn't a sales agent. He referred us to someone else, but I don't know the name. If you look at the policy, it should list the name of the agent who sold it to us."

"Grushik?" Thompson turned to Donahue. "Are you thinkin' what I'm thinkin'?"

Donahue nodded. She returned her attention to Maryna.

"Did Irina Konstantinov have anything to do with the policy?"

"Not that I know. Is there some connection between that damn policy and my husband's death?"

"Are you willing to take a polygraph about all of this, Maryna?" said Donahue.

"What's that?" she asked.

"A lie detector test."

"I'm not lying," she replied.

Donahue got to her feet, followed by Thompson.

"Stay here," she said to Maryna. "We'll set up the test, and then we'll take you home."

*****

Once they were out in the hallway, Donahue grabbed Thompson's arm.

"I think I finally figured this out."

"Way ahead of you, girl," said Thompson. She couldn't keep the smile off her face. "Petrovich and Grushik were pairing these Russian women with men who could afford to buy healthy life insurance policies."

Donahue smiled. "They must have enlisted Vlad Komarov to kill the husbands, then had him put pressure on the widows to fork over the lion's share of the payout."

Thompson shook her head. "But how are we gonna prove it, Jen? With Komarov and Petrovich dead, all we've got is a theory that may or may not lead back to Grushik."

Donahue sighed. "You saying Grushik might not have known what was going on?"

"All we know is that Grushik connected the two victims with policy agents who sold them the policies, but that doesn't prove that he was aware of what Petrovich and Komarov were up to? For that matter, we don't even know for sure that Komarov did the killings. *Hell!* Maybe Komarov got news of the deaths from Petrovich and acted all on his own. Or maybe Grushik was nothing more than an innocent conduit for selling them policies."

Donahue shrugged. "But we know from Nika's supervisor, Leigh Cherlina, that Nika discovered a connection between the girls, the agency, and the deaths of their husbands, and that she supposedly brought her concerns directly to Grushik."

"So?"

"*So*...he told us she never said anything about that to him, which means that he's lying."

"Does it? Nika can't say whether she actually told him or not, Jen. Maybe she got cold feet and never brought it up?"

"No way, Shari. I'm not buyin' it. If she didn't let him know, then why the hell would someone want Nika dead? Her killing has to be related to what she knew."

"For what it's worth, I agree with you, Jen, but by playing the devil's advocate, I think it's pretty obvious that we're gonna have a problem trying to prove that all these people were involved."

"That's why we're gonna approach this very carefully."

Donahue looked around briefly, then made a decision. "Let's go back and talk to Irina. I want to know what she knows about the insurance."

They returned to the interview room where Irina was still waiting.

"What's taking so long?" she said with a frown. "I want to go home."

"The examiner is setting the polygraph up now," Thompson told her, "but we need to clarify a few more things with you."

The two detectives took seats at the table.

"You haven't been completely honest with us," Thompson began.

Donahue leaned forward. "We need to know right now about the life insurance policies that Milan arranged for some of your clients as a wedding present."

"Sure," Irina said with a nod. "What do you want to know?"

"Who was involved? How was it set up?"

Irina looked from one to the other.

"Milan became friends with one of our former clients, an executive with an insurance company here in Los Angeles. His name is Nicholi Grushik. Nicholi told Milan that he could arrange for our clients to get life insurance at preferred rates, so Milan thought we could offer to set our clients up with policies that would provide protection to our girls since the men tended to be much older than the women they were going to marry." She flashed Donahue a tight smile. "The clients got protection at preferred rates, and we got the good will of having helped them arrange for it. Everybody was happy."

"What did Milan get out of this?" Thompson asked. "Was he getting some kind of a finder's fee for arranging a meeting between the clients and the insurance agents?"

"Not that I'm aware of," she answered. She locked eyes with Thompson. "I know it might sound like there could have been better gifts we could have given to our clients for using our service to find their love match, but as I think I told you before, we're dealing with women from Eastern Europe. The chief concern of these young women is security. They just want to know that they're going to be taken care of by someone who really loves them, so what better way for a man to show his love than to provide his beloved with a measure of security for after he's gone?"

Donahue locked eyes with Irina. "Are you aware that several of your clients have passed away since their marriages?"

Irina nodded. "I know of one case. I believe the husband died in some kind of an accident while on a trip to Europe. Milan was very saddened when he heard about it, but at the same time, he said he was proud that he had a part in arranging for the husband to secure the kind of coverage that was going to protect his wife's future."

"How many of your clients took out policies under the guidance of Milan and his contact at the insurance company?"

"I have no idea. I've never been involved in that aspect of the business." She smiled nervously. "I know nothing about insurance, and all of my focus at the time was on recruiting the male clients who become our paying customers."

"How well do you know Mr. Grushik?" Thompson asked.

"Not very well. He came to us as a client several years ago, but he didn't fall in love with any of the women, so after his contract with us was up, I really had no further connection with him."

"And Milan? Did he keep up the friendship?"

"So far as I know, he did," she said with a nod of her head. "I have the feeling that Milan occasionally set him up with some of the newer girls, but I didn't say anything. Mr. Grushik was a good client when he was with us, and because Milan liked him, I didn't feel it was anything to worry about."

She folded her hands in her lap when she realized that both of the detectives were studying her.

"I'm confused," Irina said. "What does the insurance have to do with your investigation?"

"Maybe nothing," Donahue said quickly. "We're just trying to cover all the bases."

Donahue leaned back in her chair. "Before we put you on the poly, Irina, I think it's time you leveled with us about Komarov's connection with Milan."

Thompson said, "He didn't just show up out of nowhere a few days before Milan's death, so why don't you just level with us about what was going on between the two of them?"

Irina sighed, no longer able to find the strength to continue lying. She looked from one to the other.

"Before he went to the police, Milan told me that he met Komarov well over a year ago at a nightclub called *Siberia* in Hollywood. He was recruiting young women for our agency, and Komarov befriended him. Milan thought he might be a part owner of the club, so he offered him a finders fee for referring the right women to our site."

"By *'right women'* are you referring to prostitutes?" Thompson asked.

"No, they were supposed to be young professionals who were truly interested in marriage and family."

"How did this arrangement work?" Thompson asked.

"It was free for the girls, the only requirement for them was to actually agree to go out on a date with the men who were directed to call them. If things worked out, and a relationship blossomed, then everyone was happy. The girls were professionally photographed, they filled out a brief questionnaire, then went on with their lives until they got a call and went out on a date." She looked over at Thompson. "Of course, the men paid us for these introductions. That's how we made our profit."

"Go on," Donahue urged her. "What happened next?"

Irina held her stare.

"He said that the arrangement worked well for about six months, but after that, everything changed. Komarov approached him socially and asked him a lot of questions about our business. Milan was apparently intoxicated, and he told him a great deal about our financial situation. A few weeks later, Komarov approached him again and said he wanted to invest in our agency. He offered Milan a hundred thousand dollars for a partnership share. Milan, of course, turned him down."

"Hold on for a second," Donahue said. "Was your business having cash flow problems at that time?"

"Not at all. In fact, we were doing quite well."

"Then why would Komarov think that Milan would be agreeable to selling him a share of the business?"

"I asked Milan about that, and he told me that Komarov was a drug dealer who invested his money in clubs. He thinks he was looking for a business that would enable him to launder some of his illegal profits, so when he mistakenly told him about how well we were doing, he unwittingly opened the door to the offer."

"Is that when he went to the police?" Thompson asked.

"No, he said that Komarov seemed to back off, at least, until that other bastard showed up." Then, off the detective's curious look, she added, "Martun Hagopian."

She turned her attention to Thompson.

"Milan told me that the night Komarov introduced Hagopian as a friend, Hagopian pressed him for details about the business, as if he was seeking confirmation of what Komarov had already told him. Milan said he didn't tell him much, but he came away thinking that Hagopian might turn out to be a problem."

"Did Milan know that Komarov was Vor?" Donahue asked.

Irina nodded. "But he seemed to be more concerned with Hagopian."

"So when did he go to the police?" Thompson asked.

"A month or so after that," Irina said. "Komarov approached Milan and told him he was going to buy him out. Milan turned him down, and he told me that Komarov was angry." She looked over at Donahue and gave her a nervous frown. "I warned him that Komarov was dangerous and that maybe standing up to him just wasn't worth it, but Milan was stubborn, so that's when he went to the police."

"Why didn't you tell us about this when we first spoke with you?" Donahue asked.

"And end up dead? I told you, it's not worth it."

"What about Hagopian?" Thompson asked.

Irina looked disgusted. "What do you want me to say? The man's a pig. He's going to drive me out at some point, and when he does, the business will be nothing but an escort service."

"Is he recruiting prostitutes?" Thompson asked.

"I think so." She looked from Thompson back to Donahue and shrugged. "I know that Milan brought in some women with questionable backgrounds. He was proud of the fact that he'd helped get them set up on a path that would lead them to a normal life." She smiled tightly. "Milan had a golden heart. He was a soft touch for women who needed to be rescued."

"Is Hagopian a Vor?" Thompson asked.

"I believe so."

Donahue glanced over at Thompson. Both women shared a knowing look. They'd gone about as far as they could for the moment with Irina. It was time to take a break and discuss where they were at.

The two detectives got to their feet.

Donahue said, "We'll see about that polygraph test, Irina. Make yourself comfortable. Someone will be in to get you in just a few minutes."

*****

Donahue and Thompson were greeted by Roberts in the hallway who saluted them both with high fives. "Nice going," she said. "It's starting to sound like we're getting to the bottom of things."

"We're still not there, Mitz," Donahue cautioned. "All we've managed to do is uncover a possible motive for the killings of Nika and Eliska. We still don't know who did the killings or even if they're truly related."

"My money's on this Hagopian character," said Thompson. "He shows up, and we start finding bodies all over the place."

"You may be right," Donahue replied, "but the fact that we've got nothing on him means that we're going to have to rely on the Russians to give us some info on his background."

"Should we get SIS to put him under surveillance?" Roberts asked.

"I'll run it by the Captain, but in the meantime, you two stay on top of the poly exams. We need to know if any of these women are holding back on us."

As Thompson and Roberts headed off to get the polygraphs started, Donahue located Gibson, filled him in, and the two of them went hunting for the Captain.

Elwood was behind his desk, and when all three of them were seated,

Donahue filled him in on what they'd learned during the most recent interviews.

"It looks like Petrovich or Komarov, or both of them together were running an insurance scam that was predicated on securing life insurance policies on the wealthy male clients who were about to get married to the Russian women they were introduced to. Once the insurance was in place, and the women were named the beneficiaries, someone killed the husbands, the women collected the payout, and Komarov recouped a significant share."

As usual, Elwood began by pointing out the holes in her theory.

"Where to begin?" he said with a shrug. "I'm not doubting what you're telling me, Jen. I just don't see that we're any closer to knowing who's doing the killings."

Donahue nodded, then smiled. "I want to focus on this guy Hagopian. He's got no record that we know of, but he's been in LA for all of our local killings, and he's the only one we know of who's profited by Komarov's death."

"What about the murder in London? Do we know where he was when that occurred?"

"I'll get Don Flynn to look into it with his contact at Homeland, but in the meantime, I'd like to have SIS tail him for a while. We need to know everything we can about his contacts, his hangouts, and what he's up to."

Elwood leaned back in his chair and put his hands behind his head.

"Did the FSB get back to Flynn on Komarov?"

Donahue nodded again. "Flynn called me and said that the prints came back to one Anton Sorokin. He's got a record in Russia, and it's being translated for us now." She looked at her watch. "Hopefully, I'll hear back from him a little later today."

"How about Hagopian?" Elwood asked.

"Flynn sent his prints to the FSB, but we haven't heard anything back. However, our guy in OCI, Yuri Pavienko, told Thompson that they checked him out with FSB, but that the Russians said that he's got no record."

"That doesn't make a whole lot of sense," Gibson said. Up to this point he'd been quietly listening to Donahue's recitation, but he was clearly concerned that they were still stumbling around in the dark.

"I agree, boss." Donahue turned in her chair to look at him. "I'm pretty sure that all of this revolves around the money being made by that agency and the proceeds of the insurance. But the only one who stands out is Hagopian and considering that Komarov was living here under a false identity, it wouldn't surprise me if Hagopian is too."

Elwood sat up straight in his chair and leaned forward.

"Okay. I'm convinced. I'll get SIS to tail him for a few days. In the meantime, get back to Flynn and see if we can do anything to speed up the process with the FSB."

*****

Donahue returned to her desk. She pulled out her phonebook and dialed Flynn's office number.

Flynn's secretary buzzed him to tell him that Donahue was on the line.

"Ah, Jennifer," he said from the chair behind his desk. "I was just about to call you. I got the translation of Vlad Komarov's arrest record and background information."

"Oh? Anything enlightening?"

"You better believe it," he said. "As we already know, his actual name is Anton Sorokin. He was born in *Makhachkala*, in the *Republic of Dagestan, a* part of Russia that's located in the North Caucasus region. He is ethnically a Chechen."

Flynn paused for a moment. He knew Donahue was a note taker, so he was giving her time to get it all down.

"Aren't the Chechen's considered terrorists by the Russians?" she asked.

"Not all of them, of course, but there's been a low-level Islamic insurgency in Dagestan since the 1990s. The report says the *Shariat Jamaat* is the group responsible for much of the violence, but it's more than that. The tensions are rooted in an internal Islamic conflict between the traditional *Sufi* groups who advocate a secular government, and the *Salafist's* who preach the implementation of *Sharia* law in Dagestan."

Donahue was scribbling notes like crazy. She decided she would worry about her spelling after their conversation, so she was writing the non-English words phonetically in hopes that she was close.

"So where does Komarov figure into all of this?" she asked.

"Their records indicate that as a young man, he was imprisoned in central Russia for robbery. He did eight years in prison, four of them in a youth facility, and four in a traditional labor camp. While in the prison system, he became a member of the *Vor,* a loose-knit prison group that consider themselves thieves forever. He apparently rose to the level of a Captain. He was suspected of numerous acts of violence and sexual assault while in prison, including two murders, but there was never enough evidence to convict him." Flynn looked up from the report. "Apparently, the witnesses who were prisoners themselves refused to testify."

"No surprise there," said Donahue.

"After his release from prison, he returned to Dagestan, where it was believed that he joined up with the *Shariat Jamaat.* Now here's where it gets interesting. He apparently was connected to several attacks on Russian soldiers in two different ambush scenarios, so of course, the Russians got back to us right away to demand that we send him back to them for prosecution."

Flynn spun slowly around in his chair and gazed out through his office window at the Potomac River; a view he cherished at the end of long days of paperwork.

"At that point, I had no choice, so I told them he was dead, and they'd like us to send them photos plus prints and a DNA sample for confirmation. Can you help me out with that?"

"Of course."

Donahue's mind was already racing. If Komarov was trained as a rebel fighter by a group of foreign terrorists, then how the hell had he gotten past immigration and into this country?

"I know what you're thinking," Flynn said. "I've already alerted our Homeland Security contacts, and they're looking into how he got a phony passport that somehow got him here with no red flags. Their best guess at this time is that someone within the Russian bureaucracy provided it to him, but they'll open an investigation and see what they can find out."

Donahue put down her pen and sighed. This was all very interesting, and it certainly pointed up problems within the immigration setup, but it really didn't do much to help her investigation.

Flynn wasn't finished.

"The revelation that Komarov was using a possible forged passport has the Russians really concerned. They've also opened a priority investigation, and to that extent, if you have Komarov's passport, the one that uses the name Vlad Komarov, they'd like to get it back as soon as possible for analysis to see if they can use it to track down the source."

"I don't see why we'd need it. I'll get a certified copy made of the pages for our files, then I'll forward the original on to you."

"Great," Flynn said. "And as for the other guy you wanted checked out? This Martun Hagopian? Well, any fears I might have had about them shutting the cooperation down if they learned that Komarov was dead went flying out the window. The FSB has promised to expedite your inquiry. Apparently, more than a few of the guys they're looking for have conveniently dropped off their radar during the last ten years, so they're going to start a review of all passports issued to see if they can track down any of their most wanted, and since they've got our inquiry on Hagopian and a set of his prints, they're going to bump him up to the top of their search list."

"He's now our suspect number one," Donahue said. "I just hope there's something there."

When she got off the phone, she leaned back in her chair and shut her eyes. Her brain was completely exhausted. The in's and out's of this case were slowly driving her mad, and the stress she'd endured over her cancer scare had taken a toll. She was supposed to find out today about the biopsy results, but her doctor hadn't called. She didn't know if that was a good sign or a bad one, but she decided it was out of her hands, so there was no sense in worrying about it.

She felt thoroughly exhausted and knew she was done for the day, and it crossed her mind that she should just go out and get smashed on tequila, but then her good sense kicked in and she vetoed the thought. The lump in her breast, although likely benign, had been a wake-up call; a warning from the higher power that she needed to pay serious attention to her physical health. This was an opportunity to turn over a new leaf, and for the moment, she would use this scare as motivation to bring about change.

She decided she would head on home, get out of her work clothes, then go down to the beach for a five-mile run. Running gave her the time to process her thoughts, to think things through; something she desperately needed to do on this case.

"I'm outta here," she said out loud to no one in particular. She gathered up her belongings and headed for the door.

CHAPTER 47

November 3,   9:45 a.m.

Donahue walked into the office to find Thompson already seated at her desk.

Shari got to her feet and stood at the cubicle divider.

"Your doctor called this morning," she said, handing her the written message.

Donahue scanned it quickly, looking for some indication of the result, but there was only the doctor's name and phone number. She put her purse down on the desk, took a deep breath, then took a seat and dialed the callback number.

Thompson whispered, "I'm here for you," then returned to her own chair to give Donahue a measure of privacy.

When the call was answered, Donahue said, "Dr. Carter? It's Jen Donahue."

"Take a deep breath and relax," Carter said. "It's benign. You don't have cancer."

Donahue had trouble reacting. Her hands were shaking and she couldn't speak. She'd been so sure that the news was going to be bad that she hadn't considered how to react if the news turned out to be good.

"Are you okay?" Carter asked. "I can't hear you breathing."

Donahue started silently crying.

"I'm fine," she finally managed to say. "I hardly know what to say."

"It's okay to have a good cry," Carter told her. "I know how stressful this has been, and I'm sorry you had to wait an extra day to get the results. They finished the lab work yesterday, but someone forgot to enter the results into the computer."

Donahue didn't care. All she could think about was the fact that she didn't have cancer and that from this moment forward she was going to try to live her life as if there was no tomorrow.

"It doesn't matter," Donahue told her. "As long as it's not cancer, the delay was worth it."

Carter laughed. "Funny how good news has that effect."

Donahue noticed that Thompson was standing at the divider, a look of real concern on her face, so she flashed her a broad smile and a thumbs up, and Thompson reacted with a smile of her own and a fist pump salute.

"Come in and see me next week," Carter said. "We'll talk about what comes next."

"Next?"

"Yes. We need to decide whether to remove the lump or just leave it and watch it. I'm gonna suggest we just leave it and watch it, Jen, but we can discuss it in detail when you come into my office. But just relax. It's definitely not cancer, and if you decide you want to have it removed, we can take care of it in my office."

"Thanks, doctor. I'll call back later and make the appointment."

She hung up the phone and Thompson came around the cubicle wall and gave her a giant hug.

"That's so great, Jen. How about we go out tonight and celebrate?"

"Can we put if off for a day or so? I didn't sleep well last night, so when I get home tonight, I'm just gonna crash."

"Fair enough. Let's grab a cup and talk about where to go on our case."

Donahue got to her feet, did a little dance of celebration, then led Thompson to the coffee room where the two of them got their coffee before making their way to an empty interview room.

When both were seated, Donahue said, "I spent a lot of time thinking about this case last night—"

"I thought you were gonna crash and not think about anything?"

"Yeah, well I went for a run and I gave it some thought, and I'm pretty sure the insurance angle is the key to everything."

Thompson took a sip of her coffee, then, "How so?"

"Look. The agency charges its male clients an average of ten thousand dollars apiece. How many guys can afford that kind of tab?"

"In this town? Probably quite a few."

"Maybe so, but while collecting ten grand at a time is good money, it's sporadic and slow. Then there's the office and staff expenses, plus the partnership split. A guy like Komarov gets maybe a grand or so from each client that goes through the operation."

Thompson nodded. "I see where this is going. You get a few of these clients to pay for insurance and once they're dead, the payout is huge."

"That's right, and Komarov collected... what? Nine hundred thousand from the two policies we know about? That's huge, Shari. Much better than the money he'd get from a piece of the agency. So the key to this whole mess has to be the insurance payouts."

"I agree. So where do we start, Jen?"

"With Grushik. He was the contact for Petrovich, the loose thread we need to pull to unravel this whole thing."

"Shall we pick him up?" Thompson asked.

Donahue shook her head.

"I think it's better if we go and talk to him again at his office, Shari. He's a smart guy. He'll lawyer up if we bring him down here."

"I'll get the car. You want to fill in Gibson?"

Donahue nodded. "I'll grab the info we got on the insurance policies and the payout and I'll meet you downstairs in ten."

After a trip to her desk for the file, Donahue went hunting for Gibson, but he wasn't in yet, so she left him a terse note saying where they were going and who they were going to see.

CHAPTER 48

November 3,   11:00 a.m.

Donahue and Thompson were escorted into the office of Nicholi Grushik who was seated behind his desk. Grushik was dressed in a thin pinstripe navy blue suit, a crisp white shirt, and a red silk tie. Impeccably groomed as always, Donahue tried to look past the image of the man she had previously thought of as a shining example of a truly outstanding citizen; one who cared enough about those less fortunate to actually do something to help them.

She chided herself for getting ahead of the known facts. Nicholi was still innocent until proven guilty. She needed to keep that in mind.

"This is getting to be a pleasant habit," he said as they were finally seated in front of his desk. "If I'd known you were coming, I could have arranged for lunch."

"We need to clarify a few more details, Nicholi. The last time we were here, you told us that Nika Kaminski never brought to your attention the fact that several young women at the Trophy-Wife Agency had filed claims relating to the deaths of their husbands."

"That's right. I did say that, and it's true. She never brought that to my attention." He looked from one to the other before his eyes returned to Donahue. "What's this all about, detective? Has someone said something to the contrary?"

Thompson leaned forward, drawing back his attention.

"Shortly after Nika made this discovery, she told people she was going to bring it to your attention, and a short time after that, someone decides to kill her." Thompson paused to give him time to absorb what she was saying. "Do you see where this is going? We've yet to discover a reason why she wouldn't pass this on to you?"

Grushik shook his head.

"Well, I'm sorry to disappoint you, but she never brought this information to my attention." His eyes latched on to Donahue's. "I suppose you'd like me to take a polygraph examination?"

"That would certainly clear things up," she replied.

"Then I'll be happy to take one. I'm telling you the truth."

"We'll set one up," Donahue said, although she was pretty sure he'd back out at the last minute after speaking with an attorney. "But in the meantime, we have a few more questions. I understand that you were once a client of Trophy-Wife Match. Is that correct?"

Grushik smiled. He placed his right hand over his heart.

"Guilty as charged, but I must tell you, aside from the embarrassing name, it was quite a nice experience. Expensive, but nice."

"Did you know Milan Petrovich?" Thompson asked. She had no intention of letting him steer the conversation off course.

"I did. In fact, we became friends for a while. He allowed me to go out with a few of the young women even after my membership expired."

"Did you give him anything in exchange for that benefit?"

Grushik frowned. "What do you mean by that? A quid pro quo? Absolutely not."

"You said you were friends *for a while,*" Donahue said. "Did something happen to end that friendship?"

Grushik's face split into a grin.

"As a matter of fact, I got engaged to be married. And my wife-to-be at that time did not endorse my hanging out with a man who ran an agency that was full of beautiful young women who catered to single men."

"Did you meet your fiancee through the agency?"

"Actually, I met her at church. She's a fine lady, two pre-teen children. We're very happy together."

Donahue smiled tightly. "I guess congratulations are in order."

Grushik looked genuinely embarrassed. He brushed off her compliment with a wave of his hand.

"The truth is that the women introduced to me by the agency were too young for me. They all seemed to want to go out to fine restaurants and night life venues. I did all that when I was a much younger man, so I found the experience somewhat boring."

"Can you tell us about the insurance connection?" Thompson asked.

"Certainly. What do you want to know?"

"Whose idea was it to give insurance policies to couples getting married through the agency?"

"I don't know. I guess you could say it was both of ours. I was hanging out with him one evening, and we were talking about the agency and he mentioned how important it was to the women from Eastern Europe to have security in their lives. I knew what he was talking about. My family was from the old Soviet Union and they can tell you no end of stories about how difficult it is for both men and women to grow up in the post-communist world."

He looked over at Donahue and smiled.

"I think I might have said something like 'that's not a problem here' or words to that effect because American men seem to be acutely aware of how important it is to have insurance to provide for their loved ones in the event of a tragedy. Milan thought that sounded like an idea; that maybe the agency could foot the bill for the first month's premiums on a policy as sort of a wedding gift to the newlyweds. I told him that wasn't practical, that depending on the amount of insurance, the age of the insured, things like that, he could be talking about quite a bit of money in premiums. Instead, I suggested that we might be able to get the clients preferred status, which would reduce their yearly premium bill, assuming, of course, that they met our preferred criteria. That way, the client would be saving money on the coverage, the agency would be getting the good will for arranging the reduction in premiums, and we, of course, would benefit from the commissions."

"So how'd that work out?" Thompson asked.

Grushik shrugged. "We sold a few policies, not enough to even think about actually, but it really was all about the goodwill."

Thompson smiled. "Actually, I meant to say, what were the mechanics of the plan, once someone decided to take Milan up on his offer to arrange for this opportunity to get such an interesting deal?"

"*Interesting?* You make it sound like we were doing something wrong, detective. We weren't. Anyone who met our criteria for preferred status got it. We didn't close our eyes and let just anyone pick up a policy. That would be ludicrous and costly to the company."

"I understand that, Mr. Grushik. What I was referring to, facetiously perhaps, was the fact that these clients really got nothing special from you or the agency that they couldn't get for themselves out on the open market."

Grushik shrugged, then smiled.

"That's probably a fair statement."

Thompson enjoyed a moment of short-lived satisfaction. She'd gotten him to admit, albeit reluctantly, that the so-called gift wasn't really a gift but rather a salesman's ploy.

"So let me ask you again. Mechanically, how did all this work? Did you personally meet with the clients and write up the policy applications?"

"Of course not." Grushik laughed. "That's not my specialty area."

"Then how did the process work?"

"I'm pretty sure I had Leigh coordinate everything with Milan Petrovich. He would call her and she would contact our outside sales agents and arrange for the application and the physical to be set up for the client. After that, the application and medical records would go to our underwriting department, and if they gave the approval, the company would process the application and issue the policy." He locked eyes with Donahue. "After that, we had no further connection with the policy or the clients."

"Did Petrovich know when a policy was issued to one of his clients?"

"That's confidential information. Only the insured and our agents know when a policy's been issued." He hesitated. "I suppose the clients might have thanked Milan after the fact, in which case he'd know that the policy was issued, but other than that, I can't think of any other way he could have found out."

"You've been a big help, Nicholi," Donahue said. "I'll arrange for our polygraph operator to call your secretary to make an appointment. I'd like to set it up for tomorrow. I want to clear your good name so that we can focus our investigation in another direction."

"Am I a suspect of some kind?" he asked in a voice that suddenly sounded a bit shaky.

"Not at all," Donahue replied. "It's just that my Captain requires that we poly all of our witnesses so that we can rule them out of any involvement."

She gave him her most charming smile.

"Relax, Nicholi. You've got nothing to worry about. I completely believe you."

Grushik immediately relaxed.

"Thank you, Detective Donahue. I'll take the exam, and if I can help you with anything else, please feel free to call."

*****

Outside in the car, Thompson said, "Well, that went nowhere."

"I disagree. We got Nicholi to agree to a poly, and if he goes through with it and passes, then we can start to look elsewhere."

"And if he backs out of the poly?" Thompson asked.

"Then we'll tear his life apart, piece by piece, and if he was getting a cut from Komarov, Mitzi will find it. That woman's relentless when it comes to searching for a paper trail."

"Amen to that." Thompson hooked up her seatbelt. "You wanna get some lunch?"

"Yeah, sure. You still buying?"

"Absolutely. You up for Sushi?"

Donahue shot her a look. "Have I ever turned down sushi?"

"Great!"

As Donahue started up the car, Thompson said, "Head over Coldwater Canyon to Beverly Hills. There's a place there called *Sushi Sushi.* It's one of the best-kept secrets in the sushi world."

Donahue pulled away from the curb.

"If it's such a big secret, then how do you know about it?"

"*L.A. Magazine,* girlfriend. '*Top ten best kept secrets in the culinary world.'* Don't you read anymore?"

"Who's got time?"

Thompson smiled. "Beauty shop. While your hair is drying. And speaking of that, you really do need to do something about your roots…"

*****

CHAPTER 49

November 3,   2:00 p.m.

After lunch, they parked a block away from the PAB in a police garage and walked to the building past several homeless people who'd made their daytime place of residence the stretch of green directly behind the building. Initially intended for use as a small park, it had become the favorite spot for neighborhood residents to freely run their dogs. The lawn wasn't faring too well, and needless to say, few people, except the occasional oblivious transient, ever spent time lying out on the grass.

The squad room was busy, so they went straight to their respective desks, expecting to spend a few minutes settling in, but before they could even sit down, Gibson approached and told them to follow him out to an interview room. It wasn't so much that he was worried about being overheard, the squad was just so busy and noisy that if you wanted to have a serious conversation without distractions, it was always better to find a quite place where you wouldn't be disturbed.

Gibson opened the door, let Donahue and Thompson walk in, then shut the door behind them. The three of them took seats at the table.

"I got a call from Don Flynn during the lunch hour. He got the info you requested on Martun Hagopian."

Donahue's eyes widened. "Anything good?"

"This guy Hagopian is a real piece of work. His true name is *Dimitri Federenko.* He was born in Dagestan, he ran away from home at fourteen and hopped a freight train which took him to Saint Petersburg. He got caught stealing food and did two years in *Kolpino,* a regular gladiator academy. At sixteen, he was released, but he was picked up a month later on an armed robbery charge. For that offense, he got eight years. He was sent back to *Kolpino,* and when he hit twenty-one, he was transferred to the *Black Dolphin Prison* where he finished his term. According to Flynn, it's the most dangerous and toughest prison currently in existence. The average temperature there is fifty below. It's a place where cannibals, terrorists, and killers go to live out the rest of their days."

"If that's the case," said Donahue, "how come he had to serve his time there?"

"I asked Flynn the same thing, and he said that the FSB agent told him that Federenko's father was a known Chechen leader in the *Riyadus-Salikhin Reconnaissance and Sabotage Battalion of Chechen Martyrs,* so the boy was put there to rub sand in the eyes of his father."

"Holy cow!" said Thompson who shook her head. "I would think that doing that would only make matters worse?"

"Apparently, it did. Federenko returned to Dagestan when he got out of the Black Dolphin and joined up with his father's group where he received basic training in weapons and improvised explosive devices. According to our State Department, the training was paid for by IIPB, the *Islamic International Peacekeeping Brigade*, a primary channel for Islamic funding of the Chechen guerrillas, in part through links to al-Qaeda-related financiers on the Arabian Peninsula."

Gibson looked up from his notes.

"In short, this guy 'Dima' Federenko, known to us as Martun Hagopian, is a bonafide Chechen terrorist."

Donahue rolled her eyes in disbelief. They had a major terrorist running around Los Angeles as free as a bird. How the hell did he manage to go under the radar?

She said as much to Gibson, who replied, "Flynn says Homeland Security is looking into it. They suspect he was traveling on a legitimate passport, one likely stolen from official channels."

"Is our government going to do anything about this guy?" Thompson asked.

Gibson smiled.

"Needless to say, the Russians want him bad, and according to Flynn, the FBI has been notified and they're gonna pick him up sometime later today."

Donahue looked over at Thompson.

"With explosive training, he might be the guy who blew up Milan Petrovich."

There was silence around the table as all three of them considered the implications of what they'd just learned.

"How's this sound?" Donahue began. "Komarov arrives in this country under a false passport and sets up business as a pimp running Russian girls in Hollywood. He meets up with Petrovich, sees opportunities that Petrovich never envisioned for the agency, and decides to muscle in to change the business to a high-end escort service. Then he learns about Petrovich's arrangement with Grushik to furnish the successful matches with insurance policies. He knows the Russian girls will be easy marks for intimidation, so he has a few husbands knocked off and discovers how lucrative the scheme really is."

"So where does Hagopian fit in with all of this?" Gibson asked.

Donahue frowned. "To answer your question, Gibby, both Komarov and Hagopian are organized crime figures, so maybe Komarov sends for Hagopian, has him knock off Petrovich, and as payment for the killing, he sets him up as a minor partner in the agency business."

Thompson smiled. "That makes a lotta sense, Jen, but take it a step further. They say there's no honor among thieves, so maybe Hagopian decides he wants more than just a junior partnership. He wants the whole thing. So he bumps off Komarov, moves in on the agency, and once he understands what's going on, he will probably get rid of Irina Konstantinov and runs the entire operation on his own."

Donahue looked over at Gibson. "I like it. It's a pretty tight scenario, but we're woefully short on actual proof."

"What about the murders of Nika Kaminski and her girlfriend, Eliska Rodinova?" Gibson asked. "We can assume that Nika realized what was going on with the insurance scam and that she told Eliska what she knew, but who killed them?"

"Komarov, or perhaps Hagopian....or maybe someone they hired," said Donahue. We may never figure out who did it, but it all comes back to the insurance."

Gibson scratched his chin in thought. "Okay. So what do you propose we do from this point on?"

"I guess we let the Fed's take Hagopian down," said Donahue, "then we search his place for anything that will connect him to our cases."

"Sounds good to me." Gibson turned his attention to Thompson. "You want to add anything?"

"I think we should bring Yuri in to work with us on the search. Maybe with his expertise, he'll notice something that we've missed?"

At this point, their case was nothing more than supposition, so it made sense to bring in an expert. But Donahue wasn't crazy about the idea. So far Yuri hadn't been much of a help, and he was certainly a distraction for her partner, but she had to admit that they were completely in the dark when it came to the cultural aspects of the Russian mob, so having someone with real knowledge to advise them and to be a second set of eyes during the search could end up being a distinct advantage.

"I see no problem with that?" Gibson looked over at Donahue. "You agree?"

"Why not? Maybe he can be of some assistance."

Gibson stood up. "I'll brief the Captain. Jen, you call the local office of the FBI and find out what they have in mind? And Shari, see if you can find out where this guy Hagopian is living. Maybe the FBI will know. Once you get that info, put together a search warrant. The Fed's will probably do one, but we're looking for stuff they might not include."

Gibson made his way out of the room, and as the two detectives got to their feet.

Donahue put her hand on Thompson's arm. "If we bring Yuri into this, you keep it professional, okay?"

"Yeah, sure Jen. I know you don't approve of my after-hours social life, but you don't need to question my professionalism."

"We still don't know about his partner, Shari, and until Homa and Magarian get finished with their investigation, I think it's important that we don't risk feeding Yuri's partner with information that could compromise our case."

*****

Clay Young arrived at the Hollywood Police station, parked in the secure

321

lot to the rear of the building, then made his way in through the back door and into the room used by the detectives assigned to Hollywood Homicide.

When he entered the squad room, he was immediately met by Andrew Magarian and John Homa, who introduced themselves as being from the Internal Affairs Group. Young was then led to a nearby interview room where the three men took seats around a small metal table.

Magarian spoke with Donahue a mere twenty minutes before Young showed up. During his conversation with her, she'd filled him in on Komarov's true name—Anton Sorokin—the man's background, and the surprising news from the FSB that Hagopian's true name was Dimitri Federenko, a man with explosives training who was also believed to be a Chechen terrorist. She told him how they planned to do a search warrant for Hagopian's office at *Trophy-Wife Match,* as well as his residence, and she invited him and Homa to come along.

In return, Magarian said that they'd called Clay Young in for an interview, and she'd asked him to let her know if he had anything important to say about Martun Hagopian.

Magarian briefed Homa who was itching to put the screws to Young. Homa was completely convinced that Young was involved in criminal activity, but Magarian had cautioned him to be circumspect, as they didn't want Young to know the extent of their knowledge about Komarov and Hagopian.

When all three men were settled, Magarian broke the ice.

"We invited you in here Clay to give you the opportunity to clarify a few things for us."

Clay silently laughed while looking from one to the other.

"Invitation?" He slowly shook his head. "I'm only here because I'm required to show up."

"That's right, sport," said Homa. "And just so we're all on the same page, you're required to answer our questions fully and completely. Failure to do so will result in a trial board, probable loss of your job, and possible prosecution." Homa studied him carefully. "Are we clear on that?"

Clay nodded.

"I understand you've decided not to have a representative from the Police

Protective League present with you during this session. Is that correct?"

"I don't need anyone to sit in. You're recording everything that's said, right?"

Magarian nodded. "That's right, but you're entitled to have a representative from the league with you if you so choose."

"I understand." Clay pulled out an iPhone and set it down on the table in front of him. "I'm sure you don't mind if I record our conversation…just in case something were to happen to your copy somewhere down the line." He hit the record button on the *Voice Memo* application, then leaned back in his chair.

Homa looked over at Magarian whose expression seemed to be saying *Do you believe the balls on this guy?*

Homa shook his head, then reached out and snatched up the iPhone, shutting off the app that was recording their conversation.

"Let's get something straight here, sport. You will not record this conversation. If at any time we decide to go forward with a case against you, you will be provided with a copy of the recording to do with as you please. But until that time, you are required to cooperate fully and answer our questions. Any more of this bullshit attitude of yours and we'll see to it that you're suspended by the end of the day. You got that?"

Sufficiently chastened, Clay was not about to antagonize these guys any further. It crossed his mind that he might have made a mistake in not contacting the league and getting a rep to assist him with the process, but it was too late now. He was here in their office and they were ready to go, and if he asked for a rep at this late moment, they just might suspend him out of spite for attempting to delay the process.

He locked eyes with Magarian.

"Okay, Lieutenant. I'm sorry if I came off a little heavy, and I don't really know why you've called me down here, but I've done nothing wrong, so go ahead and ask your questions and I'll answer them all as best I can."

Magarian held Young's glance. Now that it was clear that they had the upper hand, he would see how cooperative Young intended to be.

"We've taken a look at your tax records and your credit reports for the last three years. It appears to us that you seem to be living well beyond your means.

Can you explain how you're able to afford that boat and the new truck and other items that have recently come to our attention?"

Clay looked from one to the other in astonishment.

Was that what this was all about? My standard of living?

When he'd gotten the call from Magarian to come in and see them right away, he'd called Yuri to tell him what was going on. They'd met in a parking lot behind a CVS Pharmacy store, and Yuri had coached him once again about the telephone calls the night of the bombing that killed Petrovich, and that he should insist that he never knew that Komarov was working as their informant. They had both been relieved to realize that it must have been IA who'd been following them around, but Clay was filled with a sense of dread that he wasn't able to articulate. He'd done nothing wrong, he was pretty sure of that, so when they asked about his standard of living, it came as a wave of relief.

He almost laughed out loud.

"You want me to explain my standard of living?" His glance went from one to the other.

"That's what the Lieutenant asked you, sport," said Homa. "How is it you have money enough to pay for that boat of yours?"

Clay's eyes narrowed.

"My wife's father passed away last year. He was a physician. My wife was his only living relative. She inherited almost two million dollars. We set up an educational trust for the kids, invested a chunk of it in a stock portfolio, and I bought a boat, a truck, and some other things with part of it."

He fixed his eyes on Homa. "Any other questions, *sport?*"

Homa was seething at the mimicry. He was ready to reach across the table and throttle Young, but Magarian put a hand on his arm.

He locked eyes with Young. "You failed to report the money on your joint income taxes. That's a violation of the Department's reporting rules."

But Clay was ready for that question.

"On the contrary, Lieutenant, it was inherited money, the bulk of which was from a life insurance policy. According to my tax attorneys, the money derived from life insurance is not reportable as income, and since it was hers and not mine, I'm not required to report it to the Department."

He leaned back in his chair, arms folded across his chest, confident that he had just taken the wind out of their investigation.

Magarian gave what Young had to say some serious thought. If his wife had indeed inherited the money, it explained the type of expenditures the family was making. With a little basic information, it should be easy enough to check out, and if it turned out to be true, then the investigation would be closed.

"We'll need the details relating to the inheritance," he told Clay. "I'm assuming an attorney was involved, so if you'll contact him and waive your right to confidentiality, we can probably wrap this up in just a few days.

Clay provided the requested information and was just about ready to leave when Homa told him they weren't finished yet.

"I have a few more questions to ask you," he said.

"Fire away."

Clay had taken an instant disliking to Homa, but he'd answer the questions as quickly as he could just to get the inquisition over with.

"How well do you know your partner?" Homa asked.

The question caught Clay off guard.

"Well enough. Why?"

"Your partner says that Vlad Komarov was working for him as an informant. Did you know about that?"

Clay looked from one to the other. This was where things got tricky. If he lied to these guys about anything, it could cost him his career, and while he believed in loyalty to his partner above all else, he was having second thoughts about putting his career on the line over a stupid agreement his partner had with an acknowledged criminal.

"I knew he was cultivating the guy to be an informant," he said carefully.

"Did Komarov ever give you guys any substantive information?" Magarian asked.

"What do you mean by substantive?" asked Clay, stalling for time.

"Really?" Homa shook his head. "You have no idea what the word substantive means?"

Clay shrugged and hung his head. It was the moment of truth and his career was on the line. If he fudged the truth now and these headhunters could later prove it, he'd be through as a cop...and for what? Because a criminal who was now dead didn't want his name to be known as an informant? That didn't make any fuckin' sense. The guy was dead, and it was Yuri who'd made his deal with Komarov and stood behind it when Komarov was alive. Did he really want to risk everything behind a stupid, ill-conceived deception that Yuri was responsible for?

"Look. I'm gonna level with you." He sat up straight and directed his attention to Homa. "Komarov was providing Yuri with low-level intelligence, very little of it was earth shaking, but the deal was that Yuri could never say anything to anyone. Komarov was *Vor.* You know what that is?"

"We do," said Magarian.

"Then you know that even a suspicion that he might be an informant would result in his death." He looked from one to the other.

"These guys don't fool around. They're animals. If they think you might be a snitch, they'll kill you without a second thought. Komarov agreed to work with us because Yuri swore he'd never reveal his name to anyone, not even to our Captain."

"You said the information was low level. Did he ever give you anything of real value?"

Clay shook his head. "If he did, I never heard it. Yuri handled all of the contacts with Komarov. I was always nearby just to watch his back."

"Did Yuri ever tell you that Komarov was interested in the *Trophy-Wife Agency?"*

"No, I knew that Petrovich was recruiting young women for the agency out of the clubs, but the first time I knew that Komarov was connected in any way with Petrovich was when we got the call from Hollywood telling us that Petrovich had complained that Komarov was trying to muscle his way into a share of the business."

"How close was Yuri to Komarov?" Homa asked.

"They seemed to grow closer over time. I'm sure Yuri had nothing to do with him off duty, if that's what you're getting at, but on duty, I think they got along well enough."

Magarian said, "On the night that Petrovich was killed, Komarov called your partner on a phone that was checked out to you. Is that correct?"

"I was never in possession of that phone. When they signed 'em out to us, we must have been given the wrong phones." He looked over at Homa and shrugged. "A simple mistake. They all look alike."

He tried to laugh it off, but Homa's expression, one of distaste, never changed.

"What were the phone calls about?" Homa asked.

"I don't know. Yuri waived me off when I asked him about 'em."

"Did your partner ever intervene on behalf of one of Vlad's hookers?"

Clay looked confused.

"I don't know what you're asking?"

"I'm asking if your partner ever attempted to help out one of Vlad's street hookers. Did he attempt to get one of them into rehab?"

Clay shrugged. "If he did he never mentioned it to me."

Magarian thought that was significant. Clay's partner apparently trusted him enough to let him in on the big secret—that Komarov was an informant—but he wouldn't tell him what Komarov wanted when he called him on the night that Petrovich was killed?

That fact alone put Yuri's version of the calls in the suspicious category. He would have to pass that tidbit on to Donahue.

"What do you know about Martun Hagopian?" he asked.

"Nothing, really. Komarov introduced him to my partner. Said he was gonna run a few girls and sell a little dope in the clubs, but that was it. I ran the guy's info through a contact that Yuri has with the FSB, but they had nothing on him."

That's interesting, thought Magarian.

"Did you send them prints from Hagopian?"

"No. We didn't have 'em. I just gave them his DOB and a physical description."

Magarian decided the prints had made the difference when it came to getting the true identification.

"Has your partner ever talked about his background before coming onto the Department?"

Clay studied Magarian carefully, looking for signs as to where this was going.

"Why are we talking about my partner?" Clay asked. "Is he under investigation or something?"

"Just answer the question," said Homa.

Clay shot him an angry stare.

"I know he was in the military. That's about it."

"Before that," Magarian said. "Did he ever talk about his time in Russia?"

Clay shook his head. "He said the weather sucks over there. Too cold. He likes the beaches here, and he likes the women, too."

"So he never talked about his time in Russia? His family? Any issues he may have had while he was there?"

Clay looked at him skeptically.

"No. Why? Is there something I should know?"

Magarian looked over at Homa. He had no intention of telling Young what they knew about Komarov or Hagopian, and since they had what they needed to verify Clay's story about his wife's inheritance, they could let him go until they checked things out. As far as his partner Yuri was concerned, all the questions they'd been asking about him were nothing more than simply fishing around for anything that might not be kosher, but it was obviously nothing more than a waste of time.

They wouldn't be opening an investigation on Yuri, they had nothing to go on—no suspicion of wrongdoing of any kind—but it was best to keep the fact that they'd asked about him under wraps. No sense in causing the guy any unnecessary anxiety since they had nothing to go on anyway.

"We're done here," he said to Young, "and if your info checks out about the inheritance, we'll be closing our inquiry down. But I want to caution you that what's been said in here is completely confidential. You're not to discuss anything about this interview with your partner, your wife, or anyone else. Understand?"

Clay nodded.

"I need your answer out loud for the tape," said Magarian.

"I understand," he said.

"Do you? Because if we find out you told him we were asking questions about his background, you can kiss your job and your pension good-bye."

"I know the rules," Clay said flatly. He didn't appreciate having been placed in the position of having to talk about his partner, but he was pretty sure this guy Homa was going to keep digging around in spite of what the Lieutenant had just said about shutting things down. He didn't trust Homa. He would probably tap their phones to see if Clay said anything to his partner.

Magarian got to his feet, followed by Homa and Young.

"We'll get back to you soon," he said to Young. "You can take off now. Thanks for coming by."

Clay shook his head and left the room.

"You believe this guy?" Homa said when they were alone.

"His story is easy enough to check out," Magarian replied, "but there's something about these two guys that still bothers me. I can't put my finger on it yet, but my gut is telling me that something's wrong."

"So we gonna keep working 'em after all?"

Magarian smiled.

"Damn straight."

CHAPTER 50

November 3, 9:00 p.m.

By nine p.m., the warrant to search Hagopian's apartment in Hollywood was signed and in the possession of Mitzi Roberts. She walked into the auditorium at the PAB and held it up for Gibson to see. He was standing on the stage, addressing a large contingent of officers, and when Roberts gave him the high sign, he announced to the room that the warrant was in hand.

Gibson had handled the logistics for the operation.

Irina had provided them with an address for Hagopian and SIS had verified that her information was accurate during the day while Hagopian was working at the agency. SIS was still on him, and at last report, Hagopian was presently sitting in a club in North Hollywood, a Russian bar called *Glasnost,* entertaining a couple of young women, completely unaware that he was under close surveillance.

He would be taken out of the bar while his place was being searched, and he would be brought down to the PAB where Donahue and Thompson would be waiting to ask him questions.

Thompson had tried to get her usual babysitter to take care of her kids, but the woman was not available, so she'd spent the better part of an hour contacting young women on the list of babysitters that Donahue had given her before finding one who was available on such short notice. She met the young woman at her house, felt comfortable with her level of competence and confidence, so she'd left her saying that she'd be home before midnight.

She'd given Yuri a call before heading home. When he answered his cell, he sounded as if he'd been sound asleep.

"Did I wake you?" she asked.

"It's okay," he told her, sitting up in bed. "I'm up."

She explained to him that they'd shifted their focus to Hagopian. She let him know that the FSB had discovered that he was really a guy named Dimitri Federenko, a Chechen terrorist now wanted by the Russians.

Yuri got out of bed and began pacing around the room.

"So what's going to happen now?" he finally asked.

"We're gonna do a warrant on his place, and SIS is on him since earlier today. Once the warrant is served, we're gonna pick him up. The Russians want him held until they can get the paperwork for an extradition."

"Once you pick him up, let me know what he has to say. Okay?"

"If you want you can come down here while we talk to him. You can watch him on the closed circuit TV screen, so you won't blow your cover, and if you think there's something we should ask him about, someone here can pass us a note. It could be helpful, Yuri, and we really need help to unravel this mess."

"I'll think it through," he said. "Give me a call when you guys pick him up."

"I will."

*****

Yuri hung up the phone. He was alone in his apartment, wearing nothing but a pair of boxer shorts, and he was struggling to make sense of what he'd heard. He'd been sound asleep when Thompson had called, and while he had come to a state of instant clarity at the news that they'd discovered the true identity of Martun Hagopian, the ramifications of such a revelation were still a jumbled mess in his brain.

He decided that he was in a state of shock.

He took a deep breath, sat down on the edge of the bed, and tried to come up with a focused line of thought, and once he considered all of the possible scenarios that might play out, he developed a mental list of his priorities, several of which needed his immediate attention.

He raced into the bathroom, stripped off his boxer shorts, and stepped into a cold water shower. He needed to be completely awake, and from his childhood in Russia, where hot water had been an occasional luxury, he knew from personal experience that nothing enabled the senses to focus better than being immersed in ice cold water.

Twenty minutes later, after making a quick phone call, Yuri left his apartment, made his way down to his building's underground garage, got into the motor pool car that he'd taken from the station the night before, and drove out of the building. When he reached the street, he looked carefully around, but there were too many parked cars, and the street was too dark to know if he was under surveillance. Clay had called him at home that morning, advising him that he was on his way to a meeting with the scum at IA, but he hadn't heard back from him yet, and that was worrisome. Once he got to the station, if Clay was not already there, he would give him a call and see what his interview had been all about.

*****

As Yuri pulled out of his apartment building's parking garage, the transponder signal on Homa's laptop screen began to beep. He sat up straighter and started up his engine. He was parked more than a block away, but the transponder signal which overlaid the map of the city enabled him to follow Yuri's vehicle without any possible chance of detection.

Because of the interview with Yuri's partner Clay Young, both he and Magarian had felt that there was something unsettling about these two investigators. Clay's attitude hadn't helped his cause. He was too cocky, the kind of in-your-face approach that tended to piss people off and Homa was a man who had no patience for such individuals.

Homa was a former Marine. He'd seen two tours in Iraq, and he'd spent his first few years with the LAPD working patrol in south-central Los Angeles. After that, he'd done a stint in the Metro Division, three years in SWAT, followed by his most recent assignment in Internal Affairs. He was married to a real estate attorney whose income was such that most of his take home pay went out again in the form of income tax, but that didn't bother Homa at all. He loved his job, the challenges it presented, and his two young kids, a boy, and a girl, thought his job as a cop was ten times more exciting than the career that was held by their mother.

He was a very private man, one who rarely talked about his accomplishments. He never spoke about the Medal of Valor he received for saving the lives of a woman and a baby from a burning wreck on the Santa Monica freeway. He also never talked about his hobby which was *knitting*, a skill he developed while he went through rehab at a hospital in Germany for wounds he'd sustained during a combat incursion while he'd been in the hellhole known as *Fallujah.*

And at the moment, he was working alone.

Magarian had a back-to-school night for his eight-year-old son, so he wasn't due to come back on duty until ten p.m. Magarian wanted Homa to wait to start his shift until they could work together, but Homa had successfully argued that they would have a better chance of knowing what was going on if they followed these two guys when they weren't on the clock. Magarian eventually agreed, so it was decided that this would be the final night of an on-duty surveillance, for starting tomorrow, they would be on these two guys while both were off duty.

But Homa had jumped the gun. He didn't believe in wasting time, so he sat on Yuri's residence—after having hooked up the transponder on the car he'd taken home— just waiting to see if he went anywhere before he went in for his scheduled shift.

He assumed the guy had been sleeping. Yuri was expected to go on shift at eleven p.m., so his leaving at nine was not overly suspicious. He suspected the guy was gonna stop to get something to eat, or maybe he would go somewhere for a pre-shift workout. But he wasn't overly concerned. If working IA had taught him anything, it was patience, so he figured he'd follow the guy to work, then head on home to catch some sleep so he could pick him up again when Yuri went off duty in the morning.

But Yuri didn't go directly to work, and he didn't stop off at a restaurant or a gym. When the transponder signal became stationary, Homa's curiosity got the better of him, so he drove to the location where the transponder signal had come to a stop and discovered that it was a parking lot behind a Shell gas station.

Hello, he said out loud to himself as he drove past the station. *What do we have going here?*

He didn't dare stop. Yuri was too good a cop and the risk of detection was just too great, so he circled the block, coming around from the North, where he took a parking spot that offered him complete concealment. He got out of his car carrying a small camera bag. He decided he would get as close as he could, and hopefully, he could figure out what Yuri was up to.

It had taken him almost five minutes to get into position, and during that delay, he had no idea what Yuri was up to. When he finally found a spot between parked cars in a small pocket mall across the street, he could see Yuri seated quietly in his car, talking to someone in the passenger seat.

The angle he was at did not facilitate the taking of a photo. Even with a telephoto lens, he was too far away to get a good shot through the front windshield of Yuri's car which was reflecting back the overhead lights in the parking lot. He decided he would just have to wait until the meeting was over to be able to get a decent shot.

He had the camera ready at his side when he was suddenly aware of someone coming up from behind.

"Hey, you," said a gruff and guttural voice. "What you up to?"

Homa spun around and saw a black uniformed security guard who was quickly approaching. The man was obese, three hundred and twenty pounds at least, and he had his right hand on the butt of his pistol that was thankfully still in his holster.

"I'm LAPD," Homa said. "You wanna see my badge?"

The man stopped in his tracks. He hadn't expected that particular answer.

"Yeah. Let me see your hands," the big boy told him.

Homa wasn't going to argue with the man. Situations like this could easily escalate, and he had no desire to let things get out of control.

"Take it easy. I'm holding a camera." Homa held it out. "I'm on a surveillance. You want to see my identity card?"

Big boy studied him carefully. He was close enough now to see that it was a camera, so his hand moved away from the butt of the gun.

"Let's see the ID," he said, and Homa carefully obliged him. He opened the front of his jacket and revealed the badge that was clipped to his belt. The big boy relaxed.

"We good?" asked Homa.

"Yes, sir," said the guard. "You need any help?"

Homa smiled. The guy was just doing his job, and he'd done it professionally. There was nothing to be gained by blowing him off.

"No, I'm good. And I want to compliment you on your professionalism. You were right to approach me to see what I was doing. You've got good skills."

"You think I might make a good cop?"

Homa knew that question was coming. He gave the man a smile.

"You need to get yourself in shape. Get into a gym, lose some of that excess weight, get those muscles of yours firmed up, and you might make a pretty good candidate."

Big Boy smiled. "Thanks, boss. I'll give it a try."

He turned away, and Homa quickly looked back over at the parking lot where Yuri's car was parked. But Yuri was in the process of driving off, and there was no sign of the person he'd been talking to.

Homa cursed to himself from under his breath as he made his way back to his car. The encounter with the security guard had messed up his chance for a telephoto shot. But one thing seemed sure. Yuri was up to something. A clandestine meeting in a parking lot behind a gas station just couldn't be on the up and up. There had to be something the guy was concealing, and Homa was bound and determined to find out what it was.

As he got back into his car, he suddenly had a thought. He drove over to the gas station, pulled into the now empty lot, and scanned the building until he spotted what he hoped would be there.

It was. A closed circuit TV camera was set up to monitor the lot.

He laughed to himself as he got out of the car. If the camera was working, the person Yuri met would have been in the camera's view.

Could he get so lucky?

*****

By ten forty-five p.m., everything was ready for a takedown of Hagopian's residence. SWAT was in position down the street, and SIS had reported that the light from a TV was on, which indicated to them that Hagopian was still inside the apartment.

Donahue, Thompson, Gibson and Elwood were seated together in the Captain's car several blocks from the apartment location. They planned to wait until SWAT had taken down the apartment. The natural tendency of all detectives was to be on scene, but SWAT had insisted that they remain outside the kill zone just in case the operation went south.

The SWAT commander gave the "go" order and the team of well-trained officers made their way over to the building. Once they were on scene, they acted like a well-oiled machine. They quietly climbed a flight of stairs, tossed two flash-bang grenades through the front room window, then knocked down the front door using a cement filled, hand-held battering ram appropriately referred to as "the key to the city."

The first team of officers entered quickly, and when they didn't find anyone in the front room, they carefully searched the rest of the two bedroom apartment, checking out cupboards, closets and bathroom tubs, anywhere where their target could be hiding. But Hagopian wasn't inside, and it soon became apparent that he'd managed to leave the apartment before they arrived on the scene.

No one was angrier about the situation than the SIS Lieutenant who'd been assured by his team that Hagopian was in the apartment. He vowed to get to the bottom of things while the search of the apartment was underway.

Donahue, Thompson, Gibson and Elwood arrived on the scene as soon as the all-clear signal was given. They were distressed to know that he'd gotten away, and what to do next became their topic of discussion.

"You think someone tipped him off?" Thompson asked.

Elwood shook his head. "More than likely, he made the surveillance, and since the SIS guys don't wear uniforms and don't drive around in recognizable vehicles, he might have thought that he was being followed by rival mobsters." He sighed heavily. "Just a bad break. That's what I'm thinking."

"Hopefully, we'll get something good in the search," said Gibson. "In the meantime, I think we should also assume that he might be on the run. I'm gonna suggest that we notify the airline carriers at the LAX, Orange County, and Ontario airports. We should also alert security at the LA Amtrak station."

"We can send out his photo to all units citywide, as well as the Sheriff's and the local PD's," Elwood added. "We might get lucky."

"We know he's been using a phony ID," said Donahue, "so we need to assume he has access to others."

"This is going to be a mess." Thompson shook her head. "You think he might try to go back to Russia?"

"I doubt it," said Donahue. "He knows what will happen if the Russians get ahold of him. My best guess is that he'll stay in the States."

"Well, we better get on it." Elwood caught Donahue's eye. "Contact the Feds. If the Russians have confirmed his identity, then the Feds can issue a warrant for him for passport fraud. And let's make sure that we've got a warrant issued just in case he's spotted by an agency that doesn't get our BOLO. (Be On the Look Out).

"I'll get it done right away."

Donahue turned to Thompson. "You want to oversee the search?"

"Sure, I'll hang out for a while, but after that, I've got to go home." She shrugged. "My sitter has school in the morning, so I've got to be in by midnight."

Donahue smiled.

"Catch you later, Cinderella."

*****

By the time Homa had finished with the clerk in the Shell station, he was ready to hit somebody. The girl was a foreigner from central Africa or somewhere like that and she didn't yet have the hang of the English language. It took him almost twenty minutes to get her to understand that he was a police officer, and another ten to get through to her that he wanted to see the video feed from the camera that was positioned in the parking lot. The girl insisted on calling her boss, a Pakistani male who also had a problem with English, but he finally seemed to understand, and Homa was allowed to take the video.

He drove back to his office, pulled out a video player, hooked it up to a flat screen monitor, and started a painstaking review.

The tape was time stamped, so he ran it forward on high speed until the daylight faded and nighttime arrived. He then slowed down the tape and settled in for what he assumed might take hours to find what he was looking for.

At just after midnight, he found the spot where Yuri drove into the parking lot.

Homa watched with interest as a female appeared from the side of the screen, probably coming from around the side of the building before entering the front seat of the car.

Yuri's car was positioned in full view of the camera, and the tape revealed the woman while she was leaning in for a kiss.

"God damn it!" said Homa out loud. "It's just a fuckin' girlfriend!"

He stopped the tape, folded his arms across his chest, and leaned back in his chair. He'd wasted the entire evening on this, convinced that Yuri was up to something sinister, only to discover it was nothing more than a probable romantic tryst.

It occurred to him that the whole setup was strange, but then he concluded that the woman was probably married and lived nearby in the neighborhood.

"A fuckin' waste of my time," he bemoaned.

He turned the machine back on and watched the rest of the encounter, but nothing of note took place. The two of them talked for about five minutes; then she gave him a kiss—a good one by the looks of it—before getting out of the car and going back in the direction from which she'd arrived.

He stopped the tape and noted her description. Shoulder length brown hair, a good looking face, nice body; maybe late twenties or possibly early thirties.

Thoroughly disgusted, he put the tape in his top desk drawer, left his office, and headed for home.

CHAPTER 51

November 3,   11:45 p.m.

Martun Hagopian forced himself to stay just under the speed limit. He was cruising down the 405 freeway, just passing through Carlsbad, on his way to San Diego.

He had no idea how the authorities had uncovered his true identity, but it was clear that the fabricated persona of Martun Hagopian was no longer going to work.

He looked down at the speedometer, noted that he was just above the posted speed limit, so he eased up on the accelerator, just enough to conform to the sixty-five mile per hour limit.

When he'd gotten the phone call, he had momentarily panicked before gathering up his wits and focusing on the task at hand. He hadn't bothered to secure a backup identity, believing that there would be no need. But now that his cover was blown, he was cursing himself for not spending the additional ten thousand Euros to secure a second passport under a new identity. He would soon rectify that mistake, but he needed a place he could stay without drawing the attention of law enforcement. If he could get settled somewhere, he could make a call to a contact in London who would secure the necessary documents for him through a government source in Moscow. But he would need to send photos, as well as a transfer of funds, and it would likely take a week or so before the finished product was delivered by Fedex or UPS. That made finding a safe location of paramount importance, no easy task without advance preparation.

The search of his apartment would yield nothing of an evidentiary nature. Before fleeing in his new Toyota, he grabbed his computer and gathered up all the loose mail and paperwork. He took the keys to a storage locker that contained a small amount of methamphetamine, a quarter pound of high-grade cocaine, and what remained of the PVV-5A plastic explosive that he had used to eliminate Petrovich. He'd gone to great lengths to have the plastique smuggled into California by members of the same cartel that had furnished him with the drugs he had planned to resell, so leaving them behind was only a temporary situation. Once he had his new ID and knew where he planned to go, he would swing by the storage facility and clean it out.

He wracked his brain to figure out how anyone could have known that he was wanted by the Russians, or that he might have had a hand in the killing of Petrovich? But no easy answer came to mind.

At first, he thought that someone must have tipped off the authorities, but that didn't make any sense. Very few people knew his true identity, and those that did were *Vor,* so the idea that one of them might have been an informant was almost beyond his comprehension. But there was another way that they might have found out, and that was if someone in the Russian Passport Office had gotten into trouble and given him up to get more lenient treatment. That was always possible, but he thought it unlikely, for such a person would eventually pay the ultimate price, a fact that was known to everyone.

He shook his head. It had to be some other way, and he decided that when he had the time, he would figure it out and see to it that whoever was responsible got what was coming to them for cooperating with the police.

In the meantime, he needed to get as far away from Los Angeles as he could, and he needed to get rid of his old passport and identification. He would burn them once he got to San Diego, and if his luck held out, he would catch a flight to Las Vegas, a crossroads of the world, where it would be easier to hide out until he could get his hands on a new set of identity documents.

Fortunately, he had plenty of cash on hand, and there was a great deal more sitting in a safe deposit box. He would pay his way with cash for a while so as not to leave a credit card trail.

He felt the handle of the .45 cal. handgun that he'd wedged between the seat and the center console. He hoped he wouldn't have to use it, but he would not let them take him back to Mother Russia where the guards at the *Black Dolphin* would welcome him home while they made the rest of his life a hell on earth.

*****

Yuri showed up at the RHD squad room at 11:50 p.m., in search of Shari Thompson. When Roberts looked up from her desk and saw him standing and talking to one of the male detectives, she knew right away who he was, so she walked over and re-introduced herself.

"Are you looking for Shari Thompson?" she asked.

Yuri smiled. He remembered her from the bakery.

"I am. She told me you were going to pick up Hagopian and she asked me to come down in case I could be of assistance."

"Unfortunately, he wasn't around when we served the warrant, so Shari went home, but her partner, Jen Donahue, is still around."

With Thompson gone, he wasn't sure he could be of any help, but he decided to check in with her partner to make sure that he wasn't needed.

"I've never met her," he said. "Can you point her out for me?"

"Follow me."

Roberts led him through the squad and directly over to Donahue's desk.

"Hey, Jen," Roberts said.

"Yeah, Mitz?" Donahue looked up from her computer screen.

"This is Sergeant Yuri Pavienko from our OCI unit. Shari asked him down here to listen in on your interview with Hagopian."

Yuri retrieved a chair from a nearby cubicle and rolled it over next to Donahue. He sat down, facing her, then smiled.

Roberts, who had been watching from behind the partition wall, said, "By the way, Jen, before I forget, we sent his photo out statewide to all police agencies and all news outlets."

"Did we get it to Homeland down at the border?"

"They're completely on board. The FBI office there is coordinating things with Customs and Immigration."

"Great, Mitz. Thanks."

"One other thing. I ran him through DMV under the Hagopian alias. He drives a new Toyota. I sent a flash out statewide with the vehicle info, so if he's on the run, maybe we'll get lucky."

"I hadn't thought of that, Mitz. Nice going."

While Roberts headed back to her cubicle, Donahue said to Yuri, "I suppose

341

you heard, he wasn't home when we hit his place."

Yuri nodded. "So how'd you discover his true identity? My partner ran his info through our contact at the FSB and he told us that he had no record."

"He didn't, under the name Hagopian, but we sent along a set of his prints and they discovered his true identity."

Yuri nodded. He hadn't considered that.

"So you think he's on the run?" he asked.

"Don't know for sure, but he wasn't home so we have no idea where he might be. Got any suggestions concerning where we should be looking?"

"Well, if he's in town, he'll be in a Russian-dominated neighborhood. He'll be looking to bed down with a friend. The guy's a player, so maybe he'll be with one of his whores."

"You know who any of *those women* might be?" Donahue asked. She had intimate knowledge of the way that Russian organized crime made use of kidnapped women, so to call them whores, when they were actually slaves, was an insult that pissed her off. She was not in the mood to correct him now, but she filed it away to mention it later when she had more time to speak her mind.

"Not really. Maybe Vice might have a clue."

Donahue sighed. They'd already done a check with Vice, but none of the girls they'd talked to in the last few hours had any idea who he was.

"Anywhere else he might go?" Donahue asked.

"He's got contacts among the *Vor,* and there are a number of them in the greater LA area, so he could be anywhere."

Donahue flashed a tight smile while she studied Yuri's face. They guy was no help at all, but maybe she was being too hard on him. There was no way he would have specific knowledge of where a wanted felon would be, so perhaps she was expecting too much for him to be of any real assistance.

"Well, thanks for your ideas, Sergeant. If you can think of anything else that might help us find him, your thoughts would be more than welcome. I'll give you my cell phone number and you can give me a call."

She pulled out a business card and wrote her cell phone number on the back of the card before handing it to him.

Yuri reached out and took the card.

"Did you get anything during your search that would connect him to any of the homicides?"

"His place was clean."

Yuri frowned. "So what do you have that links him to the killings?"

"Nada," she said, then off his confused look, "We got the Feds to issue a warrant for using a false passport to enter the country. It's a temporary charge while they wait for the Russians to file a detainer. They want him on terrorism charges."

Yuri got to his feet. "It was nice meeting you, detective. Good luck with the search. Let me know if you pick him up?"

"We'll give you a call," she promised.

Yuri made his way out of the office and Roberts got to her feet and came over to Donahue's desk.

"So what do you think?"

Donahue looked up. "About what?"

"You know…him?"

Donahue leaned back in her chair.

"He's a pretty boy, but he's got me wondering why we have an intelligence unit? I think we know more about Hagopian then he does, and if it wasn't for his language skills, I think he'd still be working in patrol."

Roberts nodded. "Well, on that note, if you don't need me for anything urgent, I'd like to go home and get a little sleep."

"Go ahead, Mitz. Thanks for working over. I'll see you in the morning."

"You headin' out of here too?"

"Not for awhile. I've still got to finish my report on the search, but I won't be long."

Roberts returned to her desk to gather up her things leaving Donahue to think about the fact that this day had been full of pleasant surprises. Not only was she not a victim of cancer, but they probably had a pretty good idea of who was responsible for their bombing murder case.

All in all, it had been a good day, and she was looking forward to getting home and climbing into bed where she could have a real cry of relief.

CHAPTER 52

November 4,   12:20 a.m.

Martun Hagopian turned on his cell phone. He was still on the freeway, just passing the turnoff for Pacific Beach. The city of San Diego was still a few miles away, but he was close enough now that he would soon have to think about where he could get a room to lay low for a couple of days.

His cell phone rang and he quickly picked it up.

"What?"

"Get a different car," said the female voice. "They're looking for your Toyota."

She hung up the phone and Hagopian felt his stomach knotting up.

How the hell did they know what he was driving?

He put the phone down on the center console, intent on getting off at the very next off-ramp, when the sound of a siren made him jump.

A blinding white light flooded into the car, preventing him from using his rearview mirror, but there was no mistaking what was going on. The car was suddenly filled with a flashing red light. The police were on him, and a voice came on over a loudspeaker telling him to pull over on the next off ramp.

He turned on his right side turn signal, hoping that the police were not really after him, but as he began to pull off the freeway, the police car behind him stayed right on his bumper. As far as he knew, he hadn't committed a traffic violation, so they must have made his car.

All that mattered now was that he had to find a way to get away from this *politseyskiy* before others arrived to back him up.

He reached the bottom of the off ramp, quickly scanned the road ahead, then made a right turn and pulled his car over in the nearest and darkest spot he could find. The police car pulled up directly behind him, and he was sure that the officer was already getting out of his car.

"Driver, turn off your engine." It was a command that came over the police car's loudspeaker.

If he turned off the engine, he was done for.

Hagopian stepped on the gas and accelerated as fast as he could get the car to go. He managed to get a jump on the police car, which confirmed his belief that the officer had already stepped out of the car.

In his rear view mirror, he could already see that the police car was closing in rapidly. He would never outrun him in the Toyota, so he made another hasty decision. He pulled over to the side of the road and quickly jumped out of his unit.

*****

The call had gone out from the Highway Patrol Officer that he was in pursuit of a suspect who was wanted for murder, and to say that created a stir was an understatement. All unnecessary radio chatter was put on hold. Units of Highway Patrol and the City of San Diego Police Department were provided with the direction of the pursuit and the location of the suspects fleeing vehicle in real time, enabling them to close in on the chase from a number of different directions.

When the suspect pulled over for the second time, the officer quickly put out the call that the suspect had bailed out and he would be going in foot pursuit.

Other units were close by, and one of them was even close enough to see the suspect running. The two officers in that car saw him run between two houses, followed by the officer who'd called in the pursuit, so they stayed in their car and drove around the corner to the next block over to cut the suspect off.

*****

Hagopian knew that he didn't have a chance of escaping. He could hear other units arriving in the area. He was on a residential street, running up a driveway that divided two houses. He was going to be trapped. There was no way out.

When he got to the backyard, he ran a few steps to his left, then took a dive on his stomach, spinning as he did so, so that he could get a shooting angle for

345

the *politseyskiy* who was coming up the driveway behind him. He was not going to let them take him into custody. He would rather die than go back to the Gulag, and if that was how it was going to be, he might at least take one or more of them with him.

He lay on the lawn in the dark, eyes glued to the edge of the house by the driveway. The officer who was chasing him would be coming around the corner in a matter of seconds. He would be backlit by a streetlight out in front of the house. The shot would be clear and it would give him time to get away by going over a back fence into a neighboring yard.

Hagopian sighted the gun with two hands and tried to calm his breathing. He had one chance to pull this off, and he was not about to blow it.

*****

The two patrolmen with the San Diego Police Department had screeched to a halt in front of a house that was directly behind the house where they'd seen the suspect run. They bailed from their car and immediately ran up the driveway and into the backyard where they made their way through total darkness towards what they suspected would be a back fence. Neither one used a flashlight, as they did not want to give their position away. One of the two crouched down, and since they hadn't seen the suspect exit from the house they'd parked in front of, they were pretty sure that he was still in one of the two backyards.

*****

Hagopian tried to slow his heart rate, but slowly exhaling didn't help. The officer who'd been chasing him had not yet appeared at the corner of the house, and he was starting to sweat. Could the guy be coming at him from another direction? He didn't dare look around, because if he timed it wrong, the man might appear and he might lose the advantage.

What he didn't know was that the Highway Patrolman was not some gung-ho rookie who'd be running on adrenalin but not thinking about his personal safety. He was a former Marine, one who'd seen combat in Iraq, and he knew better than to race headlong after a possibly armed murder suspect, especially one who had entered a pitch-black backyard.

Instead, he approached the edge of the house from the driveway by pressing his body up against the wall. His plan was to lead with his flashlight in one hand, the gun cradled tightly in the other on top of the flashlight. He would shine it around the corner without exposing any more than his hands.

As he got to the corner of the building, he gave out a warning yell.

"Police! Show yourself with your hands up or I will turn the dog loose and you will get bitten!"

He was bluffing, of course, but it was all he could think of to say. When no one responded, he cautiously led with his flashlight and gun and inched his way around the corner of the building.

*****

Hagopian heard the officer yell and he heard the threat about the dog. But since he was planning on shooting the officer, shooting the dog first did not trouble him at all. He lowered the sightline of his handgun in order to catch the dog as it rounded the wall of the house.

Suddenly, everything went from bad to worse.

A floodlight went on, lighting up the backyard as if it were daytime. The occupant of the home, a Gardner with a wife and four kids, had heard the police car pull up in front of his house, and he heard the responding sirens. Believing that the police were chasing someone into his own backyard, he got out of bed, walked into the hallway, and switched on the outdoor light.

As the light went on, Hagopian fired in the direction of the figure now coming around the building. He squeezed off four shots from his semi-automatic handgun, all of which missed the mark because the sudden brightness of the backyard light had been momentarily blinding.

From the yard behind him, the two San Diego officers, who as it turned out were only thirty feet away, were able to see him clearly through a chain link fence. They could see the intended target at the corner of the house, and both men quickly drew down on Hagopian.

One yelled "Police!"

Hagopian heard the yell from behind him and rolled over on his back, intending to shoot.

The two officers opened fire, emptying their handguns as fast as they could fire. The chain link fence deflected some of the shots, but eleven of the twenty-one fired made it into their target.

An ambulance was called, but that was only done to comply with their Departmental policy.

The subject of the statewide manhunt would never take another breath.

CHAPTER 53

November 5,   1 p.m.

Thirty-six hours later, a meeting of the task force was called by Captain Tommy Elwood to reassess the posture of the combined cases. In light of the most recent developments, including the deaths of Vlad Komarov and the shootout death of Martun Hagopian, Elwood wanted to know where they stood, and what, if anything, still needed to be done.

The meeting had been delayed to enable Donahue, Thompson, and Gibson to get a little well deserved rest. They'd been putting in very long hours, so with the death of Hagopian, their primary suspect, it was felt that a break of some kind was warranted. Once everyone was rested, work would begin to link him up with one or more of the homicides. The pressure to stop him before any more killings occurred was now off. They would have the time to do all of the follow-up work that was put on hold due to the pace they'd been forced to work.

They gathered together in the conference room: Grayson, Tucker and Red MacLean from Hollywood Division; Joel Price from West Valley; Larry London from WLA; Donahue, Thompson, Gibson, Roberts, Jackson, and Bengtson from RHD; and Magarian and Homa from Internal Affairs. Running the meeting was Tommy Elwood.

"Listen up," Elwood said, calling the meeting to order. The chatter immediately stopped as they gave him the respect his rank deserved.

"I've asked you here today so that we can determine where to go from here? The death of Hagopian leaves a lot of unanswered questions, so I though we might start by sharing what we do know about this guy, and by that I mean what do we have, if anything, that connects him to any of the crimes?"

He looked to Donahue. "Jen, can you bring us up to speed on Hagopian?" Donahue leaned back in her chair.

"Well, according to the information provided to us by the FSB, as Dimitri Federenko, had training with explosives during his time with the Chechen rebels. His place was clean when we searched it, but there was a storage locker key on his person when San Diego PD took him down, so Rich Bengtson drove down there and picked it up. Once we determine the location of that locker, we're gonna get a search warrant and see what's inside."

Bengtson raised his hand. When Donahue looked his way, he said, "I located the locker. It's at a facility out in Panorama City. I've started putting together a warrant, so Jackson and I thought we'd serve it later this afternoon."

Donahue checked that one off her list of things to get done. She looked around at the rest of the group.

"Hagopian had a laptop computer in his car." She locked eyes with Bengtson. "Have you had a chance to look into that yet?"

Bengtson nodded. "I took it to the lab. They're going to get into it for us and give us a call."

"I'd like Shari to go through it," Donahue said.

Thompson nodded. "I'll call them as soon as we're done here."

"What else?" asked Elwood.

"His body was loaded down with tattoos," Donahue said. "San Diego PD is going to take extensive photos and send them to us later today. Hopefully, Shari's expert over at USC can interpret their meanings, which might give us a little more insight into this guy."

"What about his phone?" Elwood asked. "Did he have one on him when he bought the farm?"

"Bengtson brought it back and gave it to Mitzi." Donahue looked over at Roberts. "Any luck with the phone yet?"

Roberts nodded. "I've looked at the call log on his phone for the last twenty-four hours before he died. There were almost a dozen calls, so I've got my contact at AT&T checking on the numbers for us, and I should have a list of subscribers later today or early tomorrow."

"What do you hope to find?" Price asked.

"We're looking to see who he ran with," she said flatly.

Everyone at the table understood that it would be nothing more than a fishing expedition, but experience had taught them all that you just never knew what you'd find.

Elwood smiled. "You'll stay on top of that for us, Mitz?"

Roberts nodded. "I've got something else to bring up. When Komarov was arrested, Shari found a piece of paper in his wallet with Cyrillic writing on it. I had a chance to look it over yesterday, and I called up Shari's contact at USC. Dr. Ulyana Chirkoff, the language expert, says it appears to her to be a bank account number."

Almost to a man, everyone seemed to sit up straighter. When there was the possibility of money involved, there was usually a trail one could follow.

"What bank?" asked Gibson.

"The piece of paper only had four letters followed by a series of numbers. The four letters were FCIB. I looked it up, and if it is a bank account, FCIB might stand for First Caribbean International Bank."

Elwood was as excited as everyone else. This was as good a lead as they could hope for. He looked over at Donahue.

"Why didn't we check that out sooner?"

Donahue took a quick look at Thompson before saying, "We had too many things going on, boss. It was on my to-do list, but I just didn't have time to get to it."

Elwood nodded.

"Mitz, I want you to keep working on the cell phone numbers." He turned to Jackson. "You think you can follow up on the bank account lead?"   Jackson nodded. "I know someone at Homeland Security whose been working on the off-shore tax avoidance cases. Maybe he knows someone who can find out who holds the account?"

"Get what we have from Mitzi," Elwood said. He thoughtfully rubbed the side of his face. "Did we ever finish looking at the phone records of our murder victims?"

"Still working on it," said Grayson. He and Tucker had been assigned to yet another Hollywood homicide case and hadn't had time to check things out.

Elwood leaned back. "Okay then, what happened on the lie detector tests?"

Gibson said, "Irina Konstantinov, the partner in the agency, passed the poly, as did the two wives of the murder victims, so it looks as though from the insurance perspective, it all comes back to Komarov."

"An independent operation?" Elwood asked.

Gibson shrugged.

Elwood looked around the table.

"You guys in divisional homicide are gonna have to dig harder if we're gonna find out who killed Nika Kaminski and her girlfriend, Eliska Rodinova. Since Komarov seems to be the guy who was running the scheme, I need you to go through those phone records to see if we can find any link between either of those two women and Komarov."

A few heads were nodding.

"Okay, then, thanks for coming in."

Elwood got to his feet and walked out as did the others, and most of the detectives from the outlying divisions, including Magarian, left the room.

Homa walked up to Thompson and Donahue and said, "Have you got a minute?"

"Sure." Donahue flashed him a smile. "What's up?"

"Got something for you. Can we talk in private?"

Thompson assumed he wanted to speak only to Donahue, so she said, "I'll catch you guys later."

"No, this concerns you too," said Homa.

Donahue led them to a nearby interview room, and once the door was closed, Homa handed Donahue a DVD.

"Last night I was working a surveillance on Yuri Pavienko. I had a tracker on his car, so I waited outside his apartment. I wanted to know what he did when he wasn't on duty."

"I thought we decided you guys had nothing on him?" said Thompson.

"We were leaning that way, but the LT and I just can't shake a gut feeling that he and his partner have something going on."

"So what's on the DVD?" Donahue asked.

"He left his residence and went to a Shell gas station. He parked behind the building, waiting for someone. A female came out from a nearby apartment complex and got into the front seat of his car."

"A prostitute?" Donahue gave Thompson a quick look.

"I don't think so. She was only with him for a couple of minutes. They were doing a lot of talking. However, he did give her a long kiss before she got out of the car, but that was about all the tape shows."

"A girlfriend?" Thompson suggested.

"Looks that way, but who meets their girlfriend in a parking lot behind a gas station?"

"Maybe she's married?" said Donahue. She was still looking at Thompson who shot her a nasty look.

"Maybe, but it just seemed odd. Anyway, I talked it over with the LT, and he felt we ought to give you a copy, but keep it out of your case folder and out of your reports. Our investigation is going to stay open."

Donahue thanked him, and she and Thompson left the room and headed back to their desks.

"Let me look it over," said Thompson, holding out her hand.

"You wanna get a look at the competition?"

"Damn straight."

Thompson grabbed the DVD from Donahue's hand and slipped it into the slot on her computer.

Donahue stood behind her, and the two of them watched the screen. The camera had covered the lot behind the gas station, but the lot was well lit, and the camera was high resolution.

They could tell it was Yuri. They could see his face.

"Is that his car?" Donahue asked.

"I don't think so," Thompson replied. "They've got access to a lot of under-cover vehicles, so I doubt if he drives his own."

They continued to watch the screen. The female came into view from the back of the building and made her way over to the car. When she got into the front seat, she leaned in and kissed Yuri on the lips.

"She looks familiar," said Thompson.

"I was just thinking the same thing," Donahue added.

The woman and Yuri had what appeared to be a serious conversation before she pulled out her phone and punched in a number. The phone then disappeared below the dashboard.

"Is she talking to someone on the speaker phone?" Thompson asked.

"Maybe."

The woman then leaned over and held the back of Yuri's head as she kissed him passionately.

A few moments later, she opened the door and stepped out of the car.

Thompson froze the screen, catching a full view of the woman's face.

"Holy shit!" said Donahue. "It's Leigh Cherlina."

"Sure is," said Thompson.

"This changes everything, Shari."

CHAPTER 54

November 5,   3 p.m.

From that moment on, to say that the investigation went into overdrive would be an understatement. Once Donahue explained the possible connection between Leigh Cherlina and LAPD's Yuri Pavienko, Elwood authorized the use of whatever resources were necessary to examine the relationship with a fine tooth comb. He wanted to determine if there was any possible way that Yuri Pavienko, or his partner Clay Young, were involved in any way with the crimes they were investigating.

Mitzi Roberts was once again asked to get phone records, this time for Leigh Cherlina, Yuri Pavienko, and Clay Young. For Cherlina's records, she began by running her through the Department of Motor Vehicles where she obtained the basic information. She then used that information to run Cherlina's credit history from which she determined that Cherlina's phone carrier was AT&T.

Several calls later, after a few markers were called-in, Roberts had a search warrant signed and served on AT&T's security operations. Within two hours, they had a complete list of Cherlina's phone calls—both those that were made and the ones she received—for the previous sixty days.

To get the phone records for Yuri Pavienko and Clay Young, she used the phone numbers for the phones assigned to them by the department. A quick warrant was used to obtain their call logs for the same six month period.

Roberts then set about running through all of the logs, looking for any numbers that were immediately identifiable. She quickly spotted the number for the LAPD cell phone being used by Yuri Pavienko. It showed up many times on Cherlina's incoming and outgoing call logs.

Thompson used a yellow marker to identify the calls she knew were of immediate significance, the ones coming in and going out, carefully noting the time of the calls. Ten minutes later, she hurried over to Donahue's desk and spread the phone log pages on Donahue's desktop.

"I've developed a sort of a timeline I think you should see."

Roberts came over from her cubicle, and all three of them studied the log sheets.

"As far as I can tell, on November third, Yuri Pavienko took an incoming call about nine p.m. from a number assigned to our unit."

"That must have been my call," said Thompson who looked over at Donahue. "Remember, we wanted him to know about Hagopian, and I invited him to sit in on the interview we were going to do."

"I remember," said Donahue.

"Okay," said Roberts, "now look at the outgoing call sheet for Yuri. At 9:27 p.m., he called the number we pulled up for Leigh Cherlina." She pointed out the number, then locked eyes with Donahue. "What time did he meet with her at the gas station?"

Thompson said, "Let me look." She went back to her desk, followed by the other two detectives, and after calling up the video, she noted the time stamp in the corner which showed Cherlina getting into his car at 9:50 p.m.

"Nine-fifty," said Thompson.

Roberts was holding Cherlina's call log. "At 9:52 pm, she called Hagopian on his cell phone. A one minute call."

"Oh, shit!" said Thompson. "She warned Hagopian that we were gonna hit his place with a warrant."

"She called him again, later that night," Roberts said, "at about 12:20 p.m."

"Yuri came in here about 11:50 p.m.," Donahue said. "He was looking for you, Shari. He said he was invited down here to listen in on the Hagopian interview."

Thompson nodded. "But if he warned Hagopian about the search and the fact that we knew his real identity, then he had to know that we missed him and didn't pick him up."

"Then why would he still come down here?" Roberts asked.

"Maybe he just wanted to get an update on the search," Donahue suggested. She was cursing herself for ever having spoken to that guy. "He was right next to me Mitz when you told me about the car we believed Hagopian was driving."

She glanced over at Thompson. "Yuri probably used Cherlina as a cut-out to have her let Hagopian know that we put out an APB on his car."

They consulted Cherlina's call log again. She had received a call from Yuri only two minutes before she placed the 12:20 a.m. call to Hagopian.

"We've got to let the Captain know about this," said Thompson. "We need to pick her up right away."

"Not so fast," said Donahue. "We bring her in and confront her with the calls, and she'll say she wants to speak with her attorney." She held Thompson's stare. "We've got nothing but our suspicions. We're gonna need more before we pull her in."

"What do you suggest?" Thompson asked.

"I want you to call Magarian and Homa. Get 'em back down here right away. We need to run this by them and see what our options might be."

*****

While Thompson went off to call Magarian and Homa, Donahue slipped out of the squad and went down to the Personnel Division which was located on the second floor. She spoke with the Chief Clerk, a heavyset, very friendly African-American woman, telling her that they needed the personnel package for Yuri Pavienko; that he was being considered for a transfer into RHD.

Ten minutes later, the clerk produced the file and Donahue signed it out. She then went upstairs to her cubicle where she opened it up, located a set of his prints, then headed for the privacy of an interview room so that she wouldn't be overheard by anyone in the immediate vicinity.

Flynn's secretary advised him that Donahue was on the line, so he immediately answered the phone.

"Did the info we gave you do any good?" he asked.

"Hagopian is dead, Don. He got in a shootout with the police in San Diego."

"No kidding?" Flynn leaned back in his chair. "What happened?"

"He was tipped off that we were coming for him. A CHP officer spotted him on the freeway and attempted to get him to pull over. After a short pursuit, Hagopian was about to open up on the officer from a backyard not far from where he bailed out of his car. Unknown to him, two San Diego officers were approaching him from behind. When they identified themselves, he rolled over and tried unsuccessfully to get a shot off at them."

She didn't need to tell Flynn that the cops had turned him into Swiss cheese. That went without saying.

Flynn was silent for a few moments.

"I guess I should notify our liaison with the FSB. Can you get me the name of the lead detective in San Diego? We're probably going to have to provide the Russians with a complete set of reports, photos, and prints."

"I'll take care of it, Don, but I really need to ask you for another favor, a big one."

"Oh?"

"Yeah. This is completely confidential, but I think that Hagopian was tipped off by one of our officers. His name is Yuri Pavienko. He works in our Organized Crime Intelligence Unit. He's had access to our investigation, and we have phone records that have aroused our suspicions."

Flynn's demeanor abruptly changed. He was now all business. He reached for a pen to take notes.

"What do you need, Jen?"

"I pulled a set of his prints from Personnel. Can you arrange for your contact at the FSB to check him out? We'll need to know what they've got, if anything, as quickly as possible."

"Scan the prints and email them to me. I'll call the Bureau guy in Moscow and fill him in. Maybe he can convince the Russians to speed up the process."

"Thanks, Don. I'll get back to you if anything else pops up."

*****

Magarian and Homa arrived at the PAB about six p.m. Donahue was waiting for them, but Thompson had gone home to try to arrange for a babysitter for her boys. Roberts was still working on the phone records, and Bengtson had been pressed into service to put together whatever public information there was on Leigh Cherlina.

Donahue led them to an interview room, and for the next twenty minutes she described in detail what they knew about Hagopian, how he had died, and then she showed them a copy of the Cherlina phone logs and how her calls were connected to Hagopian and Yuri Pavienko.

"I knew these guys were dirty," said Homa. "I could feel it in my bones."

Magarian shook his head. "This may connect Pavienko with Hagopian, but there's nothing yet to link Clay Young."

"We can bring him in and put him on the box," said Homa.

"I have an idea," said Donahue. Both detectives stopped talking to listen.

"Can we get a wiretap for their phones?"

"Whose phones?" Magarian asked.

"Pavienko's and Cherlina's?"

Magarian thought it over. "I don't see why not?"

"I'm thinking we can put a scare into Cherlina and maybe she'll say something incriminating to Pavienko."

"Might as well give it a try," Magarian said. He looked at his watch. "We've got to jump through a few hoops to get everything set up. I would guess that we could have everything in place by early tomorrow afternoon."

"Good, that'll give me time to figure out how we're gonna spook her."

*****

That evening, while Donahue went for a long run around her residential neighborhood, she ticked off in her mind what was underway and what still needed to be worked on. The Captain had arranged to have SIS, the Special Investigation Section, an elite tactical detective squad, follow Leigh Cherlina around twenty-four hours a day. At last report, she was having dinner at a moderately priced restaurant with several women of her own approximate age. Magarian and Homa had spoken with their Captain, and she had authorized an around-the-clock surveillance on both Yuri Pavienko and Clay Young. Magarian and Homa were scheduled to take the evening off—they needed to get some rest —but others in the elite IA surveillance unit were well up to the task and would follow the men around throughout their scheduled evening shift.

Donahue ran hard to clear her mind. She was on pace for a seven-minute mile, and she pushed herself until she felt utterly exhausted. For the first time since the cancer scare, she felt full of life and as if she was finally living in the present. It was a wonderful feeling, one that she never wanted to lose.

She decided that she and Thompson would pay Cherlina a visit at her residence the following evening. That way she would likely use her own phone to contact Yuri. Yuri's phone would also be tapped, so even if she used a phone they didn't know about, they still had a chance to catch the conversation. Hopefully, one or both would say something incriminating; something that would enable them to place one or both of them under arrest.

She decided she would need to procure search warrants for both of their residence locations as well as their work locations and cars. She would have to get that done in the morning to have the warrants ready for service after they'd given her ample time to put a call into Pavienko.

But what to do about Nicholi Grushik?

As expected, he'd spoken to an attorney who persuaded him to decline the opportunity to submit to a polygraph examination. A refusal to take the test was not indicative of his guilt, but to officers of the law, it was always considered suspicious, and that meant that his life and activities would soon be placed under a very large microscope.

He might believe that his refusal was the end of things, but their interest in him was far from over.

If he had taken the test and passed, she would have been grateful for his help, especially in light of the apparent involvement of Leigh Cherlina in what was going on. They would now need to go over her possible role in the insurance killings, and they would need to backtrack through her work files to see if there were other killings that they had not yet connected to Komarov.

But focusing on Grushik now before talking to her might be a major mistake. Once under arrest, if she was sufficiently frightened, she might implicate Grushik in some aspect of the case. At this point, Donahue didn't trust Grushik nor anyone beyond her partner and the others in the close-knit unit of RHD, so she decided to put on hold any further approach to Grushik. For the moment there were too many other aspects of their investigation more immediately pressing to deal with; and besides, because of his lucrative position with the insurance company, she suspected that Grushik would not be going anywhere soon.

There was still the matter of the storage locker key that Hagopian had in his possession at the time of his death. She would talk with Bengtson in the morning to find out if he'd found anything. She would also need to speak with Jackson about the offshore bank account, and with Don Flynn about Yuri's early life in Russia.

Donahue sighed. There was so much to do that she was starting to feel guilty that she was not down at the office working on the warrants. But that thought quickly passed when she remembered that she needed to put things into perspective, and taking care of her own physical health was a new reality that had to come first.

She continued to run for another thirty minutes, then made her way home during the cooling down phase. When she entered her apartment, she found a message on her cell phone that Bengtson had called, so she quickly called him back.

"You ready for some good news?" he said when she answered the phone.

"I'm always ready for good news. What'd you find, Rich?"

"Drugs. Meth and Coke to be precise. Quantities he was likely breaking up for sale. There was also a small amount of plastic explosive. I don't know the make, we had to bring in ATF, and they took possession of it, but they'll let us know sometime tomorrow if it matches the stuff used in your bombing case."

"You just made my night, Rich. That's fantastic!"

"There was other stuff in there. It was a very small locker. The rest was just junk. Some old clothes, an old suitcase, things like that. I'll give you an inventory sheet tomorrow morning."

"I owe you lunch," she told him.

"That you do."

She put in a call to Thompson who had just finished putting her boys to bed. She explained what Bengtson had found, and Thompson was equally convinced that their bombing case could soon be closed out as a solved.

"How about Cherlina?" Thompson asked. "What's the plan?"

"We'll pay her a visit at her home tomorrow evening, right after she's finished at work, so line up a sitter, will you? I want you along when I talk with her."

"I wouldn't miss it, Jen. See you in the morning."

Donahue smiled as she hung up the phone. At long last, things seemed to be falling into place.

CHAPTER 55

November 6,   8:30 a.m.

Donahue walked into the squad room with a cup of Starbuck's coffee and a whole new attitude. Today was going to be the second day of her new plan to put her personal health ahead of everything else. She brought along a gym bag and had every intention of spending her lunch hour working out in the gym that was down in the building's basement. Nothing was going to deter this plan, at least that's what she thought.

Rick Jackson approached her before she even sat down at her desk.

"I thought you might be taking the day off," he said.

She gave him a curious look. "Now why would you think that?"

"I don't know. You're usually in here by eight."

"I stopped off for coffee," she said. "New me."

"I kinda liked the old you. More dependable."

Donahue shook her head and smiled. "So what's up old man?"

Jackson handed her a piece of paper. "I heard back from my source at Homeland. It seems the old rules of secrecy in the banking world have informally changed. He says the banks are cooperating with us because they're afraid if they don't the US will clamp down on them under our anti-terrorism laws."

Donahue studied the piece of paper. It contained an account number, a name, and several amounts.

"What's this all mean?" she asked him.

Mitzi was right on the mark. FCIB did stand for First Caribbean International Bank. The number on that piece of paper from Komarov's wallet was for an account in the name of someone named Alexei Kuznetsov. I asked him for the account information and he said it would take a federal warrant, but he pulled a few strings and told me that there had been two money transfers into the account over the past two years, each one was for a hundred thousand dollars."

Donahue's mind was racing.

"Do we know the dates of the transfers?"

Jackson shook his head. "Nope, and until we get a warrant, we can't get that information. But I think we need to follow through with this because with a warrant, we can get the account number and bank information that will let us know where the money came from."

"Can I get you to follow-up on that for me, Rick? I've got too many irons in the fire."

"For you, anything," he said.

Donahue took the paper and sat down at her computer. She typed in the name of Alexei Kuznetsov, but after searching through the local data banks, she didn't come up with a single hit.

Disappointed, she left the paper on the top of her desk and headed off to find the Captain to brief him about her plans.

When she arrived at Elwood's office, she found John Homa and Andrew Magarian seated in front of the Captain's desk. Elwood looked up from their conversation and waved her in.

"I was just going to come out and find you," he said. "Grab a chair."

Donahue acknowledged Homa and Magarian, but she was momentarily thrown off by their appearance. She'd been working closely with them and there had been no apparent problems, so why did they go over her head to the Captain with whatever they were here for instead of coming first to her?

"I called them in," Elwood said, recognizing the concern on her face. "I had an idea last night and I wanted to talk to them first before I even brought it up with you."

Donahue nodded. She didn't need to respond verbally. Her concerns were now alleviated and she knew that Elwood would fill her in.

"I wanted to confirm that Clay Young is off the hook. Lieutenant Magarian here says they've confirmed that his wife did inherit a sizable amount of money, more than enough to account for the purchases that he's made."

"That's a relief," she said.

Elwood nodded. "It occurred to me that instead of spooking this female and hoping that she gives Pavienko a call, why not make use of his partner? They seem pretty close, and if we bring him in, we might be able to secure his cooperation with our investigation."

Donahue thought about it for a moment, then shook her head.

"I don't know, boss. I think it might be risky."

"What makes you say that?" Magarian asked.

"He's partners with our suspect. We're asking him to turn on his partner without any way of guaranteeing that he won't turn on us and ruin the case."

"If he's clean, Jen, he'll help us out," Elwood said.

"*If* is the operative word." She felt as though she was fighting a losing battle, but she strongly felt that this was a big mistake and she intended to stop it if she could.

"We believe Leigh Cherlina was the conduit that Pavienko was using to warn off Hagopian," she said. "If we get her thinking that we're on to her, she might turn to him for advice, and if we can capture that conversation, we should have enough to take Yuri down. After that, we can put pressure on Cherlina and get her to turn on him in court. It seems less complicated to me and I think it will work."

"What do you say Lieutenant?" Elwood asked Magarian. "Have we got enough leverage on Young to get him to make a call for us?"

"I'm not sure that we do. I think Detective Donahue has got a good point. Getting a guy to turn on his partner if very tough, particularly when the evidence we've got against Pavienko is all circumstantial. The only way I can see that we can turn Young would be to have something on him that would weigh so heavily that he'd have no choice but to cooperate."

"Do we have anything like that?"

"Not that I know of," Magarian replied. He exhaled slowly, then turned to Donahue.

"When were you planning to rattle Cherlina's cage?"

"This evening. We want to have everything ready, including all your wire-taps."

"We'll have the taps in place by noon," Homa told her.

"Our delay will be the search warrants," Donahue told them, "and we need to make sure we have our search teams and security in place in case we decide to take the two of them down."

Magarian looked at Elwood.

"We can bring Young in again this afternoon and lean on him. We can tell him what we think is going on with his partner and how that could impact his future with the department. If he is truly innocent, he might be so pissed off that he's getting painted with the same brush, that he might just be willing to stiff in a call."

"How much would you have to tell him?" Donahue asked.

Magarian shifted his glance to Homa. "I don't know. I imagine we'd have to let him know that we suspect that his partner was on the take. I'm just thinking out loud here. We could tell him that we're looking at Hagopian's cell phone records, and that we plan to track down all the calls he made and received because we think that he might have been warned by a dirty cop."

"But he had Cherlina make the call," Donahue reminded him.

"We could tell him that we'll be looking at all the phone records for everyone who called Hagopian during the last forty-eight hours. We can say that we've got a new computer algorithm that will match up the calls and let us know if someone was using a cutout. Then once Young makes the call to Pavienko, you can pay Cherlina a visit and tell her that her number came up on Hagopian's phone. If she tells you about what's going on, then great, but if she doesn't, and if she puts a call into Pavienko, that will get us a second conversation which would double out chances of getting him to say something incriminating."

"I don't know," Donahue said. "What if Pavienko decides to go after her to shut her up?"

"You've got her under surveillance, right?"

Donahue nodded.

"Then we pull her in and put her into witness protection." Off Donahue's concerned look, "Look, you're gonna have to do that anyway because whether or not we use Clay Young, once she makes the call to Pavienko, you're gonna want to put her into PC until we have him securely in custody."

Donahue knew he was right. Once you put a civilian in a dangerous situation, even if that person is deeply involved in the crime, you had an obligation to keep them safe, and that trumped everything else, including the gathering of evidence for the case.

"Okay. It makes sense. But we need to make sure there are no slip-ups."

"There won't be," Magarian said. "We'll bring him down here at four p.m. He's not working today, so he'll probably be at home, asleep. I want him down here in your interview room because it will impress upon him the seriousness of his situation, and because if he does agree to cooperate, it will enable you guys to jump in and decide the best way to use him."

"I like it," said Elwood.

The decision was made, and Donahue had to agree that it did have distinct advantages.

"I like it too," she finally conceded. She looked over at the Captain. "I need to use the conference room as an operations center. I'll be in there working on the warrants." She turned back to Magarian.

"Let me know when you pick him up."

*****

At three-thirty p.m., Magarian and Homa arrived at Clay Young's home in the Simi-Valley, a residential community in the adjacent Ventura County. A surveillance unit from IA was parked down the block. They'd been watching the house since eight a.m., and they confirmed on a private tactical frequency that Young was inside with his family.

It was decided by Magarian to have the surveillance unit remain on scene in their undercover status until Young was on his way down to the PAB. They would act as a backup in case something went wrong, and as counter surveillance, if Magarian and Homa were followed away from the scene.

They approached the house and rang the front doorbell. Young's wife answered, and several of their children were standing behind her, wanting to know who had come to the door.

"Mrs. Young?"

When she acknowledged who she was, Magarian said, "I'm Andrew Magarian, from LAPD." He showed her his ID card. "This is my partner, John Homa. We need to chat for a few minutes with your husband. Can you tell him we're here?"

She stepped to the side and asked them in. After telling her sons to go back to their homework, she invited the detectives into the living room and went to get her husband who she said was still asleep.

They didn't sit, choosing instead to look around the room. There was a large screen TV, maybe seventy inches, which caused Homa to raise his eyebrows. The rest of the room was furnished with a large L-shaped couch, several comfortable recliner chairs, and Aa large coffee table that was strewn with gossip magazines.

"Nice place," said Homa under his breath to Magarian. "I'm gonna have to get a larger TV."

Magarian nodded. Both men were lost in their own thoughts when Clay Young appeared in the archway followed closely by his wife.

"Lieutenant?" he said. "What's going on?"

To Magarian, he appeared as advertised. A man in a half buttoned shirt, a pair of sweatpants, bare feet, and in need of a shave. They had obviously awakened him from a nap.

"Can we speak to you alone for a few moments?" Magarian said.

Young studied him carefully, not sure where this was going, but he had no choice. The last thing he wanted was to worry his wife, so he turned to her and said, "This won't take long, hun. Why don't you join the kids in the kitchen while the Lieutenant and I have a talk?"

She nodded slowly, then headed out of the room. Once she was gone, Young turned to Magarian and said, "You come to my home? This is harassment, Lieutenant."

"Actually, it's not," Magarian replied. "Something has come up that we figured you might be interested in hearing about. We need you to come with us right away."

"We can't talk about it here?"

"I'm afraid not. There's a big operation underway, and you're wanted downtown for your valuable input."

Young thought things over and decided that he couldn't be in trouble, he hadn't down anything wrong. This must be about something else, maybe something to do with his knowledge of the workings of the Russian mob.

"Have I got time to get properly dressed?" he said.

"You're not gonna do something stupid are you sport?" Homa kept his Voice low. "Not gonna go runner on us or come downstairs with your gun in your hand?"

Young spun around to face him and noticed that Homa was smiling broadly, but to Young it seemed contrived, and any pretense of mirth was missing from his eyes.

"I don't know what this is all about, but I've done nothing wrong, so I find your implication to be insulting. I'm gonna go upstairs and get properly dressed, and if that's a problem, then perhaps I'll say no to your invitation without the presence of counsel."

Magarian smiled. "Lighten up, Young. You've got nothing to worry about, but you know the drill. The manual says that because of our prior contact, we need to take measures to ensure that there are no misunderstandings. *Capish?* My partner here will go upstairs with you while you get dressed. I'll stay down here and speak to your wife. I'll let her know there's a confidential operation underway and that RHD needs your expert advice."

RHD? Young was confused. *What the hell was going on?*

"I'm not a suspect in anything, right?" he asked.

"If you were you'd already be in cuffs," replied Homa.

"Fine. I'll get dressed. Have I got time for a shave?"

"Later," said Magarian. "We're on the clock."

Young nodded once, then headed out of the room and over to the staircase with Homa right behind him.

As Magarian made his way to the kitchen, he thought, *I'm gonna have to speak with John about his bedside manner. He really needs to tone it down.*

*****

Young was placed in an interview room and left for a few moments while Magarian and Homa met with Donahue and Thompson out in the hallway.

"Is he cooperative?" Donahue asked.

"He believes he's down here to assist you guys with an operation that's underway," Magarian said.

Donahue smiled. "That's putting lipstick on a pig."

"You want to handle the interrogation?" Magarian asked. "I think it might be wiser. If he doesn't think we're looking at him, he might be more coopera- tive." His eyes shifted briefly over to Homa. "And coming from you guys in- stead of us, I think you'll get much better results."

Homa knew he'd pushed too far. Eyes downcast, he said, "He doesn't seem to like me."

"That's putting eyeliner on the pig," Magarian said, referring to Homa's understatement.

"Sure. We'll handle it," said Donahue. She turned to Thompson. "Take them to the monitor room. If you guys think of anything you want us to cover with him, give a written note to Mitzi Roberts. She'll be in there with you, and she can carry it into us."

Thompson left with Magarian and Homa in tow while Donahue gathered up her thoughts for approaching the interrogation.

When Thompson returned a few minutes later, Donahue asked, "We all set?"

Thompson nodded.

They entered the room, and Clay's surprise was quite evident. He'd expected another questioning by Magarian and Homa, and here he was facing two very attractive women. He smiled to himself. Maybe they really did want nothing more than his professional expertise.

After the introductions were made, Thompson said, "We need to talk with you about your partner."

"My partner?" Now he was more than surprised. "You mean Yuri?"

Thompson nodded.

"How long have you worked with him?"

"A couple of years. Why?"

"What's he like?" Donahue asked.

Clay's mind was spinning. *Could Yuri have done something that would spill over onto me?* He didn't like being used as a source of info on his partner, especially when he didn't know what was at stake.

"Can you tell me what this is all about?" he asked, looking from one to the other. "If I know what you're asking about, I might be able to give you some real help."

Thompson looked over at Donahue, who nodded.

"Okay," said Thompson. "We've discovered that Martun Hagopian has a possible source within the police department."

"What? And you think it might be Yuri?" He smiled broadly. "No way. Yuri's a good cop, and he hates these mob guys. He wouldn't do anything to help them out."

"Did he ever talk to you about Hagopian?"

Clay nodded. "The night that Komarov introduced Yuri to Hagopian, we went back to the station. Yuri told me that Komarov told him that Hagopian was a friend of Komarov's or something like that from Dagestan and that Komarov was gonna help him out by letting him run a few girls and sell some dope in the clubs." He looked over at Thompson who was waiting for more. "Yuri asked me to check him out with the FSB. I did, and they said that he had no record."

"Did that seem strange to you?" Donahue asked.

"Yeah, a little. If he wasn't a gangster from Russia, then I doubt that Komarov would have had anything to do with him."

"Who was your contact at the FSB?" Thompson asked.

Clay shrugged. "Some guy that Yuri knew. I never met him or knew his name. Yuri said the guy was someone he met years ago at a law enforcement conference. He said the guy spoke English as a second language, so he gave me a number to call, and it was always picked up by an answering machine. I would give the guy what we had on a person like Hagopian, and he would usually send back an email letting us know if the guy had a record in Russia."

"And Yuri never gave you the name of this contact?"

Clay shook his head. "Why?"

Donahue leaned forward.

"Did Yuri ever mention a woman named Leigh Cherlina?"

Clay thought long and hard, then shook his head. "I don't recognize the name, but you need to know that Yuri is kind of a pussy hound, you'll pardon my French. He's got a new squeeze every couple of weeks."

Donahue shot a quick look at Thompson, who said, "You've made the assumption that this was one of his social contacts. Did he ever mention this woman's name in relation to any type of a business or company?"

"You mean like as a lawyer or something like that?"

"Something like that," Donahue said flatly.

"Not that I remember."

"She works for an insurance company," Thompson said.

Clay actually scratched his head.

"Nope. It doesn't ring a bell."

"Let me throw a few more names your way," said Thompson. "Does Eliska Rodinova ring your bell?"

Clay looked from one to the other.

"Should I know this woman?"

"I don't know. Do you?"

"Nope. Sorry. Never heard of her."

"How about Nika Kaminski?" said Donahue.

Clay closed his eyes and seemed to be considering it.

"You know," he finally said, "I have heard that name before. I'm trying to remember where?"

Donahue sat up straight. She hadn't expected to get a hit, so it came as a complete surprise. She wanted to ask a follow-up question, maybe something to stimulate his memory, but her training kicked in, and she held her breath. She needed to hear what he had to say without unintentionally influencing his answer.

He opened his eyes, surprised to find that both women were staring at him.

"If I'm not mistaken, this woman, Kaminski, met with Yuri one evening to talk about some kind of a scam."

"A scam?" said Donahue. "What kind of a scam?"

"I don't know. Yuri took the report. He said there was nothing to it, just a disgruntled employee at an insurance company who wasn't happy with her boss."

His face suddenly grew serious, and Donahue noted that his brow became creased with concern.

"Is that what this is all about? Was there something to that woman's claim of a scam?"

Thompson leaned forward.

"So you're telling us he shit-canned Kaminski's complaint?"

"He said there was nothing to it. Why? Was he wrong?"

"Kaminski's dead," Donahue said. "Shot to death a couple of weeks ago in Hollywood. Did you know about that?"

"She's dead? No. I didn't hear about that? What happened?"

He sounded sincere enough. Maybe he didn't know.

"When you and your partner work, do you keep a log of your activities?"

"Of course. We have to account for what we do." He looked over at Donahue. "He would have written up his contact with Kaminski. It shouldn't be too hard to locate if you have a time period in mind."

Donahue would have IA look into it. They had the manpower and the authority to do that kind of a search.

"How about your off duty hours? Do you or your partner maintain any type of a diary or calendar?"

For the first time since he was in there, Clay Young smiled.

"My wife and I've got four boys. We live by the entries on the calendar."

Thompson smiled back. She knew exactly what he was talking about.

"How about your partner?" Donahue asked.

"I doubt it. You can check his computer. Maybe something's there, but if he does, I'm not aware of it."

"Okay. Sit tight for a while, Clay. We're gonna take a quick break and check a few things out. I'll get someone to bring you a cup of coffee. How do you take it?"

"Straight up. Any idea how long this is gonna take?"

Donahue nodded.

"We're just getting started."

*****

Donahue and Thompson went straight to the video viewing room where

Elwood, Gibson, Roberts, Magarian, and Homa were all seated, waiting for their arrival.

"That was interesting," Elwood said when she sat down at the table. The entire group had watched the interview with Young.

"I'm not sure what we've got," Donahue said.

"It sounds like Pavienko is up to his eyebrows in this mess," Elwood ventured.

"But is he?" said Donahue.

When everyone looked her way, she added, "Nika mentions her suspicions to Leigh Cherlina, and she tells her to take it to Grushik who says she never said it at all. So she does what? She meets with Pavienko, and he dismisses her story as not credible. It may be shitty police work, but it doesn't connect Yuri to Nika's death."

"Jen's right," Thompson said. "We've got nothing that connects him directly with any of the murders" She slowly shook her head. "We keep looking at this as if the deaths are all related, and maybe they are. But what if they're being done by more than one person?"

Gibson shook his head.

"What happened to Hagopian being the out-of-town hitter? He shows up on the scene, and all of a sudden we've got two dead girls who we think were going to rat out Komarov on a murder for insurance scheme. Then, right after that, we've got Petrovich getting whacked, likely because he wasn't willing to give up his business, and later you get Komarov himself taken out by the one guy who benefits from his death."

"Hagopian again," said Thompson, "but that doesn't explain who knocked off the two husbands whose wives were agency brides?"

"I think Shari's right," Elwood said. "There's a lot going on here that we still don't know. We're gonna have to press Young even harder. He's the guy's partner, for God's sake. He has to have noticed something that was questionable over the last couple of years."

"We can try," said Donahue, but—"

A knock on the door cut her off. Rick Jackson stuck his head in, and when everyone looked up, he said, "Don Flynn's on the line for you, Jen. He says it's important."

Elwood nodded, and she got to her feet. She turned to Roberts.

"Mitz, can you get Young a cup of coffee, black?"

"No problem. Want me to talk to him, too? Loosen him up?"

"Let Shari do the talking. She's already got a rapport going with him."

She walked out of the room, hoping that Flynn might have something of value that would help them out.

*****

"Hey Don," she said when she picked up her phone.

"You sitting down?"

"What?"

He leaned back in his chair. "I just got a transcribed report from the FSB. Your officer Pavienko isn't who he claims to be."

Donahue could feel her stomach knotting up. She had no idea what to expect.

"I forwarded the prints you sent us on to the FBI, and their guy turned them over to the FSB. The prints come back to a guy named Alexi Kuznetsov."

"Kuznetsov? I know that name. Hagopian had a Cayman Islands bank account number in his wallet when we arrested him. We ran down the account, and it's in the name of Alexei Kuznetsov. Are you telling me that's our officer Yuri Pavienko?"

"What you sent me are the prints for Kuznetsov, so if they really are from your officer Pavienko, then the two of them are one and the same man."

Donahue was still trying to process what she'd heard when Flynn began again.

"It says here he was born in Saint Petersburg, Russia. Blue collar family. His father died when he was young; the mother hooked up with an alcoholic. She did time for drug addiction, then died shortly after being released. A drug overdose. Alexi and a younger brother found themselves at the mercy of a violent stepfather who was also a drunk. Alexi was sent to the *Kolpino* juvenile prison at age fourteen for robbery and assault. He did five years for a first offense."

"They don't fool around, do they?" She was writing furiously, thinking all the while that this was making everything just that much more complicated.

"Our Bureau guy says *Kolpino* was survival of the fittest, and Kuznetsov was a survivor. He hooked up with another guy while he was there, a kid who was two years older and was there on a second beef. Together, the two of them set up a protection racket within the facility. Inmates had to pay them rent just to be there. If they couldn't get money from family or friends, they paid tribute by doing Kuznetsov's bidding."

"For a moment, I was starting to feel a little sorry for this guy, but it sounds like he turned into a little thug."

"It appears that way," Flynn said. "Now here's where it gets even more interesting. Kuznetsov got out after his five years and disappeared off the face of the earth. The Russians lost track of him. There were rumors that he caught a bullet and the body was dumped in the Neva River in Saint Petersburg, but there was never a body to substantiate the claim."

"He probably left the country and went to Sweden. Did you hear from those guys yet?"

"I did. The Swedish police say he arrived on their shores as Yuri Pavienko. They ran a check of the name with the FSB, but no one had any reason to doubt the identity. Kuznetsov had an uncle who emigrated to Sweden with his family a number of years before. That uncle was a business owner and had Swedish citizenship, so when he vouched for the kid as Yuri Pavienko, the investigation went no further, and as Pavienko, he married a Swedish citizen, and later applied for Swedish citizenship, which they gave him. He then used his new Swedish passport to travel to the USA where he enlisted in our military and got US citizenship for serving our country."

"What about his time in the service?" she asked. "Supposedly, he was something of a hero?"

"All true, as Pavienko. Looks like he embraced his new identity completely."

"So all he lied about was his true identity, that and his prison record and the stuff that he did while at Kolpino?"

Flynn paused for a moment.

"Not exactly. The FSB says that Kuznetsov and his mentor, the other boy with him in prison, were suspected in the deaths of three young inmates during Kuznetsov's five years."

Donahue stopped writing. "How strong was the info?"

"They think it was good, but they couldn't get anyone to testify against them. Kuznetsov and his prison buddy were ruthless, and at least one of the deaths they were suspected of was of a twelve-year-old boy who they thought had snitched."

"This is almost too much to take in," she said.

"As a side note, when Kuznetsov was in the juvenile prison, he had a nickname. It was *Ubiytsa.* I had it translated. It means '*killer.* '"

"God damn it, Don, what a mess!" Donahue's stomach was churning. "Do the Russians want to have a piece of him?"

"No, they've got no charges pending against him."

"How about for using a phony Russian passport?"

"If you catch him in possession of one, they might be interested, but so would we."

"I was just hoping there might have been an outstanding warrant. We're grasping at straws here, Don. We know he's dirty, but we might have trouble getting our murders to stick."

Donahue's mind was working overtime. If Yuri Pavienko was really this guy Kuznetsov, then he was possibly a vicious killer who'd somehow managed to use the flaws in the system and a false identity to get himself hired by the LAPD. Hiring someone like that, someone with that kind of a criminal background, was tantamount to putting a fox in the hen house.

"*Oh, shit!*

Poor Nika...

Without knowing it, she'd ended up talking to the one person on the department who was directly involved in the criminal enterprise.

"One more thing," Flynn said, "and this is important."

Donahue was pretty sure she knew what was coming next.

"You're gonna tell me that his partner-in-crime back in the juvenile prison was Vlad Komarov."

"Close, but no cigar. His running partner in prison was a guy named Dimitri Federenko, nicknamed '*Dimi*,' who's known to you folks as Martun Hagopian."

*****

By the time everyone was gathered around the table in the conference room some things had been made clear, and though much of what they thought was based on pure speculation, they came up with a working scenario that seemed to make sense.

Donahue was convinced that Yuri Pavienko had settled in Los Angeles and had taken a position with LAPD to have an inside track and a service he could offer to members of Russian organized crime. He had probably approached Vlad Komarov, who had seen the value of a connection within the police. It was likely that Komarov had hired Yuri to dispose of the two husbands so that Komarov could extort the lions share of the money from the unsuspecting Eastern European women who would pay up without reporting the extortion to law enforcement to protect their lives and their relatives back home.

But Komarov had gotten greedy. He needed a business to launder the insurance money, and Milan Petrovich's agency offered him a way to kill two birds with one stone. He had demanded a fifty percent share of the business, and when Petrovich had balked and went to the police, Komarov likely decided to have him killed.

She postulated that Yuri had likely used a cutout from Dagestan who prevailed upon Komarov to help out a fellow Vor who was looking to relocate to LA. When Hagopian arrived, he kept his relationship with Yuri a secret from Komarov, and Komarov—who likely learned from Hagopian about his expertise with explosives—probably believed that Hagopian was the answer to his dilemma. He would have Hagopian carry out the hit on Petrovich.

But it looked as though Yuri and Hagopian had much larger ambitions, and to accomplish their goals, they had to get rid of Vlad Komarov. Whether it was Yuri Pavienko or Hagopian who actually killed Komarov, their plan had worked, for once Komarov was out of the picture, Hagopian had taken over

Komarov's role with the agency, and it appears that Yuri was completely content to be Hagopian's silent partner.

But who killed Nika and Eliska?

For many reasons, Donahue suspected that Yuri might have done it himself.

For one thing, Nika had apparently gone to the OCI where she had been routed to Yuri because of his expertise in everything Russian. It was Nika's bad luck that the one guy at LAPD that she had spoken to was deeply involved in the scam. At some point, after nothing came of her complaint, she must have suspected that he was corrupt, hence Nika's call to Donahue and her insistence on the phone that Donahue keep their pending meeting a secret.

Telling Yuri that she had figured out what was going on was the event that likely signed her death warrant. He must have taken it upon himself to take her life, and because he was probably worried that she'd shared her suspicions with her lover, he had also seen fit to kill Eliska.

It was Thompson who decided that the connection with Leigh Cherlina had probably come about by design. She was in a position to be of inestimable help in making sure that the investigations into the insurance cases went smoothly. Yuri was a good looking guy and definitely a ladies man. He'd gotten to Cherlina, and whether she knew it or not, he was using her to further his scheme.

The group spent twenty minutes trying to punch holes in the theory, but by and large, they came around to accepting the premise.

Now they were going to have to figure out how to prove it?

It was decided to use Clay Young to stiff in a call to his partner. By letting him think they were getting close, he would be primed for a call from Cherlina that would scare him into thinking that they were closer than he suspected. They would place her into protective custody right after the call, then take him down whether or not he said anything incriminating on the phone.

They would have Roberts continue to focus exclusively on the phone records for everyone involved, and Jackson would concentrate on running down the money transfers to determine where they came from and when they occurred in relation to the murders they were investigating. If Donahue was correct, and if the deposits came from Vlad Komarov, they just might be payouts for the killings of Philip Katz and William Baker.

"We better get something when we search his place," Elwood warned, "otherwise, we might not be able to hold him for long."

"Do the Russians want him?" Thompson asked hopefully.

"No help there. Flynn says they've got nothing on him," Donahue told her.

"Jeez! We're really walking a fine line here."

Elwood scratched at his chin. "Looks like we're only going to get one crack at this, so spend the extra effort to check everything twice. Anything else?"

When no one had any more questions, the meeting broke up.

Magarian approached Donahue.

"If you guys can get someone to hang with Clay Young and monitor his call to his partner, John and I will be able to oversee the team that has his partner under surveillance."

Donahue turned to Jackson.

"Rick? You wanna oversee Young's call to Pavienko?"

"Be glad to," Jackson said.

"Okay, then. I'm going home for a few hours. I'll be back here at six. See you all then."

Donahue walked out, and Jackson said to Thompson, "Is something going on with Jen?"

Thompson caught his glance.

"No. Why?"

"I don't know. She just seems to me to be acting a little different."

"It's nothing," Thompson assured him, suspecting that Donahue was still dealing with the cancer scare she'd just gone through.

"I think she just plans to go for a run or something," she told him. "It's her new way of dealing with stress."

Magarian walked up and said to Jackson, "You ready for me to hand off Officer Young?"

"Sure. Might as well let him know what we have in mind and what we expect him to do."

They headed off with Homa to speak with Young while Thompson returned to her cubical and tried to come to grips with the fact that for all her training and life experience, she'd been incredibly careless in her personal life when she let her libido trump her common sense.

Donahue wasn't the only one who needed to reassess the way she'd been living her life.

I'm gonna have to do that, too.

CHAPTER 56

November 6,   8:00 p.m.

Teams of detectives had been working all day to get ready for the eight p.m. kickoff to the operation. Donahue had gone for a run and taken a half-hour nap before showing back up at the squad to review the final details. Thompson, for her part, had landed a babysitter she'd used once before, so she didn't bother to leave the squad, choosing instead to eat a quick meal across the street with Gibson who decided to stick around too.

SIS was covering the apartment occupied by Leigh Cherlina. Embarrassed after losing Hagopian during the previous surveillance, they had tightened up and were pulling out all the stops for this one. They followed her home from the Insurance Company and had three teams stationed in the neighborhood to insure that she couldn't slip their surveillance. They obtained a warrant to place a tracking device on her car which they installed while she was working, so they were able to tail her without getting too close by using a laptop software program.

IA's specialized surveillance unit was set up on Yuri. He'd been home for the better part of the day, and they had four teams sitting around his block to pick him up if he decided to leave. He too had a tracker on his car, just in case he slipped the surveillance.

Search warrants to listen in on their calls were obtained for Yuri's department issued cell phone as well as for his personal one. Leigh Cherlina only had one cell phone registered to her name, and that was covered by the warrant as well. Their respective lines were now tapped, and an experienced team was assembled to monitor and record their calls in case something important was said.

Clay Young had been given a polygraph exam in the late afternoon to ensure that he wasn't harboring any guilty knowledge of what they believed his partner had been up to. He'd passed the first time, so they briefed him on some of what they had by way of evidence. He was shocked to learn that Martun Hagopian had been killed by the San Diego police, but he was even more blown away to discover that Yuri may have warned Cherlina who likely passed on a warning to Hagopian.

He said it made him sick to know that his partner might be working with the Russian mob, and he was even more concerned when Jackson told him that Yuri was actually a Russian convict who'd been suspected of involvement in several murders. Young said he'd do whatever he could to help them with their investigation, so with the assistance of Donahue and Thompson, they created a tentative script that Young could follow to hopefully elicit an incriminating statement from the partner that he'd once trusted with his life.

Donahue and Thompson joined the stakeout at Cherlina's apartment. They intended to walk through the door and talk with her just as soon as they got the word that Clay Young's taped call to Yuri was complete.

Elwood had overseen the briefing that was given to members of SWAT who would be used to secure Yuri and his residence location. Bengtson was set to secure Yuri's office computer which would be searched for any incriminating information once everything settled down.

The detectives from Hollywood, West Valley, and West LA were poised to assist in the search of Yuri's apartment. Since all four teams had separate interests, they would be looking for anything unique to their respective cases.

All in all, Donahue and Thompson were satisfied that they had done everything they could to prepare for any possible unforeseen events. Now all they could do was wait to hear from Jackson, so they spent the final hours discussing the events of the last few weeks and how both of them were going to adjust their personal lives.

*****

"You ready?" Jackson asked him.

"Yeah. Let's do this."

They were seated in one of the interview rooms. It had been decided that Clay would make the call on his department-issued cell phone. To use any other line might spook Yuri who would wonder why his partner would call him on some other line.

Jackson dialed Yuri's cell phone number, then handed the phone to Clay.

Yuri picked it up on the seventh ring.

"Yeah," he said, obviously groggy. Clay was pretty sure that he'd woken him up.

"It's me. You awake?"

"Not really. What's up?"

"IA hauled me in again. I've been stuck with them for the last few hours."

"Where are you calling from?" he said in a cautionary tone of voice.

"I'm still in the PAB. I'm down on the first floor in the Chief's conference room. No one's around. I didn't want to be overheard."

That seemed to satisfy Yuri.

"So what'd they want this time?"

"They told me that they think they've got someone on the inside who's been feeding information to Hagopian. The fuckers wanted to know my whereabouts last night, and whether or not either one of us has been working Hagopian as a CI."

Yuri sat up straight in his bed.

"Oh, yeah? So what'd you tell 'em?"

"I told them I was home last evening with my wife. I said we ran Hagopian through the FSB but nothing came up, and it was then that they told me that the FSB said he's using a phony name."

Yuri stood up and scratched his head. This was not good, not good at all.

"Do they have him in custody?" he asked.

"I don't think so, but they didn't say."

Yuri started to get dressed.

"Exactly what did they tell you, Clay?" He was starting to get testy. He liked having Clay as a partner, but he tended to be long winded and took his time getting around to the point.

"They said they've got Hagopian's phone and they're gonna find out exactly who he's been talking to and who's called him."

Yuri laughed, but it sounded strained.

"Then we've got nothing to worry about, Clay. We haven't seen or talked to that guy in more than a week."

"Yeah, I know, but these guys have got a hard on for me, Yuri. They said if I know anything about what's going on, then now is the time to say so."

"Or what, Clay? They've got nothing on you so they can just go fuck themselves."

Clay was silent for a moment.

"They asked about you too, Yuri."

There was a moment of uncomfortable silence.

"What'd they want to know?"

"They wanted to know if either one of us knew someone named Leigh Cherlina?"

There was another long pause.

"And what'd you tell them?" Yuri finally said between his teeth.

"I said I don't know anyone with that name. I told them they'd have to ask you, that I don't keep up with all the women you see."

Yuri was silent, and Clay held his breath. According to Donahue, they'd reached the point where Yuri would begin to suspect that the conversation might be monitored.

"They said she works for some insurance company," Clay added, "if that makes any sense?"

Yuri was too smart to admit knowing the woman, and his suspicions were now sufficiently aroused. If Clay's call was being monitored, he was not about to give them anything they could use.

"We've got nothing to worry about, partner. We've done nothing wrong. I'll see you later tonight at the office. We can talk about it more when I get in."

Before Clay could speak again, Yuri hung up the phone.

Clay hit the disconnect button on his phone, which was attached to a suction cup that had recorded everything that was said. He looked up at Jackson and said, "I don't think that did much good."

Jackson had taken out his phone and was placing a call to Donahue. When she picked up the phone, he told her, "Clay made the call, but Yuri didn't cop to anything, and he doesn't know that Hagopian is dead. I'll notify Elwood. Good luck with Cherlina."

*****

Donahue and Thompson climbed out of their car and walked across the street to the apartment building in Encino where Leigh Cherlina was living in apartment number 306. They entered the unsecured building, going over to the elevator where they waited for the door to open.

"Watch her carefully," Donahue said to Thompson. "We're on her turf and we have no idea how deeply involved she may be."

"Don't worry about that. I've got no desire to get shot by some crazy woman."

They rode up in the elevator, got off on the third floor, then walked over to the door for 306 and pressed the button for the doorbell. They heard footsteps approaching, and a moment later an eye appeared at the peephole. When the security chain was unhooked, the door was quickly opened.

Leigh Cherlina was dressed in slacks and a light blue pullover sweater. She stared at the detectives.

"Is something wrong?"

"We need to talk to you, Leigh," said Donahue. She didn't ask for permission to enter, and Thompson followed her in. Thompson shut the door behind them while Donahue began moving into the living room, followed closely by Cherlina.

Thompson walked over to an armchair and lifted the cushion, looking for a concealed weapon. When none was found, she pushed the cushion down and gestured for Cherlina to come over to the chair.

"Take a seat, Leigh," Donahue said.

Cherlina shifted her glance between the two detectives, looking for any clue she could decipher that would help her understand what was going on. Whatever it was, there was no mistaking the seriousness of their intent.

Uh, oh, she thought.

She quickly sat down and folded her hands in her lap while Donahue and Thompson sat across from her on a couch.

"I'm not going to mince words with you, Leigh. We're here because you're in serious trouble. We're gonna try and help you out of this, but you're only going to get one chance to make things right, and if you fail to cooperate, you're going to have to face the consequences completely on your own."

Cherlina's eyes shifted from one to the other. When they locked on Thompson's, she said, "What are you talking about?"

"How well do you know Yuri Pavienko?" Donahue asked.

Cherlina's eyes went wide. She instantly suspected why they were there, but like most other people who found themselves in an untenable situation, her first reaction was to lie.

"I went out with him a few times. Nothing came of it. Why?"

"When did you last see him?" Thompson asked.

"A while ago. I don't know for sure."

Donahue shook her head.

"Ah, there. You see. That's not true, Leigh. You saw him last night when you climbed into his car. We have it on tape." She met Cherlina's glare. "You want to try again?"

Cherlina looked down at her lap. Her mind was reeling. It was plainly obvious that they'd had her under surveillance, and that was likely only the beginning of what they knew.

So once again, she tried to tough it out.

"He gave me a call. He wanted to see me. He was going in to work, so I met with him for a couple of minutes, and we did a little necking." She looked up and locked eyes with Donahue. "Is that what you wanted to hear?"

Thompson visibly shook her head. "She doesn't get it, Jen."

Cherlina's eyes turned in her direction.

Thompson fixed her with a stare.

"This is your one chance to avoid going to jail tonight, Leigh, and if you lie to us again, we're gonna take you in and charge you. Is that what you want?"

"Maybe I should get a lawyer," she replied, still holding Thompson's glare.

Thompson smiled. "Maybe you should."

She got to her feet and smiled. "Take a good look around, Leigh, and say goodbye to this place. This will probably be the last time you'll ever set foot in here again."

Cherlina's eyes widened.

"What are you talking about?"

"Murder," Thompson said without emotion. "So don't act so stupid, Leigh. You know we work at Robbery-Homicide. We're not here to question you about your social life. We're here to evaluate your role in a couple of murders, and your decision to cooperate and possibly convince us that you were not involved appears to have already been made."

Thompson got to her feet and removed her handcuffs from her waistband. "Stand up," she said.

Cherlina's thoughts were now coming at warp speed. She had no idea what they knew and she had no idea what murder they were talking about. The only thing she could imagine was that this had something to do with Nika Kaminski, and Yuri had told her that Nika was probably killed by a jealous female lover.

"Hold on," she said, raising her hands in a gesture of surrender. "I'm not involved in any murder case. I'll answer your questions. I thought you were just prying into my social life. I didn't know—"

Her cell phone, which was on the adjacent kitchen counter, began to ring. Cherlina started to get to her feet, but Thompson ordered her to remain seated while Donahue stood up and walked over to the phone.

"It's Pavienko," she said to Thompson after looking at the screen.

"That didn't take long," Thompson replied.

Donahue left the phone on the counter top and returned to the couch.

When the phone finally stopped ringing, she said, "We know you passed a message for Yuri last night to a guy named Martun Hagopian. Tell us about that, Leigh."

Cherlina knew they had her. They probably knew what she'd said, too. She couldn't believe this was happening to her, and she actually started to cry.

Donahue gave Thompson a quick look while they waited for her to start talking.

"He told me he had an informant that was working for him. He said that some Russian mobsters were after him, and if he called him directly, the phone number could be traced back to LAPD. He told me I could help him keep the informant safe, so I said I would. He said to tell him... *They know who you are. It's time to take off.'*"

"Did you make the call?"

Cherlina nodded.

"Did Hagopian say anything in response?"

"He said, 'Thank you.' That's all he said."

"How well do you know Martun Hagopian?"

"I don't know him. I didn't even know his name until you just said it." She looked down again, her hands clenched tightly in her lap.

"I called him a second time that night," she admitted. "Yuri called me and woke me up. He said the mob guys knew that he was driving a Toyota. He told me to tell the guy that they knew what kind of car he was driving and that he should get a different one."

Donahue knew they finally had her. She had volunteered the information about the second call, and while they didn't know the content of the conversation, she recalled that Pavienko had overheard Roberts when she said she going to put the car info out statewide to all law enforcement agencies.

She had to bite her tongue. That bastard had clearly been the source of a warning to a known and wanted felon. She was more resolved than ever to bring him down.

"How well do you know Yuri?" Thompson asked.

Cherlina looked up. "We've been dating for the last year or so."

"Dating or intimate?"

"Is that important?"

"We need to know how close you were to him," Donahue said.

Cherlina wasn't sure why that was important at all, but she was no longer going to lie.

"We've been intimate, " she said without emotion.

"Did he ever talk with you about Nika Kaminski?"

"Nika? Not really. I asked him once about her and he said she was probably killed by a jealous female lover." Her eyes flashed from one to the other. "Don't tell me he had something to do with Nika's death?"

"When Nika discovered that there were a couple of Russian women that she knew who'd filed claims for life insurance benefits, what did she say to you about it?"

"She told me that both women met their husbands through a dating agency and that both husbands had been murdered. When I looked the cases over, I told her that I thought it was just a strange coincidence, but nothing sinister."

"Oh? And why was that?"

"Well, because one man was killed here in Los Angeles, and the other on a trip to London. On top of that, the policies were issued by two different companies, so I didn't see any real connection."

"You told us before that you would pass the information on to Nicholi Grushik. Did you do that?"

Cherlina shook her head.

"I think I told you that I suggested that she talk it over with Mr. Grushik and she said she would."

"So you never asked him about it?"

"No."

"Do you know if she actually spoke to him about it?"

"She told me she did, and that he said that he'd look into it, but I never heard anything more about it after that."

Donahue was satisfied with Cherlina's answers. She would have to undergo a polygraph examination, but if she was telling the truth, she was nothing more than a naive female who'd been duped by a charismatic man.

But now was her moment of destiny. If she willing cooperated by making a call to Yuri, one that would be scripted, then the odds were good that she would end up a witness rather than a co-conspirator.

The choice would be hers.

Donahue leaned forward on the couch and said, "We want you to call him, Leigh. We want you to tell him that we came by here tonight and that we've been talking to you about the calls you made for him. I want you to ask him what's going on? What has he gotten you into? I want you to tell him that we are investigating the murder of Nika Kaminski, and that we think it's tied in with an insurance scam. Can you do that for us?"

Cherlina was no dummy. Yuri had apparently done something very wrong, and she was willing to cooperate fully if it meant that she wouldn't be dragged into it as well. But they were talking about murder, and she had no idea what

Yuri's role in that might be. She knew Yuri could be quite difficult. At times he'd displayed to her a volatile temper. She wasn't sure why the phone calls she'd made were such a big issue...unless Yuri lied to her and the guy she called was not an informant being chased by the mob.

Oh my God! That had to be it.

But now her overriding concern was for her own safety. If she made this call, would it put her life at risk?

"If I do this for you, will I be safe?"

"We'll see to your safety," said Donahue. "After you make the call, we'll have a team of officers move you to a hotel for tonight. By tomorrow, he'll be in custody, and you'll have nothing to worry about."

*****

When she didn't answer her phone, Yuri decided that something was probably wrong. He feared the worst, that RHD was on to her, which meant that he would soon be next.

He guessed that he'd slipped up by having her make those two calls. He could have done it himself from a pay phone, but at the time it seemed better to distance himself by using her as a cutout. But if RHD were on to her already, it wouldn't take them long to start knocking on his door.

He had no illusions that he could talk his way out of this one. He'd made a major mistake, and it was time to cut his losses.

He didn't need this job. He could vanish into the underground quite easily, and he had more than enough money salted away to last him for a very long time.

About the only thing he could do for himself now was to finish cleaning up his loose ends. He'd need to sever any links that connected him to the case, and he could do that now before he disappeared. And while it would likely not change their interest in him, if the connections were all severed, they'd never be able to charge him with a crime.

He suspected that he was probably under surveillance, most likely by the-SIS. He'd need to hurry if he was going to get away, but he had a plan in place and he kept a bag at the ready just in case this situation ever arose.

He was wearing jeans, a t-shirt and a sweater, topped off with a black leather jacket. He was armed with nine in a shoulder rig, and before stepping out of his apartment, he grabbed his laptop computer, a helmet, and a set of motorcycle keys.

*****

Yuri always considered himself a survivalist. It was in his nature to plan for the worst, and for once he suspected that his planning would pay off.

He had rented a parking stall in the garage of the apartment building next door to where he was living. His street was one continuous line of three-story apartment buildings, all of which had city mandated underground parking garages. He took the elevator down to the garage in his building, then used the stairwell to go back up to the ground floor. The stairwell had an emergency exit on the side of the building that was secured from the inside, and once he went through it, the door locked behind him. He had previously planned this escape route and easily jumped the fence in the darkened side yard, landing on the walkway of the building next door. From there, he walked around to the back of the building and used the pedestrian entryway to go into the garage. A key locked door provided security, but he'd been given a key when he rented the parking slot.

He put on his helmet, slid the laptop into a saddlebag, then left the building on his cherished Harley Davidson, a 2012 Softail Slim.

*****

Down the street, one of the parked surveillance units noticed a motorcycle pull out of the building next door to Pavienko's. The bike came their way, and they noted that the driver was wearing a full face helmet with a dark plastic faceplate.

"Is that a Harley Softail?" said the officer in the passenger seat.

"Looks like it," replied the one in the driver's seat.

They watched it slowly drive by, and both of them instinctively continued to look at it in their respective rearview mirrors as it reached the corner and turned to the West.

*****

"You ready to make the call?" Donahue asked.

Cherlina nodded. She was terrified to do it, but she knew it was probably the right thing to do. Thompson had confided to her that the man she'd spoken to the night before was wanted by the police as a suspect in a murder, and that Yuri had been helping him to get away. That angered Cherlina, and she wondered in reflecting on her relationship with Yuri just how she could have been so gullible.

Donahue walked over to Cherlina's cell phone and picked it up. She handed it to her and said, "You know what to say. Just don't get hysterical and don't try to pump him for information. All we want you to do is get him to talk with you about the calls you made last night. We want to hear his explanation for getting you to make them. Okay?"

Cherlina nodded. Her mouth was dry, so she took a sip from a plastic water bottle that Thompson had removed from inside her kitchen.

They'd taken the time to attach a suction cup to her cell phone which was wired to a tape recorder. Donahue had a set of earphones attached to the recorder, so she could monitor the conversation as it occurred. She and Thompson had worked out a signal that Donahue would give her when she was convinced that they'd gotten all they could get on the phone. It would then be Thompson who would call Gibson at the command post set up half a mile away from Pavienko's apartment, and it would be Gibson who would give the go to SWAT who would then move in to take Yuri into custody.

Donahue checked the recorder to make sure that it was working, then gave Cherlina the signal to make the call.

Leigh hit the redial button on the missed call screen and the phone began to ring. She let it ring a half dozen times before it switched over to his voicemail.

"Yuri, it's me," she said in a nervous tone. "I need to talk to you right now.

Call me back as soon as you get my message. I'm at home."

She hung up the phone and her eyes met Donahue's.

"What do we do now?"

"We wait and try again in fifteen minutes," Donahue said.

"And if he doesn't answer then?"

"Then we try again."

*****

Yuri pulled up on his Harley in front of the neighboring house; a single family home in an exclusive residential area known as Park Place in the Encino Hills. The home he was interested in was located on a mountain road of high end homes, all of them with panoramic views of the San Fernando Valley.

He parked his bike on the downhill side of the street, about three hundred feet away from the house in question. He got off the bike, walked back up the hill and made his way to the front door.

The house was an English Tudor in design, with white stucco walls, green wood trim, and a gray slate roof. The home was large, five bedrooms and six baths, with a circular driveway in the front yard. A television was on in the front living room; he could see the ambient light from the screen as it flickered on the closed window curtains.

The front porch light was also still on, so it took him a few moments, but he got the carriage fixture open and unscrewed the bulb.

He then removed his driving gloves and raised the faceplate on his helmet. He pulled out his handgun, concealed it in one hand behind his back, then quietly rapped on the door. When no one immediately answered, he knocked again, this time more forcefully.

He heard footsteps approaching, then sensed that someone was looking at him through the peephole.

"Who is it?" said a male voice through the door.

"Police," he replied. He held his badge up, literally inches away from the peephole.

A moment later, the door swung open.

Nicholi Grushik was in his robe and pajamas. He stared at the figure on his doorstep.

"Yuri? Is that you?"

Yuri brought the gun out from behind his back and shot Grushik point blank in the face. He then lowered the faceplate, picked up the ejected shell casing, spun around on his heels, and walked off.

*****

Donahue had Cherlina tried to reach Yuri a second time, but when the call wasn't answered, she told Cherlina to disconnect the call without leaving a second message. Too many messages might sound too suspicious, and they didn't want to tip their hand.

She then placed a call to Gibson who told her that he'd call her back after he consulted for a while with the Captain.

There were a lot of men and women committed to this operation, and after listening to a tape of the call made by Clay Young to Yuri, the two men were all but convinced that the odds of Yuri saying anything incriminating on the phone to Cherlina were slim to none.

"So, do we give her more time to reach him on the phone?" Gibson asked.

Elwood shook his head. "I don't think we have that option, Gibby. We know he's still inside his apartment, so let's not screw around. Tell Donahue we're gonna pick him up."

Gibson called Donahue back and delivered the news.

"Tom's going to arrange to have her moved to a hotel," he said, "so get her to pack up what she's gonna need for a few days, then I want you and Shari to bring her down to the squad until we get everything sorted out."

"You don't want us to handle the search over at Yuri's place?"

"We've already got too many people who'll be going through the place. We won't miss anything, I promise."

"Will you let me know when you have him in custody?"

"I will, and in the meantime, think you guys can handle her security?"

"I suppose so, why?"

"Elwood says the SIS guys have been on for more than twelve hours, and since we know where Yuri's at, he'd like to cut 'em loose and send 'em home."

"Makes sense. We'll hang out here until he get's picked up. Call me when that happens."

Donahue hung up the phone then turned to Cherlina.

"Leigh, I need you to get your stuff together. We're going to move you into a hotel until we get everything sorted out."

"Right now?" she asked, concerned.

"Plan for a couple of days. Okay?"

Cherlina nodded and left the room to start packing.

When she was out of earshot, Thompson asked, "They don't want her to make the call?"

"Apparently not. The Captain thinks it's not necessary. We're gonna hang here until Gibby calls to tell us that Yuri's in custody."

"Well, in that case, I'm gonna check out the kitchen." Thompson smiled. "I think I'll brew us up a pot of coffee."

CHAPTER 57

November 6,   8:30 p.m.

When SWAT got the green light to take down the apartment, they rolled by convoy into the neighborhood. Surprise was their first line weapon.

An armored vehicle led the group, followed by four black Chevrolet sedans, each one carrying two members of the team. Each officer had an assignment, and this type of assault had been practiced by them so many times before that most of them acted on auto-pilot.

The armored truck contained six officers who constituted the entry team. The rest of the units took up positions on all four sides of the building to insure that the suspect and the scene were contained.

An ambulance and several fire trucks were parked in a lot four blocks away. They were available for immediate response should something go wrong with the entry.

An hour before the assault kicked off, members of LAPD's SIS unit had tracked down the phone numbers of the other units in the building to facilitate the evacuation of the occupants. All but one of the adjacent apartments had been successfully cleared, and as the team approached Pavienko's unit, two members of the team used a passkey from the manager to enter and clear the one remaining unit whose occupants, as it turned out, were not even home.

The team in the van moved quickly to the front door of the second story apartment. Two flash-bang grenades were thrown through the front window into the living room. Seconds later, the door was taken down by force and the team made entry.

A quick search of the apartment was made but Yuri Pavienko was not inside. A check of the garage revealed that his car was still parked in the unit's assigned slot, so the leader of the SWAT team immediately notified the command post, and Gibson was advised that Pavienko was gone.

"How the hell did he slip the surveillance?" Elwood asked. "I thought we had units throughout the neighborhood?"

Gibson shrugged. "We need to get the surveillance guys in here and see if anyone remembers seeing anything unusual."

Elwood nodded and immediately got on the phone. He reached Andrew Magarian, the leader of the team that had handled the surveillance, and Magarian personally assured him that he would quickly debrief the others and would call him back within the hour.

"Shouldn't we get SIS back on Cherlina's place?" Gibson asked. "With Yuri on the loose, I don't think we should take any chances. He might decide she's a link that needs to be taken out."

"How long ago did we call 'em off?" Elwood asked.

Gibson checked his watch.

"About thirty-five minutes ago."

"Are Donahue and Thompson still with her?"

Gibson nodded. "I told 'em to hang there until we picked Yuri up."

"Tell 'em to hang tight until we get SIS back on the scene. This guy probably doesn't know that we hit his place so he might be getting dinner somewhere before coming in for his duty shift."

Gibson took out his cell phone. "While I'm talking to Jen, do you want to make the call to SIS?"

"I'll take care of it now," Elwood said. "In the meantime, just have them sit tight."

*****

When Donahue's cell phone rang, she checked the screen and knew right away that the call was from Gibson.

"Did you pick him up?" she said upon answering.

"He gave the surveillance units the slip, and just as I was about to call you, Magarian called me. He said they talked to neighbors, and it turns out that Pavienko had a motorcycle he kept in a parking slot in the building next door. The bike's gone, so we think he's on it, and one of the teams saw the bike come out of the neighboring building about an hour before we hit the apartment."

"Was that before or after Clay Young's call?" she asked.

398

"Had to be after," Gibson said.

"Did it look like Yuri on the bike?"

"The guy had on a full helmet. They never got a look at his face."

"He called here," Donahue said. "Probably right after he talked to Clay Young. We weren't ready for Cherlina to speak to him, so we let the call go to voicemail. When we tried to call him back about twenty minutes later, it went to voicemail again."

Gibson sighed. "Hopefully, he's not on his way over there."

"You think he might be?" Donahue asked, concerned.

"Not likely. He's due on duty in another hour. Elwood thinks he might be getting dinner somewhere before his shift."

"So, you still want us to bring Leigh down to PAB?"

"Just sit tight for a while. We've got SIS turning around, so they should be back at your location in about twenty minutes. Once they get there and make contact, have them escort you back to the squad."

"Will do," she told him. "See you later."

*****

Yuri rode his motorcycle directly over to Cherlina's apartment. He'd taken care of one loose end when he'd gotten rid of Grushik. As the architect of the insurance scam—a partnership that Grushik had set up on his own with Vladimir Komarov—Grushik had become a liability. He was an intelligent man, but soft, not like a *Vor,* and if he was taken into custody, Yuri was sure that he would try to cut a deal to save his own neck by informing on everyone else.

At first, they had a really good thing going. Petrovich handled the business end, Komarov provided the girls, Grushik took care of the insurance, and Yuri handled all of the dirty work. But Komarov—the greedy bastard—had pushed things way too far. Two death claims in less than twelve months had been stupid. It set off warning bells at the insurance company, where that Russian adjuster, Nika Kaminski, had gotten curious and started nosing around. He'd been forced to take her out after she had gone to Grushnik with her concerns, and to make sure that she hadn't spoken about it to her lover, he'd taken her out too.

He'd seen that things were falling apart, and in an effort to keep the scam going, he brought Dima in from Dagestan to help him clean things up. Komarov new nothing about their prior connection and Yuri had seen to it that friends from the Motherland had used their connections with Komarov to get him to agree to help Dima out.

Dima had used the alias of Martun Hagopian, and Vlad Komarov had never known his true identity.

Yuri and Dima had hatched a plan to keep things going by severing ties permanently with Petrovich and Komarov. The idea was to replace both of them with Dima, a man that Yuri could trust to do things with care, thus eliminating the possible risk that law enforcement would ever catch on to what they were doing.

Petrovich was the first one to go. It was Dima's idea to take him out, and Komarov had readily agreed. Komarov had not been satisfied with just having a piece of the agency's business, he wanted to take over the entire operation, and when he learned that Dima had worked with explosives, he prevailed upon Dima to do it with a bomb.

That too had been a stupid mistake. He'd discussed it with Dima after the fact, stressing the notion that a killing like that was too overt. The bombing had attracted too much attention, and that was something they didn't need. So when the time approached to eliminate Vlad Komarov, Yuri had done it the easy way. He had taken Vlad out for a couple of drinks, drove him up to the hills on a pre-text, and put him down with one quick shot.

It was nothing fancy, but undeniably efficient.

And Leigh Cherlina? What to do about her?

He shook his head. She was a very sweet girl, lots of fun in bed, and loyal to a fault. He hated the thought of getting rid of her, but he had no other option. He'd taken a chance by using her to get a warning to Dima, a mistake that would likely come back on him, and now that the cops had a link between Dima and Leigh, they would soon discover her link to him. She had to go. She was the only person still alive who could connect him with any aspect of this can of worms.

His career with the Department might be over, but there was still a chance, albeit a small one, that once his link to her was severed, they might not have enough to hang him with a case.

He parked his Harley at the curb around the corner from Cherlina's building. He removed his helmet, attached it to the bike, removed his handgun from his holster, checked the magazine, then concealed it in the waistband behind his back where it was covered by his black leather jacket.

He removed a baseball cap from his saddlebag and pulled it low on his forehead. By keeping his head down, he was fairly confident that he could keep his face concealed from any CCTV cameras that he might pass along the way.

As he walked down the sidewalk past the neighboring buildings, he was hypersensitive to his surroundings. If the police had surveillance units parked on the street, he would try to spot them first before they spotted him.

When Leigh had not picked up when he gave her a call, he hadn't been overly concerned. She might have been in the shower or out getting dinner or something innocuous like that. But when she'd called him back and left him a message to call, he knew that she was now at home.

Not seeing anything out of the ordinary in the neighborhood, he made his way down through her building's underground parking garage, intent on using the back stairway to get up to her floor.

*****

Magarian and Homa pulled up in front of the building, totally unaware that Yuri Pavienko had entered the underground parking garage just moments before their arrival.

Magarian stopped the car at the curb next to a fire hydrant and turned off the engine. Both men then got out of the car.

"How long until SIS gets back here?" Homa asked.

"Why? You got something better to do?"

"I'd sure like to get home and get some sleep; that's all I'm saying."

Magarian smiled.

"They should be here in the next twenty minutes. But in the meantime, since we were so close, I told Elwood we'd have their backs until the others arrive."

Homa sighed as he paused to look up and down the street.

"I hope Pavienko does show up here," he said. "I'd like nothing better then to smack him around."

Magarian smiled. Homa could be a hothead, that much everyone knew, but his weapon of choice was sarcasm, not violence, and his comment was nothing more than the inconsequential bluster brought on by his lack of sleep.

"You want to hang out down here?" Magarian asked.

"Why? You going up?"

Magarian nodded. "I'll go inside and take a look around. I want to let Donahue know that we're here."

"Okay," said Homa. "I'll catch a smoke. You go ahead."

Magarian started off, then stopped and looked back.

"Put your badge on your coat jacket pocket, John, otherwise, you might find yourself in a nasty situation when SIS pulls up."

Homa nodded and clipped on his badge as Magarian entered the building and went directly to the elevator.

*****

Pavienko had climbed the last few steps and reached the third-floor landing. He paused for a few moments to catch his breath, then pulled out his handgun, checked it one more time, then quietly opened the stairwell fire door and listened for a moment before entering the hallway.

Three other apartment units had entrances that fronted in this particular hallway. He walked slowly towards unit 306, stopping along the way to listen at the other doors. What he heard were the muted sounds of televisions in two of the units, but from the third, there was no sound at all.

He walked up to the door of 306, put his finger over the peephole, the softly knocked on the door.

*****

Inside 306, the three women were all seated at the dining room table, enjoying their cups of coffee. Cherlina had been forthcoming during their interview, and she had just agreed to take a polygraph examination.

Thompson stood up and walked over to the kitchen counter where she picked up the pot of freshly brewed coffee and poured herself a second cup.

A knock on the front door interrupted her pour. She looked over at Donahue who caught her glance.

Cherlina started to get to her feet, but Donahue stood up first and put a hand on her shoulder to hold her down. She put a finger to her lips, then signaled to Thompson to take Cherlina out of the dining area.

Thompson moved quickly and quietly. She motioned to Cherlina who silently got to her feet, crept past Donahue, then made her way into the back bedroom.

Thompson drew her handgun from the holster on her waist and moved with Donahue towards the front door.

"It's probably SIS," Thompson mouthed.

Donahue nodded. She had pulled out her handgun as well and when she reached the door, she put her eye up to the peephole. She was momentarily confused by the blackness, but then it occurred to her that whoever it was had put something over the eyepiece to prevent being seen.

She put one finger over the eyepiece and looked over at Thompson who nodded that she understood from Donahue's gesture what was going on.

Both women then quietly backed away from the front door, arms extended, guns held out at the ready.

*****

Pavienko knocked again, this time a little louder. He listened at the door, not sure if he heard any movement inside. If she wasn't home, he could leave and come back, but he discarded that idea as foolish. He had the means and the ability to break in, so he made a split decision to go inside and reassess his options where he couldn't be seen.

He got down on one knee, placed his handgun on the floor, then removed a lock pick packet from a pocket in his coat. He took out two metal picks, examined the lock, then began to work it open.

It took less than fifteen seconds for the lock to slide into the open position. He then picked up his gun, got to his feet, turned the handle, and gave the door a shove.

The chain was on, and for the moment, his attempt to get in came to a grinding halt.

*****

Things happened so quickly that it would take hours of interviews and a lot of paperwork to reconstruct exactly what occurred.

Yuri's face could be seen by Donahue and Thompson through the open space created between the door and the frame. Yuri's eyes locked on Donahue first, and he instantly realized that he'd made a huge mistake.

The gun in his hand was visible, and in response to seeing hers pointed at him, he brought it up, intending to shoot.

"Gun!" yelled Donahue.

She and Yuri fired at each other simultaneously. There were multiple shots, as both had been trained to do.

Out in the hallway, the sound of the elevator arriving momentarily distracted Yuri. He rolled to his left as Donahue and Thompson continued to fire through the door.

The elevator was flush with the wall of the hallway so Yuri couldn't see who was getting off until the person or persons stepped into the hallway.

In a fraction of a second, he had turned his body in that direction just as a hand with a gun first came into view.

Magarian heard the shots just as the elevator arrived at the floor. He quickly pulled out his weapon, a six-shot Smith and Wesson .38, and slowly eased out of the elevator and into the hallway.

Yuri fired two quick shots in his direction.

Magarian fired once, then felt the wind go out of his chest. He hit the floor, landing on his back, where he struggled to catch his breath.

In the distance, he could hear retreating footsteps as Yuri ran away towards the stairwell door at the opposite end of the hallway.

Inside the apartment, Donahue had been the first one to react. She didn't know for sure if she'd shot him or not, but when Yuri took off, she ran to the door and quickly unhooked the chain.

The tunnel vision that occurs during a shooting was something she'd experienced before. She'd been so focused on Yuri and the shots that she'd fired that she had no idea how close she also came to being hit.

One of Yuri's bullets had passed through the open flap of her suit jacket, completely missing her body. It was something that would come to light later when things slowed down and she had time to think.

She ran out into the hallway yelling "Police!" and looked both ways before deciding what to do. She acted on instinct as her mind tried to process what was happening faster than she could respond.

She knew he was gone, and that someone else was down on the hallway floor. She turned towards the victim, intent on providing whatever help she could render.

As she ran towards the inert form, she got a quick look at his face.

Lieutenant Magarian!

Oh shit!

"Call 911 Shari!" she yelled over her shoulder. "Officer down! It's Magarian! Yuri is on the run."

Thompson, who was still in the apartment, was already on the phone with 911.

"Officer down!" she said to the RTO. "Shots fired! Send paramedics. Suspect is on the run. He's a police officer. His name is Yuri Pavienko, about six feet tall, two-twenty, wearing dark clothing.... I think I saw a black leather jacket. His hair is black and reasonably short. Officer needs help, Code 3!"

As soon as the broadcast went out, she hung up her cell and yelled to Cherlina to stay locked in her bedroom, then she entered the hallway to back up Donahue.

Donahue found Magarian flat on his back, eyes closed and no longer breathing. She felt for a pulse, but there was none. She could see a bullet hole in his jacket where it struck him just to the left of his heart. She reached down to start chest compressions, but was stunned to discover that he was wearing a kevlar vest under his shirt and coat.

As Thompson arrived, Donahue yelled out, "Help me get his coat and vest off, Shari. He's not breathing!"

Thompson joined her on the floor and together they tore open the jacket, removed his tie, and ripped open his white dress shirt.

There was an entry hole in the vest, but when they stripped away the velcro straps that held the sides together and lifted the front plate off his chest, they were quick to notice that the bullet had not gone all the way through the vest.

A large bruise had formed to the left of Magarian's heart which was immediately visible, but there was no sign of a penetration wound.

"What the hell?" said Thompson as she started chest compressions. "How could this stop his heart?"

Donahue was giving him mouth to mouth, so in between breaths, she said, "The force of the bullet striking the vest gets diffused, but it's like being hit with a sledgehammer—"

She gave him another quick breath.

"—it can stop your heart."

They heard another series of shots coming from somewhere down below them, and in the distant background, the sounds of numerous sirens filled the air as units from all over began to arrive.

"You go, Shari. I'll keep up the CPR."

Thompson got to her feet and scrambled for the doorway to the stairs. She suspected that Yuri had fired at someone, and she could only hope that whoever it was had not been hit.

*****

Homa, who had been enjoying a cigarette on the sidewalk in front of the building, heard the first volley of shots.

It took him a few seconds to react, but he pitched the cigarette, quickly pulled out his gun, then ran up the steps towards the front of the building.

He was acting on adrenaline and instinct, and as he took the steps two at a time, his mind was running through his possible options. But everything came to a sudden halt when Homa, in his haste to get into the building, clipped one of the steps with the heel of his shoe and went tumbling head first, landing flat on his face on the stairs.

He struck his forehead and twisted his ankle, but of greater concern, he had dropped his gun.

He rolled over to his side and reached for his ankle. He thought for sure that it was broken, but he would learn hours later that what he had was a *syndesmotic* ankle sprain with ligament laxity.

He searched for his gun, quickly reached over to pick it up, then forced himself up to stand on his one good foot.

He was sure that his partner had been ambushed, and if that was the case, he was gonna need his help.He hopped two steps, reached the front glass doors, then used the handle on the door to help get the door open.

He hopped on his left foot into the lobby and was headed towards the elevator which was fifteen feet away when a door crashed open directly to his right.

Yuri came running into the lobby through a nearby stairwell door about thirty feet away from where Homa was standing. He was looking towards the front glass doors, oblivious to Homa, who was off to his left and now just twenty feet away.

Homa saw Yuri first, gun in hand, as he closed the distance between them on his way to the front doors.

Instinctively, Homa's gun came up.

"Police!" he yelled.

As Yuri's brain registered the warning, his head turned to face Homa. The two men exchanged a momentary look of recognition—not just of who and what they both were, but of the inevitably of where the confrontation was going.

Homa unloaded a volley of shots as fast as his finger could pull the trigger. Three shots missed, but six hit their target, and Pavienko—who only managed to get off a single shot—went down without hitting his target.

EPILOGUE

In the aftermath of the shootout, the Los Angeles Police Department conducted a full investigation of all the events leading up to the final incident. This included a comprehensive analysis of the background investigation conducted prior to the hiring of Yuri Pavienko, as well as a thorough and all-embracing study of his activities while he was employed by the LAPD.

The morning after the incident, Donahue, Thompson, Magarian, and Homa were all placed on administrative leave with pay, pending the outcome of the shooting investigation.

Five weeks later, the findings were presented publicly by the Chief of Police. The report, consisting of over a thousand pages, contained many revelations about the facts uncovered during the initial criminal investigation, as well as those revealed during the follow-up investigation conducted by Robbery-Homicide detectives.

Chief among the findings was the discovery of a receipt for the monthly payment of a public storage locker. The receipt was found in a search of Yuri Pavienko's residence, and when the locker was opened, Pavienko's escape kit was recovered. It contained a large sum of money—eighty-thousand dollars—in both *rubles* and US currency. There were also three Russian passports, each one legitimate, but all three contained false identifications designed to enable Pavienko to travel without fear of apprehension.

The discovery of the passports and the fact that they were obtained legally from the Russian Passport Agency sparked an FSB criminal investigation that resulted in the arrest of a half a dozen employees in the Moscow passport office. All of those arrested were connected in one way or another with members of the notorious *Vor* organization.

It was confirmed with a second set of fingerprints sent to Russia that Yuri Pavienko was really a man whose name was Alexei Kuznetsov. The passport he used as Yuri Pavienko to gain entry into the United States was run through the Homeland Security data banks, but other than his initial arrival in the country when he emigrated to the US from Sweden, the name Yuri Pavienko did not pop up in any of their data banks. However, when they ran the information contained in the other three false identity passports, they discovered that one of the passport identities had been used for a four day trip to London that corresponded with the date of the fatal trip taken by William Baker. In short, the report concluded that given other circumstantial evidence collected during the investigation, it was more likely than not that William Baker had been the victim of a homicidal beating at the hands of Sergeant Yuri Pavienko as part of the Trophy-Wife Matchmaking insurance scam.

Of greater importance to the detectives of RHD, and in particular to Jennifer Donahue was the discovery of a Chiappa M-9, 22LR semi-auto pistol with a suppressor. It was found in the locker along with the money and the three false passports.

The gun was traced back to a gun show in Dallas, Texas, where Yuri made the purchase directly from the dealer. The gun was never registered by Yuri, but the vendor who sold it to him was located, and he specifically remembered Yuri because of his Russian accent and his familiarity with weapons. The man had never met a Russian before, so the accent was something of a novelty that had helped him to solidify his memory of Yuri's face.

No shell casings were ever recovered from the murder scenes, so there was no way to positively connect the gun to any of the killings. But the ammunition found in the weapon was similar in caliber to what was used in the killings of Nika Kaminski and Eliska Rodinova. A GCMS (Gas Chromatic Mass Spectrometer) analysis of the gunpowder residue recovered from the bodies established the likelihood that the gunpowder came from the same batch of bullets that were discovered in the bullets that were taken from a magazine that was found in Yuri's *Chiappa's M-9*.

The comparison of the lead slugs recovered from the bodies of Nika Kaminski and Eliska Rodinova was inconclusive. The .22 caliber bullets were too damaged for a meaningful comparison.

The Cayman Island Banking records were legally obtained, and it was determined through handwriting analysis that the account in the Cayman Islands was set up by Yuri Pavienko. There were deposits made to the account over a period of several years, all of which—when totaled up—came to just under half a million dollars. The deposits to the account were made on various dates throughout the life of the account, but of particular interest to the investigators were two separate deposits totaling one-hundred thousand dollars apiece, that were made to Yuri's account within the weeks that followed each of the two insurance murders. The deposits were electronic and transferred to the Cayman Islands from an account that originated from a bank in Los Angeles where the account that was set up was in the name of *SB Trucking.*

The man authorized to sign checks on the *SB Trucking* account was identified as Vladimir Komarov.

The conclusion arrived at in the report was that the murders of William Baker and Philip Katz were both more than likely perpetrated by Yuri Pavienko and that the killings were paid for by Vladimir Komarov as part of a larger insurance scam.

The detectives discovered two other deposits to the Yuri Pavienko account that were of significance to the LAPD. Each one was for fifty-thousand dollars, and both were transfers to the Cayman Islands bank account—again from SB Trucking—within a day or two after the shooting deaths of Nika Kaminski and Eliska Rodinova. The report officially concluded that the killings of Nika Kaminski and Eliska Rodinova were contract murders carried out by Yuri Pavienko to prevent Nika from reporting her suspicions to any other officers within the LAPD. The killing of Eliska Rodinova was done as a precaution, in case she had learned about the scam from her lover, Nika Kaminski.

Although it was never proven, it was speculated that once Kaminski reported her suspicions to Yuri Pavienko, that he passed on the information to Vlad Komarov with the intent of getting Komarov to pay him to do the killings. The investigators believed that Yuri Pavienko was just mercenary enough to co vince Komarov to pay him for something that he would otherwise likely have done for free.

The report went on to state that it was highly probable that Martun Hagopian, whose true identity was Dimitri "Dima" Federenko, was the person who constructed and planted the bomb that killed Milan Petrovich. The only proof supporting this conclusion was the explosive residue found in his storage locker, and the transfer of fifty-thousand dollars from the *SB Trucking* account and Vladimir Komarov to an account set up at a branch of the Bank of America in Hollywood, an account that was created and belonged to by Martun Hagopian.

The shooting death of Vladimir Komarov was attributed to Yuri Pavienko. It was determined through the CCTV parking lot security tape that he left the OCI squad room more than two hours before the murder occurred and that he left in an undercover vehicle that was assigned specifically to the unit. Tire casts made at the scene of the homicide up on Mulholland Drive were compared with those on the Prius undercover vehicle used that night by Pavienko. The result was a match.

A .38 caliber handgun was found in Yuri's apartment, but they were never able to connect that weapon to the .38 caliber slug retrieved from Komarov's brain.

The single boot print cast, also made at the scene on the night of the murder, was matched to one of the boots worn by Pavienko at the time of the shootout and his subsequent death. Since there was no other evidence discovered to the contrary, and because his previous association with Hagopian was both criminal and personal in nature, it was concluded that Pavienko acted alone when he executed Komarov in the Hollywood Hills, and that he did so to assist his former associate who was ready to take over the matchmaking scam being run by Komarov.

As for the murder of Nicholi Grushik, ballistics testing was able to establish that the bullets used to kill him were fired from the gun used by Pavienko at the time of the shootout with LAPD. The motive for that particular killing was unclear, but two theories emerged from a series of interviews conducted with Leigh Cherlina after the shootout.

The first one was based on the fact that she said that she had introduced Grushik to Yuri Pavienko during a chance meeting at an Encino restaurant. At the time, she told Grushik that Yuri Pavienko was both a boyfriend and a police officer with the LAPD. Yuri later expressed his displeasure to her for having made that revelation, and since she was implicated by LAPD in the warnings given to Hagopian, it must have occurred to Pavienko that if Cherlina were to die, that Grushik might possibly have remembered the encounter at the restaurant, and that such an observation would have moved an investigation in his direction.

The report concluded that such a connection would have started the unraveling of Pavienko's carefully orchestrated double life, and he clearly wasn't likely to let that happen.

As for Grushik himself, no evidence was uncovered that would have implicated him directly in the insurance scam or the killings of the two husbands. However, during multiple interviews conducted with Leigh Cherlina, a second theory emerged. She repeatedly stated that Nika Kaminski had told her that she had spoken to Grushik about the killings of the two husbands and about their connection to the matchmaking agency. Given the fact that Grushik adamantly denied that such a meeting had ever taken place to detectives Donahue and Thompson, it was concluded that he had lied to them, and that he, in fact, had a role in the insurance scam. His murder was committed by Yuri Pavienko to eliminate any possibility that Grushik could ever implicate him in any of the crimes.

As for Yuri Pavienko himself, the Chief used the press conference to apologize to the general public for the failure of the Department to do a thorough background check on Yuri Pavienko when he first applied for a career with the LAPD. He said that the department had already begun a reevaluation of the way they did their background checks on foreign applicants, and that he hoped that such an obvious failure on the part of the Department would never again be repeated.

What didn't make it into the report was the fact that the FSB opened an investigation of their own to determine the identity of the FSB agent that Pavienko and Clay Young had used to get false information about suspected *Vor* members. By using the phone number that Young had been instructed to call by Pavienko, they identified a female in the FSB who was registered as the owner of the email site that was used to send Young a response. It turned out that her long time boyfriend was a member of *Vor*, and it was surmised that she and the boyfriend were receiving payments for concealing the records of the gang members being inquired about.

No outcome of this FSB investigation was ever made public, but the woman and her boyfriend were picked up by the FSB and were never seen again.

The investigation also concluded that Officer Clay Young was not part of any criminality relating the any of the homicides and he did not have knowledge of, nor did he participate in, the agency insurance scam. However, he was transferred out of the OIC operation and into the Northeast Division where he was reassigned to night watch Patrol.

All in all, with the death of Yuri Pavienko, the LAPD was able to close out six separate homicide cases, and while the Chief regretted the loss of life, he felt that it was incumbent upon the Department to publicly recognize the heroics and dogged determination of the officers who unraveled such a difficult and complicated series of crimes.

*****

Two months later, the Los Angeles Police Department held it annual Medal of Valor ceremony in a large auditorium at the Peterson Automotive Museum in West Los Angeles. The ceremony was a red carpet affair, attended by numerous A-list celebrities and professional athletes, as well as almost a thousand members of the community. Among the fourteen recipients of this prestigious award were Lieutenant Andrew Magarian, Sergeant John Homa, and Detective Jennifer Donahue.

When presented with his medal, Andrew Magarian was praised for his courage in confronting an armed suspect who was intent on killing a fellow officer.

The citation, in part, was read aloud as follows:

Lieutenant Magarian and his partner Sergeant Homa went to the location to assist Detectives Donahue and Thompson who were attempting to protect the life of a civilian witness. When Lieutenant Magarian stepped off the elevator, he immediately encountered suspect Pavienko who had just exchanged shots with Detective's Donahue and Thompson. Lieutenant Magarian identified himself as a police officer, whereupon Pavienko opened fire on Magarian who was struck in the chest. Lieutenant Magarian survived the shooting because he was wearing a bulletproof vest. The force of the bullet which struck the vest was strong enough to stop Lieutenant Magarian's heart. In the split second before he was struck, Lieutenant Magarian managed to wound suspect Pavienko in the left lower quadrant, which slowed his escape on foot and which ultimately led to Pavienko's fatal confrontation less than a minute later when he engaged Sergeant John Homa in a gun fight.

Homa was also present for the ceremony, having recently returned to duty after a prolonged recovery from his severe ankle sprain. He was awarded his Medal of Valor for "*having exchanged gunfire without any thought towards his own personal safety during the attempt to capture a fleeing and very dangerous felon who had just shot his partner, Lieutenant Magarian, after an exchange of rounds with other fellow detectives.*"

While presenting him with his medal, the Chief explained to the audience that Homa had sprained his ankle while trying to race up a flight of stairs to get to his partner. That the injury had forced him to hop on one foot to get into the building where he subsequently engaged Pavienko in a deadly gun battle. He referred to John Homa as '*Hop-along Homa,*' a remark which generated a roar of laughter from the crowd and which subsequently created a nickname that stayed with Homa for the rest of his career.

For her demonstrated courage while engaging Pavienko as he fired at her through the doorway of Cherlina's apartment, and for her role in saving the life of Lieutenant Magarian by performing a CPR breath exchange on him while waiting for the paramedics to respond, the citation for Jennifer Donahue's Medal of Valor read in part:

"—disregarding her own personal safety, and in an effort to protect a civilian witness, she placed herself between the civilian and the assailant Pavienko before exchanging gunfire with the suspect, during which encounter she was struck but not injured by a bullet which passed harmlessly through her outer clothing. She then rendered life-saving assistance, again in direct disregard for her own personal safety, to the wounded Lieutenant Magarian, while the assailant was still armed and in the immediate vicinity."

At the conclusion of the ceremony, while Gibson was busy giving a tour of the museum to Thompson's three sons, Donahue wandered outside to a court-yard with a glass of wine to get a quick breath of fresh air.

She took a seat on one of the planter walls where she thought about how nice it would have been to have someone in her life to celebrate the ceremony with.

Thompson came out of the auditorium a short time later, spotted Donahue sitting alone, and like a woman on a mission, she made his way directly over to where she was seated.

"Congratulations, Jen," she said, taking a seat next to her, "but what are you doing out here all alone?"

"Just getting some air."

"I know you, sweetie. You're upset about something. What is it?"

Donahue shrugged, then sighed. "Where are your boys?"

"Gibby got roped into giving them a tour, so I got myself a glass of wine and about twenty minutes on my own."

"Well, congratulations on that."

Donahue then raised her own glass of wine.

"Here's to Nika and Eliska. Two innocent young women who deserved so much better."

Thompson raised her glass, took a sip, then said, "That was a bit morose, Jen. I think we should be drinking to that shiny piece of metal around your neck."

"Yeah, sure. Why not? Here's to us, partner. At least we survived."

The sound of running, laughing children suddenly filled the courtyard.

"Ah, here you are," said Gibson. The three boys ran over to Donahue, and she forced them to give her a hug.

Gibson joined them, and Thompson said, "That was the shortest twenty minutes I've ever had."

Gibson shrugged. "Where do they get such energy?"

Thompson laughed. "C'mon boys. It's time for us to hit the road."

She gave Donahue a hug, made the boys thank Gibson for the tour, and off they went.

Gibson took a seat next to Donahue.

"Congratulations," he said.

"Yeah. Whatever…"

Gibson frowned. "Does this have anything to do with what's been going on with you and your doctor for the last couple of days?"

She looked at him with genuine surprise.

"Don't be shocked. I'm observant, and I know that something's been going on for the last few months."

He wasn't going to quit until she told him what he wanted to know, so she made up her mind to get it all out.

"A little lump, Gibby. In my breast. But it was negative."

"Then you should be dancing not moping around."

She inhaled deeply, then sighed, "She's gonna take it out next week."

"What? The lump?" He frowned and cocked his head. "But you said it was negative?"

"I know, but it's still growing, so she says that we should take it out."

"You mean like a mastectomy?"

She smiled. "They're not taking my breast. It's just a small lumpectomy. A cut, a few stitches. A day off, that's all."

He visibly relaxed. "Then why are you so down?"

She shrugged and looked down at the wine glass in her hand.

"I guess when you go through something like this, it makes you take a hard look at your life." She slipped into an embarrassed smile. "And mine sure hasn't been what I expected. A lump in my breast, young women who want to talk to me getting murdered, and on top of it all, it seems like every guy I go out with has feet of clay." She looked up and caught his glance. "I don't know. Maybe it's just me."

Gibson shook his head.

"Whatever *'it'* is, Jen. It's certainly not you." He put his arm around her shoulder and gave her a squeeze. "You're a great catch, Jen. You'll meet the right guy someday. Don't put so much pressure on yourself."

"Ha!" she said with a smile. "You're starting to sound like my mother."

"Well, maybe she's right."

She smiled briefly again.

"Maybe she is, but I won't be putting pressure on myself anymore. I've grown weary of the whole dating process." She looked up and pursed her lips. "I've given it a lot of thought, and I've decided I'm through with dating for a while."

Gibson snickered, "Yeah, right."

"No, really. It might take a year or two to find myself, but if I don't do it now, I'm just gonna keep on making the same old mistakes. I need to figure out who I am first and what I really want in a man." She shrugged and smiled. "Maybe then I'll finally know why my choices in men have been so bad."

Gibson nodded as he got to his feet.

"Maybe you're right. Maybe a little time off is what you really need. But in the meantime, I need you to come back inside with me, Jen. There's someone I want you to meet."

She looked up at him in disbelief.

"Weren't you listening to what I just said?"

He silenced her with a raised hand and a smile.

"This isn't a setup, okay? My friend Max is a writer and a producer. He's got a couple of successful TV shows to his credit and he'd like to talk to you and Shari about developing a series about a pair of female detectives who work together to solve complicated homicide cases."

From the look on her face he knew her interest was clearly piqued.

"He came down here today because he's been following the news about the Pavienko case and he thinks it's a storyline that will resonate with the public and the networks."

Donahue smiled. "In that case, maybe I should meet with him."

"I thought you'd say that. He's just inside."

She got to her feet and finished off the last of her wine.

"Okay. Lead on."

He walked her back into the auditorium where he spotted Max Jeffreys standing off to the side. He was alone and looked slightly uncomfortable.

Donahue studied him over the top of her sunglasses which she quickly removed so that she could get a better look.

He was six feet tall, about one-ninety, with a sculpted body and a charming, rugged look. He was probably in his early forties, and he was sporting the two-day unshaven look that seemed to be the current rage.

He spotted their approach and his eyes lit up. A warm smile quickly spread across his face.

Without taking her eyes off him, she lowered her voice and said to Gibson, "Has Shari laid eyes on him yet?"

"Not yet," Gibson replied.

A small smile began to develop at the corners of her mouth. She whispered, "By any chance, is he single?"

Gibson couldn't suppress his grin. Two years of planned abstinence had lasted all of two minutes.

The old Jenny was coming back to life!

******

*

Other Novels by Peter S. Berman

HIDDEN AGENDA

WEB OF BETRAYAL

ABDUCTION

To see a bonus chapter from "Money for Love"
visit our website at **Merseyside Press** on Facebook,
or go to my author page also located on Facebook
under the name:

Peter S. Berman

This book and others by Peter S. Berman are available at amazon.com
and other retail outlets and online stores.

IF YOU'RE WILLING, I'D APPRECIATE YOUR COMMENTS IN A
REVIEW ON AMAZON. I'D LIKE TO KNOW IF YOU ENJOYED THE
STORYLINE, THE PACE, AND THE CHARACTER DEVELOPMENT?

YOUR REVIEW WOULD BE GREATLY APPRECIATED.

THANKS

ABOUT THE AUTHOR

Peter S Berman became a Los Angeles County Deputy District Attorney in 1973. After ten years as a trial attorney, he was promoted to the position of Head Deputy District Attorney, a senior administrative position. As a Head Deputy, he oversaw the daily operation of several geographic courthouses, as well as specialized divisions, including the Hardcore Gang Division, the Sex Crimes Division, and the Career Criminal Division. He retired from the office in 2002.

While working as a prosecutor, he lectured for the National Prosecutors College in Houston, Texas; the California Department of Justice; the LAPD Training Academy, and numerous other groups. He was a technical advisor on a Paramount/NBC Movie of the Week that recounted one of his sexual assault cases. His work has been profiled on a number of television shows, including CBS's Sixty Minutes.

He has received Citations of Recognition from the Los Angeles County Board of Supervisors; the United States Secret Service; the Association of Deputy District Attorneys, and numerous other law enforcement agencies and groups.

He currently works as a Specialist Volunteer with LAPD's Robbery-Homicide Division, Cold Case Specials Unit, where he investigates unsolved homicide cases. He was honored by the LAPD's Robbery-Homicide Division as their 2008 Reserve Officer of the Year.

****

www.ingramcontent.com/pod-product-compliance
Lightning Source LLC
Chambersburg PA
CBHW051515250626
47156CB00001B/98